The Miracle Man

The Miracle Man

Maggy Whitehouse

Winchester, UK
Washington, USA

First published by O-Books, 2010
O Books is an imprint of John Hunt Publishing Ltd., The Bothy, Deershot Lodge, Park Lane, Ropley, Hants, SO24 0BE, UK
office1@o-books.net
www.o-books.com

Distribution in:

UK and Europe
Orca Book Services Ltd
Home trade orders
tradeorders@orcabookservices.co.uk
Tel: 01235 465521
Fax: 01235 465555

Export orders
exportorders@orcabookservices.co.uk
Tel: 01235 465516 or 01235 465517
Fax: 01235 465555

USA and Canada
NBN
custserv@nbnbooks.com
Tel: 1 800 462 6420 Fax: 1 800 338 4550

Australia and New Zealand
Brumby Books
sales@brumbybooks.com.au
Tel: 61 3 9761 5535 Fax: 61 3 9761 7095

Far East (offices in Singapore, Thailand, Hong Kong, Taiwan)
Pansing Distribution Pte Ltd
kemal@pansing.com
Tel: 65 6319 9939 Fax: 65 6462 5761

South Africa
Stephan Phillips (pty) Ltd
Email: orders@stephanphillips.com
Tel: 27 21 4489839 Telefax: 27 21 4479879

ISBN: 978 1 84694 416 1

Design: Stuart Davies

A CIP catalogue record for this book is available from the British Library.

Printed by CPI Antony Rowe, Chippenham, Wiltshire

O Books operates a distinctive and ethical publishing philosophy in all areas of its business, from its global network of authors to production and worldwide distribution.

For Roger Holdom

Chapter One

Gemma Goldstone died on Friday 21st March at 12.37pm when her Aston Martin V8 Vantage crashed over the Hoover Dam. It was just three days before the long delayed, state-of-the-art Colorado Bridge bypass was due to open.

News like that spreads around the world within minutes; the headlines harsh and filled with excitement.

'Glamour Queen of Talent Dies in Horror Crash'

'Final Curtain for the Lady with the Midas Touch'

'Crisis as Multi-Million-Dollar *Miracle Mile* Show Threatened.'

Etc., etc.

And that was just what happened, but despite the Hoover Dam tourists' blurred cell phone images, uploaded to the Internet within the hour, the news that it was Gemma who had been killed could not be confirmed immediately. No matter how frantic or voracious the media might be, the police were not releasing the victim's name until next-of-kin were informed.

Next-of-kin was Gemma's husband, Josh. But he was not at any of the celebrity couple's homes in Los Angeles, Las Vegas, London or the South of France, nor at the offices in London, Vegas or New York. Nobody knew where he was and nobody — to start with at least — noticed whether or not there might have been a passenger in the royal blue Aston Martin.

People often didn't notice Josh; he was more of a peaceful space than a person. Someone once described him as 'slippery' but that wasn't exactly it. He just sometimes *wasn't there.*

Despite his wife's worldwide celebrity, her charity foundations and associates, nobody knew what Josh did; if he did anything. He certainly didn't have a PA or secretary and there were no children to know where their Dad might be at this time of crisis.

Gemma's entourage never took much notice of the husband; he was the quiet accessory who accompanied their Matriarch everywhere. He had to be tolerated because she operated better when he was around and he was the only one who could deal with her occasional tantrums, which could shake the building with their violence. He had to be present for every public or TV appearance as her support and her Muse; without him, she was uncomfortable and prickly. Exactly what he actually did with himself at other times — apart from getting slightly in the way of course — nobody knew. Wasn't he some kind of a landscape designer or something? Some years ago, some bright spark had called him 'the Gardener', which about summed up his status, and the turnover within *Gemstone Inc* was so high that very few of them nowadays realized that actually was his surname. Everyone called him 'Mr. Goldstone' and if he ever bothered to contradict, no one took any notice.

Staff didn't stick with Gemma for long; they didn't quarrel, they just moved on to even bigger and better things. There was never a whiff of controversy: she was the opposite of a jinx; self-esteem bred in the air around her. Not that she would suffer fools gladly (and those tantrums were legendary) but that was just it: Gemma was a legend; an icon, loved worldwide — and rightly so because she was a ball of golden energy, talent and, unexpectedly, kindness. Gemma Goldstone was exceptional and she expected her staff to be the same. She would always say that she needed the talent to be better off-screen than ever it was on-screen. In fact, efficiency was the bare minimum required to work for Gemma. If you put a foot wrong there would always be dozens of production wannabes begging to take your place.

But if you fulfilled her criteria for an outstanding employee, once you had paid your dues, any other media company would go down on its knees to headhunt you and you were guaranteed to go far.

That was, it seemed, everyone except Josh. He didn't even have style despite the couple's money and superstar status. His shoes were slightly scuffed; his shirts always seemed crumpled on his lanky body and he looked as though he wore clothes from Wal-Mart. And, my dear — his fingernails! People in Gemma's world noticed that kind of thing. Okay, the nails in question didn't actually have dirt in them (as a real gardener's probably would have) but Josh obviously had never seen a manicurist in his life even though Gemma traveled with her very own team of beauticians. And *per-leez* don't mention the color of his teeth! What was going on with that? Appropriate flouncing would indicate group opinion of a man who had access to everything but chose not to use any of the tools provided to make himself look good.

Gemma, on the other hand, was exquisite on every level. A touch of Botox, of course, and a little liposuction. And, of course, breast enhancement. But nothing else was needed yet — she was only 36 and at the peak of her physical attractiveness. Not beautiful exactly but pixie-faced and arresting with just the right way of looking up at you through her eyelashes and just similar enough in attributes and charitable works to be compared with the long-lamented Princess Diana. Some commentators even speculated that Gemma had filled the long-empty hole in the hearts of those who sought a human icon in order to worship the Divine Feminine. Gemma herself snorted with derision in private and cooed modestly in public when confronted with that one.

What this megastar didn't have in physical stature, she had in buckets-full of magnetism and simmering fire. She was a media phenomenon; a power-ball of energy, sometimes even traveling back and forth across the Atlantic every single week when both the Las Vegas-based *Miracle Mile* and her own X-rated, mega-successful late-night British chat show were in production.

Right now it was holiday time, twelve weeks before the re-start of auditioning and just time to begin cutting back on the personal appearances, the book signings and the charity galas, and to begin thinking about gearing up again. Time to hone the diet, check out a startling new hair color and style, and pull focus before beginning a new season of spotting the extraordinary performers that her show always found, to the continuing amazement of the whole of the Western World. *The Miracle Mile* had been Gemma's idea and it remained Gemma's, not only because she owned the brand and was majority shareholder of the global entertainment franchise that ran it but also because of her style and wit and her ability to choose co-judges who complemented her perfectly. Gemma could scent the very aura of talent in the smallest mouse and she could make even the rejected candidates laugh with her precise and profound assessment of exactly why they were useless.

In the end, it was one of Gemma's fellow judges on *The Miracle Mile,* Sam Powell, the former PR and media executive, who found Josh — or, perhaps more accurately, definitively located him as lost. The Las Vegas Metropolitan Police called at Sam's Hacienda-style home in Spanish Hills with a 'routine enquiry' to see if he knew where Mr. Goldstone might be. There had been an accident, they said, but no details were being released as yet.

'Josh is with Gemma!' said Sam. 'I spoke with her this morning — when she was on her way back to Vegas from Phoenix. They were in the car together.'

'What time would that be, Sir?'

'About twelve, I guess.'

'And was Mrs. Goldstone driving?'

'Yes, it was her beloved Aston Martin. Look — what's happened?'

The sergeant sighed. It was a big story and it was going to break soon whether they found the husband or not. Now it looked very much like they weren't going to find him alive.

'Mrs. Goldstone's car was in collision with a pick-up on Highway 96 in Nevada just on the Hoover Dam.'

'Oh my God! Is she alright?'

'Mrs. Goldstone's car went over the barrier and into the lake, Sir. We have no more than that right now.'

'Jesus Christ.' Sam fell backwards against the wall; sweat beads forming on his face. '*Jeezus!*'

'And you are saying that her husband was with her? Are you sure, Sir?' the officer asked.

'Jesus Christ!' Sam's mind was reeling. 'What? Yes. She said so.'

'Thank you Sir.'

'Wait — wait. Have they found her?'

'A woman's body has been found, Sir. We have no formal identification as yet. We need to find someone who could identify her as soon as possible.'

'Oh God. You'd better take me there. Jesus wept. I can identify her. Oh Christ...'

'Thank you Sir. There's a car outside.'

Sam looked at the tiny, empty body, its cold, elfin face strangely blank, white and totally unscathed. She would have died swiftly, they said, from multiple injuries to the spine caused in the collision and, if not then, as soon as the car hit the water.

He nodded, curtly, holding back unexpected emotion. 'That's Gemma.'

They offered him terrible coffee from a vending machine. 'Don't you guys know that you can get machines now with coffee that tastes like coffee?' he said, irritated but craving the caffeine and throwing the obnoxious mix down his throat as though it were a shot of tequila. The grimace that followed was familiar to anyone who knew him — Sam Powell was known as much for his hard drinking and high life as for his TV personality. Tequila was his drink of choice and there was a running joke that when he bit the lime afterwards it was the fruit that reacted to the bitter taste of Sam.

'Jeez, I never thought I'd end up family,' he muttered as he ransacked his cell phone address book for people who needed to know the news before it hit the headlines. He gave seventeen names to the police to deal with; the remaining six he called himself.

Outside the mortuary, the press was already lining up. The accident itself was news but Sam's involvement and the cell phone footage of the Vantage were quite enough evidence with which to go live: the story was breaking all over the world.

The truck-driver, Frank Morrison, was dead too, his neck broken like a stick in the impact. Frank's truck didn't go over the impossibly high wall but its contents — boxes of chips and cocktail snacks — did. They floated pathetically over large areas of the lake all that day with all the accessible ones being salvaged by tourists before the police cordoned off the entire area. After that, they sank, slowly and dismally, to be investigated without much enthusiasm by fish and small crustaceans.

Police examined the truck and found that the brakes had failed for no apparent reason; it had the appropriate service history; the driver's body tested negative for alcohol and drugs; there was nothing to apportion blame. It was just a freak, impossible, stupid accident.

Gemma's face was on every front page in the Western World every day until the funeral and her presence lived on perpetually, across Internet forums, conspiracy sites and tribute websites. In the first week after her death, Josh was sometimes in the picture too. Gemma would have said herself that the coverage was the best she had ever had. She had never actually written the long-planned autobiography but her brother Paul, who lived in London, England, arrived at the Goldstone's Los Angeles home within 48 hours of her death and brought in a team of researchers and ghostwriters. Together they started working through Gemma's own notes and the contents of her computer. A book contract was a foregone conclusion with publication being set for as soon as possible, ready to compete with a rash of unauthorized biographies.

Gemma had been a phenomenon. She had risen from what most people chose to see as humble Jewish beginnings (but which were actually perfectly comfortable lower middle-class) in London to become a dancer, briefly a singer in an all-girl band, and then a talent agent. The girl bands she promoted were tacky, it's true, and hardly ever lasted more than one album containing three hit singles, but who minded that when the money kept rolling in and there were always more ingénues who were queuing up to become the next, greatest thing?

Gemma's great coup was to be the first one to take talent-seeking

TV back to the tradition of vaudeville, opening doors to both old and new-fashioned acts alike, and the first to take the show to Las Vegas. The theatres and casinos in Vegas always needed new stars and *The Miracle Mile* provided them in bucket-loads. And Vegas had fallen on the idea of its very own talent-seeking show where nothing was too glitzy and nothing too outrageous. *The Miracle Mile* was followed up by *Miracle Camp* for teenagers each summer, touring shows and a year-long Las Vegas-based series of concerts, circus gigs and theatrical extravaganzas from that year's contestants. Gemma's company, *Gemstone Inc,* was now as integral a part of the Las Vegas profit-making machine as any of the casinos, its conscience salved by Gemma's billion-dollar children's charitable foundation.

Others, of course, followed her — the world was flooded with talent shows — but there was no one like Gemma and nothing with as much kudos as *The Miracle Mile.*

She was married, all the time, to her childhood sweetheart. Their 15th anniversary renewal of vows was featured in *Celebrity Star* magazine (which re-decorated their Las Vegas house for free and donated five million dollars to the charitable foundation). Gemma looked golden and glorious in a series of designer outfits with her husband in the background looking vaguely bemused and uncomfortable. He had been shoehorned into designer clothing, which made him feel ridiculous.

Josh was always the boy next door, the son of an American who worked at the US Embassy in London. He was her rock, Gemma said, her best friend, her reality-check. Professionally, he was an academic and theologian and an expert in ancient languages. He had even written a textbook on Bible translations, which was published by *Oxford University Press* and read by virtually nobody. He probably even had a PhD in something obscure but nobody ever called him Doctor.

Josh worked somewhere in UNICEF at the start of Gemma's fame but, once the roller-coaster of talent shows took off, he didn't need a job and Gemma wanted him by her side wherever she went. There was never a sniff of scandal on either side.

They dredged the whole of Lake Mead but, although they found his wallet, suitcase and cell phone, Josh's body was not found. Sam swore blind that Gemma told him he was with her; the hotel staff in Phoenix confirmed that they had left together in the car that morning; CCTV confirmed that a man looking very like Josh *was* in the car moments before the crash (raising a lot of understandably awkward questions as to why he hadn't been noticed the first time anyone looked). He had to be *somewhere*. But he was not.

Chapter Two

Gemma's funeral took place, without Josh, back home in London, England. It was held at the Grade One-Listed Golders Green Crematorium where centuries of the rich and celebrated from within the Jewish community were either buried in the Jewish graveyard opposite or scattered in the elegant gardens. The crematorium was packed with the wealthy and the famous who had flocked, in designer outfits, to the event of the year (Gucci is just *so* good in black). For hours beforehand, the road outside was lined with grieving fans and celebrity seekers held behind a tight police cordon. At least six of the scream-inducing stars who came to honor Gemma had been her own creations: stars of *The Miracle Mile.* It was a tribute to her generous nature that they were willing to travel across the Atlantic to honor her — especially as the prestigious Tony Awards were only the next week. Besides, showing up for Gemma's funeral was seen to be a tremendous publicity opportunity for those whose star status might be slipping a little.

Gemma's parents, elderly and bemused, both suffering from Alzheimer's disease and uncertain what was happening, were there being shepherded by Paul. He, the nominal heir, had taken charge of everything including finding a suitably elegant female Liberal Jewish Rabbi. He had seen to all the organization and the huge reception afterwards and arranged the readings to be given by several well-known people, including Sam Powell.

Josh's father, Joe, an angular-looking man who seemed to have aged more than 20 years in the last few weeks, attended too. Josh's mother, Maria, confused and grieving but stubborn to the hilt was not there. Instead, she was holding vigil at the Hoover Dam. The Gardeners had been told that there was no hope for their son; if he could have possibly survived, he would have been found by now — and nobody *could* survive that crash over the side of the dam and down into the water. The Aston Martin had long been dredged up and Josh's side of the car was all but sliced off. But no one could convince Maria Gardener that her son was dead. 'I would *know,*' she said.

Each night that she was in Nevada — forty in all — Maria wandered sleeplessly around Gemma and Josh's luxury ranch in Queensrich, Las Vegas, her bare feet padding silently on the blue-and-white mosaic floors so as not to wake the unnervingly courteous staff who always wanted to bring her something or arrange a massage or a pedicure for her. She knew it was their way of trying to help and that they were all fearful of losing their jobs, especially the bodyguards who had been excluded from the trip to Phoenix because Gemma had wanted time alone with her husband. But she didn't have the energy to placate them. Instead, she did all she could to avoid the sleep that brought nightmares of her only child's broken body, half-eaten by fishes, lying at the bottom of the lake. By day, she sat on the scarred wall of the dam, reading out loud to him from the Old Testament — mostly from *Psalms* and the *Book of Esther* — and said the day's prayers in Hebrew from the old, navy blue, age-spotted prayer book that had once belonged to Josh's grandmother, long dead in the gas chambers of Auschwitz. To those watching, it seemed that she sat, faithful and defiant, where her daughter-in-law had died, daring God not to bring back her son. 'He's not dead,' she said to anyone who would listen. 'I would know. I would feel it in my bones.'

It was as a tribute to Maria's firm gentleness that the officers of the Hoover Dam Bureau of Reclamation and the investigating police both allowed her to be there. They would have thought it far more than their jobs were worth with anyone else, but Maria had a kind of inexplicable presence. It wasn't charisma; she was just a very ordinary gray-haired, plump, down-to-earth, elderly lady in loose shirt, elasticized trousers and sensible pumps but there was *something.* They didn't even contradict her repeated affirmation of her son's being alive. When she said, 'I would just *know* if he weren't,' they were amused by her English accent and old-fashioned grammar but they didn't laugh *at* her. In fact, they sometimes hovered around her when she was praying. Religion was increasingly thought of as only for Evangelicals and nutters these days and, if asked, they said they were just making sure no one disturbed the poor woman or objected to her religious beliefs while she was at her morning prayers — and that was true. But there was also something strangely comforting and comfortable about being close to someone who believed so strongly in a benevolent deity and who spoke in an ancient, sacred language. It was as though they felt that some of that Grace would rub off on them.

When Maria had finished reading and praying, she walked everywhere around the dam that it was possible to walk. Out of sight of interested eyes, she wept for Gemma, that funny and affectionate daughter-in-law, behind the bright, brittle light of celebrity, and said *Kaddish,* the Jewish prayer for the dead, for her soul but, more than anything, she prayed for Josh, the special, unexpected child of her late youth. He was a miracle baby, born when the doctors had said she and Joe could have no children and who, for all his spoiling as a beloved only child, had never been other than as loving and gentle as his mother.

Joe, Maria's husband, returned to her after the funeral and waited patiently at the ranch with a series of good books and the odd, slightly guilty round of golf, for the rest of the forty days while she kept vigil. Paul, the heir, raised no objections. He hadn't decided yet whether the ranch should stay or go.

Maria could sleep with her dear love beside her and such was their relationship that she could wake Joe in the middle of the night and ask for a cuddle if the nightmares returned. Joe himself appeared taciturn and a little grumpy which was his way of showing his grief. But he was unceasingly kind to his wife, so much so that he would go and make her a cup of tea in the kitchen at 3am and bring her some cookies to nibble to help her be comforted. The staff couldn't work out whether to be outraged at this lack of use of their services or relieved that they didn't have to make 'proper'

English tea with boiling water instead of using the hot water tank. It was in these night rescues of his wife that Joe discovered that Gemma had actually employed someone to clean the dust off every leaf and flower of the house's abundant pot plants two nights a week. Manuel began work at 3am so that nobody would see him. 'Ridiculous!' snorted Joe but Maria reminded him of Gemma's kindness. It might well be that Manuel could get no better work and had a wife and big family to support.

'I don't suppose Paul will keep half of them on,' said Joe thoughtfully, to his wife's horror. She berated him for his lack of faith in Josh's survival and he took her tongue-lashing without a word. Joe didn't believe Josh was still alive for a moment, but he wouldn't say that to his wife. Sufficient unto the day was Maria's despair and one thing Joe didn't believe in was the concept of false hope. 'Hope is, by its very nature, hopeful,' he would say to anyone who tried to work out why he supported his wife's pointless quest. They would go away perplexed. The quotation was undeniable but it was strangely tangled in its own meaning and few people could work out what it actually *did* mean. But it did shut them up.

While she was at the dam, Maria was sometimes accompanied (in what she considered a horrible irony) by local Christians who prayed for her son and at other times by gawkers and fans of Gemma's. She became a celebrity (briefly) in her own right as the press continued to milk the story. She spent the fortieth night at the dam with lighted candles and, at dawn on the forty-first morning, Joe drove up in the car, got out and wrapped his arms around her while she wept, and wept and wept. As soon as he could, he led her away from the prying eyes and the flashing cameras. He had arranged that they were to drive to Gemma's and Josh's home in Coldwater Canyon, California to meet with Paul to sort out what they wanted of Josh's personal effects.

As he started the hire-car, the satellite navigation system failed to update (or maybe Joe just missed the instruction it gave), and he turned the wrong way without realizing it. Maria sat hunched and uncommunicative in the passenger seat as he drove until they saw the sign saying 'Valley of Fire Visitor Center.' She sat bolt upright engulfed by a flame of inspiration.

'Stop!' she said. 'There. There! Go there!'

Joe looked at her without expression and carefully pulled off the road in order to let other drivers pass. He switched off the ignition and turned stiffly in his seat to remonstrate gently with his wife.

'Please,' she said with tears in her eyes. 'It's not just forty days, it's forty days and forty nights! And I know he's here. Please Darling, have I ever been wrong?'

Well yes, fairly frequently, thought Joe. Maria had always been what her Scottish family called 'fey' but she could also be fanciful and if it was something she *wanted* to believe she would find signs to confirm it very easily. But rarely did Maria insist on anything; on the rare occasions when she put her foot down, she *had* never been wrong.

Joe sighed, started the engine, checked the mirror, indicated out and drove on until they reached the turning. As they took the road to the Visitor Center, the sun rose over the vermillion hills and spread golden rays across the land.

So who would replace Gemma on *The Miracle Mile*? Executives from *Gemstone Inc* and the production team chewed gum frantically through meeting after meeting in their luxurious theatre, hotel and apartment compound, all linked by its own SkyTube, just north of the Las Vegas strip. This was where everything to do with the show took place, from the semi-final auditions through to the first complete public shows by the final twenty-four contestants (all of whom got cast-iron contracts to perform for the following two years) to the star-studded final itself. The final was an event that known as much for its splendid A-list party as for its magnificent parade along the Las Vegas Strip. *The Miracle Mile* complex also included the contestants' hotel and rehearsal area with cameras everywhere so that Reality TV could meet *The Miracle Mile* whenever required.

In the very early days, the most productive discussions would take place outdoors as the hard-core smokers stood just under the SkyTube sheltering from the sweltering heat. Both the standing itself and the irritation of being sent out of the comfortable air-conditioning into the hot sun speeded up the decision-making process considerably. But now very few people smoked at all; alcohol and recreational drugs had replaced tobacco as the socially acceptable addictions of choice.

There were, of course, water cooler moments and coffee machine conversations as a kind of substitute but the younger the show's staff and producers got, the less there was of light and shade of movement and discussion. Now it was all 'the brand' and 'the reach' and the advertisers rather than the talent.

Gemma was irreplaceable, of course, but the show must go on. There were three other judges ready to step up to the star-spot. Could they run the series without replacing her at all? Executive Producer Bartos Varga thought they could. As a matter of respect. Partially this was laziness and partially the fear that the rest of the panel would rebel if some new star were brought in.

'You could cancel,' his PA, Pippa, suggested but she only did it in jest. There was no possibility of a top-rating television reality program ever being anything other than milked for every ounce of money and emotion it could give.

Sam Powell, Gideon Jones, the former comedian and conjuror, and Deborah Deforge, the crazy, Prozac-ridden Hollywood musical actress, cried a few crocodile tears in public, thanked their lucky stars for being alive and for the opportunity to take Gemma's place at the top of the heap and got on with business. John Jordan, the suave and ultra-famous compère, who made almost as many world headlines as a fervent campaigner for liberating Tibet as he did over whether or not he was gay, shed a genuine tear in private. He had liked Gemma and, being a man of perception, had enjoyed Josh's quiet company behind the scenes. However, he also had to face facts.

Without Gemma the show could never be the same and John was the kind of man who could see further than a production team, that just wanted to paper over the cracks and placate the existing stars. *Gemstone Inc* had never managed to shackle John Jordan with a pair of golden handcuffs and in two more years, he'd be too old to make the grade elsewhere. John Jordan began to consider jumping the ship.

Chapter Three

Lake Mead lies below the Hoover Dam and is the focal point of the one-and-a-half million acres of Lake Mead National Recreation Area. It includes twenty-five miles of the Colorado River and a smaller lake, Lake Mohave.

It is a man-made lake, a large, flooded area of desert. Far below the surface lie the ghostly remnants of several small villages as well as relics of even older settlements. Thousands of visitors go boating, fishing, camping, swimming and hiking there every year; the weather being sunny and hot, rising to 110 °F in midsummer. All around the lake there are hidden coves and flooded canyons that can only be reached by boat.

To the north end of Lake Mead, the Valley of Fire is composed of an ancient and unnerving landscape of petrified dunes, fossilized trees, strangely shaped rocks and sandstone cliffs. At sunset here, the rocks glow and blaze like Uluru, Australia, and away from the tourist trails, canny wild animals blend easily with the shadows cast by vermillion, scarlet and golden rock.

In the beginning, Josh was in hell. He lived in a world composed of all-pervading torture, simultaneously fire and ice. Every fear and inadequacy he had ever experienced engulfed him; every uncomfortable memory from birth to the present day came back multiplied, torn apart, amplified and filled with remorse, anger, anguish and hopelessness. He — and he no longer knew who or what 'he' might be — was consumed by hatred, terror and uncertainty. How long that lasted in our time, no one could know. In his time it was a terrible, terrible eternity. It seemed as though he was being attacked by demonic forces from all sides, the agony unbearable and irredeemable. Then, one crystal-clear thought emerged. 'This is not outside of me; this is within me. I am attacking myself.'

Then it cleared and the demons were resolved. A deep harmony spread throughout the Universe that was Josh and Josh himself was healed, whole and at peace.

Most of the time that he spent in the desert, he slept or dreamt. Sometimes he walked and sometimes he sat. Much of the time he sat on one particular rock; it seemed to him to be a very nice rock. Every night he lay on his back on the ground out in the open air and watched the stars turn in their courses with a wonder that consumed him. A city boy, he had rarely seen the glory of a sky without light pollution. But this one was magical. Every star seemed to be a living being with a story to tell. There was so much to learn. The music of the spheres played in every atom of his being.

A part of him knew that he was crazy. Some of him remembered coming out of some water and standing, breathless and confused about whether those who had rescued him were actually there. He was sure there had been presences — someone, something? He had been cushioned in the fall and pulled up from the deeps by a thousand gentle hands. But on the red sand of the beach there was nothing.

There was nothing anywhere.

Nothing but the desert and the no-thing-ness.

He had walked until he was tired, then sat until he slept. He dreamt until he woke, hungry, thirsty and stiff and aware, too, that he had some kind of a head injury and that there was dried blood all over his face and neck.

Gingerly he touched the wound but he could only feel it for a second and then there was what seemed to be a rush of light and air and laughter and he knew he must be mad because it was no longer there.

Thoughts of food assailed him. Water there seemed to be in plenty: the cave behind where he was sitting contained a spring of cool, running water. He frowned for a moment; had that been there earlier? Did it matter? He went in and drank and it was cool and fresh and delicious.

A small part of his brain tried to warn him about tainted water. He ignored it.

He slept on the floor of the cave and dreamt of the pink-icing cup cakes with a bright red cherry on top that his mother had made for him in England when he was a boy. He had loved them until he discovered that they were made with cochineal — crushed beetles. Then he would never touch them again. She made the cakes with Ribena icing after that but it wasn't the same.

In the cool dusk, when he woke, there was a canvas rucksack — of a kind of a camouflage color — sitting by the rock at the entrance of the cave. He looked around but no one seemed to be claiming it so he opened it up.

Inside was a Tupperware box of pink iced cakes each with a cherry on the top.

He had eaten three before he remembered the dream.

He had eaten four before he remembered the cochineal.

He ate the rest.

'Well I'm over that one,' he thought, dispassionately observing the Tupperware box disappearing.

The tiny thoughts inside protested about that; added that this was an appalling diet and insisted that he got up and found vegetables or fruit or protein.

'What a daft thought,' he said.

Instead, he lost himself in the night sky for seven hours, orbiting the great gas giant, Jupiter, before discovering the even greater mysteries of Orion and, at one point, just west of Betelgeuse, the thought of bacon sandwiches drifted across his mind. Now Josh was not a totally observant Jew but he didn't eat pork or shellfish unless he was being polite. It had always seemed unkind to others to maintain an ancient law in the face of unwitting hospitality. After all, loving-kindness was greater even than truth — his Dad had taught him that in synagogue.

So he wasn't surprised to find bacon sandwiches in the rucksack at dawn when the light show was over and the angels had left. They were sandwiched in British white bread, still warm and totally, totally delicious.

'Okay, I'm over that one too,' he thought.

From then on, food was not a problem, though he did sometimes find that the canned orange soda got up his nose.

When they asked him later, he would sometimes speak of the demons and the incredible release when he had gone from them but he would never tell anyone all about the magic of this time. It was indescribable and, more importantly, it was none of their business. There was such joy in the memory of this ultra-real, impossible existence in the desert that often helped in the face of the imaginary world that everyone seemed to live in outside of it. He had learnt as a child not to take out treasure only to watch others tarnish it before his eyes. And how could anyone who had never experienced what he had experienced ever understand? Of course, afterwards, he still spoke with and listened to those light-forms who had talked with him in the desert and he would give a taste of what he had experienced to anyone in his new life who genuinely sought a real understanding, but they were in the minority. The phrase 'casting pearls before swine' was politically incorrect so he just said 'ask me again in a year' when questioned, which usually filtered out those seeking a quick spiritual fix or a thrill.

On some days, he talked with a bobcat that made him chuckle with its tempting suggestions. On others he talked with Gemma, his Uncle Frank and people he had known before … before … well, earlier. Sometimes he spoke with the wrens or the eagles. Mostly he just listened.

If anyone had asked him then if he knew that Gemma was dead, he would have said, 'Nobody dies' and dismissed the question. In the desert everything is very much more real.

Eventually, with a sigh and the realization that it was time to begin the work and, anyway, that his legs were getting stiff from sitting, his beard was itchy and he really fancied some pancakes and maple syrup, he got up in the dark before the dawn and walked the seven miles to the Valley of Fire Visitor Center.

Chapter Four

Behind the closed blinds of her bedroom, Maude-Lynn Sykes lay sleeping, spread-eagled on the purple-sheeted bed. Around her the detritus of a still-open wardrobe lay scattered across the floor; outfits selected, tried on and discarded in the haste to find a better, sexier one that actually fitted. Maude-Lynn was tiny but the alcohol was beginning to show on her breasts, stomach and hips. A layer of fat actually made her look sexier but she resented the change and refused to admit that her age might be the reason for her body's decision to react to her blinding self-hatred. She was only 32, still immortal surely?

At the moment, she wore an old black tee-shirt and, with her head buried in the pillow and her bum naked, she looked like a soft-porn picture of someone barely old enough to be posing. As the radio-alarm clicked on and she turned her head, the first thing noticeable on the high-cheeked, Oriental face was an expression of habitual discontent. Unhappiness oozed from every pore.

She groaned and spat an expletive at the alarm. Obediently it shut up for five more minutes and she rolled over and squeezed her eyes shut to try and stop the lids sticking to the corneas. God they hurt! She should drink more water; she knew she should drink more water. For years she had visited doctor after doctor to find out why her eyelids stuck to her eyes every night so that she woke with smarting swollen lids. In the end, some holistic doctor at a TV station had told her that it was probably just dehydration — and he was right. If she got that all-important liter of water a day then her eyes were fine (whether she drowned herself in coffee and alcohol or not).

The alarm jerked into life again and memory crept in around those sore, deep-lidded eyes. Kieran! Oh God! Jesus Christ, what a disaster. She had promised herself — *promised* — she wouldn't sleep with him and what a good decision that had been. Why, why, why hadn't she kept it?

He'd been making sheep's eyes at her for ages and she'd come to dread covering news stories where the other Network stringers were bound to turn up because he was always there. He was just such a no-go area; all lame remarks and yucky jokes and so sure that he was God's gift. Okay, he was also quite cute but she needed another notch on the bed-head like a rhino needed Botox and you just had to keep a professional distance to look — well, hell, professional. And yesterday, on one lousy story where they'd both had to work all day to get their clip (a *great* story — she knew it would be), she'd blown it. They'd had to work together to pull it off this time and it was worth the effort. Okay, so two Networks got it but without that collaboration neither would have got a thing. Afterwards, she'd agreed to have a drink because it had all worked out so well and because the crews liked each other. One drink had turned to half a dozen, to dinner and to bed.

Now she would have to hope against hope that he shut up and let it pass. She couldn't afford another one night stand becoming common knowledge; she'd had to lie through her teeth about that night with the Deputy News Editor last year. Thank God he had no cred and Maude-Lynn's ability to feign innocence had won out against his sleazy accusations that she was a heartless tart.

It was the drink; that's what it was. And the other stuff — but she rarely took that because it made her feel so out of control. The problem was that she *was* out of control even when she thought she was being so sensible with the drink. The problem was beginning to get through to her — but, so far, only after the event.

She wrinkled up her face remembering the sex. Yeah, so it had been exciting; she loved to be wanted and admired and she liked the sensation of power when he cried out as he came but, in the end, it was just another guy in bed. His bed.

'Stay,' he said, reaching out for her when she began to get up. 'Hey, stay over, it's cool. Plenty of room and we can do it again in the morning.'

She pretended she was just going to the bathroom. He muttered something and was asleep by the time she came out again, fully dressed apart from the shoes. She wasn't leaving without her shoes — Maude-Lynne had exquisite, tiny feet and reveled in high heels. These were Jimmy Choo heels and they were going home with her.

For a moment Maude-Lynn had looked down at her lover feeling a masculine sense of conquest that never worked in retrospect. It took her three minutes to find both her shoes and then she let herself quietly out of the room.

Another hotel corridor; another 3am exit; another mistake; another drive home when over the limit because she had to be alone. Always, Maude-Lynn had to get back to her own space. The drives were good. *Then* she felt powerful, exultant and alive. But the mornings were another matter.

She groaned as her cell phone began to vibrate just as the alarm radio went off for a third time.

'Yep?'

'Madeline?' It was the *Fox News* duty editor, Celine. One of a hundred thousand people who always got her name wrong.

'Maude-*Lynn*. What?'

'Have you *seen* the news?'

'Nope.'

'Well take a look and come right in willya? We need all the cover we can get on this one!'

'Celine, I'm not staff, I'm freelance! I'm not booked in today.'

'I *know.* But we've got three people out … you'll get paid.' The whiney voice receded into the background as Maude-Lynn flicked the TV remote and turned up the volume.

She watched open-mouthed for 30 seconds.

'On my way,' she snapped.

Maria Gardener always wondered whether they could have just lived a quiet life somewhere simple if they had all just gone into hiding on that first day. Joe didn't give that theory a moment's credence and Josh didn't give it any attention at all. That was what would always annoy the media most about him — he didn't care about their coverage. It wasn't that he had any false modesty; he didn't (and that was fairly irritating too). He just did what he wanted to do and, when he had had enough of everyone else, he would disappear quietly.

It began at the Valley of Fire Visitor Center. Of course, afterwards, people said he walked in shining, wearing pure white and that they could see he was obviously someone special. Others said that he was a magician and that they could see the evil intent in his hooded eyes (Josh didn't have hooded eyes). Joe said that people see what they want to see wherever they are — and if the press wanted them to say that they'd seen something exciting well, heck, they'd find something to say wouldn't they?

For Joe, it had been a terrible six weeks. There is no single bereavement worse than a parent losing a child. He knew that, in the old days, children died all the time — his own brother had died at the age of seven — but that was 60 years earlier and, in the 21st century, death is considered an insult as well as a tragedy. Maria might have been holding on to hope but Joe was not. He couldn't have said if it was worse because Josh was their only child or not; he just knew that, if Josh were dead, a great piece of himself had been cut away.

But, as he navigated the maroon Pontiac GrandAm into the Valley of Fire Visitor Center car park, narrowly avoiding a hoard of people racing back and forward between a fleet of *Forever Love* corporate trucks and the huge marquee set up for a wedding, Joe felt an unexpected frisson of hope. Maria's face was alive with joy and some of her almost religious feeling eked its way through into Joe's more prosaic reality. He swung the car into a parking space with something like his old driving style and got out without grunting at the effort.

Maria ran ahead, dodging between waiters carrying silver dishes of canapés, her 70-year-old legs carrying her without effort. She *knew.* She just *knew* although she couldn't have told you how or why. A great light filled her and carried her past the archetypal Visitor Center building and beyond into the brightly raw-red vista of the valley.

It was still early enough for that white, slightly eerie morning light that seems to blank out all detail. Maria wasn't wearing sunglasses so she had to screw up her eyes and shield them with both hands. Before her, the rocks shone scarlet, orange, purple, mauve and pink, piled up in clumsy chunks over the sparse vista of tumbleweed and red earth.

'Josh!' she called before she could help it. 'Josh!'

'Have you lost someone?' asked a Philip Glazer, a Visitor Center worker who was throwing trash into a dumpster.

'My son,' said Maria simply. '*Josh*!'

Philip looked at her sharply in case she was in trouble and then relaxed, seeing an elderly man following her. The woman looked crazy but at least she wasn't alone.

He was watching Joe, so he was able to observe the change in the old man's face as Joe's jaw dropped, his face lit up and his whole body started to tremble. The shock of the transformation made Philip turn on his heel to see what it could be that had brought such emotion.

All he saw was the dark outline of a man in a pale suit and white open-necked shirt walking slowly towards them with his arms held out. Yes there was a strange silvery light behind him — but that was the aureole expected from the Sun at that time of day — and, on later consideration, he was far too clean, neat and tidy for someone who had spent six weeks in the desert but, right then, it was nothing to write home about. In fact, he thought it must be the groom for that morning's wedding. He smiled as he saw the slightly dumpy, elderly lady run forward and heard her squeal with joy. He would have turned back to his work had the elderly man not staggered and fallen to his knees with a choking sound.

'Are you alright, Sir?' he said, dropping onto one knee. All the Center staff were fully trained in first aid and this looked like a heart attack.

The man held onto his arm with a vice-like grip. 'Alright?' he said. 'Oh yes, I think so. Just a bit breathless. Thank you.' And he sank into a sitting position with his legs to one side, not even looking towards the place where his wife and son embraced in that even brighter aureole of light.

'Would you like some water?' said the young man, anxiously. 'I could get you some water.'

'Yes, yes, water. Thank you,' said the man and Philip walked away from the scene. He did not see Josh reach out his hand to his father and raise him in a way that lifted the old man backwards in time, dissolving the slight stoop and rheumatic twinge in his knees. He did not see the mingled joy and terror of the man's recognition of the half-forgotten dream of angels from nearly 40 years before. He did not see Joe fall to his knees at the feet of his son and ask for his blessing.

You may be a *Bene Elohim* but you can't beat Federal Law and Federal Law says no food in state park Visitor Centers. Philip had brought the promised bottle of water and Joe had a Snickers bar in the glove compartment but that was it for the celebration breakfast. Joe, Maria and Josh shared both water and chocolate between them, sitting outside, enjoying the sun and watching car after car of elegantly dressed people arriving as the *Forever Love* crew made the final adjustments to their peripatetic wedding chapel. It and the marquee were festooned with flowers and the scent of white lilies (with the orange-staining stamens carefully removed) filled the air.

Hunger was sated for the moment — which was a miracle in itself. Nothing was said; it was as though they all *knew*. They sat in peaceful contentment, just people-watching as the wedding guests began to arrive. Maria observed the impractical shoes, the floaty dresses and, mostly, the discontent in so many faces even though they were here to celebrate joy. Occasionally she glanced up at the face of her beloved son, noting anew the wrinkles on his high forehead and the laughter lines around those kind brown eyes and the rather scruffy growth of pale golden beard.

Perhaps a hundred people gathered over half an hour, all wandering in and out of the marquee, drinking champagne and orange juice. They were herded regularly to their seats but, as the Bride was late, they wandered back for another drink, fuelled by the pleasure of morning champagne and the hospitality of the groom's father — who wasn't paying.

By the time the Bride, in her over-embroidered strapless dress, had arrived and been photographed a hundred times with her flower girls, page boys and bridesmaids, the wedding was running nearly an hour behind time. At last, the string quartet with additional harpist began the processional music, the Bride straightened her tiara one last time and everyone settled down as the final guest ran back from the lavatories.

'Shit, shit, shit!' Colleen Diamond, wedding planner for *Forever Love* sank down on one of the folding chairs exquisitely-covered in rose-pink satin to match the rest of the marquee. Marc, the sommelier, had just told her that the guests had been drinking far more freely than had been expected — and drinking far more alcohol than water — and the champagne had run out.

'How can it have?' she asked with a gesture of disbelief. 'Didn't you realize? Why didn't you move them on to something else?'

'The groom's father,' he said briefly. 'He insisted.'

'But why didn't you *warn* me? I could have got some more over.'

'I don't think so,' said Marc with a rather mean smile. 'Wasn't the budget being cut back on this one?'

It was true. The bride's family, realizing how costs were mounting, had put a ceiling on the free alcohol. But on the day you couldn't stop the family ordering more drink without making them look ridiculous.

'Oh *shit!*' Colleen ran her fingers through her hair. 'I'll think of something.' She stood up, automatically brushing down her immaculate gray suit with nervous hands. 'Stand by with the white wine and sparkling water and I'll see if we can get more champagne.'

She turned away and, fumbling in her all-purpose gray bag for a cigarette, ducked out of the marquee on the side facing the Visitor Center. She could call for back-up but it would take time and a cigarette would calm her down first. If only she could find her bloody lighter!

She saw the three people sitting peacefully on the bench and something took her feet over towards them. She couldn't have described it; it didn't make sense to say they were the calm in a sea of turbulence.

'Problem?' said the man in the middle of the two elderly tourists. He was holding up a light for her cigarette and he exuded an unexpected joviality that made the formalized wedding celebrations behind her seem dull and flat.

'Thanks,' she said, bending and inhaling that precious first drag. 'Just a bit.'

'You're running late,' said the woman; she was probably the man's mother, Colleen thought on automatic pilot, noting that the man, if he shaved, could be quite a looker. He wore a gold wedding ring.

She sighed. Sometimes strangers were the best people to sound off to; it got rid of the pressure — and she could feel her head beginning to throb. 'You tell me!' she said. 'The Bride was so incredibly late we're out of champagne,' she said. 'I can't believe they didn't send enough. Cutting costs.' She drew viciously on her cigarette.

'Is that going to be made your fault?' asked the man gently. He didn't move but Colleen felt as though he raised a hand to stroke her forehead, dissolving the stress and pressure.

'Oh yes,' she looked at him sharply, appreciating his understanding. 'Even though I was on a budget I'm supposed to eke everything out. It *is* my fault. I assumed it would be okay. I was too busy getting the flowers straight that I didn't supervise properly.' As she spoke, some part of her was surprised. It was her normal custom to blame others and here she was owning up to her responsibility.

'Do you like your job?' asked the man.

'Yes,' Colleen felt an unwelcome tear well up. That was surprising too; she was supposed to be tough. She took another drag and then the words tumbled out of her.

'It's my first big chance. I know I can be good at this; I've wanted this job for so long and I stepped up too soon for this one. It's staff cuts and all that; I know I need more training — it's learning how to handle the people that takes the time. You really need one person for the physical arrangements and one for the people. I just want to learn enough to set up my own firm and do it properly — so it really *works*, if that makes sense.'

She stopped suddenly, feeling very cold.

'Josh?' said the woman. 'Can you help her?'

The man smiled and looked down into her face. 'Are you for real?' he said. 'Mother, I ask you!'

She laid a tiny, blue-veined hand on his. 'Please?' she said. He patted the little paw lovingly and nodded.

Maria stood up. 'Have you got any bottled water?' she asked, putting one hand out to touch Colleen's shoulder.

'Yes.' Colleen stepped back slightly; she didn't like to be touched by strangers.

'Would it have to be sparkling, Josh?' the woman said.

The brown-eyed man threw his head back with a great bellow of laughter and suddenly all three of the strangers were chuckling helplessly. The elderly man was even having to wipe his eyes from tears of mirth.

Colleen stood there looking slightly insulted.

Then the man called Josh stood up; it was as though he unfolded — he was so much taller than Colleen had suspected. 'Go back and check the bottles of sparkling water,' he said. 'I suspect that's where you will find your missing champagne.'

She stared at him. 'You're mad!' she said. But those brown eyes were magnetic.

'Okay,' she muttered, dropped the cigarette and ground it out with her heel. Then she turned and walked briskly back towards the marquee.

'What champagne is this?' asked guest after guest as they drank the extraordinary mellow but crisp sparkling nectar. 'Where can I get some?'

'Amazing … usually the wine gets worse, not better at a do like this. What did the wedding planner say it was again?'

'She wouldn't say. Probably doesn't know. Odd that it's in plain bottles; quite a talking point! Certainly a Dom Perignon in my view.'

'Or the Widow? No, too dry for the Widow. I think you're right … a Dom.'

And somewhere in a Waffle House nearby in Bryce Canyon, three people sat eating pancakes with maple syrup, bacon and eggs. They drank coffee and hot chocolate and left a very good tip. Every now and again one of them would say, 'Does it have to be sparkling?'

And all three would collapse with laughter.

Chapter Five

This is not the story of Josh's grief for Gemma, nor of the happy years that they spent together. Those who have lost a much-loved companion know well enough the sorrow of bereavement: the moments of sudden, blinding anguish; the pervading sense of loss and distress even in laughter; the emptiness of the end of the day with no one to tell how it all went. There would be no more silly in-jokes and nicknames. Instead there would be the continual longing and the occasional heart-stopping, stupid recognitions of the long-dead loved-one accidentally perceived to be walking ahead of you in a crowd.

Josh would not have been who he had become if he hadn't known, with total certainty, that Gemma still lived in another dimension and that she had fulfilled all that she came to do in this life. He knew now that human souls can choose their moment of birth and of death and that this mortal coil is only one strand in a tapestry of existence that is constantly woven through eons of time.

He could speak with her, laugh with her across those dimensions and, in that way, he was more blessed than many other widowers but, just like anyone else who is bereaved, he could not hold her physically in his arms for that final cuddle every night before going to sleep. He couldn't make love to her or let her steal his fries; he couldn't fight over the Sunday supplements with her or ask her if she would scratch his back when there was an itch he just couldn't reach.

The link with Gemma's soul might be real but Gemma herself had moved on; free of remembrance and knowledge of the physical world with its weights and limitations. Real life had to be lived without her.

Josh would not have been Josh without Gemma; her essence was in his bones but he could not have become what he was born to be with her still by his side. This was the time to step up and step out and do the job that he had come to do.

Unfortunately, if you're any way in the public eye, you can't miraculously survive a death crash and vanish for forty days in a desert without somebody noticing.

To start with you have to account for yourself to the police (and it's a good idea to tell them before they find out later because they can get stroppy about things like that). You are also expected to be taken to hospital to be examined at length for signs that you are hurt or crazy. People will hold press conferences about you and, as the British Royal Family found out when Diana died, if you don't show up yourself, the publicity will turn bad and blame will be thrown at you like rocks.

At first, the Gardeners thought they should return to the ranch in Las Vegas. But Josh didn't want to go there so they headed instead for Coldwater Canyon, where Paul was expecting them. On the way, they discussed the best way to deal with the situation. Josh's personal effects from the car, including his phone, had been handed over to Joe and Maria but the phone was useless and Josh couldn't remember any of the direct-line numbers. Joe did have the Las Vegas office switchboard number on his phone because sometimes it had been the only way to find out where Josh was.

'Jude will probably be in LA. That's where her partner works; she calls it home,' said Josh, referring to Jude Isaacs the fearsome beast who was *Gemstone Inc's* Head of Public Relations. 'They can either patch us through to her cell from Vegas or get her to call you. We should probably talk to Jude first anyway.'

He liked Jude; she was a Samurai sword in a world of fakes. When Jude's clipped heels sounded in the corridor outside your office, something made you sit up straighter, clear your mind and drop all the bullshit.

Maria volunteered to make the call. She was, understandably, trying to organize and protect her son as a way of showing her love and her relief. But she couldn't make her cell phone work. It seemed as though the whole apparatus had died.

Joe pulled over to the side of the road only to find the same with his phone.

'That can't be right,' he said. 'They wouldn't both go simultaneously.'

With a flash of insight, they both knew simultaneously that the 'problem' must be Josh.

'Son, would you just walk away for a few meters?' Joe asked. Josh made a face at him and then grinned, reading his mind.

'That could be inconvenient,' he mused, walking backwards with his hands in his trouser pockets and watching his Dad with interest as Joe turned his phone back on.

'Watch where you're putting your feet!' cried the perennial Jewish mother in her heart. Fortunately, she clenched her mouth and left the words unsaid.

'Two meters. That's it. It's working now,' said Joe. 'It's working fine.'

'Hang on, let's just check again,' said Josh.

He took one pace forwards and the cell phone died.

'Dear God!' said Joe involuntarily.

Only when Maria had walked all around Josh with the phone (to the extreme irritation of two passing motorists) did she actually believe what was happening.

'Is it your — what do they call it? Aura?' Joe asked.

'I guess so,' Josh said thoughtfully. 'Electro-magnetic field...yes. I suppose it could be that strong.'

'Son, it *is* that strong,' said his father. 'What else is it going to affect?'

'Well, we'll find out,' said Josh. 'Do you want to make the call with me on the other side of the road?'

'No, we'll be old fashioned and find a pay phone,' said Joe. 'Belt and braces.'

They found a phone in a diner full of gambling machines and virtual reality games in Primm, on the I-15 on the border between Nevada and California. Just walking into the diner was a fairly enlightening experience as all the virtual reality machines within three meters of Josh failed simultaneously. It caused quite a furor. Josh went bright pink with the effort of trying to look innocent when nobody could possibly suspect him anyway.

'That blows the idea of it being something to do with wireless,' Joe said.

'No,' said Josh. 'They are wireless, I think. It must be something to do with vibration.'

Maria found the pay phone and made the initial call. Josh let her do it; she wanted to feel useful and he didn't feel controlled. He just made sure that she realized it was important not to tell anyone except Jude for the moment. He believed Jude could be depended upon not to leak the news, but no one else could necessarily be trusted.

The conversation went like this:

'*Gemstone Inc,* Sarah speaking. How may I help you?'

'Hello, can you put me through to Jude Isaacs please?'

'Who's calling?'

'Maria Gardener.'

'What is it concerning?'

'I'm Gemma Goldstone's mother-in-law.'

'Does Ms. Isaacs know you, Ma'am?'

'Yes of course. I'm her late boss's mother-in-law. Josh's mother.'

'What's it concerning?'

'It's private.'

'I'm afraid Ms Isaacs is currently unavailable. Do you have her cell number?'

'No, can you give it to me?'

'I'm afraid not Ma'am. I can put you through to her office extension and you can leave a message there.'

'Thank you,' Maria's voice was sounding edgy by now.

'What do I say?' she mouthed at her son who had been perusing the fluster around the virtual reality machines with interest. He saw her distress and came over.

'Hang up,' he said. 'Thanks. But maybe it just has to be me.'

He took the phone, ended the call and redialed the number.

'*Gemstone Inc*, Sarah speaking. How may I help you?'

'Put me though to Jude Isaacs' cell please. Code 54 reference Code 16.'

'What? Who's that?'

'Someone who knows what Code 54 is, Sarah. Put me through.'

Every member of *Gemstone Inc* knew the codes. They were the only thing that got people in the know through to Gemma herself or to Jude in the case of a PR disaster. Codes 1-16 were specific people (Josh was code 16) but code 54 was the great unspoken, only to be used at a time of a major press disaster — or even a death. It could only be activated on the day of such an event itself. Code 54 had been used to alert every member of the entourage on the day Gemma died but never before or since.

'Jude Isaacs.' The voice was cold iron; you could say angry.

'Jude, it's Josh Gardener. I'm alive and well and driving in to LA. I need your help and a safe house to meet if home isn't clear of the press. Keep *shtum* until we meet. This has to be managed carefully.'

'Okay Josh. Good to hear from you. I'll call you back in five.' She hung up.

'Wow, that was cool!' said Josh. 'She takes my breath away sometimes. Not a word of reaction. And I love it that she doesn't swear.'

He began to chuckle. 'Let's see how long she takes to realize I didn't call in on my own phone!' His parents looked at him with their lips pressed together. They weren't sure how to take this light-heartedness in such an extraordinary situation.

'Josh, it's going to be hard,' said Joe. 'You do know that don't you?'

'Dad, you have no idea,' said Josh. 'But it has to be done.'

They were talking at complete cross-purposes but they were both speaking the truth.

Maria hovered anxiously by the phone while Josh tried some experiments on just how far he had to be away from virtual reality machines for them to work and tried projecting silver-gold light from his electro-magnetic field on a few slot machines (which suddenly paid up a surprisingly large amount of money). He was fascinated.

The pay phone rang. Maria leapt for it and held it out to Josh.

'Jude?'

'Josh. The house is *not* safe. I've taken a suite at the Beverly Wilshire. I take it your folks are with you? You're in Primm, right?'

'Yes.'

'About five hours then. I'll be there and will wait in the room. No. 1117, name of E. Coker. Got that?'

'Yes Jude, thanks.'

'Any special orders — food? Drink? Pastrami and Brie on rye?'

'Jude, you think of everything. I'll leave it to you.'

'There's the usual press presence at the hotel — Marco Montbretia and Arianna Bel and their kids are there. Try not to come in wearing a false moustache or a rug, Josh. They're usually wise to that. Who's driving? Okay, tell your old man to drive round to the garage and ask for Herb. He'll bring you up in the service lift. No need to tip; taken care of.'

'Thanks Jude —' but the phone had cut off. Iron-heart Jude Isaacs never bothered with 'Hello' or 'Goodbye'.

Five-and-a-half hours later, road-tired but still strengthened by relief, the Gardeners were looking up at the Hollywood sign on the edge of the hill with the age-old delight of children. It was magic that never failed.

'What was the name Jude booked us in under?' asked Maria.

'E. Coker!' Josh said with appreciation. 'Amazing she remembers that!'

'What?' both parents spoke at once.

'East Coker — the poem by T. S. Eliot.'

'What about it?'

'It's one of my favorites,' Josh said. 'Oh — the Beverly Wilshire! Dad. Take the next left, two blocks, right, one block right again —

and we'll take it from there.'

'The Beverly Wilshire!' Maria had been horrified at the decision to go to such a star-ridden hotel. 'Somewhere less ostentatious surely?'

'When you want to choose your time it pays to be in the place where people know how to help you,' said Josh. 'The staff at the Wilshire have a long history of knowing how to deal with the media. And, Mum, this is going to be pretty big news. Might as well handle it as well as we can at the start.'

'You trust Jude?' Joe was curious.

'As far as it goes, she's bomb-proof,' said Josh. 'As far as it goes. This may go further than that but not yet thank God, not yet.'

Chapter Six

As Joe negotiated the last turning and spoke to the garage valet who was discreetly waiting for them at the back of the hotel, Josh sighed and leaned back, tapping his fingers on the door handle. He was suddenly feeling frustrated and very lonely. He yearned to see Gemma, not only because of how she would be loving this situation, spinning it and open to every possible opportunity, but because she would, now, be squeezing this restless hand.

'I'm here,' she whispered and suddenly his mind was filled with music: Coldplay's 2007 song *The Scientist* and the video that illustrated it flowed through his heart. The grief and joy that he could hear her — and it — so clearly caused tears to run down his cheeks.

Joe and Maria exchanged anxious looks but said nothing.

'So here's how it goes,' said Jude Isaacs, her perennial clipboard tucked under one arm and her other hand brushing back the long brown hair that always fell over her face. Jude had a dozen electronic devices to hand but she wrote everything longhand first. 'Helps me remember,' she would say if you asked. And Jude forgot *nothing.*

'First, we get you fully examined by the Wilshire's doctor — no.' She stopped Maria from speaking with a wave of her hand. 'It must be that way or Josh will be taken down to the police station. We have to be able to say that he's under doctor's orders. And if he goes to the police first, he goes to hospital. That's how it is.'

Maria nodded reluctantly. She didn't like taking second fiddle to this tall and elegant creature with talon-like fake nails and a vibrant, youthful glow that was only just discernibly due to exquisite make-up.

She also didn't like the way Josh looked at her or how he related to her. Maria was not a stupid woman and she knew that it wasn't a sexual attraction — yet. It was some kind of kindred spirit emotional link: the kind that was more dangerous than sex in her view — and so easy for outsiders to misinterpret *as* sex.

Jude was also intuitive. She turned her full charm on Maria. 'Please don't worry Mrs. Gardener,' she said (Jude was one of those rare Americans who did not automatically schmooze people with their given names without permission). 'The Wilshire is used to inexplicable calls for a doctor. Generally it's to get some drug-crazed celebrity back onto their feet in time for a public appearance — but they do have access to some of the very best — and they always come discreetly.'

'For a fee,' muttered Joe.

'But we have the money, Dad,' said Josh. 'The money is there to serve us — not for us to fear.'

'Wealth always looks bad,' said Joe.

'It's a tool,' said his son, smiling. 'Just an energy. It accepts whatever we project onto it. Do me a favor, Dad and don't add any more negativity on to it!'

'You've got your work cut out, Josh,' said his father.

'Maybe Dad — but let Jude finish.'

'Thanks Josh.' Jude brushed her hair back again. She was stunning: half Jewish, half Negro with straightened dark hair and steel-gray eyes. Or were they contacts? Maria couldn't tell. Either way, they were arresting. As was her beautifully encased bust and the coral and slate-blue woolen dress that clung to every curve. And how could anyone get away with wearing orange and blue? It was ridiculous; they should look stupid. Maria shook her head mentally, realizing she was getting a real prejudice together and tried to concentrate.

'And as soon as the doctor has finished, I call the cops and tell them that you have just shown up and that we thought we should alert them as soon as possible. I'll also say you can't be moved because you're undergoing a medical examination.

'They will come here which will start the ball rolling for the press. It looks better if it gets out through them — less of a publicity stunt.'

'Stunt!' Maria couldn't help it.

'Ma'am, everything today is viewed as a publicity stunt,' said Jude patiently. 'Folks will think that we staged this whole thing; kept Josh out of the public eye deliberately so that he'd get more press when he takes over the show.'

'Takes over the show…?' said Josh. 'Which show would that be?'

'*The Miracle Mile* of course,' said Maria with a snort.

'Yes Ma'am. But not at first. Josh will probably be approached by another Network or one of the IPTV channels and he'll be offered several million dollars to go there,' said Jude.

'Oh I will, will I?' Josh stretched his lanky legs and knotted his hands behind his head.

'To do what?' interjected both Joe and Maria.

'To take Gemma's role but in their talent shows. It's the most likely scenario,' said Jude.

'Tell me, Jude,' said Josh. 'Have you always had this gift of crafting life from your thoughts?'

'Pretty much,' she said, in all seriousness. 'I'm certainly what they call a self-made woman. My folks told me it couldn't be done but I got where I wanted to go.'

'You just darn well got on and did it?'

'Pretty much,' she said again. 'Okay, I'm going down to see the manager and fix up the doctor's visit. Any questions before I go?'

'Can I shave?' Josh rubbed the itchy mess of his beard with his hand.

Jude considered long and carefully.

'Not now, no,' she said. 'The doctor needs to see you with the beard. But once he's gone, yes. We don't want the press seeing you with a beard. It's not an image we want to get out. Anything else?'

'No Ma'am,' said Josh and he took another pastrami and Brie sandwich.

Joe and Maria exploded once she'd gone.

'What are you doing? You're behaving like a movie star/her puppet!' they said simultaneously.

'I'm allowing the world as it is here to serve me,' he said, very quietly.

'What?'

'*Allowing*,' said Josh. 'Not resisting. It's resisting that causes the pain. Jude knows what she's doing. If we were in England, I would do it differently, but we're not. It is what it is and if I'm here to demonstrate anything, it's how to make peace with now. You do that and everything else works out.'

'Can you put that in English?' said Joe.

'Dad, it's what you do all the time!' said Josh. 'Mum pushes and prods you and you don't resist; in fact you let her have her way most of the time. And by not resisting her, you give her permission to try things — and to discover for herself whether or not they don't work. Then it's her decision to do or not to do them. It's win-win. She has learnt how to live more easily and you've had no bad feelings between you because you quarreled and tried to tell her what to do.'

'I'm right more often than not,' said Maria, half angry and half impressed.

'Mum, you are right so many times it's scary,' said her son. 'Look how you waited for me! But even so, you were all tense and worried. Didn't you *know* inside that what you had to do was get on with life in England and show up on the 41st day?'

'I didn't *know* you weren't dead.'

'Yes you did.'

'Well…yes…but…'

'But you thought that if you kept vigil it might help me *not* to be dead?'

'I suppose so. I needed to do it.'

'Well that's all any of us can do most of the time,' said Josh. 'What we need to do. But I don't think it made the slightest difference to *me* whether you were at the dam or back in England. But what you *thought* did matter…because you were led by hope not despair.'

'Yes…yes I was,' she said.

'I don't suppose you thought about the times you made me cup cakes with cochineal icing, did you?' he asked with the gentlest of smiles.

'Why, yes, I did,' Maria was genuinely surprised. 'And when you found out, you wouldn't eat them.'

'I felt that thought,' he said, remembering with a chuckle. 'It did help. It did help. But it helped because it was fuelled by hope not despair. So many prayers are filled with despair.'

'Of course they are,' said Joe. 'Most people only pray when they have lost all hope.'

'East Coker,' said Josh and quoted:

I said to my soul, be still and wait without hope
For hope would be hope for the wrong thing;
Wait without love
For love would be love of the wrong thing.
There is yet faith
But the faith and the love and the hope are all in the waiting.

'That's interesting,' he said, stopping abruptly. 'I used to like that poem. Now I don't like it at all. There's no…no…*joy* to it.' He flexed his shoulders as if trying on a new coat.

'I waited with love,' said Maria.

'You *know* love,' said Josh, returning his attention to his mother. 'Most people don't. They think they do — but it is the love of the ego they know. The love of what they want people to be or love of what they think should happen. You waited with acceptance that love itself remained whatever had happened to me. That God remained. You must have done.'

'I did know that it was all perfect; that you lived whether or not you were dead,' Maria admitted. 'My ego fought that but I did know.'

'That's love,' he said and held his arms out to give her a hug.

Both parents ached to say, 'What *did* happen in the desert?' but they held their tongues. And that was real love too.

'Do you think I could have a bath?' said Josh. 'I forgot to ask Jude. I'd give anything for a bath.'

Doctor Vikram Prakash had pumped more celebrity stomachs than he cared to remember. He could never watch the Oscars, the Golden Globes or the Grammy's without snorting with derision. A load of fakes; no talent; no *discipline*.

But this one had him stumped. He had spent two hours with Josh Goldstone including accompanying him to the private medical center next door to the hotel for a full body-scan to indicate signs of trauma. There were none. Josh's eyesight, hearing, heart, blood pressure, cholesterol level, hydration levels were all textbook perfect. *Too* textbook perfect for a man of his age.

Returning to the hotel room, the doctor had repeated as many of the tests as he could by hand, mistrusting the machinery. But as he lay down the last of his equipment on the smooth marble washstand in the huge bathroom he couldn't think of what to say that would possibly keep him his job.

Josh sat patiently on the edge of the much-wanted but as yet untaken bath wearing just a white toweling robe.

'Mr. Gardener, I'm sorry to say this but you're either lying or there's a fine restaurant hidden in the Valley of Fire,' Vikram said.

'Perhaps I ate grubs, cactus and whatever I could catch,' said Josh. 'Or it could be the third option.'

'And the third option would be?' The doctor did not hide his impatience but, despite himself he was intrigued. This man was registering as perfect on every count and nobody — *nobody* — did that. What was more, there wasn't a mark on him; not a bruise nor a pimple.

'Manna from heaven,' said Josh simply.

The doctor sat down heavily on a stool by the washbasin. 'And you expect people to believe that?' he said.

'No,' said Josh, gently. 'They will probably call me a liar and think that I holed up in a hotel room somewhere; probably with another woman and that I was so callous that I disregarded the death of my wife completely for 40 days.'

'So why did you do it?'

'Do what? Hole up in a hotel room?'

'Yes.'

'I didn't. But it will probably take a week or so for the journalists to check out every motel and possible place that I could have stayed. There will probably be computer-generated recreations of the crash all over the news demonstrating that I couldn't possibly be alive, let alone be thrown clear, in a death crash like that.'

'There already have been,' grunted the doctor.

'So if that was impossible, then obviously other impossible things can happen too,' said Josh. 'I am here after all.'

'You can't have been in that car.'

'Well you're perfectly at liberty to think whatever you want to think,' said Josh. 'You won't be the first or the last. But I suspect people will have seen me in the car.'

That was true, the doctor had to admit. CCTV did show that there were two people in the car. And even if the passengers had not been celebrities, a beautiful, elegant, open-topped Aston Martin V8 Vantage re-made entirely to Gemma's specifications in metallic royal blue, could not have been missed. Eyewitnesses had seen it rear up and tip over the wall. Vikram himself had seen the footage on TV. No one had been thrown clear. The car hit the water and sank. Nobody swam away from it.

'I believe evidence,' said the doctor heavily, getting up to check Josh's reflexes. 'I don't believe the impossible.'

'Shame,' said Josh with a sudden grin. 'Life is such fun when you do. What kind of evidence would you like to see?'

'I'd like to see the man who was in a fatal car crash,' said the doctor.

'Okay,' said Josh simply.

Before Vikram's eyes the world blurred. Josh seemed to shrink and fold in on himself; his head horribly broken and crushed; his body twisted, scarred with blood and purple bruises; the right arm sheered off at the shoulder; both legs smashed beyond repair.

The doctor screamed and fell back. Staggering, he found himself crashing into the bidet. Pain shot through his hip as his sciatica flared but the emotional shock was greater. Tears of horror and compassion flew to his eyes.

When Josh, visibly whole again, reached out a hand to help him up, Vikram winced and recoiled. How could he not?

'Evidence isn't all it's cracked up to be,' said Josh gently. 'There are more things in heaven and earth, Doctor, than we can know of. There are powers greater than humanity – even greater than the medical profession!'

'You're a magician!'

'No Sir, I'm not. You asked and you were given. It's the Law – ask and it is given.'

'Who are you?' spluttered the doctor.

'I'm me. Unequivocally and indisputably me. Just me. Who are you?'

'I'm a Hindu. I don't believe in…'

'No, you're not a Hindu. You're *you.* Unequivocally and indisputably you. That may include a Hindu belief but you're not *a* Hindu. Once you say you're *an* anything you stop being an individual. What's wrong with your leg?'

'S…s…sciatica,' the doctor spluttered.

'Really?' said Josh. 'I think it's actually the shoulder that's the problem. It just transmits as the leg. Have you ever seen a chiropractor?'

'No!' Dr Prakash was not a fan of the chiropractic community.

'Put your hand into the water,' Josh ordered. 'It will help.'

'What?'

'Put your hand in the water,' Josh repeated, moving away from the now bubbling hot and steaming bath water behind him. Part of Vikram's mind registered that the water had not been that hot before and that it wasn't a Jacuzzi. In a daze, he moved forward and touched the water with the fingertips of one hand.

He gasped as a sensation he could only describe later as tasting of lemon fizzy sherbet shot through the arm and down his back. It was like being on the most amazing roller-coaster ride back in time. He felt 20 years younger and stood up taller than he had done since leaving medical school. His ego too was healed.

'Do you *know* who you are?' he said, tears falling from his eyes as his body and soul sloughed off the pain and resentment of years and his mind saw Krishna.

'Yes,' said Josh. 'I'm me. And there's nothing that I can do that you can't do either. You just need the faith. Forty days in a desert will make or break a faith.'

'They're going to crucify you,' said the doctor, wide-eyed and shaking with awe.

'Not this time,' said Josh. 'Guantanamo Bay more likely.' His brown eyes were kind as he took the doctor's hand again.

'Do you think you could talk to Jude and the police while I take a quick bath?' he asked.

Chapter Seven

'Stand by studio.'

'Five, four, three, two, one, go titles.'

'Breaking News from *Fox News* — we go live now to our Los Angeles Bureau with Alan Baylis and Susanna Doyle.'

'They're calling him "The Miracle Man". But could Gemma Goldstone's husband really survive 40 days in the desert?'

'Josh Goldstone was in *this* car as it fell over the side of the Hoover Dam. How could he survive the crash that killed his superstar wife? We hear his story in his own words today!'

'In other news, new fears over the ice-caps and global warming.'

'And California's controversial governor sets feathers flying over vegetarianism.'

'But first, the story that has all America debating. It seems that Josh Goldstone, husband of *Miracle Mile* star Gemma Goldstone, has survived the fatal car crash that took place on the Hoover dam six weeks ago.'

'Goldstone turned up in Los Angeles last night — with his parents — after apparently surviving in the desert heat of Nevada's Valley of Fire for 40 days.'

'We know that Josh Goldstone was in the car with his wife when the accident occurred from this cell phone video taken just before the collision.'

VT FX: *'Great car — look at the plate! It is — that's Gemma Goldstone — oh my God...!'*

'And *this* CCTV footage...'

'Or at least that someone *like* Josh Goldstone was in the car. There have been suggestions that spending 40 days in the desert was simply a publicity stunt. But who then was in the car?'

'Well Josh himself is about to appear at a press conference here in Los Angeles and we cross now live to our reporter Maude-Lynn Sykes outside the police station.'

'Maude-Lynn, Have you seen Josh? How did he look?'

'Alan. Susanna. I have seen him. I saw him briefly on his way into the police station. He appears surprisingly well for someone who has, apparently, been through such an ordeal. There are no visible signs of bruising or broken bones. The staff at *Gemstone Inc* tell me that he is very tired and deeply emotional about his wife's death but he is adamant that he did spend those 40 days in the desert.'

'He didn't hide out in some hotel then? Can that be proved?'

'Not exactly. This is not strictly a police matter any more. Josh Goldstone has provided the police with a statement about the crash and will appear at his wife's inquest. Here's what Chief Superintendent Jonah Blake had to say earlier this morning.'

The VT cut in:

'We have already established from enquiries within a 20 mile limit around the Hoover Dam that Mr. Goldstone did not book into any motel or inn of any kind. Someone may have taken him in to a private home but we are satisfied by medical opinion that the shock sustained from the accident was sufficient to disorientate him in such a way that he might not have realized that he should come forward and declare himself to be safe. Obviously Mr. Goldstone will be required to give evidence at the full hearing of the inquest into his wife's death. However, apart from that, we are completing our enquiries into his whereabouts and we are pleased that this missing person aspect of the enquiry has had such an unexpected, happy outcome.'

'Maude-Lynn — what was the press response to Chief Superintendent Blake's statement?'

'A very mixed response, Susanna. There are even those who are speculating that Gemma Goldstone is not dead either and it's all a massive publicity stunt!'

'Oh come now, Maude! Surely not even the most jaded of celebrity-watchers can believe that?'

'Stranger things have happened in the world of entertainment, Alan. This is almost a real-life return of Bobby Ewing in the 80s TV show *Dallas*.'

'Maude, we have news that the press conference is about to start…we're now crossing live to Los Angeles police headquarters where Josh Goldstone is coming out to face the press.'

It was Jude who stepped out in front of the cameras first. Josh stood in the wings blowing on his fingers as if he were cold; it was a habit of his when he was nervous. He was wearing a royal-blue sweatshirt and jeans; looking very ordinary; very un-famous; very un-intimidating (as Jude put it). There was nothing to offend or set the press at odds with him from the start.

Jude herself looked immaculate in a dark red suit with a crisp white blouse, her hair tied back and garnet studs in her ears.

'We must get the colors right from the start,' she had stipulated earlier. 'Vibrant blues and creamy-whites, not pure white; that would blank you out — a little green perhaps but soft green — olive green for you. Hints of all the higher Chakra colors including violet. It's weird but you'd probably look good in violet with that pale light in your hair.'

'Will they know the higher Chakra colors?' asked Josh, amused.

'Not consciously,' she said. 'I must wear low heels or I'll be taller than you.'

'Not my fault you're a giant,' said Josh easily. Jude was 6ft in her stockinged feet and Josh 6ft1in.

'Whatever we do, you mustn't look like a celebrity — yet,' she said, ignoring the previous remark.

'Well that won't be hard.'

'Josh...your private life ends here, you know that, don't you?'

'Yes. It already did.'

She nodded. Jude wasn't sentimental and she didn't expect Josh to be either. She was working on the biggest story she had ever handled and she exuded a fierce excitement.

He hadn't had to tell her about his effect on cell phones — that had become very apparent very quickly. Would that affect the press conference? She had made sure that the cameras were all three meters away, to the press's extreme irritation, but it remained to be seen whether the satellite transmissions would go live once Josh stepped out into the lights.

This inexplicable uncertainty, mixed with the tangible hunger of the throng of press in front of her brought an uncharacteristic tremor to Jude's throat. 'Get a grip!' she told herself fiercely and stepped up to the desk.

'Ladies and gentlemen, my name is Jude Isaacs from *Gemstone Inc.* I'd like to warn you that Josh Goldstone is very tired from talking with the police this morning and after his ordeal in the desert. While he has been cleared to take part in this press conference by the medical team who examined him on his return to LA, he will only be reading a statement. He will not be taking questions.'

She paused. No one was exclaiming at broken equipment so it looked like all was good on the transmission front.

'Ladies and gentlemen, Josh Goldstone,' she said, stepping back.

Josh recoiled visibly from the barrage of photographic flashguns. He looked ostentatiously normal, certainly thin but not excessively so. Many of the women watching found themselves feeling slightly protective towards him, noticing his brown eyes and self-effacing way of moving. Most of the men felt unthreatened but not superior. If you were trying to create someone who was easy on everyone's eye you could hardly have chosen a better physical vehicle.

The room erupted. Men and women raced forwards with recording devices ready to push them into his face. Questions hit him like bullets and for a moment he looked confused. He noted that some of the journalists who had raced forward had stopped dead, flustered as their electronic equipment malfunctioned and inside, he felt slightly rocked by the fear in their energy fields. Then he seemed to come to himself and simply put one hand up to encourage silence. Then he just stood and waited. Some inner part of him actually said 'Back off!'

It worked. They backed away. And then their equipment functioned perfectly.

'Thank you for coming,' he said in a voice that was quietly authoritative. 'I do have a statement but I'm not going to read it. I'm just going to say a few things.

'Firstly, I wasn't able to go to Gemma's funeral; and I wish I could have done. More than that, I wish beyond all things that she could be standing beside me now – then you wouldn't be interested in me at all.

'But she's gone and…and…well I want to tell you how wonderful she was. Not as a celebrity – though she was that as well – but as my wife and my friend and my lover. She was everything. I will…I will always love her.'

He took a deep breath. A single tear slid down his cheek. He bowed his head and wiped it off with the side of one hand. That picture raced around the world, to be seen on millions of TV and computer screens for years to come.

The silence was palpable as Josh raised his head and began to speak again.

'I'm not permitted to speak about the accident until the inquest is completed. But I can say that we both saw what was going to happen. It was one of those slow-motion moments you hear about. I had time to take her hand. There wasn't anything else to do.

'Then, it hurt – and it all went very strange. I thought I was dead for a long time and I couldn't for one moment explain what happened but I found myself in shallow water in a place that was all red. I knew what had happened but at the same time I *didn't* know – if you can understand that. I was there but not there.

'Some of you may think this is stupid but I ask you not to put your pre-conceptions onto it. I knew that I had been saved and I knew that Gemma was safe and through to another reality *because I could see her.* And she could see me. People say there's a tunnel you go through with a near-death experience. That may be so. All I saw was light and friends and loved ones. And in the whole time in the desert it was as though they told me how to find food and water. It was a miracle that I survived but it was also an extraordinary experience. I was lost and more found than I can ever explain. I heard the music of the stars and I was washed clean.'

He shrugged. 'That's it really. It was what it was. And one day I realized that I had to leave and come home. That's all. Thank you.'

'Who were you holing up with, Josh?' One harsh voice cut across the silence. There was a murmur of dissent.

Josh looked straight at the man and, despite himself, the questioner winced. They both stood their ground and the rest of the room held its breath.

'All truth is relative,' Josh said. 'You can only see in others what is within yourself. If that's your truth then no one can dissuade you of it. I have nothing to defend. Do with me and say of me what you will.'

He gave a brief nod and walked out of the room as the press corps erupted. Jude stepped forward and spoke, but to no avail; she was drowned out by the roar of 'Josh! Josh!'

Back in the Fox studios, Alan Baylis and Susanna Doyle looked at each other and then at the camera. Both spoke at once.

'What do you think of that Alan/Susanna?'

'I thought it was rather touching,' said Susanna

'Quite amazing' they added simultaneously.

'OB has the doctor who checked him out,' said the director in their earpieces.

'We gather that Maude-Lynn Sykes is with the doctor who examined Josh Goldstone. Maude?'

'Thank you Alan. Yes, I have with me Dr Vikram Prakash — Dr Prakash, you were called to the Beverly Wilshire Hotel where Josh Goldstone was staying. What were you asked to do?'

'I was asked to examine Mr. Goldstone — to give him a full physical examination to ensure that he was well enough to be interviewed by the police.'

'You didn't see the need to send him to a hospital.'

'Mr. Goldstone was extensively examined at a private medical clinic including undergoing a full body scan and tests for all possible conditions. The results show that he is entirely healthy.'

'But after an ordeal like that surely he should have some traces of trauma.'

'He is healthy Ms Sykes,' said the doctor. 'There is nothing wrong with him whatsoever.'

'Are you keeping him under observation?'

'I will remain on call but it is rest that he needs; rest and good food. Nothing else.'

'Is he malnourished?'

'He is a little thin but I cannot say any more than that. Again, his health appears to be perfect.'

'Appears to be. But surely if he has spent 40 days in the desert there should be a multitude of things wrong with him.'

'I don't know where he has been. All I can tell you is that I examined a fully healthy, slightly thin man,' said the doctor testily. 'All the tests I took returned normal. That is all I can say.'

'Thank you doctor.' Maude-Lynn swung back to the camera. 'Josh Goldstone has now left the police station, apparently for his home in Coldwater Canyon. According to his staff, this will be his first visit home since his wife's death and they are asking for press and public to allow him some privacy.'

'You'll be right there, Maude-Lynn?' cut in Alan Baylis.

'I will indeed. For *Fox News,* this is Maude-Lynn Sykes.'

'I think that went quite well,' said Jude. 'The equipment worked at least.'

'Um…everyone's calling me "Goldstone," said Josh mildly. 'My name's Gardener.'

'Trust me,' said Jude. 'You may need Gardener to hide behind from now on. If you use Goldstone for public and Gardener in private, life will be a lot easier.'

He saw the sense in this because all his and Gemma's private holidays had been taken as Mr. and Mrs. Gardener. 'But…' said Josh. He sighed. 'Oh well,' he said as the black Mercedes pulled in through the gates of the ranch-style house in the heart of the canyon. The black shields closed soundlessly behind them. Ahead was Joe and Maria's hire-car parked outside the front awning of a sprawling honey-yellow house decorated with white and terracotta tiles. Josh hoped there would be tea. An upbringing in England had ruined him for American tea. He thought that it was never made with truly boiling water and the teabags tasted like dust. He drank coffee because all Americans did but now it was tea that he craved with all the fervor of a child seeking a favorite toy.

A part of his mind was blanking out now. It knew that the sight of all the familiar things: Gemma's clothes; newspapers; letters; ornaments and their gifts to each other would be immensely painful. Something had to shut down for a while in order to be able to bear it later.

Gemma's brother Paul answered the door, nodding curtly to Josh. They had already spoken and Paul was trying hard to pretend to be pleased at the prodigal's return. The two men had never been close, Paul regarding himself as the go-getter who got nowhere and Josh the do-nothing who reaped the rewards of his wife's success.

Josh had lost his keys in the crash and it felt odd to have to ring his own doorbell. He stood back for Jude to walk in first, taking a little time to assimilate the sight and smell of home. Paul immediately began to bluster with some spiel about memorabilia and some book. Josh looked at him and away again, leaving him to Jude. Instinctively, he turned into Gemma's office to the left of the Mexican-furnished hall. There were three people in the room. He knew two of them vaguely — members of her back-up team from the office — and he knew, without understanding how he knew, that they were putting together an 'authorized biography' for immediate publication.

What he didn't know — and they didn't hide fast enough — was what else they had been doing.

There seems to be a natural inclination to walk around a computer and look at its screen. Josh did it almost absent-mindedly as the people stood paralyzed by his presence.

If he could have, Conor, one of the acolytes, would have opened a new window to hide what he was doing but, as Josh walked into the room, the laptop's wireless connection to the Internet had died and its screen remained stuck on the last connection. Josh saw the listings of Gemma's clothes and personal effects just as Paul walked crisply into the room and stood defensively in front of him.

'eBay?' said Josh, stunned. 'You're selling her on eBay?'

'We thought you were dead,' said Paul. In fairness, it was tough for him; Josh could see that. He thought he had inherited everything. But this was beyond enough.

'We listed them before you came back,' said Conor. 'Some of them sold already; we've got bids on everything; we can't just pull the auctions.'

'We haven't posted anything since we heard from you,' said Paul. 'Obviously we must discuss this. There's the matter of the autobiography too — I have a deal...'

Josh put one hand up, stopping him. There was silence.

'You've got Gemma's laptop,' he said without emotion. 'Are the other two computers full of her information too?'

'Yes,' said Conor in a relieved tone. 'We've collated everything together and backed it up on all three computers for safety.'

'Just these computers?' said Josh conversationally. 'No off-site back-up?'

'No.' Conor looked more and more like a rabbit caught in headlights.

'Would you just give me a minute?' said Josh. 'I'd like a moment alone in my wife's office.'

Nobody moved; they looked at Paul.

'Out please,' said Josh dangerously.

'Er...' Paul stepped towards him. Josh exploded, grabbing his brother-in-law by the lapels of his gray suit and hurling him round. Paul reeled out of the room and fell back against the wall. His stocky frame slipped down slowly with his jacket riding up above his head.

'OUT!' Josh roared at the others. All three acolytes scuttled out. One of them was squealing like a pig.

Jude went in five minutes later and leant against the doorpost quietly. She had a mug of tea in either hand and her perennial black bag hooked over one arm. She picked her way around the smashed computers on the floor and placed one mug in Josh's un-resisting hand. A bar of organic dark chocolate found its way onto the desk.

'Drink,' she said. 'Eat. The tea has that Rescue Remedy Gemma used in it; doesn't spoil the taste. You should be having it intra-venously right now. We've already administered it to the others. Did you get the hard drives? Did you find any CDs?'

Josh waved his hand at two short stacks that he had piled on the desk. Jude slid them into her handbag.

Josh drank deeply. A line of dried tears marked both his cheeks.

'Why are you helping?' he said. 'Surely you approve of publicity?'

'It's my job to serve you,' said Jude. 'Not Paul Goldstone. What you say, goes.'

'Thanks,' he said, running a hand through his hair and taking a gulp of tea.

'Oh that's good,' he said, cupping the mug with both hands and drinking deeply. 'Thank you.'

'I kinda thought the explosion of temper would happen at some phony religious center or the like,' said Jude conversationally, sipping at her own tea and one-handedly unwrapping the chocolate. 'Turning over the tables in the Temple — you know…'

'Huh,' Josh took some chocolate and sighed. 'They didn't have litigious lawyers, law suits and criminal damage charges in those days,' he said. 'I'll have to pay for the computers.'

'They are yours. Everything that belongs to *Goldstone Inc* is yours. Anything that doesn't, I'll take care of,' said Jude.

'And I have to stop the sales…' he faltered and stopped.

'Taken care of,' said Jude again. 'At least all that can be, will be.'

He looked at her and she looked right back.

'You know, don't you?' he said.

'Always did,' she said. 'Didn't *know* that I knew or *what* I knew but I did know. Can't explain that. Can't even explain to myself. Odd isn't it?'

'You could say that,' he said.

After he had finished his tea, she held him in her arms like a baby as he cried.

Chapter Eight

Paul Goldstone also sat drinking tea, his self-righteous soul singing with indignation. Part of him wished that he had been slightly physically hurt so that he could call the cops or sue but he was just emotionally shaken.

Poor Paul. When Josh had telephoned him to tell him that he was alive and well, there's no doubt that Paul was deeply disappointed at the news. One might even say offended. What right had Josh to turn up after so long when Paul had got everything so well organized? When he had been able to plan a wonderful, extra-prosperous and busy future for himself? When, for once — at long last — he had been the one in the driving seat instead of his super-successful bimbo of a sister who'd just got lucky in a world that worshipped celebrity.

Of course Paul had had every right to have Gemma's biography published, to sell her dresses on eBay. He could do whatever he wanted with her celebrity memorabilia — if he were the heir. But now, he had no rights at all. Perhaps he had thought that if he just continued what he'd been doing anyway, Josh wouldn't mind. Why would he mind? Josh had never amounted to anything or pushed for anything. And Paul, at twelve years older than Gemma, had always striven to be a father figure with authority especially since their parents became sick.

How he felt inside, no one ever knew — although his ex-wives spoke of tantrums and deep emotional troughs that seemed unbelievable to those who experienced his outer charm and control. Even though he was only 5′7″ Paul went through women like a knife through butter, drawing them in, chewing them up and spitting them out, depleted.

Even those who had been dumped had to admit that Paul had had this odd indescribable charm and, when he was animated, a compelling charisma. He was so very ugly that he was almost beautiful. His face had gone, mid teens, from angelic childish to asymmetrical and large boned, ruled by deep-set brown eyes under fierce satyr-like eyebrows and haunted by five-o'clock shadow. And that was without the nose. Paul had the nose to end all noses. Fagin had a snub nose by comparison. No one understood why women were attracted to him but they were, probably because he had the ability to make you his entire world when he was talking to you. What you didn't spot — until it was too late — was that he did that to everyone else too.

Paul was the archetypal Jewish Prince. He could do no wrong in anyone's eyes for far too long for a healthy ego to be able to develop and, as his parents were unassuming lower middle-class people, the academic achievements of the little Junior School Head Boy made them glow with pride. He became an architect, lived in the 'right' part of Hendon and granted his ex-wives their Jewish divorce or *get*.

It was always going to be hard for Paul to be overtaken by the little sister who had never done well at school; who had just been pretty and who had just been expected to marry into the community and have kids.

Gemma was mousey and submissive until she discovered the joys of hair color, facials and manicures and found that she could eat whatever she wanted and stay as slim as bird. She had the same childhood angel-face as her brother but her bones were kinder as she grew. And Gemma herself possessed kindness in bucket loads. If Paul had realized his lack of inherent kindness and her abundance he probably would have written her a well-structured letter complaining about it. As it was, he was proud of her in public and resentful in silence.

For Gemma became the princess over and above him in the eyes of both the family and the world. She married a Jewish boy she'd known at school and, although they didn't have children (polyps were whispered about for several years with sad shakings of the head), they remained secure and happy together while Gemma shone in the show business world.

Ponderous Paul and elfin Gemma never knew if they got on well or not; they were family so they didn't think about it. Paul cordially despised Josh who was quiet, academic and would vanish behind a newspaper or underneath an affectionate dog at the drop of a hat while Paul and Gemma remained the center of the family's attention. Paul always showed up at the right events; did the right thing and said what he truly believed were the right things.

So when Gemma died, Paul — as heir and executor — did the right thing again. Did what should be done, took over the family business, as it were, and started organizing. Their parents, now in their eighties, were incapable of coping (they lived in sheltered accommodation paid for 50-50 by Paul and Gemma which was a strain for him and nothing to her) so it was all down to Paul.

So when he was approached about the notes for Gemma's autobiography, Paul took charge again. On the 28th day after her death, naturally. All estates rely on the heir to survive the deceased by 28 days and as Josh, the original heir, was obviously dead, then it was Paul's duty to start making decisions and move on.

No one in a media-ruled world could blame him for authorizing the finding of all relevant information for a book. The advance was a quarter of a million for goodness' sake! And that was pounds, not dollars! Paul had a very pleasing meeting with the editorial director of a very large publishing company in London and was extremely flattered that they wanted him to write the first chapter and the epilogue under his own name. And now, that stupid husband had ruined it all.

Paul left the house as soon as he had finished the tea pushed upon him by Joe and Maria. They didn't know where he — or the others — went and everyone was heartily embarrassed. It didn't bode well for the future.

It's best to draw a veil over Josh's life that next week in the house where he and Gemma, his first and only love, had lived and which still carried her scent in her clothes and cosmetics as well as on the sheets and in the fabric of the easy chairs.

Josh haunted the synagogue where he and Gemma had formerly gone haphazardly. In there, he was safe from press intrusion and both the Rabbi and his wife offered genuine comfort and advice. He was invited to two community suppers but declined both, preferring to spend the evenings at home alone. After two days of being fussed over, he had asked his parents to let him be and they flew back to England reluctantly but understanding that this was time that their son needed. Every night, Maria contacted him on Skype to check that he was okay and every night he either answered or sent her a message back when he got in. Sometimes he felt frustrated by her clinginess because he knew that if she just let go of conventional communication, she would be able to hear and feel him in her heart as she always had been able to do. But the web cam link helped her to re-align herself to the fact that he was alive — and remained alive.

At the end of the week, Josh attended the re-opened inquest into Frank Morrison's and Gemma's death. It felt totally surreal, the courtroom being filled with celebrity journalists and the building surrounded by paparazzi. Mr. Morrison's lawyer was trying to blame Gemma's driving for the accident even though tire marks and the CCTV coverage showed the truck veering across the road. Josh said simply that he couldn't remember; he had no intention of landing the Morrison family with any blame. The verdict was accidental death.

That evening, Josh gave instructions to his accountant to arrange to sell the LA, Las Vegas and South of France houses and their contents, including Gemma's collection of classic cars and her multi-million-dollar yacht moored in Monte Carlo. 'I don't need them,' he said simply. 'I have more than enough. They should go to people who can appreciate them.'

The money was to go to Gemma's charitable foundation but, first, Josh set up a fund to pay one hundred per cent of Gemma's parents' costs in perpetuity and gave Paul a one-off payment of $5,000,000 in lieu of the biography fees.

'What will you live on?' said the accountant, wide-eyed. Josh laughed and pointed at the bank statements. He was still a multi-millionaire without any of those assets.

'Don't you want to keep a car? Just one?' said the accountant.

'I'm not a car person,' said Josh. 'Gemma loved the Astons and the Ferraris and the Porsches. I just need something that gets me around and I'll hire a car when I need it.'

He left the house forever with two suitcases and a holdall and the Real Estate Agent watching him go thought he walked like a king.

Most bereavement counselors suggest that it is best to let a full year pass by before making major changes or moving house. But Josh still had London, which he regarded as his true home, and that's where he was heading next.

In the next few months, a series of unauthorized biographies of Gemma's life did come out. Paul and the ghostwriters still got their advance despite what Paul ungratefully called 'the pay-off' from Josh. They came up with a very creditable biography based on Paul's childhood memories and every available photograph and media clipping. But the resentment of being denied power — and of being offered charity — burned long and hard in Paul's heart.

Josh did one recorded radio interview with an agency journalist in London. Jude had been besieged with requests including all the late night American chat shows but, for the moment at least, both she and Josh wanted to hold their cards closely to their chests. It would all unfold as it was meant to. That doesn't mean that Jude's inner PR guru wasn't champing at the bit.

'It's so frustrating,' she complained to her long-term partner Charlie, who was cooking fresh pasta in their penthouse apartment in Los Angeles. 'I quite understand that it's important to control the news and I know he needs time to get over Gemma — but I can't help wanting to jump in with Josh's own side of the story; build up his brand; get him out there in the market. My God, he could be crashing websites the world over right now!'

'And just exactly what purpose would that serve?' asked Charlie, tearing some fresh basil to make a garnish. 'He doesn't need the money; he's not a celebrity. Why would he bother?'

'Oh I don't know,' said Jude. 'It just goes against the grain. But you're wrong about his not being a celebrity. This man is going to be more famous than his wife. More famous than anyone since Princess Diana.'

'As long as he doesn't meet the same fate,' grunted Charlie. 'Come and eat. You'll be racing around the world with him soon enough.'

'You could come with me?' said Jude slightly diffidently. She might be the power-bitch from hell at work but where Charlie was concerned it was a different matter.

Charlie laughed. 'No way!' she said. 'I've got a life here; and you really, *really* don't want people to know about me.'

'Why not?' said Jude. 'It's not a sin!'

Charlie snorted. 'I know that. You know that. But in the Evangelical-driven world of America — the one that you are about to drive totally nuts with your promotion of a new Messiah — being gay *is* an abomination. You *might* get off to a certain extent because we're women,' she added, reaching into the refrigerator for the Parmesan cheese. 'But, frankly, when Josh gets going, he's going to attract every religious nut on the planet. I don't want to come in for any of their flak even if you do. No thanks. I'll stay here and get on with my own life.'

The two women sat down together and ate. But the level of Jude's commitment to Josh was a new and slightly bitter-tasting ingredient in their bolognaise. Before this, she had always had the ability to switch off and come home. Something was about to change forever and both of them knew it.

The interview by Nico Leonides did go around the world but it didn't crash any websites. At the time it was thought to be delusional and, basically, bonkers. Some British people who were old enough remembered the former British footballer David Icke being pilloried on the TV chat show *Wogan* for saying something pretty similar. Icke went on to tell the world that it was ruled by reptiles so that was about the level of credibility Josh was going to experience at the beginning.

Here's an extract:

'Josh, you spent 40 days in a desert. The only other time on record that that's happened was 2000 years ago in the Christian story.'

'I can't comment on that Nico. I wasn't there.'

'But it's an incredible story — how did you survive?'

'Well it was what most people would call a mystical experience — outside of rational explanation I suppose.'

'Would you call it a mystical experience?'

'Oh yes — I was re-built and re-formed in that time. I thought thoughts I'd never thought before. I don't think I was really conscious for much of the time — not conscious as we usually think of consciousness — all the everyday worries, repetitive thoughts, even what had happened to Gemma didn't seem to be real any more. What was real was light and hope and energy. It was like being lifted up into another world, a world where everything is possible and every thought becomes manifest.'

'As in food?'

'As in everything.'

'So what did you eat?'

'Manna from heaven I suppose.'

'In the form of what? Locusts?'

'If you're referring to John the Baptist, those were most likely locust *beans* that he ate rather than the insects.'

'Did you eat locust beans?'

'I don't know what I ate, Nico. Sorry.'

'So would you say you were re-born? Has it affected your faith?'

'Oh yes. Before, I believed. Now I *know*.'

'Know what?'

'All that is.'

'Josh, you are Jewish?'

'Yes.'

'And you've studied theology and ancient languages with particular reference to Christianity and Aramaic.'

'Yes.'

'Are you under some delusion that you are Jesus Christ come again?'

'No.'

'It seems a bit like it. Your detractors say you're making all this up.'

'Well I believe that everyone, once they wake up from what the Buddhists call *Samsara,* the grind of everyday beliefs, is a *Bene Elohim* — a son or daughter of God — and if you are a son or daughter of God then some part of you has to be Christ. Christ is a title for someone who is directly in touch with Divinity; that's all.'

'So you would say that everyone is Jesus Christ?'

'No, that's the mistake many people make — in my view. They only associate Christhood with Jesus. Jesus was a person who attained Christhood and Jesus himself said that we could all do the same.'

'And you have.'

'We all have. We are all Christ. Shinto calls it 'Kami' and that's probably a less controversial word to use. Some know it; some don't.'

'And you do know it!'

'I'm working on it, just like everyone. So are you whether you know it or not.'

'So if you're Christ come again, can you end wars and poverty?'

'Um...I'm not Jesus Christ come again; I'm someone who is working on himself — there are many people doing the same world-wide; people like Eckhart Tolle; Jerry and Esther Hicks; Byron Katie, Mike Dooley, Deepak Chopra — dozens of them. And war will exist as long as we all have war in our hearts. The secret is not to misuse faith to create war — as religion so often does.'

'So have you got a solution to the Middle East crisis?'

'The solution is always love and the moving away from the ego's need to be right. Jesus taught that; Buddha taught that; it's in the early translations of the Koran and the Baghavad Gita. It's the same at the heart of all the holy writings. But we have to do it ourselves not worship someone who's going to do it for us. That's the difference between an icon — an image that helps us find our own way to God — and an idol, which is something we worship instead of God.'

'I'll repeat the question: have you got a solution to the Middle East crisis?'

'Yes, clear the anger out of my own heart and encourage others to do the same. If we didn't hate and make war in everyday life then peace would spread. What we see in the Middle East and in other places is exactly what we have inside of us.'

'So meditate and say 'OM' and the world will be at peace?'

'If we all did it, it would.'

'Josh Goldstone, thank you very much.'

Jude winced when she heard the recording. 'Not good,' she said to Josh on Skype, which was proving pretty useful as long as Josh was at a computer cabled to the Internet. Giving him a new cell phone or a wireless connection was a total waste of time.

'Best I could do at the time,' he said, unfazed by her criticism. 'It's so complicated Jude...and yet it's so simple.'

'I understand that you shouldn't cast pearls before swine,' she said. 'But what's the point of cobbled-together fluffy, semi-religious preaching?'

'Hmm.... Swine before swine then? I'm so lucky you're not politically correct or polite to me!'

'Josh, don't get even holier than thou than thou art already.'

'Sorry Jude. It's not easy not to sound like a complete idiot.'

'Well try harder.'

Chapter Nine

Josh only paused in London for long enough to do the interview and pick up Gemma's ashes. He didn't even go home this first time, just stayed in a hotel and took the next available plane to Tel Aviv. Technically, he 'should' have gone into the London offices of *Gemstone Inc.* He also 'should' have contacted Gemma's usual team of minders to look after him and one of the company's PAs to either book him a flight or hire him a jet. That's what stars and their spouses do. Instead, he went underground. Jude had arranged for his flight to London but he'd not told anyone his plans after that. He thought that tickets to Tel Aviv would be easy enough to book on the Internet and it was only at Heathrow that he realized that he had booked Economy class by mistake.

'I *thought* it was cheap,' he said to himself as the check-in girl upgraded him to Business without even asking for payment. *That* had never happened before.

'Shouldn't I pay you some more?' he asked, suddenly aware of how out of synchronization he actually was with the world.

'No, we upgrade single passengers quite often if there are spare seats,' she said.

'Thank you,' said Josh, completely unaware that she had been feeling really depressed that morning but for some reason, when this perfectly normal guy in baseball cap and shades reached her desk, her heart had lifted and life suddenly seemed worth living again.

He managed to stop himself from making his way to the VIP lounge and wondered quietly to himself how people managed to cope with the hustle and bustle of airports. Usually, he and Gemma had flown privately.

As he wandered through Duty Free, feeling slightly amused at his effect on the cell phones that he passed, he thanked God that he didn't interfere with aircraft communication systems. There had been a nervous moment about that as he walked onto the plane in LA and he had wondered whether or not he had the power to switch himself off in some way if it did happen. But nothing did and the flight was fine. Luckily, it had been full of business executives who thought themselves too cool to seek out possible celebrities and his quiet demeanor didn't identify him as someone who might be all over the news. What he didn't quite realize was that he had the ability to become virtually invisible when he wanted to. That would turn out to be very useful.

Gemma and Josh hadn't talked about death much except at other people's funerals. But they did have an agreement that they would like to have their ashes spread on the Mount of Olives outside Jerusalem. Luckily, Gemma had written this desire in her will or she would, most likely, have been spread in the gardens at Golders Green crematorium before Josh returned to the world.

Orthodox Jews are buried not cremated and the most religiously observant like to be buried close to Jerusalem so that they can rise up at the end of days when the True Messiah comes. The practice of burial is important because a bodily resurrection is expected, so an orthodox Jew's body must be whole when it is buried. If you lose a leg or an organ, that must be buried in your grave too — probably before the rest of you. It follows that it is very important to book a plot early.

In the mid 20th century, Muslims set a graveyard before the gate into Jerusalem through which the Messiah is believed to be planning to enter. This was a provocative action because the Messiah was to come from the Cohen branch of Judaism — the priestly class. Religious observance said that a Cohen could not cross a graveyard but, hopefully, the Messiah will be able to rise above that when the time comes. He/she may decide to update the rules a little. After all, as Josh was to say as a virtual mantra, God may not change but human perception and understanding of God can and will change and that can make God *appear* to change.

Josh didn't usually call God, *God,* as he realized that people often have big issues with their own personal concept of God whether it's

God the Judgmental or God the Warmonger or God the Exclusive — 'You must worship me this way or you are damned' or God the Meek — 'You must live in poverty to prove you're worthy.'

He liked the way that Jesus had called God, Abba or Father but, in the modern world of equality, that wasn't going to work. Anyway, Jude expressly forbade him to do it.

He also did a doodle about the pronoun for God — She? He? It? And had a good chuckle when he said that out loud too fast. In the end, he called it the Source. Apart from anything else, that allowed the pronoun to be 'It'. He thought 'Source' up himself but he wasn't the first to call It that and it was probably all to the good that he adopted a name used by spiritual teachers who were already known. Josh had been raised in Britain with British food and condiments including Lea and Perrins and HP Sauce so he invented his own little joke referring to God as the Higher Power Source or, simply, the HP Source. Nobody else thought it was funny.

On the Mount of Olives, he sat for perhaps three hours looking over Jerusalem with the pot of Gemma's ashes held in his arms, waiting until that part of the graveyard was empty of visitors. At last, he sighed and stood up, donning his kippah and the blue and white silk tallis that Gemma had given him on the day of their wedding. He scattered her dust under a tree at the far edge of the Jewish graveyard while singing the *Kaddish*, the Jewish prayer for the dead. Some part of him was deeply, compassionately detached as he sang the Hebrew words and Josh was very grateful for that as he wasn't quite sure he could have got through the prayer otherwise.

Afterwards, he walked and walked and walked. He made his way down the Kidron Valley on land owned by the Palestinians but guarded by Israeli soldiers. The political reason for the soldiers' presence is that if the Palestinians cannot harvest their crops (mostly olives) on this land then it can be ruled to be fallow and settled by Israelis. But Josh was not thinking about that until he saw some Israeli soldiers with guns held ready, walking towards him from a distance.

He froze for a second and then resumed walking. Very clear in his head was the knowledge that he must keep walking. In less than a minute he came upon a dip in the ground containing a small well. A young Palestinian woman was crouching down by the rock wall there with a large half-filled water sack in her hand.

She looked at him as if she were a wild beast at bay and at once he understood what was happening. She was being hunted by the enemy — his people. Probably her village had no water of its own because of the great security wall erected between the two nations and she had to sneak onto what was actually her own land to fetch water.

He sat down, making his movements smooth so as not to frighten her even more and asked her gently, in English, for a drink. As he did, he took the kippah out of his bag and put it on his head, securing it with a kirby-grip. As he closed the bag he made sure that the tassels of the tallis hung out for anyone to see.

She stared at him with hostile brown eyes. She said nothing but her body tensed, knowing that the soldiers would see the two of them.

As they approached, they saw Josh, the Jew, with the Palestinian girl and hesitated.

He stood up and smiled at them.

'I need water,' he said in Hebrew. 'I asked this girl to show me the nearest spring.'

'What are you doing here?' said one of the soldiers. He was the burly one, the sergeant who was intent on just doing his job. His companions hung back, too war-scarred and hesitant to get into yet another wrangle if they could help it.

'I've been to the Mount to my wife's grave,' said Josh. 'I went walking so far that I'm thirsty. I asked this girl for help.'

'You asked a Palestinian?' The man spat.

'Water is water,' said Josh.

The burly man took a step towards the girl who shrank back. Josh put his arm out to her. 'Please give me the water sack,' he said in English, hoping that she would understand him. Reluctantly, she did and he tipped it up to pour some into his mouth without touching it with his lips. He drank long and slowly.

'Thank you,' he said, lowering the sack onto the ground. 'Now I will escort you home.'

'Leave the bottle,' said the soldier.

'Why?' said Josh. 'It's mine.'

He stood there, every bone in his body strong and peaceful, smiling at the men. He owned this land and it showed. One of the soldiers felt an instinctive urge to salute. He took half a step back and whispered something to his colleague.

'What?' said the sergeant impatiently. All three conversed briefly in whispers to Josh's unexpressed amusement. The first soldier then tried to make a call for instructions but, of course, his phone wasn't working. However, in the meantime recognition had sunk in. The sergeant's face went purple with combined fury and interest (a very unusual expression that is rather hard to describe).

'Mr. Goldstone?' he asked.

'Yes,' said Josh. He'd given up correcting people and now was a good time for name-dropping. He just hoped they liked Gemma's show.

'*Miracle Mile*!' said the two soldiers in English. 'Is good. Is good. So sorry for your wife's death.'

'Thank you,' said Josh, also in English. He took a roll of signed photographs of Gemma out of his rucksack. 'Would you like one of these?'

The men would, thank you very much! There was much shaking of hands and nodding. Bidding them *Shalom*, Josh picked up the water bag, turned away and, touching the girl on the shoulder gently indicated that she should walk with him.

She did. 'Why did you help me?' she said, eventually, in good English.

'Why shouldn't I?' he asked.

'You could have got your own water.'

'Surely there are peacekeepers round here who are Jewish?' he said. 'Others who would help you.'

'Not here,' she said. 'In some areas, yes.'

'They will increase,' he said. 'There are more and more people in the world who understand that you do not need to own land to worship God — that this hill and even Jerusalem — mean nothing to real faith. Allah is spirit and in truth and the Source of Light for us all.'

The woman said, 'But Allah is not the Jewish god.'

'Allah is One,' said Josh smiling at her. 'It's the Source. It's all One. We are cousins you and I. Our father was Abraham. One day it will all be healed, I promise you.'

'And who are you to promise that?' said the woman. Then she put her hand to her mouth and stopped, her eyes wide.

'It's not up to me,' said Josh. 'It's up to us all. Every heart carrying hatred or resentment creates this war. Will you help me with another drop of peace towards your enemy?' As he spoke, he handed her the water bag.

The woman began to shake. 'I know you,' she said. 'I know you.' She dropped the bag and began to run away.

Josh sighed, picked up the sack and followed her at a respectful distance until she reached her tiny village. Then, as she looked back at him, he placed the water bag down on a large rock just outside the tumbledown buildings. It tilted and he had to catch it before it fell. He lowered it gently to the ground, nudging the rock with his foot by accident. Clear water gushed out. After checking it wasn't just a fractured pipe, he nodded to himself and turned to walk away.

Chapter Ten

He got about a quarter of a mile before the woman's brother caught up with him. As the Palestinian had a truck it didn't take him long once the decision was made: Josh was only walking.

With a mixture of bad English and sign language he communicated that they wanted Josh to come and eat with them — a singular honor. Josh thought for a moment about the wisdom of being a lone Jew in a Palestinian village and, for another moment, about his lonely hotel room and accepted.

He was to stay with the Palestinians for two days that both he and they came to treasure. There wasn't much room in the house so he ended up sleeping in the kitchen area on a straw mattress after eating a delicious dinner of spicy lamb and pickles with taboun smothered with labneh that had been cooked by three generations of women in the same kitchen. The house was owned by the eldest son, Yasser, the girl-from-the-well's brother and twelve of them lived together in as much peace as any family can. The men ran a garage and the women farmed and cooked and raised the children.

The village had about 100 inhabitants, most of whom had already heard about this miracle man and who flocked to see the new source of water.

'Water is life,' said Yusra, the girl, proud to have been the means by which it had happened and enjoying the kudos that being able to translate from English for her elder relatives gave to her. 'Water of life,' repeated her friends and relations.

'The water of life comes from what you think and say,' said Josh. 'If you ask for something, believing it can come, then it will come. Love brings good things, and hatred bad things.' Nobody heard or understood him but it didn't matter.

The men tested the water from the new spring and found it good. They cleared the earth around it and built a proper well. Probably 50 people came up and shook Josh's hand. He wondered if he could ask to join them in their tiny mosque for the evening prayers but he didn't want to risk offending them so he didn't push it.

He slept like a baby, unsurprised to find when he woke that two cats had curled up with him under the blanket and that there was a chicken examining his shoes. All that next day, he spent with the women, threshing and cooking, all of them talking in as many languages as they could muster and listening and being happy. He felt good doing physical work.

They brought him the babies of the village and asked him to bless them so he did. They said it was a shame that no one was sick for he could have healed them and he smiled and said, 'Better to be well to start with.' The children climbed all over him, loving how he felt and moved and he loved them back with a passion that was new to him. Josh had never been much into kids before.

Yasser drove him back to Jerusalem the next morning enjoying a brief and unproductive but good-humored banter about the nature of war. They parted the best of friends and, after a bath and shave at his hotel, Josh paid his bill and bought a bus ticket to take him back to Tel Aviv welcoming what could be the last anonymity he would know. Part of him couldn't believe that he could ever be famous in his own right but deep inside, he knew that he had a job to do and, in the modern world, he would not be able to do it in secret.

It was an hour before his bus was due to leave and tradition as well as desire took him to the Western Wall, the last standing wall of the Second Temple, built by Herod the Great. It was the place where the great Rabbis including Hillel, Gamaliel and Jesus had all taught.

Most of the men at the Western Wall were Hassidim, striking and seriously orthodox in their black coats, white shirts and black or fur hats. These most fervent of Jews were founded by the Bal Shem Tov, the Axis of his Age, in the 19th century and named after the Hebrew word for 'loving-kindness'. The Bal Shem Tov taught that love, joy and dancing were integral to spiritual reality in a time of great persecution and depression. His legacy, ironically, was just the opposite (although the Hassidim still dance like crazy); ending up in orthodox fundamentalism in following the laws of the Old Testament and in the Hassidic tradition for women of shaving their hair and wearing wigs as soon as they marry.

It was only the ultra-orthodox on both sides of Judaism and Islam that were so stuck in what was 'right' that they had forgotten about love, thought Josh noticing a group of Jewish men snarling at a white, female tourist who had accidentally stumbled up against one of them. She wasn't to know that the Law taught that in touching an unknown man she had made him unclean in God's eyes. The man must now go to the *Mikvah* or ritual bath to be cleansed before he could go to Synagogue.

The foreign woman said 'sorry' and reeled back under the unexpected hostility. Josh didn't move but he caught her eye and smiled at her and saw her recover her equilibrium and find her way to the women's section of the wall where she began to pray quietly.

He too went to the wall, on the men's side of course, and leant his head against the ancient stones. He could feel the centuries of prayers in there — mostly impassioned pleas for help but some grateful acknowledgements too. Many asked for victory in the war and he found himself shaking slightly at the hatred they carried. What use was it to carry hatred to the Source?

With a sigh he stood upright and, as he did, a piece of paper fell out of the wall just to his right. He caught it and turned to see who had put it in. A distinguished-looking middle-aged Hassid bowed to him and held out his hand to receive the paper again.

'It is important,' he said. 'My son is sick; it must go in the wall now.'

'It has already reached its goal,' said Josh without thinking. 'It is answered. Your son is well again.'

Disbelieving, the man stared at this slender, inconsequential-looking man who spoke with such calmness. Subconsciously he noted the well-worn kippah and the tallis tassels hanging from the bag.

'You either believe or you don't,' said Josh. 'If you have faith and you have asked, then the answer is given. It is yes.'

Impasse.

Then the man's eyes widened and he put his hands up to his head. 'Yes,' he said. 'Yes, I do believe. Thank you. I'm going home.'

Later, as Josh looked out of the window while his bus maneuvered itself out of the suburbs, he saw what could quite possibly be the same man (but with the identical clothing it was hard to tell). He and some friends were dancing in the street outside a big house. He smiled to himself, leant against the window and closed his eyes. Beside him the father worrying about his family in the seats in front and watching out for suicide bombers, felt himself relax. There was nothing to worry about; this bus was perfectly safe.

And at the airport, as Josh stood scanning the departures board to find out just how seriously delayed his flight to London was going to be, he found himself standing next to an anxious young man in a new-looking suit who'd got a standby ticket for the same flight.

Somehow the two of them migrated to the bar where they had a drink to pass the time (estimated at being a seven-hour delay due to a fault on the airplane). The anxious young man, who normally wouldn't have spoken to a stranger, let alone poured his heart out, lost his inhibitions in the warmth and generosity of Josh's energy field and began to talk. His name was Jesse and he wanted to study in London — it would transform his life — but to do so he had to get to the preliminary selection process and this delay to the flight would get him there just too late.

He couldn't believe it; he could only afford standby and he was sure he'd come early enough.

Josh listened and tested the water to see if the young man was open to suggestions. He could see that Jesse was blocking himself with self-doubt and financial worries but you couldn't just throw advice at strangers; they don't like it.

'Is there anything that you need to do, or present at the selection process?' he asked eventually as Jesse finally ran out of lamentations and paused to take a drink of apple juice.

'Oh yeah!' I've got a whole Power Point presentation to put together. I'll do it when I'm on the plane. No point in doing it if I'm not going to get there.

'Can you believe this happened exactly before? I tried to go a year ago and exactly the same thing happened.'

'Did you need the same Power Point presentation then?'

'Well that or something like it.'

'Did you do it?'

'No of course not.'

'Hmm.' Josh took a drink.

'I tell you what,' he said. 'How about doing it now so that you can email it to them with an explanation of why you're late?'

'Do it *now?*'

'It would pass the time...wasn't it Goethe who said about kick starting things so that providence could help you along?'

'What was that then?'

Josh quoted from memory:

'The moment one definitely commits oneself, then Providence moves too. All sorts of things occur to help one that would never otherwise have occurred. A whole stream of events issues from the decision, raising in one's favor all manner of unforeseen incidents and meetings and material assistance, which no man could have dreamed would have come his way. Whatever you can do, or dream you can do, begin it. Boldness has genius, power, and magic in it. Begin it now.'

He put down his drink, smiled at the young man and moved away. Jesse was deep in thought.

Ten minutes later, Josh saw him typing busily on his laptop at an Internet port. He smiled to himself as the airport announcer advised passengers for London Heathrow that an alternative aircraft had been brought in and boarding would begin in 20 minutes. Jesse saw Josh in the queue at the gate and grinned at him with pure joy.

Back in the celebrity-driven world of Hollywood, the first auditions for *The Miracle Mile* were not going well. The show had always began the hunt in LA, working from the belief that Hollywood was always filled with would-be stars, including the most deluded who made such good television. But it seemed, increasingly, that there was less natural talent and more arrogant and mediocre 'want it alls' who were only interested in being pop stars. Sam, who was top dog now when it came to the judges for *The Miracle Mile,* was both bored and worried. If they didn't have Gemma and they couldn't find enough talent, the show was doomed.

He couldn't blame the kids; they were blinded by the cult of celebrity and everyone wanted their fifteen minutes of fame. But the older talent, the ones that made up the vaudeville element, the ones who had been struggling for years but who now had a real chance to make it, were getting thin on the ground. And they, together with the very young super-talent, were the reason the show was such a success.

*The Miracle Mil*e and other shows like it had been running for more than a decade now and many genuine stars had been created. Well, be honest, he said to himself a few *genuine* stars. Most of them fizzled out in less than a couple of years but they had had their chance of fame and it was their fault not the show's if they couldn't sustain it. Most of the finalists thought they knew more than the agents, managers, record companies and handlers who sorted them out and after they finished their water-tight, golden-handcuff contracts to perform in Vegas they went their own way to spectacular failure. They were probably right in that they were being ripped off right, left and center by the people who promoted them but Sam's motto was always, 'better 20% of a million dollars than 100% of twenty five dollars and twenty cents.'

The Miracle Mile focused on finding raw talent and nurturing it through the series including a final two-weeks of broadcasts running on prime time every single night. They were a fine source of all-round entertainers including acrobats or clowns for Cirque du Soleil, variety acts, comedians, conjurors, dancers, animal acts, actors, mimes, and musicians. One of their most popular winners had been a ventriloquist. Everyone (that is, everyone without any brains, in Sam's view) said a ventriloquist was a stupid thing to promote but they had been popular once and could be again. And Ally Jolson was, frankly, brilliant. She now had her own children's TV show and a syndicated cartoon for her main doll, Nasty Norman, and she had so much work in Vegas that she had moved there full-time.

Sam thought *The Miracle Mile* was a good name. People wanted miracles that would make them rich and famous. The 'original' Miracle Mile, however, was not in Las Vegas but in Los Angeles. It was the name given to Wilshire Boulevard where hundreds of thousands of aspirants to fame and fortune have driven or worked. Originally it was an unpaved farm road through bean fields that was transformed into a super-highway by a developer called A. W. Ross. Ross realized that this undistinguished farm track could become the Yellow Brick Road. It just needed a bit of a re-think and a smart injection of money. During the 1920s he developed the Wilshire area to rival and then out-rank downtown Los Angeles, making it a symbol of rags-to-riches. His secret weapon was the car. For the first time, automobiles were given priority on a stretch of road in a manner designed to influence the whole world. Wilshire Boulevard was choc-a-bloc with motoring 'firsts' including shops with their own parking lots, dedicated turn-left-only lanes, timed traffic lights and shops whose the architects were instructed to make sure they appeared at their best through the windscreen of a car.

When Gemma, already a celebrity and competition show producer in England, began talks about developing *The Miracle Mile* in the USA, everyone had advised her to make LA her focus. But Gemma was savvy; she knew that the all-round talent show had a big place in the future of entertainment. Other judges' comments to many a contestant that they sounded 'like cabaret artists' was music to her ears. Cabaret was a sure and steady place to look for income and Las Vegas didn't have its own Network TV show. Vegas would be the place to go; Vegas was hot for its own chance at making celebrities.

She was right. She was so very right! And she made sure that she was the major shareholder in everything she developed over the next five years so she became quite as wealthy as she was right. Las Vegas has its own famous Miracle Mile — firstly a shopping center but then a generic phrase. The show of the same name now had its own luxury $5 billion dollar public resort. Every room had its own private massage section, every guest had the opportunity to audition for a place in one of the three shows presented every night in the private theatres. They also had the option of a Big Brother-style Reality TV package on DVD of them filmed during the whole of their stay (some of those films made it to TV as well). They could swim, gamble, ride on rollercoasters, ride, play golf, take the SkyTube, shop and, at the right time of the year, watch the official contestants on *The Miracle Mile* without even leaving the compound. The hotel was totally dedicated to entertainment.

At the second auditions of the new season, in Minneapolis-St. Paul, they continued to miss Gemma. Her professional knowledge, her mix of kindness and devastating wit were the lynch-pin of the show and she had worked so well — and so spikily — with fellow judge Deborah Deforge. Deborah was in her fifties, a former star of musicals, both stage and screen, and so lifted you could hardly remember the original features of her face. Once called 'A musical mix of Bette and Joan' she had a nasty tongue and a tendency to lay down the law without humor or kindness. She was vicious to the contestants, out of what she said was the desire to toughen them up. Often she'd have someone (and not only the girls) in tears with her cruelty. Gemma had acted as her antithesis. She could croon and comfort or use her style and wit to make Deborah look dumb (though fortunately both for the show and herself, Deborah rarely spotted what she was doing) or she could argue with alacrity and conviction.

Sam and Gideon were also counter-weights to each other. Sam

the powerful bastard (he was devastatingly handsome) and Gideon the softie. Gideon knew his stuff about performance, charisma and star-quality but he didn't have that bite that would make him great. However, he was just what was needed to soften Sam and the two often went head to head on air — and off.

Without Gemma, Deborah was interfering with Sam and Gideon's on-screen relationship without contributing anything in return. She just sounded petulant and even stupid. And neither man dared to face up to her in quite the way that Gemma had done.

Meanwhile, John Jordan, the compère, who usually did his best to adjudicate, charm and paper over the cracks, was phoning in his performance. He was being courted by two Network Heads of Talent and, as soon as he got an offer big enough, John would be off like a shot. The only reason he hadn't been poached already was his political activism. It might be fashionable to support *Freedom for Tibet* but to get yourself so notorious you were black-listed by China and several other countries was tricky.

Sam knew that Bartos was worried and had had several top level talks lined up with the Network bosses. They were deeply worried that John Jordan's contract was leaking badly and they had no power to keep him if he wanted to go. Losing both Gemma and John would be the death-knell.

Sam too considered abandoning ship. Better to get out while the going was good. His contract was irrelevant; that's what lawyers were for and he could always say it was out of respect for Gemma.

But he didn't want the program to die; he had a great financial stake in it. Even more, he didn't want to defect to the other side. Sure they would have him, but he'd slept with the female judge on the rival show and 'his' place as Mr. Nasty was already taken. It would look bad even if it didn't feel bad.

He was relieved rather than worried when Bartos asked him out for lunch on the day they returned to Las Vegas after the second round of auditions. Bartos knew Sam could be trusted and it looked like he was planning to run some names past him for replacing

Gemma. Better they looked callous than they failed to get the ratings.

Sam got his driver to stop at the news stand next to the hot new Argentinean restaurant where anyone who was anyone now had lunch. All the new periodicals would be out today and, although they were delivered to his home, Sam liked to cast his eye over where each one was placed on the stand. Stan, the news guy had an unerring eye as to what would sell and arranged his stock according to the best-selling pictures and stories.

What he saw made him stop dead in his tracks. It was Josh's face that was looking out from more than half of the glossies.

'The Miracle Man.' That was repeated *six* different times.

'Gemma's Josh Out of his Mind with Grief.' (even more important than the latest girl-band lead singer's cellulite, thought Sam, noting the rest of the magazine's cover and its habitual expose of star imperfections).

'Are These Stigmata?' (*The National Enquirer* of course).

'Peace-Maker Josh.'

And just under the main series of headlines stood *US Weekly* blaring:

'Global Networks Bidding for Gemma's Josh.'

Sam snatched it up together with five others and went into his lunch. He was suddenly feeling very bullish.

Chapter Eleven

Josh and Gemma's home in London was a beautiful gray stone Georgian terraced house that, in springtime, was covered in purple Wisteria. It stood on a previously forgotten quiet back street in Dartmouth Park where there was even room for a small but reasonably sunny back garden. Fourteen years earlier, Josh had fallen in love with it at first sight, his enthusiasm enhanced by the fact that it was less than five minutes' walk from Hampstead Heath. Gemma had baulked a little simply because the nearest tube line was Tufnell Park which wasn't as salubrious as she would have liked it to be. Josh had his way because, already, Gemma was used to being picked up by chauffer-driven car or, at the very least, a taxi, so he could talk her out of Tufnell Park being a problem. They both thought that the house itself was glorious. It was four floors of beauty and space, including a basement (they had a live-in house-keeper) and plenty of room for parties and guests and visitors.

Before Gemma became famous, they had lived in Stoke Newington in an ugly second floor 1960s flat and then in a semi with a pebbledash front in a cul-de-sac full of cherry blossom in West Finchley. Always there had been somewhere for Josh to walk. Firstly with his Rhodesian Ridge-back, Harvey, then with Harvey's successor, Flame the Labrador. But, for the last five years there had been no dogs because Josh and Gemma were all over the world.

In Stoke Newington the local walk had been Clissold Park with its flat grass area and pool. In Finchley, it was the enchanting Dollis Walkway, alongside the Dollis River, winding north and south for miles on end. Finally, there was the glory of Hampstead Heath. Here, Josh and Flame would meet with a camaraderie of dog-owners who walked in the early mornings. Once, walking with a fellow dog-owner and her Tibetan Terrier, Josh had seen a flock of more than 20 goldfinches and they had both stood, entranced, for a whole ten minutes.

Even though he didn't have a dog any more, Josh found that there was solace in walking. For the first three days back in London, he walked and walked and walked. He walked the Heath, the Camden canal tow path; the Dollis Walkway, into and out of the city and the shopping areas killing mobile phone calls by the thousand and, without even knowing it, causing everyone who came within three meters of him to stop and collect themselves for a moment. The un-made calls prevented a thousand quarrels, business misunderstandings and gave people time to reconsider decisions before acting. It even achieved one marital reconciliation and the prevention of an affair that would have destroyed three people. The local papers picked up the fact that there was some electro-magnetic interference in localized areas of London, but why would anyone connect it to one fast-walking man whose face was focused in determination as his mind and soul did all they needed to be cleansed?

The house itself felt big and empty, and despite Mrs Dawes' best efforts to look after him, was just too much. It would take a while for Josh to stop expecting to hear Gemma's voice raised in greeting as she burst in through the front door in a fireball of energy.

Sarah Dawes cooked and cleaned for him and took messages; it was all she could do. Usually, she and her husband Fred, who was a barman at the Delfont Arms just up the road, did all that was necessary (Fred mowed the lawn and grew some vegetables in the little walled garden at the back) and kept out of the way. If Gemma had a big party she got caterers in. As a job it was a sinecure but Gemma chose staff wisely and she had had a friend and a trustworthy helper in Mrs Dawes.

They always called her by her title and surname — most people thought it archaic but Mrs Dawes liked it. It maintained a slight distance between the two couples and implied a respect for her work that she appreciated. Mrs Dawes was 68 and technically should be retired but everyone was very happy with things as they were so it never happened. Now, of course, might be a very different matter and, when your whole home is at stake as well as your job, life can become quite scary.

Nothing would have happened until probate was granted on the will but it was unlikely that Paul Goldstone would have kept the house on. It's fair to say that both Mr and Mrs Dawes saw Josh's resurrection as a true miracle.

The grapevine had kept them well informed about the impending sale of the American houses including the fact that the staff there were to be kept on in the meantime and, if the new owner didn't want to hire them, were to be given a full year's salary in lieu of notice. The Americans were mostly non-residential staff however and, although the Daweses had always meant to save for an eventual retirement they certainly didn't have enough to buy a new home.

In the meantime, the telephone messages were a bit of a problem. There were dozens of requests for interviews and nothing to do but take messages and apologize that Josh didn't have a mobile number. In London, Josh didn't have a Jude to field them for him. Gemma's power bases had been in Los Angeles and Las Vegas and her London PR, Susannah, hadn't yet picked up on Josh; why would she? He wasn't a *Goldstone Inc.* employee.

There were the letters too — most of them forwarded on from various agencies and TV studios. Some were from cranks; some from those seeking a guru; some very nasty — and quite a few sorrowful ones commiserating with him for the loss of Gemma. He answered all the coherent and vaguely sensible ones slowly but surely. It helped to pass the time.

On Saturday, he walked to Synagogue. Josh was still a member of his local orthodox Synagogue although Gemma understandably had preferred the Progressive at Finchley where they could sit together and women participated in services.

He was met with obvious pleasure by the Rabbi and several others including an old school friend, fair-headed, blond-eyelashed Simon and his darker brother Andrew. Both men were tall and lithe and worked as security officers. They had always made Josh laugh at the most inappropriate places in services with whispered irreverences and Simon's thirst for information had always interested Josh too. The Rabbi told Josh that it was a *Mitzvah,* that he was here as Isaac Diamond, who was going to sing Haftorah and to tell them after the service about his trip to Massada, could not come that day after all. Could Josh sing the Haftorah and perhaps say a few words at the Kiddush?

How could he say no?

It was the 48th day of the Omer and the reading came from Zechariah 2:14-4:7

It would be fair to say that Josh got a fairly dry throat while singing it and he thought, 'This will put the cat among the pigeons...'

This is what part of it said:

He showed me Joshua, the high priest, standing before the angel of the Lord, and the Accuser standing at his right to accuse him. But the angel of the Lord said to the Accuser, 'The Lord rebuke you, O Accuser; may the Lord who has chosen Jerusalem rebuke you! For this is a brand plucked from the fire.' Now Joshua was clothed in filthy garments when he stood before the angel. The latter spoke up and said to his attendants, 'Take the filthy garments off him!' And he said to him, 'See, I have removed your guilt from you, and you shall be clothed in priestly robes.' Then he gave the order, 'Let a pure diadem be placed on his head.' And they placed the pure diadem on his head and clothed him in priestly garments, as the angel of the Lord stood by.

And the angel of the Lord charged Joshua as follows: 'Thus said the Lord of Hosts: If you walk in My paths and keep My charge, you in turn will rule My House and guard My courts, and I will permit you to move about among these attendants. Hearken well, 0 High Priest Joshua, you and your fellow priests sitting before you! For those men are a sign that I am going to bring My servant the Branch. For mark well this stone which I place before Joshua, a single stone with seven eyes. I will execute its engraving — declares the Lord of Hosts — and I will remove that country's guilt in a single day. In that day — declares the Lord of Hosts — you will be inviting each other to the shade of vines and fig trees.'[1]

It didn't put any cats among pigeons because nobody noticed or, more accurately, it never occurred to them that anything from the scriptures could happen *today.* As the Rabbi's wife had once said to a child (may the Lord forgive her!) 'Miracles don't happen *now.* They happened *then.*'

What did cause a furor was the unfortunate — or was it providential? — fact that the world is now over-run by the Internet. Someone had posted an article on an Israeli blog about the Palestinian village and the girl and the soldiers and someone else had followed it up with a video on YouTube showing the new well of water.

Only those seeking something negative to chew over would have found it — or passed it on — but there are always plenty of those.

The Rabbi had asked Josh to say a few words afterwards about his faith and the experience in the desert. But Josh had spoken only for about three minutes before being interrupted by a young would-be Zionist who wanted to know why Josh was supporting the enemy when he should be on the side of his own people.

If Jude had been there, that would have been the moment to step in, hands raised in conciliation using the time-honored phrase, 'No questions people, thank you. Mr. Goldstone is not taking questions.'

But Jude was not there and Josh, totally unassuming, said mildly that the hospitality he had received from the Palestinians had been wonderful and that their patience and kindness with someone of another religion had been both inspirational and comforting to him.

Three voices spoke up expressing outrage that he had actually accepted Palestinian hospitality. Josh looked down, frowned and rubbed the ball of his right foot back and forward on the ground; a sign that he was getting irritated. For some reason, that gesture silenced the group.

He raised his head: 'I found more generosity and honest faith there than I find here right now,' he said.

A barrage of voices was raised to him and he waited for it to die down until he spoke again.

'I think that if we followed the rule of loving-kindness we would do better than depriving these people of the harvest and the water of their own land. Two wrongs don't make a right and we are worshipping the same Lord whether or not he has the same name.

'If the Lord were truly on our side don't you think he would have given us victory by now? If Joshua could take the Promised Land then surely we could regain the Holy Land as swiftly — *if* it were what the Lord wanted.

'Perhaps he knows that we are bigger than this; that we are wiser than this; that we can think of creative solutions rather than retaliation. Perhaps, now, He wants us to forget tribal differences and learn to live together in peace. Perhaps now is a time of personal responsibility rather than blame.'

Pandemonium.

Provoked? Yes, you could say that. We all want to be right and most of us want to avenge a wrong. But, in Josh's view, two wrongs made more wrongs and, even if the first person to suggest the olive branch of peace were stoned, at least the first word had been spoken.

It was unfortunate that Josh was speaking during the Kiddush because that meant that there was food to throw — and the furor was such that some people did indeed throw food (but not the smoked salmon or the gefilte fish; those were too delicious to waste). The Rabbi was deeply upset and offended by his congregation's behavior and stepped in to try and stop them while his daughter quietly spirited Josh away round the back into the ladies' lavatories and out of the window.

Behind him it sounded like hounds baying for blood.

The girl was both embarrassed and defensive. Josh laid one hand on hers in thanks before he began climbing and said 'It would be just the same at a mosque. It's not just our people it's all people.'

Nevertheless he felt quite shaken as he dropped down into the car park to find two men below, waiting for him. But it was Simon and Andrew, who were acting as the synagogue's security men, and who steered him out of an old, forgotten, ivy-covered hole in the fencing that they had used as children and, together, they loped off around the corner before continuing walking briskly until they reached what they considered to be a safe distance.

For as long as they were moving, none of them said anything. The two brothers kept intending to speak but they knew that Josh wasn't listening. His arms and legs were moving but his face had an expression that Simon was later to call the 'seriously engaged' look.

Nowadays, Josh often had conversations with the Source. Mostly (unlike the rest of us) he listened rather than speaking. If you asked him what he heard he would probably wrinkle his nose up and say it was more like hearing colors or seeing vibration rather than a voice. There were words in his head which were probably English but the problem in explaining it was that we need words to think — and without the words it's hard to think — but if we got communication in our heads that *wasn't* words but was perfectly understandable it wasn't easy to put it into words.

And of course it's hard to tell the difference between the inspiration and the subconscious (which was currently telling him that he was a dumbcluck). The subconscious can put forward some very believable ideas and rationales and is very good at covering up its resistance.

What was most pressing right now was the feeling he was getting that they should go to another Synagogue — which was frankly ridiculous.

On Golders Green High Street they stopped. Around them the shops and people bustled with *Goyim* going about their usual business. Plenty of food shops were open but none of them were Kosher.

'I could murder a smoked salmon bagel,' said Simon wistfully, looking into the firmly shut and empty bakery beside them.

'Yeah, right,' said Andrew. 'As if anywhere where we can eat is going to be open today!'

'You never know,' said Josh, who was also ravenous (they had all missed out on the delicious-looking Kiddush at the Synagogue).

'We could eat non-Kosher,' he suggested mildly but neither Simon nor Andrew was impressed.

'?' said the voice in his head.

'Yes please,' said Josh.

Almost at once, the side door of the baker's which made the best bagels in the world opened and a girl came out with a tray of smoked salmon and cream cheese bagels.

'Oh!' she said, obviously startled.

'Are you going to throw those away?' asked Josh.

'They're yesterday's,' she said. 'We can't sell them tomorrow.'

'May we dispose of them for you?' asked Josh with a twinkle in his eye. She looked back and smiled, holding out the tray.

'Thank the Lord for the Eruv!' said Simon as the three men gratefully took two bagels each and Simon stuffed the rest into a carrier bag he found in his pocket. Traditionally, Jews aren't allowed to carry things on the Sabbath except within the confines of the Synagogue. The Eruv is a designated area in many Jewish settlements that can be regarded as sacred space so that children can be carried and pockets can contain keys and carrier bags can be filled with unexpected smoked salmon bagels. Golders Green High Street is, thank the Lord, within an Eruv.

As they walked along the street, eating their bagels, Josh knew they had to go to the Progressive Synagogue in Finchley. He turned to tell the others so just as a car pulled up beside them. Inside were three men who hailed Simon.

'Hi John, James, Mr Zellinger,' Simon replied, bending down to look into the old Volvo. 'What are you doing out in the car?'

'Not so *frum* as you!' said John. 'We're off to the Progressive in Finchley. Do you want to come?'

'Yes please,' said Josh before the others could introduce him. 'That's just where we were heading.'

Simon and Andrew hesitated. They were quite orthodox and riding in a car on Sabbath was almost as bad as eating non-Kosher. But when Josh looked at them, they felt their resistance dissolve.

The three men clambered into the old Volvo but it was a very tight fit and Mr Zellinger got straight out the other side of the car.

'You youngsters go ahead,' he said. 'You're going to be too crazy for me, I can tell it. I'll head back home — no don't worry boys, it's fine. I can catch up on some reading. Have fun.' He turned away before his sons could persuade him otherwise and walked briskly over to the opposite pavement.

'He didn't really want to come anyway,' said the driver, John, conversationally. 'Bless his little cotton socks; the Progressive isn't really for him.'

Introductions and bagels were exchanged.

'Oh, you're the guy who came back from the dead!' said James with great interest. 'Amazing stuff.' Then he remembered who hadn't come back from the dead and colored up.

'You're going to see more amazing stuff than that!' said Simon who had a knack of not noticing nuances. 'This guy can just manifest what he wants whenever he wants it.'

'Have you noticed that all the traffic lights have turned green just as we came up to them?' interjected Andrew. John had but he wasn't going to comment — yet.

In Finchley they could barely park within half a mile of the Synagogue. It held a special family service at 2.30pm that was obviously very popular.

'Why are we coming here?' said Simon. 'Isn't one service enough in a day?'

'Haven't you ever been here?' asked Josh amused. 'It's very different.'

However, it didn't seem different to Simon to start with; it was like *deja-vu*. The Rabbi welcomed Josh like an old friend and asked him to sing Haftorah and to speak. Josh declined the first but agreed to the second.

This time as he stepped up, it was during the service itself, not afterward. And half his audience listened spellbound as he talked to them of love, compassion, direct contact with the Divine and of the importance of rising above the tribal consciousness that made one group 'right' and another one 'wrong.' It wasn't just because they were more open minded, more that Josh was getting better at explaining himself.

The other half suffered what they thought were his rantings in silence.

'Who *is* this man?' John whispered to Simon.

There was a scraping of chairs and an elderly man staggered up the aisle just behind them.

'I know you!' he cried.

'Shhh…' said the congregation. Simeon Zachary's daughter got up to take his hand and pull him back to his chair. Her poor Dad had had a stroke and could hardly speak through his lop-sided mouth and the beginnings of Alzheimer's was adding to his distress but he'd never done this in public before. She was rigid with embarrassment. Two friends got up to help.

'What do you want with us Son of David?' croaked the man. 'Have you come to destroy me, Anointed of the Lord?'

Josh looked over to the man and held out his hand. Ignoring the scarlet, embarrassed face of Sarah, Zachary's daughter, and the efforts of the others to calm old Simeon down, he spoke gently, so gently that only those close to him heard.

'Shush,' he said, as if to a frightened child. Then raised his voice, saying, 'Come out. Be gone!'

Simeon fell onto his knees convulsing and crying. Sarah yelped and reached out to him, staggering herself as she failed to catch his weight. The old man went down like a log, the breath knocked out of him in a strange howl.

The sharp intakes of breath around the synagogue were audible. Most people were shuffling in their seats to see what had happened to Simeon but some just stared at Josh. It was as if they could see colors around him and light scorching down the aisle.

'What? What happened?' said Simeon's voice from the floor. It was his normal voice. The voice he had not used for years. 'Darling, did I fall? I'm so sorry; how embarrassing for you. Darling, what's the matter?'

He looked aghast at the tears running down his daughter's face then shrugged off the helping hands that were offered to help him rise.

'I'm not in my dotage,' he said. 'I can get up. Goodness, what a spectacle I've made of myself, eh?' He put one hand to his face then grinned broadly. The slippage had gone; his mind was clear and his voice was perfect.

'Well blow me!' he said. 'I'm cured.'

Chapter Twelve

The extraordinary events around Simeon's recovery made the front page of *The Jewish Chronicle* although Josh declined to be quoted. Even so, the paper ran quite an extensive article on Josh and the miracles, which were beginning to mount up past the point where they could be ignored. Simeon Zachary was pictured, smiling broadly with all his family, and the Palestinian well was mentioned — with some comment from both sides of the divide on that — plus, of course, there was the now perennially-mentioned miracle of Josh's escape from the car crash. The local London papers picked up the story and magazines would surely follow. Already, *Celebrity Star* and five other magazines had offered upwards of $2million for Josh's own story.

It could only get worse (or should that be better?), thought Josh. Within 24 hours of the synagogue visits, home had become less of a refuge than a prison. Simply to go walking, he had to arrange for a taxi to pick him up and take him half a mile away and soon, it was likely, the paparazzi and the satellite trucks would be under orders not only to try and doorstop him but to chase him as well.

He 'should' have had Gemma's minders but, for the first weeks at least, he tried very hard to live an almost normal life and refused any offer of help from *Goldstone Inc.* They, bullied remorselessly about him by the press, became more and more confused and even resorted to Gemma's particular bugbear of saying 'No comment'.

Josh had plenty of visitors who *were* celebrities, mostly friends of Gemma's, so the press coverage was rewarding for the photographers even if Josh wouldn't speak to them.

So, when Jude called Josh on the landline and told him of the three Networks bidding upwards of $125million for his non-existent talent as a TV judge, he sighed, looking around his home, and said 'Okay, *The Miracle Mile* it is.'

He sat for a good half hour with his head in his hands when the call was finished. Josh had never liked Las Vegas and this was the end of any kind of peace. But, he had a job to do and there was no good in trying to avoid it. Gemma's face beamed down at him from the picture above his desk. 'Oh Honey,' he said. 'How did you ever do it?' He knew her answer before he had finished speaking: 'Because I had you.'

The next day, Josh was expected at the Knightsbridge-based London offices of *Gemstone Inc* where Gemma's now defunct British chat show had been produced. The office would stay open — *Gemstone Inc* had plenty of British celebrity clients — but it had a lot of ground to make up and, currently, no ideas of how to do it.

Not surprisingly the company had called another Extraordinary General Meeting with Josh's return to life — he'd already had informal meetings with Philippa, Gemma's successor as president, but nothing further. Josh was a non-executive director of the company and nominally a Vice President but these had, until now, all been courtesy titles and Gemma had always structured the company so that if anything happened to her, even though Josh inherited her shares, Philippa would step up without question in the interim until there was clarification as to what would be needed.

Realizing that he couldn't face being surrounded by *Goldstone Inc's* idea of protection, Josh called Simon, John, Andrew and James and made them an offer they couldn't refuse.

The four men were already feeling magnetically drawn to Josh — and he was quite happy about that; some male bonding was very helpful right now. But to be asked to walk away from their work in England and spend the next twelve months in the USA (taking their families if they were prepared to go) was a lot to take in.

Even so, all four men said yes. For Simon and Andrew it was perfectly logical; they ran their own security company and had other staff to keep things ticking over, so taking on a long-term bodyguard job was really just a good business opportunity. John, by far the youngest, had just finished law school and was actively seeking work — and James had just given in his notice at the restaurant where he worked as chef. Simon and Andrew said they could train the other two on the job. To their nonplussed families, they all just said, 'This is how it is — I have to go! Are you coming?' The idea of frequent free holidays in Las Vegas was a small sop to the familial outrage but neither Simon's nor Andrew's wives were willing or able to come full-time so some friction was bound to be felt. John and James were single and both glad to get away from parental pressure to find a nice Jewish girl.

Even if they hadn't witnessed at least one miracle at the Synagogue in Finchley, what happened to Simon's mother-in-law at the end of that the first Sabbath with Josh would have converted all four of the men.

Simon had invited them all to supper at his and his wife Mariah's home. Mariah's mother, who lived with them in a basement Granny Flat over the garage at their Golders Green semi-detached house, had been in the kitchen with her daughter when all five men arrived. Adele was not-so-very-affectionately known as 'the parrot' for her incessant chatter. Her mouth worked feverishly without stop with a flood of words constantly tumbling out without her brain engaging in the slightest degree. If you could get Adele to shut up and listen she had a perfectly good mind but over-ruling it was this constant flow of inanity and inconsequence. It was at its worst when visitors came, although Adele even chattered when there was nothing to say while cooking with her daughter.

'There is no harm in her, she just rattles,' said Simon despairingly as he warned the others what was likely to happen as they opened the door. 'And she never takes a breath at the end of a sentence when you could get a word in edgeways.'

As the men came in through the front door, all together, Adele launched herself at them like a puppy seeking affection. A torrent of banalities shot out of her mouth, all irrelevant but they had to be attended to for politeness' sake. She simply could not stop the words from tumbling everywhere. What made it worse was that if you looked closely into Adele's eyes you could see that she was trapped inside this torment. Those eyes held a desperation that would have touched any soul that actually looked. But the armor of the chat was so strong that hardly anybody did.

'Goodness, look at you four all without sweaters on. It's very cold today though the weather forecast said it would be warmer. I'm surprised you've not got a jumper on between you. Not that it hasn't been very warm for this time of year but you never know do you? And it's wise to take a good coat, that's what I always say. Or a cardigan. Not that so many men wear a cardigan nowadays. Such a sensible and useful garment but I suppose it's just not the fashion. Not that the summers haven't been getting warmer. I've noticed it myself with the garden and the pot plants whatever they say because you can never know whether they know what they're talking about. Not to say that they don't because what you can learn from the television now is quite amazing don't you think? But that's not to say that the radio isn't very good though I've never been a fan of Radio Four — quite above my touch! No, I still like Radio 2 though not that interview lunchtime show where there are just too many complaints. I turn over to one of the local stations then. But of course I'm often out around lunchtime or sometimes I simply don't listen. Silence is a lovely thing. Though of course in London it's never really silent is it?'

And horribly unaware of the irony, she rattled on and on and on.

Poor Adele rattled physically too with tablet after tablet from the doctor to try and stop her head and hands shaking. It was as though she had Parkinson's Disease although she didn't — or at least they'd never been able to diagnose it — and she would tell you all about that at the drop of a hat too. And that recitation included a catalogue of sixteen years of medical appointments, history, misdiagnoses and general time-consuming nothingness.

Or, at least, it used to.

Simon introduced Adele to Josh, who took her hand in his. Adele looked up into the friendly brown eyes, breathed in the light that surrounded him, opened her mouth, closed her mouth; shuddered from head to foot and lost 16 years of unhappiness in one second.

'You're the one they're calling The Miracle Man. I saw you on TV!' she said, tears springing to her eyes. 'You've healed me. Oh. Thank you! It's been so awful.'

And then she shut up! She stood in silence for a full minute, still holding Josh's hand while the others stood, waiting. Then she bustled into the kitchen to take over the preparations, shooing Mariah out. In half an hour, Adele had served up a wonderful meal with evident enjoyment and sat with them all talking occasionally, sensibly, relevantly and with great humor.

Simon and Mariah sat there with their mouths open. While they had loved Adele as much as they could, she had exasperated them for so long that they simply couldn't take it in.

The effect lasted. Adele was happy again; Mariah was happy; Simon was happy. And now, Simon, James, John and Andrew had every intention of sticking with Josh through thick and thin whether he liked it or not. Luckily, he more than liked it.

So, as Josh turned up at the offices of *Gemstone Inc* at 10am sharp, he arrived with two brand new minders. They were tall, strong-featured men in navy blue suits and sunglasses and the change of image did Josh no harm at all.

At the meeting of *Gemstone Inc* were the Acting President, Philippa Denton and her PA Jo Sears; Executive Producer, Bartos Varga; Managing Director (Goldstone Music), Simon Zeller; Manager, Artists and Repertoire, Tadaeo Tanaka; Project Coordinator, Thomas Didier; Head of PR (UK), Susannah Drummond (UK PR) and Director of Television (Goldstone TV), Jamie Johnson.

Bartos was Hungarian-American with an accent as thick as toffee, Susannah's Irish brogue was soft and enchanting and all the rest of them bar Financial Director, Mattie Jones, were American. Mattie was not there, to Josh's regret. She was still over in the US, re-organizing, re-grouping, leveraging, consolidating, and all those other official business words that cover the phrase, 'What the hell do we do now?' Susannah was based in London and both Philippa and

Bartos juggled lives between London and Las Vegas but all the others had flown in on the Red-Eye, timing their arrival with Jude's call to Josh. If he had said 'no' on the phone, they were planning to convert him en masse.

Ironically, if any persuading had been needed, Mattie would have been the only one who could have done it. Josh liked Mattie. He found her normal, very down-to-earth and practical and not in the least intimidating. Philippa scared him a bit, Jo was rather over-stately for his taste and Bartos practically had 'I'm Hungarian, have you got a problem with that?' hung on a placard round his neck.

Simon was fiercely enthusiastic; Tadaeo ruthlessly efficient; Thomas a noted detail-aholic; Susannah a perpetual Earth Mother and Jamie stylishly and decoratively relaxed and cool. And Josh? Well Josh *was* a non-entity who never made a decision. *Was.* Now he even walked differently, with his previously gangly nothingness transformed into a kind of calm, assertive power. There were already legends and a series of inexplicable happenings linked to him, not to mention the powerful stigma of widowhood.

Bartos and Tadaeo had looked up the places where Josh had been lost and found on a map of Arizona and Nevada. It wasn't possible for a man to swim that far or walk that far or to live that long in a desert. He *must* have been somewhere else when the car went over. But *Gemstone Inc* had not had any trouble getting the CCTV footage on the dam and it was certainly Gemma, probably Josh and absolutely the Vantage. Its distinctive number plate M1RACLE had sheered off in the impact (and was sold for $1m on eBay four weeks later courtesy of Paul Goldstone).

Everyone in the building made an excuse to sneak a look at the unexpected hero of the hour through the corridor window onto the boardroom which, in turn, had a view of *Harrods*. Everyone saw something different. Several came up to Josh to talk to him about Gemma and he was touched by the genuine sorrow and concern they expressed. A part of him found the change in their attitude towards him confusing. Now they were offering him respect whereas before he had just been part of the wallpaper. What he didn't realize was how different he, himself, was.

In the boardroom Susannah found herself double-checking the food and drink. She had ensured that exclusive multi-colored bottles filled with fizzy water were arranged decoratively around the boardroom table; canapés were served by the catering staff as were wine, tea, herbal tea or coffee, fruit juices and sodas. Everyone had a complimentary pad and pen; there were elegant, spiky pollen-free flowers (in case of asthma or allergies) and, everywhere, a slight sense of over-orchestration and effortless strain. 'It should be more *homely*,' she thought. 'Those flowers are too…too perfect. We should have scented roses and delphiniums.'

Every one of the executives gathered had been feeling somewhat resentful at the way things had turned out. They could now see a long hard haul ahead where, before, it had all been so easy. And what of Josh? Could he cut it?

But as Josh walked in, the men found themselves straightening up. Their clothes somehow felt heavier like robes and in their unacknowledged souls they felt the deep swell of inexplicable joy as though some great music were being played.

The women felt beautiful for no reason that they knew of…if there had been music it would have been so very tempting to begin to dance.

Even so, nobody knew what to say.

The air felt heavy. Bartos suggested opening a window and everyone agreed even though there was air conditioning and it was hardly hot. As he did so, a sparrow dived in to the room and crashed into the glass of the window on the opposite side of the room. It fell in a shattered clump of feathers at Josh's feet.

Susannah squealed; everyone else took a sharp intake of breath and froze.

Josh leant down and picked up the sparrow. He sat down at the table with the tiny body cupped inside his hands, giving it the whole of his attention. This seemed so natural that everyone else sat down too. There was silence. Every eye was on Josh and, when he stood up and walked to the open window, held out his hands and the sparrow flew, joyfully up and up and up and then away, there was a tangible sigh.

Susannah burst into tears. 'That was the moment that the demons of fear and hatred and lack left us,' she said later and no one contradicted her.

Josh gently closed the window and went back to his seat. Still not one word had been spoken. Philippa thought for a moment that she saw a golden aureole of light around him.

'Shall we begin?' he asked.

How hard is it to talk to a purveyor of miracles? Children would find it easy. They would say, 'How did you do that? Can you teach me how to do that?' Adults tend to stuff the unusual into a corner and paint it to match the walls so it's conveniently hidden.

Philippa hastily called the meeting to order. The *real* question (and even that was hard to voice) was would Josh be any use on TV?

The nurturing of the talent itself wasn't a problem; the machine that was *Gemstone Inc* could do that. Stylists, voice coaches, personal trainers were on constant standby. But could Josh take the pressure of the cameras? Could he be witty; urbane? Could he shine the way Gemma did?

'Yes,' they thought as one, each as surprised as the others. Even allowing for the fact that the public's appetite for the sensational was insatiable and the grieving and elusive widower would be hot copy, Josh now had something tangible of his own. His previous lack of charisma had dissolved into a certain indefinable — they hesitated to say majestic — style. He had his own entourage too. Even though they just stood there and looked fierce, they looked prosperously fierce. And, for God's sake, the man could do miracles! What could he do for the contestants? And what would that do for the ratings?

The program was dead in the water without him if John Jordan were successfully headhunted. But now, wonderfully, there was hope. Real hope. They believed in Josh. He didn't say very much but when he did, they listened and everything he said had sound judgment and kindness in it. It occurred to one and all that they heard Gemma's voice in him — and they realized at last how much of Josh had been in Gemma.

There was no time to lose. USA production was well under way so, at the top of the piles of administrative decisions that swamp most meetings, was the one vital requirement that Josh should be on the corporation's private plane to Las Vegas the very next day. As should Philippa, Bartos, Jamie and Thomas — they needed to be there both to support him and to watch.

And Simon, James, John and Andrew?

'They're coming too,' said Josh. 'That's the deal.'

'But *Goldstone* has its own minders!'

'That's the deal,' said Josh. 'Take it or leave it.'

They took it.

'You should be called Peter!' said Susannah to Simon afterwards, clapping her hand over her mouth as soon as she'd said it.

'That's my other name,' said Simon, surprised. 'How did you know?'

She stuttered something about the names of the disciples of Jesus. Simon looked blank.

'I wouldn't know. I'm not a Christian,' he said. But there was no offence taken and nobody else took any notice.

'We'll live in the resort staff condominium as usual,' said Philippa.

'It's already in hand,' said Jo. 'Re-decoration is finished. Josh, what about you? I gather you have sold the house. I can find somewhere for you — an apartment by the lake?'

'No, I'll stay with you,' said Josh.

'But...'

'I'll stay with you,' he said firmly.

It was only later that any of them realized that they had all bowed their heads in assent.

Before he left England, Josh went to see both his and Gemma's parents. Joe and Maria were peaceful and companionable with him, hiding any anxiety they might be feeling at what might be ahead and just glad that he would, at least, have companions in the form of Simon, James, John and Andrew. He made sure that they knew they could fly over to see him any time they wanted.

'You go and do your best to enjoy yourself,' said Joe. 'It's nice of you to ask but we didn't hang on your coat tails when Gemma was alive and we're not going to now.' Both Josh and they knew that Maria would be on Skype nearly every day to start with but that would fade away as the work got busier.

'Don't shine too bright,' Maria whispered to her son as he left, a touch of fear in her voice.

'I don't really have a choice Mum,' he answered. 'It shines through me, not of me.'

She nodded. 'I'll pray for you,' she said and he smiled at her lovingly. 'You do that,' he said.

Gemma's parents didn't really know who Josh was when he went to visit. It was really all too confusing. Once they had identified him, they wondered out loud where Gemma might be and why he had come alone. He considered for a moment and then realized, with compassion, that maybe they were best off confused as they were. Clarification might hurt too much and they had chosen to let go of everyone else's reality — which was their right to do. But whether he wanted to help or not, something still came through him and they understood much more clearly (and stopped feeling their arthritis half as much) by the time he had to leave.

He also went to see Paul. It was a good meeting where Paul could express in full his indignation and frustration at Josh's condescension in paying for his parents' care and in giving him money. The tirade fell on ears that were untouched by the bitterness but Josh registered a lesson learnt. He was beginning to realize that the more he *wanted* to help or heal, the less he could do so. It was not up to him but some kind of deal between the Source and the person (or animal) with him acting as a clear transmitter. Pushing healing — or for that matter, money — was interference and that could not be beneficial to either party. But, even so, every time he heard anyone speak, he found that he also heard the truth underlying their story and he was beginning to wonder how he would be able to bear seeing so much of the world's pain.

Paul's pain, in particular, was like a smudged Jackson Pollock painting with hundreds of twisted, tangled strings of offence taken and anger absorbed. Josh knew that if Paul gave his permission, one end of that string could be pulled to dissolve the whole. But he also knew that Paul's choice — right now — would be to re-bind the string. The silence and emptiness of peace would be too alien to him.

Josh could respect that and allow it. It wasn't that he didn't want to interfere but he knew it would do no good and it would probably rebound.

'And there's going to be enough of that!' he thought with a wry smile.

But he was able to leave Paul feeling listened-to and understood and that was a salve to the restless man's heart if not to his soul. He felt vindicated and was able to return to despising Josh cordially which was an outcome much better than it might have been.

Paul expected *The Miracle Man* to fail dramatically without Gemma. As he looked through the eyes of memory rather than of the moment he saw nothing different. Josh had no style, he thought. It could never work. How often people set themselves up for disappointment, he thought, never realizing he was talking of himself.

The last thing to do before leaving England was reassure Mr and Mrs Dawes that they had a life-long tenancy of the flat downstairs and that even if Josh decided to sell the house, the flat would remain theirs. So there were quite a few soothed hearts in London by the time Josh left for Las Vegas.

On the aircraft, bitterly familiar in a way that was surprising to him whereas Gemma's office had barely registered at all, Josh hid away in what had been her private office space, which was now his. He drank champagne and freshly-squeezed orange juice, ate fillet steak and watched the unwavering glory of the sky outside, aware that these hours were probably his last moments of being just him. He slept for a while and then watched the welcoming video that they provided for guests. 'The Entertainment Capital of the World' it called Vegas as well as 'Sin City'. The video included excerpts from a show featuring long-legged, big-breasted devils and angels, laughing at the city's image. Josh was beginning to know about angels — not the fluffy replacement for the saints that were so popular nowadays but the clear, strong energies of the Divine. Demons he wasn't so sure about but, one thing he did know, they were usually very good at disguises and generally extremely attractive.

'O how art thou fallen from heaven, O Lucifer, Son of Morning,' he muttered to himself as he saw the shining, pulsating, energized city of Las Vegas below as they came in to land.

Now it would all begin and continue until the perfect end.

Chapter Thirteen

Maude-Lynn Sykes had been busy. The instant antagonism she had felt at first sight of this holy-moly insult of a man who was setting himself up as some kind of guru grew and grew, hard as a diamond in her heart.

She alerted every celebrity stringer she could to update her with news of where Josh went and what he did. She got permission to do a little traveling herself and filed several poisonous little reports that went down well with the Network. They didn't need their celebrities to be good people, they needed celebrities to do daft things and Maude-Lynn was touching an important sore-spot on the human psyche — the one that says, 'He's no better than he should be. Who does he think he is?'

Of course it would have been better if Josh were female, young, and preferably sleeping around, but it was pretty good as it was.

First she had reported on the scattering of Gemma's ashes on the Mount of Olives, pointing out the hypocrisy of a Jew who was willing to have his wife cremated (against the Jewish law) but then took her ashes to the place where the orthodox fully-bodied were buried. Several locals were very willing to comment on that.

Secondly she took a scientist to the Palestinian well in order to try and prove that the water had been there all along and that what the locals thought was a miracle was just a trick. She managed to fudge over the expert's obvious perplexity and, instead, suggested that Josh had a sexual relationship with the girl concerned.

Then she reported (via a stringer) on the fracas at the synagogue in Golders Green and the 'staged' recovery of the elderly man in Finchley. Good editing managed to make the Zacharys look credulous and a little added innuendo about stage-managing a normal event to make it look special and some vox-pop comments from local Jews made it all rather snide. To be honest, that wasn't her best report but she was on a roll so it went out anyway.

The revelation that Josh would become a judge on *The Miracle Mile* made the news with a bullet and Maude-Lynn was now the official expert.

She camped out with the family of Frank Morrison, the driver of the truck that struck the Aston Martin on the Hoover dam, in order to leach out every bit of pathos she could — think of Gemma Goldstone, rich and beautiful with a charmed life (apart, of course, from dying brutally in a car crash), and Frank Morrison's family who got no compensation and no help even though they were downtrodden and poor.

Frank's widow Stephanie was suspicious of the reporter and wanted to keep her kids away from her but Frank's sister Maisie was happy to talk and to say that Josh should help the family out. Frank actually had life insurance so Stephanie and the kids were going to be okay financially, if not emotionally, but that aspect wasn't highlighted.

Once she had sucked that story dry, Maude-Lynn turned her attention to *The Miracle Mile,* interviewing Sam, Gideon and Deborah. Sam was bullish about the idea of another man on the show and dropped an interesting little bit of poison about Gemma saying that Josh used to do a lot of her thinking for her. Gideon was non-committal: they would see what they would see — although he thought another woman would have made a better balance to the show.

Deborah just hoped, fervently, that Josh would be kind to the people and understand their problems and therefore have a steadying influence on Sam's harsh words and unkindness. Her blindness to her own vicious cruelty was well known but this really took the ticket. As to the reported miracles, she didn't believe a word of it! Deborah never trusted what she saw or heard on the news and even if there were anything to it, it would just have been clever PR from *Gemstone Inc.*

Maude-Lynn did everything she could to spread rumors about Josh's miracles being bogus. She worked hard to gather together people who didn't like him and joyfully discovered the computer-smashing episode in Coldwater Canyon over Gemma's biography.

Paul Goldstone, to his eternal credit, did not say an openly negative thing about Josh and refused to speak to Maude-Lynn or any other reporter directly. Unfortunately he did issue a rather pompous statement saying that wished Josh well while noting how painful it had been for him and his family to have been allowed to believe that Josh too was dead for so long and how they would never have dreamt of trying to sort the estate out if they had known the truth.

Unspoken but palpable behind every single story was a drip feed of the belief that Josh was trying to con people. Just why he should spend 40 days hiding out and then constructing a series of tricks was inexplicable — unless of course it was the result of some brain injury. That was possible, but who treated him after the accident and who took care of him for that month and a half? Jude shuddered to think what would have been said if she hadn't called in Dr. Prakash, although the testimony of one doctor was never going to be enough to silence the detractors. Heck, the testimony of a team of surgeons, pathologists and a coroner's report hadn't been enough to stop the conspiracy rumors about Princess Diana's death.

Jude and her *Miracle Mile* team were kept busy enough every day with a simple Google alert on Josh's name. They were stretched to keep up with all their more general promotions work. Jude herself had always focused on Gemma's own PR and simply transferred allegiance to Josh but even Gemma had never had this level of attention across the Internet. More conspiracy theories were thrown up by the day. Jude wasn't surprised to see the story growing but even so, she found herself feeling unsettled by the power of the belief in the only-to-be-expected theory that Josh had planned the car crash all along in order to murder Gemma. Obviously it wasn't Josh in the car at all (who was the patsy — a blow up doll? wondered Jude, and where did the truck driver come in?). CCTV and the cell phone video were discounted as easy to fake.

The theories as to why Josh would commit murder were varied and mostly unimaginative: Gemma was having an affair; Josh was having an affair; they were secretly bankrupt and it was a ruse to get the life-insurance; one or both of them was an alien or one of the lizards that secretly ruled the world. Opinion was verging more towards Josh being the lizard rather than Gemma — lizards being well-known for surviving in desert conditions.

Jude chuckled at that one. There would almost certainly be anti-lizard placards at the audition-spots for *The Miracle Mile*.

She had a file on Maude-Lynn by now and scarcely a day went past without a request for a comment on one of her latest stories. She thought the reporter was a nasty little weasel and the feeling was fully reciprocated. Charlie thought a catfight between those two would be something to see.

'It would be a rout,' snorted Jude but Charlie wasn't so sure.

If Maude-Lynn had believed in miracles, she would have seen the blowfish incident as Divine Intervention. She was eating blowfish herself in exactly the same Las Vegas restaurant when it happened so the story fell right into her hands.

Fewer than 20 restaurants throughout the entire United States are licensed to serve blowfish. The reason for that is that it's more than a thousand times more poisonous than cyanide. The poisonous parts from just one fish could kill up to 30 humans.

But human beings, being what we are, find this fascinating and enjoy the challenge of trying to eat blowfish without dying. It's perfectly possible because it's mainly the skin, ovaries and liver of the fish that are poisonous. The emphasis there being on the word *mainly*. The Japanese blowfish — the fugu — is the one most commonly eaten and every one caught is supposed to have the toxic parts removed before being freeze-flown to the USA under license, in purpose-built, clear, plastic containers. The fugu chefs for U.S. restaurants are specially trained and, in the case of raw fugu — *sashimi fugu* — it appears that the desired outcome for the diners is to get *just a little* poison in order to experience intoxication, lightheadedness, and numbness of the lips.

In Harry McDonald's case the dosage went slightly wrong and he ended up paralyzed and seemingly comatose while totally conscious. This made the news on the day before Josh got on the plane to Las Vegas and, the news being what it is, it made some pretty big headlines. These ruined the career of the chef who was just doing what he was paid to do, lost jobs for fugu-preparers in Japan, and seriously affected the financial year for that particular restaurant and shipping company.

Maude-Lynn, having Oriental blood in her — and being a professional risk-taker — knew quite a lot about blowfish poisoning. She'd experienced the intoxication several times and she understood the risks. In fact, hers was the first call through to 911 when she heard the man at the next table complain that his tongue didn't seem to be working properly and that he felt oddly dizzy.

Thanks to her and to six other cell phone owners, the paramedics were there by the time Harry's heart rate had accelerated off the scale, his blood pressure had dropped dangerously low and the muscle paralysis had begun.

For Harry, the feeling of stasis creeping through him was the most terrifying experience of his life. He didn't know enough about blowfish to realize what was happening, he thought he was going to die. Fortunately, he also didn't know that even partial blowfish poisoning would mean that for at least next 24 hours he would be fully conscious but unable to speak, move his eyes or indicate in any way whatsoever that he was awake.

He flailed like a fish as the strange, prickly sensation spread through his body and fell awkwardly off his chair, taking the tablecloth and two plates of blowfish with him as he crashed onto the floor.

But he lived, thanks to the paramedics. For a few moments, until the situation had been fully explained to her — as in 'Shaddup, he's dead if you don't get out of the way!' — Harry's botox-blown wife was considering suing the paramedics for assault as they shoved a breathing tube down her husband's throat. Her own desperate fear made her retreat behind an automatic panic mode that manifested like a wide-eyed mongoose on a screaming rampage and impeded everyone whether they were trying to help or not.

Maude-Lynn carefully took transmission-quality video with her cell phone, filed the story and then followed the ambulance to the hospital where she was met by a film crew. Her dining companion, an old friend from college, had given up on the evening already; he knew Maude-Lynn in reporter mode. For fairly obvious reasons, he didn't fancy finishing his own blowfish but, given that his evening was already ruined and the restaurant was frantic to keep its other customers, he happily accepted a complimentary replacement meal with wine and dessert — and coincidentally hooked up with a lady who had been dining alone and who was later to become his second wife.

Harry did not recover within the specified 24 hours but neither did he die. His wife, the mongoose Becky, all power bosom and stretched skin, couldn't move her own face muscles enough to show her intense distress so she screeched instead. Her anguish was genuine enough but it managed to alienate virtually everyone except Maude-Lynn who was seriously on the prowl for a good story that would stitch up Josh Goldstone and seeing a very good opportunity here.

Maude-Lynn talked to the doctor in charge who said they had done all they could, maintaining Harry's heart, blood and renal functions and that it was simply a matter of time.

'Could he still die?'

'Unlikely,' said the doctor. 'But we have no way of knowing how long the paralysis may last. Perhaps another 24 hours, maybe more. And it also depends on the strength of his body. His liver is not good which doesn't help.'

This is how Maude-Lynn's mind was working:

'If we get Josh Goldstone here and he can't cure Harry (which of course he can't) then I can show him up as a fraud. If Harry recovers then it's just the normal state of affairs for blowfish poisoning and Josh claiming a miracle also shows him up as a fraud.'

But could she get Josh Goldstone to the hospital? For that she had to enlist Becky's help.

Poor Becky, finally silenced by exhaustion and sitting bolt upright like a rabbit frozen by headlights, had not left the hospital once. She was Harry's third wife, had no children of her own and absolutely no friends in Las Vegas. They were just visiting on holiday to celebrate their first wedding anniversary. But now, Harry's sister and cousin were there — and two of his kids had shown up too — and Becky was determined that Harry shouldn't recover with them present and her absent. She wasn't even going to go back to the hotel to get a change of outfit in case that happened and none of Harry's relatives was going to go and fetch fresh clothing for her. For a start, they wouldn't know what to get and she would not want them rummaging through her wardrobe.

Maude-Lynn was canny. She arranged for a one-hour dry cleaner's to come and fetch all of Becky's clothes while Becky had a shower in Harry's private bathroom. Becky was so grateful, especially when a hairdresser also arrived to perk up her drooping curls and some good-quality make-up manifested itself unannounced as well.

So when Maude-Lynn suggested asking for Josh's help, she did not baulk. She wondered whether Harry's family would approve but decided that she didn't really want to ask them. They had never really taken to her and were still in league (in her view) with Harry's first wife who was the mother of his children. The kids were always distantly polite but she found them pretty intimidating.

But this could be her chance to show them that she mattered! She was Harry's next of kin after all and what she said went, according to the hospital and Harry's *Medicare* at least.

Becky had heard a little about the purported miracles around Josh Goldstone and she had been a big fan of Gemma's and of *The Miracle Mile.* As Maude-Lynn had suspected, she was happily credible of most things and an avid reader of *The National Enquirer*. Gently, Maude-Lynn pushed Josh's ability to heal at her and Becky, too flattered to be in the confidence of a well-known TV journalist to recall that Maude-Lynn had only ever filed hostile reports about him, was entranced.

'Well it stands to reason that the government is lying to us,' she said. 'There's so much out there that we don't know about. I believe in flying saucers and angels and crystal magic and that TV show *Heroes* showed us that regeneration is possible after all. And if this man is a wonderful healer, then he'll heal my Harry!

'And I have an even better idea,' she said playing unwittingly into Maude-Lynn's hands. 'We'll take Harry to the airport! Expense is no problem and the amount we pay *Medicare*, they can sort out a portable life-support system. Yes,' she said, nodding and feeling powerful. 'We'll go there. After all, Josh might not want to come all the way over here.'

'Perfect,' said Maude-Lynn. It didn't even take that much arranging. Fortunately, Harry's family objected which only strengthened Becky's zeal and, after she had told Harry excitedly what she was doing (and Harry heard every word with horror), she arranged with the doctors for him to be sedated so that the journey wouldn't trouble him.

Maude-Lynn was elated at Becky's stupidity. If Harry were sedated, even if he did suddenly recover as the poison wore off, he wouldn't be getting up. It was going better than she had ever imagined.

Chapter Fourteen

Maude-Lynn's film crew was waiting outside the airport arrivals hall. Jude swung past them, assuming they were there for Josh but thinking no more of it. There were three more crews expected by the airport's PR people but that was nothing exceptional. Jude was excited to be seeing Josh again and, as she said furiously later, the blowfish incident never entered her consciousness.

To Becky's and Maude-Lynn's amazement, the miracle happened while Harry was in the private ambulance. He began to twitch slightly and move his arms. As he was three-quarters asleep it was hard for them to tell exactly how profound the recovery was but Becky was ecstatic, the medics pleased and Maude-Lynn hugged herself with glee. She had witnesses that Harry was already well on the way to recovery and when Josh came over and did his healing he'd be shown as an impostor and a fool. It couldn't be better!

The ambulance pulled up outside the main terminal five minutes after Josh's plane was due to touch down. The film crew, eager as Maude-Lynn, had reported back that the timing was perfect and, to put the icing on the cake, the newsroom was prepared to link live.

The only fly in the ointment was that Becky took a little persuading that Josh needed to be involved at all now that Harry was recovering. But Maude-Lynn was skilled in ego-massage and had the wonderful carrot of an appearance on live TV to offer. And after all, no one knew just *how* much better Harry was did they? She helped Becky apply a little more make-up — matte foundation for the cameras — and patted her hand reassuringly.

So it went like a dream…up to a point.

Harry was unloaded from the ambulance just as Josh was coming through customs. The private paramedics pushed him through the doors into the arrivals hall with Becky hovering anxiously behind Maude-Lynn. The other film crews hesitated but widened their focus just in case.

Jude, waiting for Josh, saw them and frowned but before she could move, Josh and the others were through.

'Go live!'

Maude-Lynn, microphone in hand started up like a well-rehearsed actress.

'Here at Las Vegas International Airport, Becky McDonald, wife of blowfish victim Harry McDonald, has come to find a miracle. She believes that Josh Goldstone, The Miracle Man as he's now known, can heal her paralyzed husband.

'Josh! Josh! Can you heal this man?'

It will take longer to read what happened than it took to occur. Firstly Jude stepped across Maude-Lynn with her hand held out, saying 'We're not here for any publicity stunts. Back off!'

Then Simon and John stepped in front of Josh. With a little signal that they were come to know well, he indicated that he wanted to be accessible. They obeyed and stepped back again.

Becky, schooled by Maude-Lynn, ran forward and grabbed Josh's sleeve, her eyes wide with excitement.

All the film crews focused in on the scene, pushing away the casual observers.

The trolley bearing Harry was propelled forwards until it was right beside Maude-Lynn.

'It's okay Jude,' said Josh calmly. He stepped over to Harry and looked down at the recumbent figure.

'Hello Mate,' he said and squeezed Harry's hand. The long-held leg pain from a car accident 24 years earlier healed instantaneously as did the bruising from his fall in the restaurant; his cholesterol balanced itself, his hardened arteries softened and the sedative cleared out of his system.

Josh turned to Becky and said, 'Your husband?'

'Yes,' she was breathless with excitement.

'He's already better,' said Josh, his every word clearly transmitted to everyone listening though not to *Fox News*. 'The blowfish poison's going out of his system and, if he weren't sedated he'd probably be sitting up now. What's his name?'

'Harry,' she whispered.

'Harry,' said Josh. 'Harry, get up and stop worrying your wife!' He smiled and walked away, his entourage closing ranks around him to block out the cameras.

Behind him, Harry McDonald sat up slowly and took a deep breath. Before his wife threw herself at him, he said, 'Good God, I feel wonderful.'

It was only after Josh walked away that Maude-Lynn and her team realized that the live broadcast had failed totally. Nothing had been transmitted.

'That sniveling little weasel,' said Jude, looking back over her shoulder to where Maude-Lynn was frantically covering ground and interviewing Harry and Becky with a camera that suddenly worked. 'She was trying to trap you, wasn't she?'

'Can't blame her,' said Josh. 'It's her job.'

'Oh stop being so holier-than-thou,' said Jude but Josh had stopped walking. Andrew and Simon bumped into him, the entourage's momentum blocked.

'Hang on a minute,' he said. 'I've got to go back.'

'Are you mad? They'll eat you alive!'

'Probably.' But Josh headed back to where Maude-Lynn was just finishing her interview with Harry and Becky.

'This job is *not* going to be a sinecure,' hissed Simon to Andrew.

'But my sciatica's gone!' Harry was saying. 'I've had that more than 20 years. It's incredible.'

'Sciatica can come and go,' said Maude-Lynn, a touch of desperation in her voice.

'Well maybe. All I know is that I feel great and I wasn't feeling great when I went into that restaurant,' said Harry. 'I was feeling distinctly under the weather. And my back! I really hurt my back in the fall and now it's fine.'

'Thank you Harry and Becky McDonald,' said Maude-Lynn turning to the camera. 'Miracle man or complete fraudster, is this what we have to expect every time Josh Goldstone seeks publicity for his show? This is Maude-Lynn Sykes reporting from Los Angeles International Airport.'

Josh waited behind the crowd until the red-eye of the camera was off and Maude-Lynn had said goodbye to the McDonalds. She handed her microphone back to the cameraman and turned away. He saw the unshed tears of hurt pride in her once-pretty almond eyes. It had all gone horribly wrong.

Something made her look back over her shoulder and she saw him. Anger filled her eyes, then uncertainty and then a kind of calmness. She blinked; the tears had gone.

'One,' he said softly. Maude-Lynn heard the word across the crowds but was perplexed by it. She hesitated, then shook herself slightly and walked away.

Having four judges on *The Miracle Mile* meant that, in the preliminary auditions, the voting could go two-all. It was a rare occasion as talent was talent and practically everyone could spot it. But there were always a few borderline cases according to personal taste.

To overcome this problem, Gemma — the acknowledged star of the show — had held a casting vote.

With Gemma gone, the first auditions had not faced the old problem as the voting had been, at worst, two-to-one. But now it was back to the original formula, and the production team was wondering if Gemma's casting vote should be given to Josh.

'Absolutely not,' he said when meeting up with Bartos and the others. 'It should be Sam if anyone. He's the senior judge now.'

But *Goldstone Inc* didn't want Sam to have the job or the kudos. In the end, they came up with a new system of voting: each Judge could award zero to three votes per contestant. Those who had eight votes or more went through and those with seven and under were out. Bartos and Jude were excited because it was something 'new and improved' and anything 'new and improved' meant a publicity push and was a potential ratings booster. Sam, Deborah and Gideon were pleased that no one got to be top dog and both Sam and Deborah enjoyed the idea of giving lousy contestants a zero. Josh simply wasn't bothered.

Philippa and others from *Gemstone Inc* on the other hand were very bothered by Josh's lack of ambition.

'Couldn't you have accepted the casting vote?' Philippa asked Josh.

'No,' he said gently. 'It was time to move on. I'm not Gemma.'

Too right. And that wasn't the last of their disappointments over Josh.

Where Gemma was driven everywhere in a stretch limo (and Josh, by her side, had been too), Josh tried hard to veto the celebrity star cars.

'A tinted window black saloon will do fine,' he said. In vain did they argue that the limousines were required for his entourage. 'I don't need an entourage,' said Josh.

These cars were his due: what his fans would expect. 'What fans?' said Josh. 'They can learn to expect something else.'

But, they reiterated, he would need the space inside the car for all his staff to consult with him and advise him between locations.

'I want to think for myself,' said Josh.

Where Gemma had a personal entourage of twelve, apart from security — make-up, speech consultants, personal assistants, wardrobe mistresses, drivers, hairdressers and personal fitness trainers — Josh just wanted one PA.

'I can work out what to say myself, I don't need people to pack my bags for me and I don't need anyone to make me do press-ups at 6am,' he said. 'What Gemma did was right for her; I'm going to be right for me.'

He wanted to sell Gemma's Lear Jet and give the money to animal welfare centers. Philippa nearly had a fit over that one. She thought that the jet was essential for image and for easy transport.

'But I like real airplanes with real people,' said Josh. 'Anyway, it's my Jet and I can do what I want with it.' He didn't say that sulkily or aggressively, he just said it. And it was just true.

He won on that one. But he didn't win on the issue of hiring private airplanes for transporting the team and the production people around the USA as it could be proven quite easily that using a private plane was actually more economical than going by scheduled flights.

'And you really are going to be so famous you simply won't be able to go on a scheduled flight,' said Jude.

'I know,' he said sadly, making her laugh out loud at the stupidity of the situation.

'Most people would give their eye teeth to be as famous — and as wealthy — as you,' she said.

'I know,' he said, again, this time with a sigh.

'Well, I can spin it easily enough,' she said. 'The world has just recovered from a major recession and you want to contribute all you can to the continuing recovery.'

'Jude, I don't like spin,' he said warily. 'I just don't want to do things to excess. It just gets too complicated.'

She smiled her tight smile at him and turned crisply away on her four-inch heels.

The private plane fight was the only one Josh didn't win. In nearly all things, if he didn't like what was being suggested, he had a way of not resisting that outlasted everyone else's insistence.

As he also developed an astonishing habit of manifesting free private flights, gifts, food and other transport that saved the company a lot of money, he drove everyone totally crazy over organization.

'It's not as if we *need* to save money!' said Mattie, the Financial Director, as one of the accountants asked her how on earth he could get the books straight. 'It just increases the tax we have to pay. And, frankly, I'd rather pay companies and people for services than pay the IRS.'

There was another problem too. Gemma's super-efficient senior personal assistant, Marjorie, had left after her boss's death, taking with her the majority of her staff. She was setting up her own production company and would be a force to be reckoned with in a year or so's time. Josh was offered any number of bright, Botoxed and beautiful assistants (and that was just the boys) who worked at *Goldstone Inc* and he could have headhunted anyone he wanted. But he didn't want any of them. 'I don't know what I want,' he confessed to John Jordan over lunch.

'I think you want a friend,' said John who knew Josh a little better than the others. 'Someone who doesn't care what you — or they — look like. Someone who knows what cookies you like and when to leave you alone.'

'Yes!' Josh brightened up. 'But where do you find someone like that?'

'Oh I think I can find someone,' said John.

He could. Her name was Mary-Beth Oliver and she had worked firstly as a runner and then as a production assistant for *Goldstone Inc* for three years, while both looking and feeling like a fish out of water. She would be perfect for Josh.

'Last year, I recommended she moved her skinny ass to *Habitat for Humanity*,' said John, referring to a local housing charity. 'There, she could look a mess and do a real good job and she did just that. I wouldn't recommend her to anyone but you but she's kinda nice with that subtle grizzly bear loyalty of the ugly girl.'

'Subtle grizzly bear?' Josh was confused.

'Well, if she takes to you, she takes to you in a big way,' said John. 'But she doesn't get girly or pre-menstrual at you. She just defends you from other people like a grizzly protects its cubs.'

'How do you know?'

'She did some work for me,' said John evasively.

'Tibet?' Josh knew all about John's activism. 'She's not too political is she?'

'I don't think so,' said John. 'She doesn't seem to have *opinions*. She just does what you ask her to — even the impossible — and then asks what's next.'

'Even the impossible?'

'Yeah.' John Jordan looked evasive. Josh read his energy field carefully and relaxed a little. 'The impossible' would not have been unethical, just ever so slightly illegal.

'Well I'll see her if you like,' he said. 'But isn't she happy where she is?'

'Well yeah,' said John raising an eyebrow. 'But this is a kinda rather bigger gig!'

'And she'd care about that?'

'Now you've got me!' said John. 'The fact that she wouldn't care a damn is exactly why I think you might like her.'

'I think you're right.'

Chapter Fifteen

Josh never knew how John persuaded Mary-Beth to come and be interviewed and on first sight he couldn't see why John had suggested her in the first place. The woman who showed up at Starbucks took up less space than her body had actually been allotted on this planet and her energetic field almost bent backwards on itself to be inoffensive.

She was as skinny, as was required in the modern media world (two aspirins on an ironing board was the phrase that sprang to mind) more than thirty years old with a furrowed brow. She appeared totally lacking in physical charm, having no prepossessing features, a pointy nose, very white skin and slightly frizzy hair that couldn't quite make up its mind if it wanted to be curly or straight, auburn or a very slightly odd sort of brown. And she was so obviously a worrier who tried so hard not to fuss that she fidgeted with her feet almost all the time.

John Jordan introduced her to Josh in between signing autographs and joking with the Starbucks staff. Everyone knew and loved John, he was a Las Vegas favorite; no one — just yet — knew Josh well enough to recognize him on sight, they just felt very relaxed when he was around. Looking carefully at the woman who was almost invisible inside John's aura, Josh stood up, as his parents had always taught him to do for a lady, and held out his hand as if offering food to a frightened wild animal.

Mary-Beth Oliver took the proffered hand gently as if Josh, too, were a frightened animal. They contemplated each other gravely in silence. When she had made up her mind, she nodded, briskly. 'Yes,' she said. 'I'll take the job. Thank you.'

Josh threw back his head and roared with laughter. Mary-Beth stood there completely unoffended until he had finished and then looked up at him cautiously.

He twinkled down at her. 'Monday?' he said.

'Monday.' She nodded. 'Seven-thirty.'

'Um...I don't get into the office until eight.'

'Why not?'

'Oh...you know. Um. I meditate.'

'Okay. But I'll be in at 7.30.'

'You don't want to know anything about money or terms — or that kind of stuff?'

'I doubt you know any of it to tell me,' she replied, matter-of-factly, making him laugh again.

John Jordan observed, while appearing to be totally absorbed in a cell-phone conversation with his agent who was firming up his still top-secret new contract with a rival Network. He saw exactly what he expected to see: Mary-Beth taking one look at Josh and offering him her heart and soul without either of them realizing it for one moment.

'All you really need in this business is a friend,' he said softly so that no one could hear him. He might not be able to do much for Josh before he left for his new job but what he could do, he had done. Josh would now have someone who would be able to understand and take care of him — and he would need it.

However, the first weeks of being Josh's PA were pretty terrifying. Mary-Beth Oliver might have knowledge and ability but working for the new, miracle-making boss who used to be the also-ran whom even she had ignored a few times was no sinecure.

'How are you coping?' he asked her at the end of the second day.

'I'm making it up as I go along.'

'Me too,' he said.

'Yes, but I'm taking notes,' she replied. 'Probably in a week or so I'll be able to tell us both what we're meant to be doing.'

That was a problem. She didn't know what to do and he didn't know what to do either so she made him coffee and, when she found out from others that he didn't like coffee (why didn't he *say?*), she made him undrinkable American tea which he drank politely until he managed to teach her the importance of boiling water on real tealeaves instead of a pot of rapidly-cooling water with a teabag waiting forlornly on the side.

She re-arranged his office (formerly Gemma's) which was exquisitely decorated in cream and green, buying new desk lamps and pictures and having the carpet cleaned. He carefully arranged it back and found the old pictures, replacing the new ones slightly apologetically, saying he liked familiar things around him.

Organizing the office itself, she had to admit, was hell. First of all there was the cell phone. She got him the latest. It wouldn't work. And the Blackberry wouldn't work either. Neither would the wireless Internet. When Josh told her rather bashfully that it appeared to be because of him, she didn't contradict or disbelieve, she just sighed heavily and telephoned the chief technical officer, Jon Taylor, a normally dour Scot with an a collection of really bad jokes for those he liked, to try and work something out.

Jon, a worshipper at the shrine of Apple Mac, was bemused. As he said, it wasn't as though Microsnot (his words) was involved; these were good machines! There was a two meter exclusion zone all around the office whenever Josh was there. And everything worked when he wasn't.

'Actually I rather like it like that,' said Josh mildly. 'It means that when people want to talk to me there are no interruptions.'

'A wee problem with the Internet however,' said Jon. 'And your phones aren't cabled so they don't work either.'

Jon sighed and then brightened up. This was a challenge! He was not in his first youth and could remember a time with cables like spaghetti and computers you couldn't fit in your pocket. The good old days!

'I'll have some old stock you can use,' he said, rubbing his blonde beard with one hand; his eyes twinkling with pleasure at all the re-systeming he would have to do.

'Can you do with an old G4 to start with? I've got a couple in my storeroom. I can add plenty more ram and a separate hard drive.'

'Sure,' said Josh watching Mary-Beth's outrage at the outmoded equipment Jon was suggesting.

'We're going to look like someone from the stone-age!' she wailed. Mary-Beth's own office was within the exclusion zone too and she hated the thought of losing her state-of-the art technology.

'Nothing wrong with the old stuff!' grunted Jon getting down on his hands and knees under the desk and working out the availability of power points.

He had Josh fitted out within three days and, had it not have been for the flat screen monitors, Mary-Beth's prediction of returning to the stone age would have been correct. As it was, half a ton of spaghetti in wiring had to be bound together with gaffer tape and hidden as best it could and spaces under desks found for old and large machinery with noisy fans.

'But we can afford the brand new stuff!' Mary-Beth wailed again. 'There must be *something!*' But Apple, like everyone else, had long outgrown cables and the old stuff it had to be.

Despite all this distraction and worry, and somewhat to her surprise, Mary-Beth found herself happy at work. She was entranced by Josh's gentleness and wry sense of humor and although worrying how to look after him properly made her forehead more crinkled than ever, her devotion did mean that Josh's paperwork was tidy, he always had the cookies that he particularly liked and his appointments were screened with a passion.

She tried to stop the Financial Director from seeing him for as long as she possibly could, having been taught that accountants were the devil incarnate — always trying to chop expenses and budgets. Josh was enough at sea as it was.

But eventually Josh did get the message that Mattie Jones wanted to see him and he set off, quite eagerly, into the financial heart of the multi-million-dollar fake art-deco building with its incongruous Feng Shui prosperity-bringing peacock and phoenix motifs.

Mattie was getting herself a coffee from the vending machine from hell just outside the swing doors of the accounts department. She had her own office and two PAs and could order coffee at the drop of a hat. But she preferred to take time and walk out of the office to the less-ornate open space of the stairwell where the vending machines lurked. It was the equivalent of a cigarette break and it cleared the head almost as well.

'Josh!' she said, her smile lighting up a very ordinary, clear-skinned face surrounded by rather too much doubtfully-colored brown hair. 'What are you doing here? *I* should come and see *you.*'

'Oh Mattie, there are too many shoulds,' he said ruefully. 'I'm surrounded by 'should' and 'ought' and 'must.' I'm quite lost.'

She was touched by this openness and vulnerability and, remembering that he wasn't an 'auto-hugger,' refrained from offering him a hug to demonstrate just how much she could empathize with him.

'You're feeling overwhelmed,' she said. 'It's quite natural in a new job. And with no Gemma...oh God Josh; I haven't seen you since then. I'm so sorry; you were together as long as Neil and I.'

'If anyone understands, you do Mattie,' said Josh gratefully. Mattie's husband had died three years earlier and he remembered someone wondering, fourteen months after Neil's fatal heart attack, why Mattie had a blotchy tear-stained face at work. Memories were horribly short in show business and the beautiful moved on fast. But ordinary, unexceptional accountants went through the long, natural process of mourning and still missed their husbands long after they had gone.

'Why did you want to see me?'

Mattie tried to look severe.

'You seem to have hired four people with no jobs,' she said. 'It would be useful to know what they are meant to do and what they actually do do.'

'They're friends,' said Josh. 'In England they are bouncers — minders. They're doing that for me. But mostly they're here for moral support.'

'Well you're going to need both,' said Mattie, sensibly. 'The trouble is that we are awash with security guys and they're going to need Green Cards as security men which means that I have to give good reasons why they are better than Americans at the job. You should have local people really.'

'They wouldn't know me or be able to anticipate me,' said Josh. 'Mattie, it's going to get harder and harder. I'm…' his face crumpled and he rubbed his eyes with the back of one hand. 'Mary-Beth is great but it's all new. And...well...the thing is…'

'The thing is that you're bereaved, exhausted and appear to be able to do miracles,' said Mattie briskly. 'You're not a charlatan — I know you well enough to know that — and you've not got a charlatan's thick skin.

'Come into my office for a while? It's pretty safe. I can get your friends sorted right away if you like.'

'I'd like that,' said Josh, taking a deep breath and following her into accounts and to the little glass-screened room Mattie called her own. It was filled with pot plants and crystals.

'Good for the electro-magnetic field,' she said gruffly as he looked around. Her Internet connection quietly switched itself off, as did her phone. Josh smiled.

'No angels,' he said, interested. People who were into crystals and energy balancing usually had images of angels everywhere.

'I deal with the head guy,' said Mattie simply. 'Not the staff.'

She fingered the cross around her neck slightly nervously. Mattie went to church and believed in the Scriptures but she didn't actually expect them to be real – nor standing in her office. For all his talk of being lost and uncertain, Josh held a presence that made everything around him glow.

'He doesn't know how powerful he is yet,' said a voice in her head that made her shiver.

'It's still you, isn't it Josh?' she said.

'I think so!' he said with a smile that reassured her.

'Well, you're just as scruffy as ever!' she said, passing over the fact that his scruffiness was somehow magnificent.

'Oh Mattie!' Josh relaxed. 'I'm so lonely. It's not just Gemma — it's the old familiar voices in my head. They're not there any more! It's silent. Most people have thoughts running around all the time — running them really. And now they've gone it's so strange.'

'Not filled with God?' said Mattie quietly.

'Oh yes. Filled with light,' said Josh. 'Yes the light is always there — and it's calling me back right now; it's incredible. But there's a little me in there too — and the light is so big and so, so *light.* And it's like not having my own private room any more. I live in the light — and don't get me wrong, it's blissful but sometimes it's just *too much.'*

'You want to go home,' saxid Mattie.

'Yes. Both homes,' said Josh. 'The old one and the new one.'

'Are you going to die?' asked Mattie gently. 'I mean…people like you don't tend to hang around very long; you seem to have a job to do and then get assassinated or just drop off the planet.'

'I don't know. Actually I don't quite *get* time any more either,' confessed Josh. 'It doesn't seem to be linear in my mind. I know quantum physics says it isn't and believe me, I know a fair amount about quantum now! I couldn't actually tell you most of the time whether I'm alive — that is technically — or dead. I'm just me.

'And I'm you too. And the Source; and the plants…And I can kind of switch myself off and on and be visible and invisible...and yet…' he tailed off looking confused.

'I expect,' said Mattie prosaically. 'That it's hard enough to conceive of how you feel, let alone rationalize it, let alone explain it. So I have a suggestion. You just sit here with an orange juice or something that Sally can fetch you while I sort out your minders' employment status and then we'll go and have lunch with my colleagues. Accountants are boring, predictable and very, very rational. Even in the cyber-age we still talk spreadsheets and math. We'll have you grounded in no time.'

She smiled; a lovely bright expression that lit up her initially mundane-seeming face from top to bottom and side to side. Josh sighed.

'Thank you Mattie,' he said.

So the new star was seen in the studio restaurant with *accounts* instead of going out and eating sushi or egg-white omelets in celebrity watering holes where everyone wore sunglasses, ordered $450 dollar bottles of wine, $40 bottles of water and bought a Ferrari or a pair of Manolo Blahniks on the way back to the office. It was worse than his fabled appearances at Starbucks. It was appalling. Not one of the staff members who were acting as unofficial spies for the other Networks could think of anything interesting to report about it at all.

Chapter Sixteen

The next day, there was the issue of the makeover. In the era of the worship of beauty and youth, Josh simply wasn't fit for national television. His teeth, his clothes, his pasty skin! He urgently needed tooth whitening, tanning, Botox and Restylane. There wasn't time for bletharoplasty for his eyes, a neck lift or pectoral implants — they could substitute a body pack until he had hit the gym and with luck most of the physique could be dealt with through a personal trainer between the auditions and the finale. And as for his clothes! He needed an image and he needed one fast.

Four of the eight auditions had already been held, with Seattle, Chicago, Miami and Denver still to come. They had less than a week to get Josh into some kind of shape.

Teeth first.

'No,' said Josh.

'What?'

'No.'

'What do you mean?'

'I have to be authentic,' he said.

'*What?*'

'Authenticity. You've heard of it!' He laughed, but no one else in the room was laughing.

'You can't be authentic with yellow teeth,' said Colin, the head of the makeover department and previously Gemma's much-valued assistant in such matters. Colin knew *everyone* and everything they had had done to their face or body. He understood every single trick in the book. Given a free rein he could have done enough to have made Josh fit perfectly in to the celebrity world in just three days.

'Be reasonable Josh,' he said, quite kindly. 'You are the youngest of the judges but you look the oldest by far. It's perfectly acceptable — even required — for men to have work done nowadays. Sam and Gideon do!'

But Josh was having none of it.

'Someone has to stand up for the human body,' he said. 'I'm not interested in hiding my age or my face or my physique. You see these lines here?' he pointed to the laughter lines around his eyes.

Colin shuddered. Certainly he saw those lines.

'These were made laughing with Gemma. These lines on my forehead are also part of my life with Gemma. Why would I want to get rid of her legacy?'

'Because it looks bad,' said Colin's assistant Chris. 'It's wrong!'

'Are you telling me that I should be fake?' said Josh, smiling to alleviate the accusatory phrase.

'Yeah!' said both Colin and Chris, neither seeing any cause for offence although their preferred word would have been 'faux'.

'Why not? Real is just gross!'

'But I am real,' said Josh. 'So are you.'

That was a mistake because Chris had never spent a day being real in his life. He didn't actually know what the word meant.

Josh laughed, looking at Chris's immaculate face and beautiful body.

'Perhaps not!' he said. 'You look great but it's not the right image for me.'

'Well what is?' said Colin, exasperated.

'*Me*. I'm what someone looks like naturally if they have lived this many years in a pretty happy life,' said Josh. 'Some laughter lines, some pain lines from love gained and lost. The look of someone who isn't afraid to be himself.'

There was silence.

'What in God's name are you talking about?' said Colin.

'I think people change their faces and their bodies because they are unhappy with their lives,' said Josh. 'Because they're trying to hide self-doubt and pain under image.'

'Well get real! That's how it is!' said Colin. Chris nodded in agreement. They didn't get Josh at all — and he didn't really expect them to.

'Look I want to look like just who I am,' he said calmly. 'I think you guys look great. Sam looks great; Gideon looks great; Deborah looks...looks...' he stopped dead as Colin's face began to crease up.

'Like that Biblical thing — *new wine in old wineskins,*' he added suddenly understanding it for the first time. Josh burst out laughing.

Colin began to laugh too. Deborah drank like a fish and she was so lifted that it was a miracle her ears didn't cross on the back of her hirsutely-enhanced head. Nothing could move except her mouth. Chris still didn't see the joke but now there was a point of contact between the two other men. Colin submitted with good grace (he did like a gently dominant male).

'Whatever!' he said rolling his eyes with mock exasperation. 'But even so some things must be attended to. There *will* be trimmed eyebrows. There *will* be a manicure; there *will* be a facial and a haircut; there *will* be chiropractic and massage — and deportment training for that stoop — and we really, *really,* need to go shopping.'

'Okay,' said Josh meekly. 'Ready when you are.'

Three days later, in Seattle, he stepped out of the car into the flash of cameras outside the sports stadium where auditions took place, looking calm, assured and surprisingly handsome in a fresh cream open-necked shirt, dark blue jeans, maroon cowboy boots, killer shades and — what was to sum up his image for all time — a simple necklet of royal blue lapis lazuli set in gold that Gemma was known to have worn. On Josh it lay just below the clavicle of a surprisingly strong neck and both the gays and the females watching thought it looked simultaneously strong and masculine and emotionally vulnerable. Copies of the necklace were in the shops within a week. Josh looked good enough on TV but in person — well that was something else. He exuded a presence that spoke of courtesy, kindness, strength and, despite his sadness, there was an air of unquenchable joy that sang in the very air around him. You felt cheered and hopeful just through shaking his hand. It was impossible to pinpoint or explain but it was infectious. Without surgery or make-up, Josh Goldstone made it to pin-up status within a week. It wasn't because he was gorgeous; it wasn't because he was tall or had a wonderful voice; it wasn't because of anything that anyone could name. That was because words like 'honor,' and 'joviality' had long gone out of fashion.

'Every move you make, every step you take, I'll be watching you...' quoted Jude softly as she stepped out of the car behind. Jude's cell phone never stopped vibrating with requests — more like demands — for Josh to appear here, there and everywhere on every TV show in the country.

'I'll do Salema's show after I've done Seattle,' Josh told her. 'Nothing before then. Tell them I've got to find out if I can do the job before talking about it.'

She did just that. They didn't like it but it did mean they could have a lot of fun speculating and attempting to dig up dirt. And Jude could have a lot of fun being a bitch. 'Best time of my life!' she told Charlie. 'Once it all *really* breaks it will be even better.'

Everyone was doing all they could to adapt to Josh and the new situation. Simon, Andrew, James and John worked out a routine for cover, working well (after initial friction) with the *Gemstone Inc* contracted security team. They all had to resort to walkie-talkie radios to make communication with each other and outside sources when working with Josh. Jon Taylor had spent two days shadowing Josh while hung from head to tail with appliances to see what would work and what would not. Jon was having the time of his life — and that only got better when he met up with Mattie on one of Josh's visits to the accounts department for time-out and talk. Two very ordinary-seeming people with what would be regarded as boring careers and uninteresting histories, met under the light of Josh's smile and knew that there was a future for love and laughter again.

It was a Sunday when Josh arrived in Seattle and one of the people there to meet him was Ernie Simmonds, caretaker at the stadium where the crowds were already queuing for their chance to audition. Ernie had been a big fan of Gemma and was an assiduous autograph-hunter. His wife, Geraldine, tutted at him for thinking that Josh was a celebrity. Surely he was just the two-bit husband of a star? But Ernie knew that Geraldine was way behind the times on that one. Celebrity passed between people like stardust and, anyway, he remembered Josh for himself. They'd watched a tape of Ernie batting in his first season at the Colts together over a beer two years ago. Nice guy; knew his baseball pretty well for a half-Brit.

Ernie had been given a college scholarship for his baseball skills. A backwoods boy from the mountains on the border with Idaho, he'd been quite a sportsman. He told Josh all about his youthful hopes and dreams during that shared beer and how he'd had to give it all up when the bomb went off too close to him in Vietnam. His right hand had never fully recovered with the muscles in the arm withering so that it appeared foreshortened and the hand could not grip very well.

Ernie could still hold a steering wheel or a frying pan but he couldn't pitch and he couldn't bat. So that was that. And it wasn't the kind of world where you could sue for compensation back then — or even be offered charity.

But his son, Nate, had found some old TV footage of Ernie playing and made it into a DVD for him and, whenever Ernie could find a willing viewer, he would sit and watch it with great enjoyment. So many years had passed that he had lost any bitterness. As he said, it would all have been long over now anyway and he didn't live in a time when the wages were all that great so he'd most likely just be where he was now, caretaking the stadium. He had no complaints.

So Ernie, remembering Josh, was by the front door with his autograph book and a wry smile. He could see the irony of asking the guy he'd watched TV with for his autograph and he was sure that Josh would see it too.

'That is, if he recognizes you,' scoffed Geraldine.

'He will,' said Ernie. And he was right.

All the film crews and all the cameras saw Josh greet Ernie, laugh out loud at the idea of the autograph and grip Ernie's hand with a strong shake. All the world got to see Ernie wince and Josh try to drop his hand at once, remembering that it was disabled. And then there was the slow delight dawning on both men's faces as Ernie returned the grip and shook and shook and shook Josh's hand.

'What did you do?' said Ernie looking at the robust, fully working sinews, tendons and muscles and the strong, smoothened skin.

'God knows,' said Josh quietly. 'I have to go in now, Ernie. We'll have a beer later, yes? Don't say anything if you can.'

Don't say anything if you can! Ernie shouted it from the highest hill. It made the local news with a bullet, and Jude gave the order to go live with the Josh Goldstone website.

Meanwhile, Maude-Lynn Sykes sat cross-legged on her bed in LA, surfing the Internet, feeling deeply uncomfortable and eating an awful lot of chocolate. She was seeking the perfect Evangelical preacher to set up against Josh. It had to be done; it was exactly what was required — and it was what she wanted to do. She wanted to bring him down and get the recognition for doing it.

The trouble was that the Evangelicals themselves made her feel nauseous. Maude-Lynn had never given much thought to religion, having been raised in a home where it wasn't discussed and going to a school where it was barely on the curriculum. Her family moved to the USA from Hong Kong when she was four so if any religion were prominent in her parents' life it would probably have been Buddhism. Fundamentalist Christianity came as a bit of a shock. It required most of a packet of Oreos, a Snickers bar dunked in coffee, six cigarettes and, as the shadows lengthened, most of a bottle of Napa Valley red.

She surfed on her laptop, sitting crossed-legged on her bed. It wasn't that she didn't have a living room in her apartment but that was kept for best, not for work. Maude-Lynn would be the first to admit that she didn't understand why she was so tyrannical about it but the living room didn't even have a TV or a computer and she never *ever* smoked in there. The living room, kitchen-dining room and bathroom were all immaculate, the main room furnished in white leather with copper-colored lacquer tables and chairs and stark Chinese calligraphy framed in copper on the walls. The bathroom and kitchen walls had sea-green and white tiles. It was very Zen.

It might have made sense if she had used the spare bedroom as an office but that was white from top to bottom and either carefully tidy or covered with washing according to the day of the week. All her media equipment was in her bedroom which was strewn with papers, post, TV screens (she had four), newspapers and magazines. The room had French windows, a balcony, and a huge air-conditioning unit.

Sex, on the rare occasions that she had it at home, took place on the settee or in the spare bedroom, never here — despite the purple sheets. That was just the way it was. Maude-Lynn didn't think about it but she enforced it rigorously. That she was as much a fundamentalist in her own way as many of the Christians she was researching, never once crossed her mind.

Of course she *knew* about Christianity. She had been to enough Episcopalian and the like funerals. She knew the bit about 'I am the resurrection and the life' and all that stuff but she'd never really thought about it. That was something you considered — maybe — when you got old or were dying. Not *now*. Not in this world.

Her lips moved as she read the precepts of one of the churches in the Mid-West. Somehow it could only sink in if she read it out loud.

'Being estranged from God and condemned by our sinfulness, our salvation is wholly dependent upon the work of God's willingness to offer us grace. God credits His righteousness to those who put their faith in Jesus Christ alone for their salvation, thereby justifies them in His sight. Only such as receive Jesus Christ and are born again of the Holy Spirit can become children of God and heirs of eternal life.'

Maude-Lyn's sensual mouth trembled as her unacknowledged

soul registered an unknown discomfort. This was all new to a journalist from the secular world. At the back of her mind the sneaking thought crept in that, if this were the norm, perhaps Josh wasn't all that bad. She bit her lip and read on, finding *Trinity Broadcasting Network* and listening, aghast, to the songs about Jesus and viewing with amazement the video clips.

It was weird and horribly exclusive and the forums were so filled with such a mixture of obsessive love and hatred that she had to go out on the balcony and breathe deeply and watch the passing traffic below for a while, feeling personally attacked for her life choices and lack of faith. But she could see the attraction too. All the websites and all the televised Churches invited you in. If you would only believe in Jesus as your savior you had friends and you had a community. No matter who you had been, you could be saved. The lost, the lonely, the hurt and the desperate could all receive love and be born again. Just one condition…Jesus or hell. Your choice.

Even so, it wasn't enough. She needed more. She needed a real fire-and-brimstone evangelist with his own local TV show. Someone who wasn't afraid to come out with all guns blazing, who would knock the wind out of the sails of Joshua Goldstone. Ideally someone who wasn't too cheesy with obvious false teeth; someone appealing as well as dangerous.

Just before midnight, she found him on *Salvation Hour* hosted by a local TV station in South Carolina.

The preacher of the Church of the Resurrection of the Righteous was not only fanatical and loquacious, he was hot — in a kind of Russell-Crowe-meets-Harrison-Ford-in-his-prime kind of way. He was a big man in his 40s with powerful features, a strong, lean body, his own whitened teeth, plenty of his own hair and a voice that — when unprovoked — sounded like deep red silk velvet with a twist of bourbon. There's not a dry seat in the house when a voice like that cajoles women to believe.

When provoked, the pastor's velvet purr became a powerhouse of rage that made the hairs on the back of your head stand up. He was white too, which was what Maude-Lynn wanted: even after Obama, it was better copy for Middle America. And he was hot on apostasy and demon-worship in the modern world too. He saw it as his personal job to alert people of the hell that they were heading for in not following the word of Jesus. His name was Joseph Sadd.

'I am justly named SADD,' he roared on *Salvation Hour*. 'I must be SADD you see, because of the sins of the world. SADD because of the destruction that is coming. But GLAD for the salvation of the righteous.' It was a great catch phrase and he had *great* charisma.

Maude-Lynn hastily checked the back catalogue of shows. Fantastic! He had even attacked Gemma when she died. Perfect. She sat back and sighed as she watched the archive footage warning that Gemma's fate was exactly what was in store for other sinners who lived lives of apostasy and excess.

Gemma, who had lived a life of sin and celebrity had met a violent death unrepentant and damned. He was SADD, he roared, about her eternity in Hell but what could he do? She had met her just desserts — the wages of sin! The fact that Gemma was a faithful, loyal wife was not mentioned. Nothing could mitigate her Jewish mis-belief and her hedonistic lifestyle. Her husband only missed out on the flak for being mostly invisible.

That, thought Maude-Lynn, was going to change.

She booked a flight to *Greenville-Spartanburg International Airport* the next morning, packed carefully to make sure she would look like someone Joseph Sadd could deal with (she had taken a good look at his congregation) and, after a delicious 2am Chinese delivery from her favorite restaurant, she slept the sleep of the just.

Chapter Seventeen

It took Maude-Lynn just 24 hours to be sitting in Pastor Jo's wood-paneled office, ostensibly asking to do a profile for him for *Fox News* but gently dripping the poison about Josh by commenting on the Pastor's piece about Gemma and wondering if he had any comment on Josh's miraculous time in the desert.

Joseph Sadd was not stupid but his ego was huge. He knew full well what Maude-Lynn was trying to do; that she was not a believer and that she wanted a story. To do her justice, Maude-Lynn never implied that she was a Christian, just that she was 'concerned' about people's reactions to Josh.

That didn't fool Pastor Jo either.

'That polluted little madam just wants a story,' he said to his African-American wife Beulah who led the Church choir. But as far as he was concerned God provided the means to the end – and Pastor Jo, devoted servant of God, preacher of the Truth – was up to the task of making it to national television. He had previously heard of Josh's escapade in the desert but discounted it, assuming he had hidden out as a publicity stunt. But now, this man too was a celebrity; worse, a Jew and, according to this reporter, *one who could be seen to be aping Christ!*

Within the next 24 hours, the ultra-faithful of the Church of the Resurrection of the Righteous had surfed the Internet, plotted the events surrounding Josh and provided their Pastor with all the information he needed for a real, roasting television rant. If there had been a dearth of 'real' Josh news, they might not have had their day of fame but, as it was, the story of Ernie's hand hit the headlines, Josh Goldstone was public property and all heaven was ready to break loose.

'Right,' said Josh, his throat dry as he looked up and around a stadium filled with more than 5000 people, all of whom were either auditioning or accompanying a contender for *The Miracle Mile* and all of whom had seen or heard what had happened to Ernie. They saw him come out of the players' tunnel with Jude and were roaring his name.

'Josh! Josh! Josh!'

'Any idea what I should say?' he muttered out of the side of his mouth while waving to the crowd.

'Do I look like I have a script?' asked Jude.

'Not exactly.'

'And would you read it if I did?'

'No, but a bit of preparation might have helped.'

'I don't think so,' said Jude. 'Straight from the heart I think. Just shine, Josh, shine!'

Technical problems with the set up of the auditions for *The Miracle Mile* in Seattle meant that the crowds, clustered together in the stadium had had to wait far too long for the beginning of their audition time and it was the new boy, Josh, who was asked to stand up and address them, just to pass a little time…

He swallowed hard and stepped up to the wired microphone set up by the sound recording team. As he held out his arms to the crowd, something golden, peaceful and glorious streamed from him. Five thousand people fell silent in waves around the stadium.

'Okay,' said Josh. 'Here's the thing. You're not all going to qualify.'

'Oh dear God,' said Jude involuntarily.

She was wrong. A steadily-gathering impulse of amusement and then outright laughter rippled through the crowd. They heard the words but they were also aware of the light of *bonhomie* that was streaming from Josh. There were no losers in that light and for a few precious seconds each felt his or her true worth.

But a few whispered the caveat to themselves 'I *will* qualify.'

'I'm sure you've all been told that you're brave for being here,' said Josh. 'And you are. But you know, unless you write and promote your own material, to be a performer in the modern world means be at the mercy of your manager, your agent and, if you are a singer, your record company. You will have to empty yourself of all desire to be who you think you truly are and be what they can sell. You'll have to put aside some of your own views and prejudices — because they would not look good in print and they could damage your career. This can be a good thing because it may make you think about what you are thinking and saying. But, consider before you audition, are you willing to jettison everything, and become the puppet of the celebrity machine? The long-lasting stars are able to hold on to who they truly are, deep within, because they want to serve — to offer pleasure and maybe even enlightenment to others. Those who only serve their own wish for fame are eaten by their own desire. They don't last.

'You know, don't you, that even if you win, wealth and fame aren't going to make you happy? Happiness is within, it can't be created from outside.

'If you are truly at peace with yourself so that the opinions of others do not hurt you; if you are willing to go along with what is required of you as a star — realizing that with celebrity you can influence others who are lost by demonstrating your own inner truth — and without imposing your ego on them — then you are a winner already and your talent will serve you for the whole of your life whether you qualify in the next two days or not.

'For those of you who are turned away, it will hurt a great deal but most of you are very young and the lesson may be to learn how to overcome challenges like this. If you are authentic and talented and you don't get through then perhaps this is just not the right path for you. It's a real opportunity to be able to walk away from rejection, confident in yourself and knowing that there is no need to blame others. You've seen the show — and if you aren't as good as you think you are, although rejection will hurt, it may teach you to learn to be better or even to seek a different kind of life where you *will* shine.

'It's wonderful to hunger and thirst for your right livelihood; to feel passion for your work and to know that by shining yourself, you help others do the same. If you are your authentic self and that shows — then either you go through or you don't need us.

'As you look around you, you may see others that you, personally, wouldn't send to Vegas in a hundred years but be kind while you are waiting; they have valid dreams as well as you. If you have a genuine suggestion that may help their act, pass it on. It won't take away from your own likelihood of getting through. But if you just think they are stupid, keep that to yourself. For all you know, you may look as ridiculous to them as they do to you.

'Clarity, authenticity — I can't say those words enough. Be you, purely you, not a clone of your favorite artiste or singer. We're not interested in imitations. Being *you* is the key to all happiness. And it is the key to winning through here.

'If you are dissed by anyone, even by us, the judges, it can't hurt you if you genuinely know your worth. It's only when the criticism pushes a button that's already there or if you secretly agree with it that it hurts. So keep your calm and hold on to dignity. We don't have wars in this world just because governments want them. We have wars because we fight those people we don't like…and because we feel attacked when someone else has just expressed an opinion that we don't agree with. It's only their opinion. It can't hurt us unless we allow it to make us feel inadequate and we will only feel inadequate if we are not authentic in the first place.

'So don't worry if people diss you. They are either helping you to become less a carbon copy and more you — or they are only seeing you through their own inadequacy. Grace is when you don't attack back but allow them their opinion. It's theirs and they have a right to it just as you have a right to yours.

'You showed up today; you risked it. You did well. In the world we have created there are what we call 'winners' and 'losers'. Not all of you are getting through today. If it's not your turn today seek somewhere else where your light *will* be recognized.

'But there are rules to *The Miracle Mile* and to get through to the next round, you have to follow them. If you don't agree with them, then you don't get through. If you don't have the discipline to apply them then it's your responsibility. So stand away from your ego and let your real self shine.

'And if you *do* get through — well God help you because I wouldn't want to be in your position!'

He stepped back — to a stunned silence. Luckily he was authentic enough in himself for that not to bother him. He'd said what he had to say and that was all that mattered.

Jude looked at him in simultaneous awe and horror. It was a terrible speech; it was an amazing speech. It was so over their heads it was ridiculous. But that was who he was. It came with color — beautiful, golden, smooth, warming love that was impossible to describe. You might not understand a word but the *feeling* was wonderful.

Slowly, faintly, applause built up, initiated by a small group of people dotted here and there. They were the ones who got it. Jude wondered if she could work out from the CCTV later whether they were the people who would get through the audition or whether they changed their minds and quietly left to go home and live their life without celebrity. Even she momentarily wanted to go home and raise Appaloosa ponies, the power was so great.

Once the clapping reached a tipping point, it exploded so that the place was roaring with appreciation. Jude shook her head, awed by the power of this unassuming man by her side. It wasn't because the crowd were just celebrity-sycophants, he had actually found the heart of his listeners — when most people would only have tried to appeal to their ego.

The crowd started chanting and clapping in time. 'Josh, Josh, Josh!'

'They want more?' said Josh in surprise.

'Sounds like it. Try some sound bytes this time if you can,' said Jude. 'There are cameras on you after all and the news can't cope with more than a minute at a time.'

'Yeah, right! Like I even know what a sound byte is,' he said stepping up to the microphone again.

'You want more?' he asked.

'YES' they roared.

'Why?' he asked. The whole stadium rippled with laughter.

'Why not?' they called back.

'Well, then I would say that I wish you luck,' he said. 'But actually I wish you that feeling of quiet satisfaction from knowing that you've done your best and that you know it deep inside. There's no point in showing off to others and telling them how amazing you've been. That's just covering up for inadequate feelings inside.

'And don't worry if you miss your big chance and think that you will never be able to be wealthy and happy. Remember, wealth and happiness have very little to do with each other. You know that saying about the lilies of the field and the birds of the sky being looked after. Well it's true! You be your own beautiful self and you will always have everything you need to get by comfortably. It's called the Law of Attraction. You shine as *you* and the Universe must deliver. You get what you are focusing on. You push *against* whatever it is that you *don't* want and focus on the negative and you get what you are focusing on. It's a simple law but, in the world where image and marketing is everything, it's not easy to understand. But you can't be angry or negative or critical or judgmental of others and draw to yourself anything that you want. You can't serve two masters and judgment, greed and negativity will just pay you back in kind. As will love — so obviously love is the one to seek. Just be yourself today and do what you love; tomorrow will take care of itself.

'Actually, you know what I *really* want to say to you? Don't stay here and audition to be a star — get out there and live a real life as you! What do you want us to judge you for? We can't validate *you*! Only you can do that!

'If you are seeking fame, you are really seeking self-esteem so ask for that, not for my approval or Sam's or Gideon's or Deborah's.

What do we know? Pearls before swine!' he said.

'Oh great,' muttered Jude. But Josh was still speaking.

'You know, you are all part of the Source,' he said. 'God isn't popular nowadays but whatever you believe, there is a life force; a force for good. This world turns and prospers every day. If you are true to yourself, you can't help but prosper too.

'Enjoy — and if you're still daft enough to audition, I'll look forward to meeting you later!'

He stopped as laughter rippled through the crowd, waved and turned away.

'Okay,' he said, nodding curtly to Jude and the gob-smacked entourage as applause and cheers flooded over their heads. 'What's next?'

At exactly the same time that Josh was speaking, Joseph Sadd stepped up to the microphone. *Salvation Hour* was on the air and Maude-Lynn Sykes was standing just behind the *Fox News* Satellite uplink.

Pastor Jo also took the Beatitudes for his theme but in this case, it was a conscious plan. He was too smart to launch an attack directly at Josh without a solid weight of theological certainty behind it. Pastor Jo knew his Bible and he knew that this one always worked.

'Blessed are the poor in spirit, for theirs is the Kingdom of Heaven,' he began softly, his voice gentle but husky with emotion. 'The poor in spirit…the lost…those who do not know the truth…but those who will listen to the truth. The Great Truth of our Lord Jesus Christ. Those who humbly admit their wrongs and come to his table to be saved. Those are the ones who will be redeemed in the Kingdom. But those who seek to set themselves above others…those who seek fame and fortune without the goal of enlightening others and bringing them to peace…those are the fake in spirit! Those are the charlatans, the raisers of false hope! The celebrities who think they are important but who know nothing of the Kingdom and live their lives of sin and hopelessness in the light of fame! How they will fall! How they will repent when the Kingdom comes!'

'Amen!' moaned his congregation happily. This was going to be a good roaring thunderer, they could tell.

'Blessed are they that mourn, for they shall be comforted,' whispered Joseph, leaning down from the stage and holding his hand out to Sarah Bright whose husband Dan had died just two weeks earlier. With tears in his eyes, he kissed Sarah's hand and shook his head lovingly. 'We feel for you so much in your loss,' he said gently. 'But we know,' he stepped back and let his voice rise in crescendo. 'We *know* that Dan is with Christ. We *know* that he is in the Kingdom and we are glad!'

'Aaaah,' said the audience in unison, agreeing and anticipating what was on its way.

'Yes, we are glad for Dan although we grieve with Sarah. We are GLAD!'

Joseph's voice dropped an octave and hardened.

'But we are SADD for the man whose wife died unshriven as her car was knocked off the Hoover Dam. We are SADD that he hid out in the desert — who knows with whom? — and came back to take his wife's tainted place in the world of so-called Talent TV. Did he mourn?'

'No!' said the audience more hopefully than anything else. They weren't quite on board with this one yet and the 'Sadd' hadn't been quite loud enough.

'He did *not* mourn!' roared Joseph. 'He stepped out for his own fame in his dead wife's footsteps! What should he have done?'

This was an easy one. 'Pray!' yelled the congregation. That was *always* the right answer.

'Yes pray! PRAY for the soul of his wife the unbeliever! Weep for her fall into hellfire. If he *knew* the truth, he would mourn indeed. And maybe...maybe then there would be hope for him.'

Maude-Lynn whispered Josh's and Gemma's names to a bemused-looking member of the congregation at the back who hadn't a clue what Pastor Jo was talking about. The man beamed at her and nodded and whispered enlightenment to his neighbor.

'Blessed are the meek, for they shall inherit the earth,' said Pastor Jo tenderly. 'The meek. Those who are willing to bow their heads to Christ. Those who are willing to learn; willing to understand that we are *nothing*.' The word came out in a long, sensual hiss. '*Nothing* without Christ. *Nothing*.'

'Amen!'

'Blessed are they who hunger and thirst after righteousness,' roared Joseph. 'Do you *hunger?* Do you *thirst?*'

'Yes! Yes!' shouted the congregation happily. This was getting better and better. 'Yes! Yes! YES!'

'Then you shall be filled! Filled with the light of Christ! The one, the only, the true light of Christ. You shall be *saved*!'

'Amen, Amen, Amen!' the congregation leapt to its feet, stamping and cheering. 'Hallelujah! Amen!'

Joseph stood, silently, waiting for them to calm down. One bead of sweat shone on his forehead. He put one hand out, palm down and his audience sat eagerly.

'Is the search for fame a search for righteousness?' he asked, softly.

'No,' came the whisper back.

'Do those who hunger and thirst for fame, hunger and thirst after righteousness?' the voice was soft and powerful.

'*No*!'

'Do those who hunger and thirst after worldly gratification, hunger and thirst after righteousness?'

'NO!'

'Too right they don't,' he said, an entrancing smile lighting up his normally stern face. Several women felt themselves go slightly dizzy. Even Maude-Lynn was mesmerized (albeit in a way that felt horrible).

'Blessed are the merciful,' Pastor Jo was in his element now. His voice, perfectly warmed up rang like a bell. 'What shall they obtain?'

'Mercy!'

'I can't hear you.'

'*Mercy*!'

'Again!'

'MERCY!'

'Hallelujah!'

'Amen!'

'Blessed are the pure in heart!' Oh it was going well now! Everyone was back up on their feet, calling out 'Hallelujahs' and 'Amens.'

'The *pure* in heart! The pure who take Christ for their savior — *for they shall see God.'*

Pandemonium ensued for a good five minutes with Beulah and the choir chorusing 'Amen!' behind Pastor Joseph.

Then Joseph held his hands out and the congregation settled down happily. This would be the best bit, the bit about those who *weren't* pure in heart.

'But I have to tell you, my brothers and sisters, I have to tell you about a man who is claiming healing powers that do not come from the Lord!'

'Ohhhh.' This would be a good one.

'A man who does not even *claim* to be a Christian!'

'Wooaah!'

'A man who is using tricks and lies to give himself fame and deceive the innocent, the poor and the needy!'

'Shame! Shame!'

'This man is a judge on a television talent show *The Miracle Mile*.'

'Ooooh-er.' Some of the congregation watched *The Miracle Mile*. There was a moment's unease in case they were all in for one of Pastor Jo's blanket condemnations.

'Josh Goldstone! A Blasphemer who is masquerading as the Christ!'

'Who-ho-phew-what?' Really? They were in the clear then and this Josh Goldstone was in serious trouble. This was the *best!*

'I do not deceive you Brothers and Sisters! My staff have been watching this man. He is pretending to copy the miracles done by

Christ himself!'

'No! Shame! Shame!'

'Even worse!'

'Whooaaah!' Could there be worse?

'He is using Satan's — *yes! Satan's* — power to cure these people.'

'No!'

'Oh yes! It is happening my friends. The great deceiver will help anyone fallen enough to call upon his hideous powers.

'Jesus said,' He softened his voice and paused for the Hallelujahs to die down. 'Jesus *said*! 'Beware of false prophets, who come to you in sheep's clothing, but inwardly they are ravenous wolves'. The Gospel of Matthew, Chapter Seven!'

The congregation was stamping its feet and shouting.

'Jesus said!' Pastor Jo was in his element. 'Jesus said, 'There shall arise false Christs, and false prophets, and they shall show great signs and wonders; insomuch that, if it were possible, they shall deceive the very elect'. The Gospel of Matthew, Chapter twenty four!'

'Waaah!'

'But my brothers and sisters!'

He had to say this ten times before the shouting and crying out died down. Women and children were hysterically screaming 'Save us Lord!'

'Hush! Hush!' said the velvet voice of Pastor Joe. 'There is good news!'

They hushed, slowly but steadily.

'For although this man — Joshua Goldstone — is surely the servant of Satan!'

'Oooh!'

'He is heralding the coming of the End Times!'

'Aaaaah!'

'The Book of Revelation!'

'Hallelujah!'

'The Book of Revelation says!'

'*Hallelujah*!'

'The Book of Revelation says that Satan will make people sick by casting his spell on them in order to remove it to make it look as though there has been a miracle!'

'Aaaaah!'

'The Book of Revelation says,' Pastor Jo took a deep breath and thundered, "'He doeth great wonders, so that he maketh fire come down from heaven on the earth in the sight of men, And deceiveth them that dwell on the earth by the means of those miracles which *he had power to do*."'

He took a much-needed breath.

'So my Brothers and Sisters! How can we distinguish the false from the true?'

'Pray!'

'Yes! But Scripture tells us! The Book of Isaiah says!'

'Hallelujah!'

'The Book of Isaiah says, "To the law and the testimony: if they speak not according to this word, it is because there is no light in them.' There is no light in Joshua Goldstone! He has not been saved! He is not a believer in Christ! He will be cast into *Hell!*"'

'Hallelujah!'

'The Book of Revelation, Chapter Nineteen: "And the beast was taken, and with him the false prophet that wrought miracles before him, with which he deceived them that had received the mark of the beast, and them that worshipped his image. These both were cast alive into a lake of fire burning with brimstone."

'I tell you my friends, the Anti-Christ is coming and Joshua Goldstone is his messenger!'

Total pandemonium.

'Oh yes,' said Maude-Lynn quietly, her body quivering with the lust for the kill.

Chapter Eighteen

Some of the congregation later noticed that Pastor Jo had not finished the Beatitudes. He never got to 'blessed are the peace-makers, for they shall be called the children of God' or 'blessed are they who are persecuted for righteousness' sake, for theirs is the kingdom of heaven.' Or even 'blessed are ye, when men shall revile you, and persecute you, and shall say all manner of evil against you falsely.' But it obviously wasn't relevant.

Back in Seattle, Mary-Beth found John the security-disciple poring over a Bible in his office. She'd gone to find out why he hadn't turned up for lunch.

'It's all here,' he said as if to no one, pointing at the text. 'Everything he said. It was just changed for *now* so it made sense to them.' His eyes were suspiciously damp.

'What do you mean?'

'Josh's speech today. They were listening to the Sermon on the Mount! Every word. Every bloody word.'

Silently Mary-Beth put her hand out to hold John's. 'He's so young,' she thought, wanting to stroke John's hair like a parent.

'What are we going to do?' he said. 'This is going to explode. How can we protect him?'

'I think that forces greater than us will protect him,' said Mary-Beth softly. 'We just have to show up, do what we can and let whatever it is unfold.'

'I wish I had your faith,' said John, squeezing her hand gratefully.

'I wish I had it too,' she said. 'It's lunchtime; you need to eat. There's chilli today. You like that.'

Pastor Jo's roaring, tear-strewn, emotional and prayer-filled service was much better visually than Josh's quiet hand-shaking or gentle words about personal responsibility and authenticity. And the miracle of Ernie's hand was the perfect excuse to let Pastor Jo have his day in the spotlight. The growth of Christian fundamentalism over the last decade gave him the platform he needed. Not even Maude-Lynn had expected her visit to South Carolina to have quite such an effect but she had not reckoned with the power of the Christian Right. Joseph Sadd was big news: he was on every Network for days; he had his own blog, his own Facebook fan page and was offered a book contract. He was here to stay.

The pastor's celebrity even made it in the UK — to be equated by some with the Rev. Ian Paisley, scourge of the Irish Catholics at the height of the IRA conflict between Britain and Ireland. Not that Paisley had been a healer (more, some said, a wooden plank in his own eye than a remover of specks from the eyes of others). But the sheer determination and the timbre of the voices were similar. Pastor Jo did have Irish ancestry and, in the weeks that followed, a slight brogue descended onto him as a gift from God.

In the meantime, Josh started being a judge on *The Miracle Mile* and, to his great surprise, was enjoying himself immensely. He was feeling his way most of the time but his gentle honesty was a good foil both for Sam's egotistic, assertive, dismissals and Deborah's callous vitriol. His confident malleability and Gideon's balanced and professional views gave a much-needed balance.

Not all 5000 contestants from Seattle and surrounding areas could possibly make it before the cameras and the judges so there was a filtering system where everyone had a first audition with a series of producers. Not only the good ones were passed through. With the cheerful cruelty of the modern media-led world, the pathetic, the deluded and the arrogant who would make good TV were put through too. Of course they thought a 'yes' at that stage meant they had talent which made the fall even harder later on.

As Colleen Mason finished her painfully off-key rendering of 'I Will Always Love You' and stood back with 17 years of self-satisfaction pouring from her spoilt, over-made-up face, the judges began to make the first good quotes of the day.

'Have you quite finished that caterwauling?' asked Sam, who

usually led the comments. 'Are you truly deluded enough to think you actually have a voice?'

'What?' Colleen's shock was palpable. She had expected a repeat of the sycophantic enthusiasm of her family and friends.

'Well you don't.' Sam sat back with arms crossed. 'Worst voice of the auditions so far.'

Colleen's face closed down as Deborah added her venom.

'You're ugly; your hair color is totally inappropriate for your own coloring and you have no talent whatsoever,' she said.

'Cheer up,' said Gideon, misreading fury as distress in the girl's face. 'You'll make a perfectly good cabaret singer in your own town. But a star in the mainstream you are not.'

Josh said nothing, looking long and hard at Colleen whose face was now violently stormy.

'Josh?' Deborah raised her eyebrows in irritation at his slowness.

'Why are you here?' he asked.

Colleen exploded with anger towards this seemingly easy target.

'Because I *have* got talent!' she yelled. '*Everyone* says so! You're just a load of outdated, old-fashioned know-nothing f***wits! You know *nothing!*'

'So why are you here?' said Josh. 'If we're — what did you say? — Outdated, know-nothings. Why come and expose yourself to our ignorance?'

'Because I want to be a star!' wailed Colleen with tears of anger and hurt pride running down her cheeks.

'A star needs to have dignity,' commented Deborah with a sneer.

'Like you'd know,' retaliated Sam.

'Now, now,' interposed Gideon.

Josh leant forward looking closely at Colleen.

'You're just being lazy aren't you?' he said.

Colleen stared at him. '*What?*'

'You've got a good brain in that head and you could be quite a success in business. But you can't be bothered to study and you think that being a blonde country singer would be easy.

'Well you're wrong about that. I suggest you stop trying to fit into the mould of celebrity cheerleader because you don't fit. Try being an intelligent woman with ambition in your career. You could do that and do it well.'

Colleen stared at him. 'What the f*** are you talking about?' she said. '***hole.'

'Internet marketing or something like that,' said Josh, chattily, completely un-moved. 'But not singing. And don't start a charm school either because that really wouldn't work.'

As Colleen stormed out of the audition room, Bartos and the rest of the production team felt like punching the air with joy. 'He'll do,' said Bartos, famed for his understatement.

Outside, the second unit filmed Colleen's return to her parents. She was tear-strewn, furious and vituperative. And yet…after a few minutes of ranting she calmed down and said, 'Dad?'

'Yes Sweetheart?'

'Could I go study marketing? At college?'

'College? You want to go to college?'

'Yeah,' she said. 'Only stupid people want to be celebrities and I'm not stupid!'

Andy Marshall had no real talent either. He was auditioning as a comedian, using tired unfunny jokes that were too old for him. He was smart enough to know that he wasn't that good and sane enough to be terrified of the judges' caustic wit. He wasn't quite sure how he had got through the first level of auditions. But he couldn't let his Uncle Mac down so it was a relief to have got this far.

'Pathetic.' Sam sat back with arms crossed. 'Totally unfunny; completely the wrong material but, frankly, I think the only way *you* could be funny would be if you tried to sing.'

'Son, you're not a natural comedian,' said Gideon. 'I'm not really sure why you think you are. And I have to agree with Sam that the material you chose was the worst! Go and get a couple more years' experience under your belt, find a decent writer and come back and see us again.'

'To what end?' said Deborah turning to Gideon in amazement 'His delivery was appalling. No talent, no style, no elegance. Atrocious.' She turned back to Andy, standing round-eyed, like a stunned herring in front of them. 'Not even good writing could help you.'

Andy's damp eyes flickered to Josh and he tensed even further for the deathblow.

'Andy,' said Josh, thoughtfully. 'Is there someone in your family who used to be a comedian or who really wanted to be one?'

'My…my…my uncle,' stammered Andy.

'What happened to him?'

'Nothing…that is…he…he didn't make it to the big time.'

'And you wanted to make it to the big time for him?'

Andy twisted his hands together with embarrassment.

'Kinda,' he said.

'Andy, you can't live other people's lives for them,' said Josh kindly. 'It just means two ruined lives instead of one. What do you really want to do?'

'I'd like to be a vet,' said Andy with sudden enthusiasm. Then he slapped his hand over his mouth in horror at letting out the unacknowledged truth.

'Well, it's a 'no' to comedy,' said Josh. 'I think we're all agreed.'

'Indeed we are.'

'Yes.'

'Absolutely.'

'Is your uncle outside?'

'Yes,' said Andy miserably, twisting his feet this time.

'I'll come out with you,' said Josh, standing up.

'Really?' Andy felt a frisson of hope.

'Josh!' Deborah thought he was being ridiculously soft. 'We don't have time!'

But Josh was up and round the desk and walking out with his arm around Andy's shoulders.

Mac Marshall didn't receive a healing as such. But he did understand, for the first time, that Andy had been trying to succeed for his Uncle's sake, not for his own.

'You stupid boy!' he said affectionately. 'I thought you wanted it for you.'

Dumbly, Andy shook his head.

'I'll leave you two,' said Josh. 'That's a good lad you've got there. Very talented with animals I think. He'd make a wonderful vet.'

'A vet? No one in our family has ever gone into medicine!'

'Worth trying,' said Josh. 'A lot more reliable than show business.'

For a while, the judges despaired of finding anyone with any talent at all, but halfway through the afternoon they met Melissa Brown. Melissa was exquisitely pretty, absolutely tiny, and packed a voice like Aretha Franklin. She had also been an epileptic since she was three and really should have disclosed that on her application form. If she had, she would never have been accepted — there are plenty of bright, flashing lights in Las Vegas.

Josh could see something amiss in her electro-magnetic field when she came in, shaking slightly from nerves. Melissa didn't have much self-esteem and she was painfully aware that she should have owned up to her disability. After all, even studio lights could set off a fit — and as for tension! But her Mum believed she had talent and Melissa loved to sing so much that she managed to find the courage to show up.

She couldn't start her song (Mark Ronson and Amy Winehouse's old hit 'Valerie') because her voice dried up from nerves and she felt the familiar symptoms of an on-coming attack which froze her to the spot. While Sam drummed his fingers on the desk and Deborah raised her eyes to the ceiling, Gideon and Josh exchanged glances. They both thought the girl had possibilities.

'Melissa, come here,' said Josh gently holding out his hand. The girl managed to step forward. She placed her tiny, long-fingered hand into his and energy flowed through him dissolving the nervous tension and reprogramming the cells of her body to delete the epilepsy completely from her DNA.

Melissa thought only that she had fallen deeply in love (at seventeen a crush is always 'love'), stepped back and sang like Aretha. It was maximum points leading to screams of joy and floods of family tears outside the audition door.

It was only after a fit-free week and all the news coverage about Josh and Ernie that Melissa began to put two and two together. She was one of the rare ones who hugged her miracle to herself as a private source of joy. She never mentioned it, never had another fit and always, throughout her life, kept a little picture of Josh by her bedside as a talisman.

That miracle passed the media by but the guy in the wheelchair was too startling for anyone to miss. His name was Hamish McTaggart and both he and his wife Freda had come with their son Simon even though Simon really didn't want them there. Simon was a cool dude, a break-dancer who thought he could take the competition by storm and, when he proved to have neither talent nor discipline, took it out full-throttle at the cameras waiting outside. He made so much noise, swearing and shouting, that Sam went out to give him a well-televised dressing-down.

As Simon stormed off, Hamish managed to back his wheelchair in through the door to see the other judges and to plead for his son.

They took his well meaning but ill-informed views of Simon's precocious talent with a justifiable pinch of salt but were courteous due to his paralysis.

Josh asked him what made him have to sit in a wheelchair and Hamish answered that it was a car accident 10 years before when he had broken his back.

'I was driving Simon to camp,' he said. 'And a truck hit us.'

'Driving to camp? Isn't there a bus?' asked Gideon.

'Well yeah, but Simon didn't like going on the bus. He got bullied. He was a sensitive kid.'

'You know, Mr. McTaggart, you should try standing up for yourself,' said Josh. 'You can't live your life looking after your son.

You've got to let him go so he can be who he wants to be — and he doesn't know what he wants to be yet. All kids want to be stars at his age.'

'I should try standing up for myself?' said Hamish torn between outrage and disbelief. 'Did you *say that* to me?'

'I did,' said Josh smiling. 'Why don't you try?'

Hamish could feel heat in his legs and hips. His big, anxious face went red as he fought the sensation of belief that was working through him. He was paraplegic! He couldn't move his legs!'

But he could. And with Gideon stepping out from behind the desk to offer a hand, he stood up.

'Good God,' was all he could say again and again. 'Good God. Good *God!*' He walked round in a circle and then almost ran out of the audition room.

'Are you going after him?' said Gideon. Deborah was open-mouthed with astonishment.

'No,' said Josh. 'Sam will be back in a minute and we can get on. We're already behind schedule.'

'Imagine that,' said Deborah. 'A man who would fake being in a wheelchair just to get us to give his son a second chance. Who would credit that?'

'Not many people,' said Josh, laughing.

One of the assistants asked if he should wheel the wheelchair out of the room. Josh and Gideon nodded assent and Gideon sat down again, looking at Josh quizzically, his honest dark face sizing up his fellow judge.

'I think we are in for an interesting few weeks,' he said.

'Oh do you?' Deborah was totally impervious. 'Dear God I hope we are. So far it's been dire.'

That night Hamish and his family were all over the news — as was Pastor Jo decrying the cheap publicity stunt — and from then on, Simon, James, Andrew and John were pretty much run off their feet. Their work as minders in the UK hadn't quite prepared them for celebrity bouncing (as they called it) or holding back the hoards begging for a miracle but they were fast learners and had a knack of co-ordination with each other that made it look as though they had taken to the new life like ducks to water. They dressed casually and were easy to lose in a crowd, taking it in turns either to guard Josh obviously or do surveillance work. Simon and Andrew both had army training and James was a natural. John found it really weird but he stepped up to the line pretty well and was by far the best at warding off the hysterical women.

'Hysterical women?' said Josh in disbelief as he was almost manhandled into the car at the end of the next day. 'For *me?*'

'I didn't say rational, sensible women,' said John. 'I said hysterical ones.'

Chapter Nineteen

Nobody could decide whether Salema Abdul was the new Oprah Winfrey or the new Larry King. Whichever it might be, she was very, very good. She let the interviewee tell his or her story without needless interruptions and she got the point of what they were trying to say but she didn't let them get away with anything.

Gemma Goldstone had appeared twice on her show, in New York, so Josh had met Salema before. She had flirted subtly with him, which he always found surprising as he was used to being a very married also-ran. He liked her Arabic beauty, the deceptively sleepy-looking black eyes, slender neck and, off-air, her self-deprecating manner.

Salema was a Sufi — a mystical Muslim — and, as such, had done much good work in helping calm Christian-Muslim fears over the previous decade. She did not object to wearing her hair covered in order to interview an orthodox Muslim and, in her days as a reporter, had sometimes worn full Burkha if it meant she would get into the heart of a Saudi, Iranian, Afghan or Iraqi story. She always dressed modestly with arms, legs and throat covered and wore her smooth black hair tied back. She let it be known that she regarded this as courtesy to her fellow Muslims rather than her own belief but, the truth was, she suffered from psoriasis and it was both helpful and convenient for her to keep covered up. Nothing had worked for years and it was testimony to her calm and disciplined style that the itching and discomfort of the disease never distracted her from conducting a fair interview.

This time, Josh and Salema met in make-up surrounded by the angst and fuss of the pre-show bustle. Josh was being what he referred to as 'foundationed-to-death and blow-dried to high heaven' and couldn't concentrate very well. He was forbidden to smile at that point so Salema just waved at him and moved on to her own make-up area.

So, it was live on air that they touched and kissed. She whispered in his ear, 'Josh, can you heal me?' so quietly that the microphone could pick up nothing.

'Done,' he said just as quietly, feeling Grace flood through him. 'Don't tell a soul.'

Even though the joy, as her skin was softened, soothed and relaxed all over her body, was so great that she wanted to scream it from the rooftops, Salema sat down in the stylish maroon armchair, smiled serenely and arranged her long skirt. This would be a complex interview to do well and she needed to give it her full attention — after the initial lovey-dovey stuff of course.

'Well Josh,' said Salema, once the audience pandemonium had died down. 'It's been quite a year so far. I am so sorry about Gemma. She came to see us less than a year ago. It was a terrible tragedy.'

'Thank you,' Josh wriggled a little in his own armchair until he was comfortable in the seat. Sometimes the light that flowed through him during a healing was so strong that it took him a moment or two to get back to himself.

'So many people love Gemma,' he said 'And it's really touching that their love for her rubs off on me.'

'You still refer to her in the present tense. I've noticed that in several interviews.'

'I'm sure she still exists,' said Josh. 'Death isn't the end, it's just a different dimension.'

Oops. This was going too deep too fast. Salema reined back.

'Gemma was the one in the public eye but you were always there too even though you never made the headlines,' she said.

'I was always there, in the background, yes.'

'You were her rock, she said.'

'I hope so. I tried to be.'

'Well before we talk, I've got some footage here that shows just how much a rock you were — and not only to Gemma.'

Josh had been warned by Jude that Salema's staff had asked for any footage *The Miracle Mile* might have of him but he had not seen the VT and was surprised and interested to see that they had cut together more than a dozen incidents over the last few years where he was shown comforting or talking to one of the contestants who had been sent home.

He made a mental note to get a copy of the VT for later — there was one face there that struck a chord…

What also struck a chord was an image of him and Gemma embracing. Oh how he missed that — and how beautiful he thought Gemma was. There was a tear in his eye when the camera came back on his face. That didn't hurt his image anywhere; thousands of women watching wanted to offer him comfort.

'So, Josh,' said Salema. 'You were there all the time?'

'Oh yes. Just a backstage guy.'

'Well, whether you were just a backstage guy or not — and I suspect not — your face is now on the front of more magazines than Gemma's ever was. You're being followed by the press everywhere you go; you are The Miracle Man. And I'm so honored that you've chosen this show to tell us your story.'

'Thank you.'

'So, Josh, let's start at the beginning. What did happen to you in that accident?'

'I wish I could tell you Salema. I really don't know. I remember what we were talking about — we'd taken a special detour to go over the dam for the last time before the by-pass opened.

'I remember the moments before the crash — ' Josh put one hand to his head and closed his eyes tightly as if to squeeze out the pain of the image. 'And I remember crackling sounds, heat and tremendous pain and then there were just dreams for a long time. At least I think it was a long time. I was with Gemma in the dreams.'

'Did you think you were dead?'

'Yes, I was sure I had died.'

'Did somebody rescue you from the water?'

'Some*thing* did.'

'An angel perhaps?'

'Something like that; there were presences — or at least there seemed to be. And I knew that I was alive and that Gemma had gone. And that she was okay. And that I had to go on.'

'And then what?'

'I don't really know. I did eat and I did drink but mostly I watched the sky and my mind tortured me until it had dissolved itself.'

'Tortured you?'

'Yes, you know those thoughts that think themselves inside your head?'

'I guess we all have those.'

'Well I think the purpose of a vigil or a retreat is to quieten those voices so that you can think clearly and consciously instead of having them think *you*. And mine seemed to be attacking for a long time until they thought themselves out...and went away. And once they'd gone, I could hear...'

'You mean you don't have those thoughts any more?'

'Yes, that's what I mean. That old grinding of worry and irritation and fear and even hatred has all gone. My mind is mostly clear now. Of course, there is sadness now and then as memories come up of Gemma and our life together. But any other memories or thoughts are purely impartial ones — they just present the image without the comment that would have been there before.'

'That must be amazing.'

'It's a little disconcerting — still. But it's peaceful.'

'Were you examined by a doctor?'

Josh smiled. 'Yes I was. But I take it that you mean if I don't have thoughts trying to rule me through worry and fear I must be insane?'

Salema laughed. 'You sound pretty sane. And you do miracles.'

'Well *I* don't do anything. I'm just a conduit — a catalyst if you like. I can now see people as perfect — I see them in all sorts of colors and I can see where the colors don't fit but that it's just on the surface. The blueprint is always perfect. And I guess they see their own perfect reflection back. If your cells believe they are perfect then they can't be sick so you can't be sick.'

'But miracles are happening all around you.'

'I guess so. It depends on what we see as a miracle. If someone's aligned to the Source then they are aligned with all wellbeing. So they will be healed. It's misalignment with the Source that is the problem. If you amend that then the solution is automatic.'

'But the miracles wouldn't be happening if you hadn't shown up.'

'I don't know,' said Josh simply. 'I think miracles happen all the time. We just don't notice them.'

'What do you mean?'

'Well think about the miracles of what *doesn't* happen. Given the way we think and the bombardment of news and negativity that we are hit with I think it's amazing that we don't go wrong all the time. But we don't!'

'What do you have to say to Pastor Joseph Sadd and the Christian community that is saying that you are fraudulently trying to make people think you are Jesus Christ?'

'Well I'm not Jesus Christ. I'm not pretending to be Jesus Christ. I'm Jewish but that's the nearest it gets.'

'Are you an observant Jew?'

'I used to be more observant than I am now. Gemma preferred Liberal Judaism but I was okay with orthodox. But since the desert I eat bacon (though I don't eat shellfish because I actually don't like shellfish) and I don't find I need to go to synagogue as much. You see, it's the thoughts in our heads that think us that are the things that block out God. If they aren't there, you can hear the music of the spheres; you can hear the voice of God and you are a part of it all. You don't need to go and find God in some special place. It's just the noise and constant chatter of life here on Earth that drowns out the Source. God's speaking to everyone all the time — it's just hard to hear for the fear.'

'God speaks to you?'

'To everyone. Not me more than you — or anyone here. God speaks all the time.'

'What does He say?'

'*It* says whatever you can hear, I think. Perhaps, if you are a Christian, it speaks as Christ. Perhaps if you are a Hindu, It speaks as Brahman; if you are a Moslem, It speaks as Allah. It speaks to me as the Source because that's the filter I like to use.'

'The filter? And you call God 'It'?'

'The filter is the form we are comfortable with. Like Christians are comfortable with Christ. It's whatever we call the Source Energy. The Source Energy doesn't have a sex. It's not a big man in the sky looking down on us!'

'Did you think like this before the accident?'

'No. I don't think I thought much at all. My thoughts thought me.'

'But you are a theologian — you've studied ancient languages; the lives of holy men such as Jesus. You even speak Hebrew, Greek and Aramaic.'

'Yep.'

'So are you using all this for what you're doing now?'

'Maybe some of it. But mostly I just listen and talk directly.'

'To God?'

'Well...yes. To the Source. To Love.'

'Love?'

'Yes but even that's complicated. You see, we use the phrase 'God is love' but it's *agape* — spiritual love not *eros* or *phileo* which mean sexual or brotherly love — and both the words *God* and *love* are so loaded in the modern world. If you say 'God is love' people so often think of the love they had from their parents or from their partners. So, in so many cases, for them, God means 'authoritarian' or 'not there' or even 'cruel' or 'possessive.' And love can mean just the same — it can mean 'abandonment,' 'pain' or 'terrible let-down'. So it's really hard for people to align to 'God' or 'love' with that level of pain around them so perhaps it helps to be with someone who can align — to show the way if you like.

'I tend to call God 'Source' because that's got less loading on it.

And if you can align to that Source energy, it's love like nothing else. It's totally unconcerned as to what religion you are or how virtuous you are or think you are. We are all loved equally no matter what we do or believe. And miracles are just a perfectly natural part of it. If you are *there* then you must be healed.'

'Wow. Do you see angels?'

Josh laughed. 'Not really. I'm going to quote someone else here and say that I tend to go to the boss not the staff. Angel work is fine but an angel is a messenger and if talking to it aligns you to your authentic self then you're talking to the Source anyway.'

'What would you say to the Christian groups who say you're a blasphemer and a magician?'

'Nothing, because they wouldn't listen to anything I did say.'

'Josh!'

'Well, okay…I'd say try reading the Gospels on the assumption that Jesus wasn't talking from his ego. The ego is the mask or personality that we wear and someone of the level of Jesus was talking about Spirit not ego. If you read the Gospel of John as a personal meditation I think you can see that Jesus is begging you to rise up out of ego — to be born again if you like — and to understand that you too are a child of God as Jesus was. If you do that, then his words are your words and you can do as much as he did or more — just as he said.'

'Just as you're doing?'

'Just as he asked us all to do,' said Josh. 'There's nothing in me that is in any way different from what's in you — and in everyone. We are all children of the Divine. We are all perfect, all healers. We just forget because we get mired in all the chatter.'

'Would you say that to someone suffering from cancer? To someone with a disabled child?'

'I guess I probably just did.'

'Could you heal someone with cancer?'

'I don't heal anyone. If they wanted to be healed they would be healed.'

'Why would someone *not* want to be healed?'

Josh sighed. 'That's hard to quantify when we live in a world where death is judged as wrong,' he said. 'We think that length of life is more important than quality. We think that you must live more than 80 years or it's unfair. We think that we begin at birth and end at death. If you believe that, then it's going to seem impossible that someone might not want to be healed. But if you know on a soul level that there's somewhere pretty wonderful that you're going — going home — then why wouldn't you want to go? Particularly if you are tired or find life here hard.'

'Because of the pain of the people you're leaving behind?'

'Well it hurts,' he admitted. 'I know it does. But in a world where people die, we will grieve; it's part of the deal of living on a planet. But if you don't go — don't die — because you don't want to hurt the people left behind then you are living more of their life than you are yours...and if you do that, then you're not aligned to the Source. You're not living truly as you. So that's probably why you don't feel so good in the first place.'

'A lot of people will be very angry with you for saying that.'

'You know something? If they're angry, they're angry with themselves, not with me. And anyway, anger is fine — it might get them up and doing and help them get back to who they really are.'

'Do you know there have been death threats against you?'

'Really? No, I didn't. Well there've been some nice letters too. Swings and roundabouts.'

'Aren't you afraid?'

'No.'

'Just no?'

'Why would I be afraid? One day I'll go home. I'll miss the pancakes though...'

Salema laughed.

'I should talk to you about *The Miracle Mile,'* she said.

'Yes, I think I'm meant to be here to promote that,' he said with a smile.

'I gather that you refused to have your teeth whitened.'

'Yeah, I've seen the magazines saying I have 'English teeth,'' he said grinning again without a flash of white.

'Why not? You're a celebrity.'

'Well I just want to be me. I'm not ashamed of my body or my teeth or my skin. I'll admit I had all the mercury taken out of my teeth when Gemma first got famous and we could afford it. But that's it.'

'So what do you think of the Hollywood faces and the surgery and all that?'

'I think everyone should do what they want to do but understand that it won't make them happier or more authentic. It *might* make them prettier; that's all.'

'Your picture's being touched up on the magazine covers anyway!'

'Oh is that what it is? I did think I'd got surprisingly good-looking all of a sudden.'

'And how has the show itself been so far?'

'Okay I think. There are a lot of people out there who have mistaken their talent — and who think that fame would make them happy. But that's only to be expected.

'Obviously I'm a complete beginner but Sam's being rude enough to me to make me think there's hope — he'd be totally ignoring me if there weren't. Deborah is unique and outrageous and great fun to be with and Gideon is a saint.'

'And you've done a miracle already!'

'Which one would that be?' he asked politely, drinking some of his water.

'There's been more than one?'

'I have no idea how many people have found themselves…but I expect you mean Hamish?'

'I did mean Hamish.'

'Well a miracle happened. Personally I think that one was Gideon.'

'And if someone here needed a miracle, could you help them?'

'They could probably align themselves yes. But not live on TV right now.'

'Why not?'

'Because TV lights and all that kind of stuff makes it pretty hard to be aligned — and if someone wanted a miracle and didn't get it, it would hurt a lot. I wouldn't like to put them through that. People are not performing seals.'

He threw his head back and laughed. 'I'm going to get slated by the 'honor the feelings of the performing seals' society now, aren't I?'

'Well you're certainly creating some controversy.'

'But all that's just make-believe isn't it?' he said, leaning forward. 'When we hate someone for what they say it's only because some of it is within us. If anyone hates the idea that they can align to their perfect self it's because they secretly want to. If anyone thinks I'm blaspheming it's because they feel imprisoned by their faith. It's all in us — the trouble is all in us. It's not *out there.* When we think it's out there, we feel helpless and frustrated and that leads to more fear within us.

'We try and fight wars against what we see is evil — and just create more anger and hatred. There's nothing outside of us. It's all in the terrifying thoughts that rule us. We don't think evil things — they think us.'

'You think there are demons in us?'

'Not external demons, no, but demonic thoughts and feelings, yes. Anything that leaps up inside us and hates is a demonic thought and it causes terrible pain.'

'Where does it come from then?'

'Repetitive thoughts of anger that build and build on themselves. Repetitive thoughts of fear that rise up and engulf us. Wanting to run with the crowd or wanting to be accepted. All sorts of reasons.'

'Maybe we should all spend six weeks in a desert to exorcise them.'

'It probably wouldn't take you a whole six weeks, Salema. I think

I was a particularly difficult case.'

'So do you not actually feel fear, hatred or anger?'

'Not as such, no. I still get a bit judgmental but only as in, 'I don't like that so I'm not going to go in its direction.' I don't think that's too bad.'

'You don't judge people?'

'Not at the moment. But who knows what I might do tomorrow?'

'Who knows indeed? Josh Goldstone, thank you very much for talking with me today — and I know there are a lot of people outside waiting to see you. Will you talk to them?'

'When you turn the cameras off, yes.'

Salema kept her word. The cameras were turned off and the production staff excluded when Josh saw the people who asked to meet him backstage. Only Jude, James, John, Andrew, Simon and the new men seconded in to help, were there. So no one (except them) knew what took place backstage and anyone who tried to take a sneaky photograph found that their cell phone wouldn't work. However, for once, when Josh asked the people not to speak of what happened in public, they agreed and kept their word.

But the cameras were on again as he left and, when Cameron Bruce, head of security, waylaid him just before he got into his car, the microphones caught the whole of the conversation.

'Sir, Sir!'

Josh stopped and turned. Generally he would have said, 'Call me Josh,' but he could sense Cameron's army background and knew he was being treated as a superior officer. To contradict would not have helped the situation.

'Can I help you?' he asked, seeing the heightened colors of tension and frightened love around the man's physical body.

'It's my son, Sir. He's sick. He's got leukemia.'

'Josh, we're behind schedule already,' said Jude. To give her her due, she felt like a total bitch but they did have a plane to catch.

'Just give the word, Sir,' said the man. 'I know my Bible. I know you can do it.' Tears began to run down his pitted, tanned cheeks.

'You're a man holding the authority of God. Well I understand that; my men obey me. I know you just have to give the word. Please Sir!'

Josh watched in open-mouthed delight as the man's faith aligned him to the Light and all love and healing raced through him down the emotional cords between him and his son.

'Damien,' he said. 'He's Damien — right?'

'Yessir!' Cameron stood rock straight and saluted. 'Thank you Sir!'

Josh nodded, acknowledging the salute and got into the car.

'Really?' said Jude as the door shut and the car glided off. 'Even when you're not there?'

'Easier, or so it would seem,' said Josh. 'Interesting isn't it? I think that one was filmed? If so, we'll find out soon enough.

'Jude, Did you get that VT Salema showed?'

'Yes, it's here,' said Jude, taking a CD out of her big black bag. 'Do you want to watch it on the way to the airport?'
'Yes, there's someone in it I remember and I need to know why.'

'Oh I can tell you who and why,' said Jude dryly. 'The doo-doo is about to hit the fan, Josh.'

'Oh well, it was bound to,' said Josh sitting back. 'I'll watch it anyway. There might be something even worse than you think there is!'

'Worse than a girl confessing to you that she had an abortion in order to compete in the show? And you comforting her and telling her she'd done nothing wrong?'

'They didn't show that!'

'No, they didn't but this is the unedited tape and you can bet your life it will leak pretty soon.'

'Are you going to leak it?' said Josh quietly.

'Do you want me to?'

'No, but I want you to do your job the way you see it best,' he said, peaceably.

'No, I won't leak it,' she said. 'But there's a small Oriental weasel right on our tail and she'll get it or I'm a salted pretzel.'

Chapter Twenty

Maude-Lynn looked at the images of Josh comforting the distraught girl with delight. Worth every penny she had paid for it!

Even so, part of her was touched with compassion despite herself. It was strangely moving to see Josh's kindness for the 18-year-old girl who had been through hell in order to follow her boyfriend's ambition for her — and who had failed the audition. Josh's comforting words and completely non-judgmental attitude over what she had done helped the girl to feel herself again instead of a failure both as a singer and a lover.

But there was no room in the professional world for sentiment. Maude-Lynn hissed through her teeth to toughen herself up. Now, should she take it directly to Joseph Sadd or find the girl out first? Hmmm. Yes, it should be Pastor Jo. The girl could wait. Maude-Lynn felt great. Her career was really taking off. She had a plane to catch and a juicy carrot to dangle before a fearsome preacher.

Back in Las Vegas, Josh was having lunch with the accountants again. Really, he was having lunch with Mattie and enjoying the peace of her calmness and the ability to sit in silence but, as all the accounts department tended to sit together, it looked to outsiders as if he was either in a stew with the tax man or a serious fan of number-crunching.

'How bad is it?' asked Mattie.

'Oh it's not bad,' he protested. 'Not *bad.* Just all a bit fast and overwhelming. I got back to find Mary-Beth submerged in a pile of letters and awash in emails asking for healing. She's got a hive of people in to help her sort them. Literally thousands of them — letters, not people!

'That's not to mention the Facebook fan pages, YouTube and Twitter of course.' He sighed and shrugged. Until now, Josh had never bothered with anything much on the Internet.

'Have you looked at any of them?'

'A few. Some are heartbreaking; some just weird.'

'And can you do anything for them?'

'Oh yes — mostly. If the letter is just a rant or a long moan then no, because they're too attached to what's going on. They've got too much of a pay-off for being sick. There's one I read where the lady is so entrenched in her problems that she wrote six sides about all 'her' illnesses and 'her' tragedies and all the talents she couldn't realize because of them. I suspect that the talents were fantasies and the disease and the personal difficulties are the excuses for not exposing that. That letter made me feel ill to read it — she's too powerful for me!

'But some of the others — the clearer ones — will probably heal themselves just by writing. I don't know if the Internet works that way; there's no direct link, which there is with a letter, but…well, I guess it will all work out,' he said, hopefully.

'Hmmm.'

'Hmmm?'

'There are a lot of people in the world who will blame you if they don't get healed,' said Mattie. 'And they'll expect you to visit or at least to write back. If you don't they'll join Pastor Jo.'

'They'll all get an answer; whether they'll like it is up to them. But Mattie, that kind of thing happens all the time. They love you but they don't get what they want from you then they blame you, even hate you. And, anyway, the dissenters are already getting most of the publicity — they're bound to aren't they? The good guys are always boring. The bad guys or the complainers make much better copy. The press is an entity in itself — it builds you up then knocks you down. I'm better news if I'm the bad guy.'

Mattie had typed 'Josh Goldstone' into Facebook search as he was speaking and blanched at the amount of negative traffic it showed.

'You really don't mind?'

'Well, no. It's not about me, is it?'

'Yes, Josh, it is! And the girl Jude calls 'The Oriental Weasel' is obviously stirring it as much as she can.'

'It's called 'the plot' Mattie! It thickens. And then it all turns out right in the end.'

'That's fiction Josh!'

'Fact is based on fiction; fiction is based on fact. It will be what it will be. But in the meantime I'm boring and good and I'm hanging out with you because you're boring and good too.'

'You pig!' Mattie was only half-outraged. 'But I know what you are trying to say — all the actors say they want to play the bad guy not the hero as those parts are much more fun. Unless you're James Bond or the like.'

'Basically it's not fun unless you get to kill people?' asked Josh, smiling.

Mattie's eyes widened. 'I think you're right!' she said. 'Oh my God, Josh. Have you had any threats?'

'None that matter,' he said, softly, putting his hand on her suddenly worried little paw. 'They are par for the course, you know.'

The death threats certainly had started — as well as the disparaging, insulting and hatred-sodden letters and Internet postings. Josh may have been on Salema's show, but, primed by Maude-Lynn on the abortion story, Pastor Jo was on every news program on every Network across the USA. For many years, certain Christian groups had campaigned against abortion although, since born-again Christian Scott Roeder was sentenced to life imprisonment in 2010 for murdering late-abortion provider Dr George Tiller — a Lutheran Christian — no one had actually died. The name of the girl whom Josh had comforted the previous year was, so far, still secret — all the staff at *Fox* and *Gemstone Inc* were made very aware that their job was on the line if it got out. It certainly would do so — and soon — but, at the moment, Josh was the better target.

Pastor Jo was enjoying himself (although he would never had admitted it). He was 'Sadd' to see that the credulous people could be taken in by charlatans and tricksters, he was 'Sadd' to see Christianity mocked and Jesus profaned and faith denied. He was relieved that Josh was shown at last as the tool of Satan that Pastor Jo had predicted. He threw his righteous wrath at the man who claimed to be holy and who sanctioned the murder of the unborn child. He was a hell-threatening, ratings-grabbing preacher armed with the justified wrath of God. And he was really, really hot!

The pastor was looking forward to this week's *Salvation Hour.* He needed to start with the Old Testament for this one — 2 Kings 14:6; 'The Lord commanded, saying, The fathers shall not be put to death for the children, nor the children be put to death for the fathers; but every man shall be put to death for his own sin.'

Add to that, Revelation 11:16: 'Thou shouldest give reward unto thy servants the prophets, and to the saints, and them that fear thy name, small and great; and shouldest destroy them which destroy the earth.'

And finish off with 1 John 3:9 'Whosoever is born of God doth not commit sin; for his seed remaineth in him: and he cannot sin, because he is born of God' — and he had a thunderingly good basis for a lot of shouting.

To be fair to Pastor Jo, he might be telling everyone that Josh Goldstone was the spawn of Satan but he wasn't intending to tell anyone that they had a God-given right to take Josh out and earn eternal salvation. But it has to be said that several people thought that's exactly what he did say and death threats came flooding in to the offices at *The Miracle Mile.*

Pastor Jo got speaking engagements all over the USA and his *Salvation Hour* was taken up by the *Trinity Broadcasting Network.* Donations flooded in to the Church of the Resurrection of the Righteous. It was all very good.

Back in Vegas it was time to expand security and to bring in the local police. 'It's not the threats we have to worry about,' said Simon to the local protection squad. 'It's the ones that don't bother to make any threats.'

'Assuming they can get through the wheelchairs and the crowds baying for healing,' said Andrew.

So now Josh got police protection as well as his minders. He didn't mind; Thomas, Philip, Jodie and Adie were all pleasant enough. When he went to Mattie's for supper he was surrounded by a bigger entourage than what he called 'real' celebrities. The house had to be searched from basement to roof before he could go in.

'Is it going to be like this for ever?' asked Jon Taylor, the other guest whom Mattie, with slight embarrassment, introduced as her new boyfriend. Jon was rather enjoying the fuss.

'Not for long, I suspect,' said Josh. 'Just until it's over.'

Mattie started to say something but Jon put his hand on her arm. Somehow he knew that wasn't a line of conversation that needed to be followed. Instead he started talking to Andrew, Simon and Josh about how he was setting up a system that was independent of all their computers so no one could hack into Mattie's financial files.

'Bloody hell, Jon, you're a good man!' said Josh. 'Know how I know?'

'No...'

'You're *really* boring the pants off me, that's how,' said Josh.

But the next morning, in Jude's office, the price of goodness was a different kind of boredom; the tedium (to Josh) of working out what should be said in this press statement and what should be added to that hand-out; whether there should be a weekly press release or a press conference; how much input Josh should have on his blog and all his other Internet pages, what should be ignored; what shows Josh should appear on; what shows should be turned down; what could be done in person and what could be done via satellite; which inaccurate allegations should be denied and which let go; how much blog-bombing there should be to block out the most offensive sites on Google and whether Josh should go head-to-head with Pastor Jo on *Fox* live, recorded or not at all...

'You've got a job to do despite all this stuff,' Josh said admiringly as he watched and listened to Jude, the complete professional, dealing with files, letters, messages and assistants like a six-armed goddess.

'I can't work out whether it's harder or easier that you don't care,' she said. 'Gemma would tell me what to do; we'd argue and half the time she'd win and half the time I would. You just say 'whatever' all the time.'

'Not all the time,' he said thoughtfully 'I do have some odd ideas.'

'You're heading for Miami Beach tomorrow, right?' she said.

'Yes.'

'And I take it that you have an odd idea?'

'Yes.'

'Which is?'

'One-to-one live with Pastor Jo, hosted by the Oriental Weasel.'

'You are not serious!'

'Yes I am. It could be fun.'

'*No* Josh!'

'Okay…whatever.'

Josh may not have worried but Mary-Beth did. Her hot, passionate little soul had linked itself firmly with Josh's and now, despite spending most of each working day in his warm white-gold aura, she found herself filling up with worries about Josh's safety. She was flooded with angst over the piles of letters; concerned about whether she was doing her job properly and whether she was drafting proper replies and referring to the right departments. She found it really hard being in charge of loads of assistants and she was run ragged by the telephone — and adamant that Josh should *never* answer it himself. He got round that when he sent her to make tea (she wasn't going to delegate *that*). But then she got a kettle and a fridge in the office. After that, he had to make up errands for her just to get a few moments alone without the burden of her all-encompassing concern. But Mary-Beth just made sure that Sally, her new assistant, either ran the errands or stayed behind to answer the phone. Josh found Mary-Beth quite amusing. If she could only have given in to not worrying (she could spout the theory of non-attachment, he knew from talking with John) she could have relaxed and enjoyed her job but her determination to fret was refusing her healing nearly all the time.

What with Mary-Beth fussing over him every hour that he was awake, both at the office and at the adjoining apartment complex and with Simon, Andrew, James and John hanging around all the time checking that there were no letter bombs or anthrax or people with guns, machetes or martial arts equipment within half a mile, Josh found increasing solace in the thought of five hours on an airplane where he could pretend to be alone. He had taken to waking up earlier and earlier each morning so that he could meditate and contemplate before unlocking the door from his bedroom. The moment he stepped outside, his life was not his own and, he thought, without that haven of peace when he reconnected with the Source, he would surely go nuts.

Eighteen years earlier, John and Venus Delmar, from Tampa, Florida, had named their only child Isaiah. John, being a fervent Catholic, loved Biblical names. Venus, being eighteen years old, naturally shy and totally in love with John, did whatever he suggested. She usually called the baby Isa rather to John's distaste; he thought it unsuitably feminine but then he didn't really like his wife's name either. Venus seemed rather pagan so he called her Honey instead. John made sure that the young Isaiah's hair was kept trimmed very short as the baby had abundant, dark, naturally curly hair and could easily be mistaken for a girl. He and his mother, who was part Native-American Indian, were a picture of beauty together.

John adored his son and, for a while, the little family was exquisitely happy. But, unfortunately, Venus grew up. By the time Isaiah was going to school, she was less interested in going to church and more attracted to fashion, less interested in the dominating father-figure she had first adored in a husband and more concerned with going her own way. The die was cast when she bought a book on witchcraft back into the family home. To be fair to Venus, she was only paying attention to what some of her contemporaries at the office were talking about — they cast spells for love and to get pay rises. Neither seemed to work but they, and all the TV shows about witches and magic, were hot topics around the water-cooler and, when Jo-Anne had offered to lend her the rather dog-eared tome, Venus had been willing to give it a go. She was looking for a better job and if casting a spell would be less trouble than getting her CV together, it sounded like a good plan.

John tore the book up in front of her. The childish part of Venus was impressed by his strength; John was a fine figure of a man in his mid-thirties but she was also outraged at his cavalier attitude to somebody else's property. Another part of her was insulted that he would not let her find things out for herself.

'There's nothing to find out,' said John. 'Jesus is your savior. This is Satan's work. That's it.'

The marriage went downhill swiftly after that as Venus became more and more independent (and awkward) and John became sterner and more dogmatic. Little Isaiah, torn between the two, tried to become the perfect child, in order to win each of his warring parents' approval.

He was five when they finally split up and John went to live in an apartment rented to him by the church. Divorce was out of the question, but an annulment was possible if Venus would affirm that she had been too young to get married and was unaware of the level of commitment she was entering. The now magnificent, independent woman snorted in derision at the very idea that divorce was 'wrong'. In law they had to be divorced anyway as a Catholic annulment did not count in legal terms. But, she had to admit, with the knowledge of herself and the magical lore that she was beginning to pick up, that she hadn't known what she was doing when she married John. She *was* way too young and innocent. She also realized that whatever the Bible might say, two people tearing each other apart didn't help anything and if John were determined to get an annulment, she was better off not resisting.

It wasn't so much Venus or John who was suffering through the break-up but Isaiah. The very idea that his beloved father could leave caused nightmares and hysterical tantrums. In vain, Venus tried to explain and reason with the child — she was a great believer in Indigo children who were believed to be beings of a higher nature who were coming in to help humanity along its path to enlightenment. Indigo children did not need boundaries and reacted badly to being told what to do and the enlightened mother allowed the child to discover the world for itself. In reality, it meant that Isaiah ran her ragged and respected her a lot less than he did his rule-enforcing father. With John, Isaiah knew where he was, who he was and what he was allowed to do. With Venus, he got his own way.

With the main trauma of separation over, Isaiah became the typical child of a broken family. His mother and father squabbled over access; child care; money and visiting rights with John fighting hard every step of the way 'for Isaiah's soul as much as for his company' as he said to friends. As is so often the case, his ex-wife became the bitch from hell and, to Venus, John became a monster.

Every second weekend, John collected Isaiah from his mother's and, until he put his hand into his father's on the doorstep, Isaiah pretended to his distraught mother that he didn't want to go. And, when he was back home with his Mom, he pretended he'd had a horrible time.

The weekends spent with John were the most magical time for the little boy. Then, he was the *big* boy, the one and only son, with special responsibilities and treats and his own pew at church. Isaiah didn't mind going to church because the singing was pretty and he was allowed to read a book or play quietly with his knights on horseback when the preacher talked for a long time. But even then, Isaiah knew that he was special because he heard and saw things in the church that even his revered father didn't seem to be aware of. He saw colors around people's heads and how they changed and moved with every thought. He knew who liked whom whether or not they behaved appropriately and he caused considerable embarrassment after one service by asking why Michael Phillips was marrying Carrie Dunn when his colors were all wrapped around

Susan Chester.

Within a couple of years, John was ordained a deacon and Venus became a white witch and a past-life therapist. Each held the other's beliefs up to ridicule without realizing what effect their despising and condemning might have on their son. Venus took a series of lovers, which confused Isaiah and introduced him to the emotions of jealousy and resentment although he found out pretty swiftly that if Mom spent time with other men, more often than not, he got to watch more TV. And, if he really didn't like the man, he seemed to be able to repel him without doing anything more than throwing a dark color at him.

John married a fellow Christian, Stephanie, who was three years older than Venus. Isaiah quite liked her; she would tempt him with toys, ice cream and pleasing flattery — already Isaiah was a very vain little boy. He liked playing one family off against the other when he could although, nowadays, Venus never seemed to have enough money to treat him and thought he was wonderful whatever he did, so it was Dad and Stephanie whose praise was really worth working for. He viewed their house as heaven and his home as sadly lacking.

When he was nine, Stephanie got pregnant. Isaiah didn't really understand what that meant, but he liked the idea of a little brother or sister who would look up to him. He was as surprised as anyone else when the baby turned out to be twins. 'You never said anything about two!' he said reproachfully to his father when taken to see Stephanie and the babies in hospital. 'Can't you send one back?'

Evan and Ada were the twins' names and they were two perfect children in a perfect marriage as opposed to an increasingly inconvenient extra little boy who was proving expensive in maintenance money. Of course it wasn't as simple as that but Isaiah lost ground in his father's heart from the day the twins were born and it became easy for John to let the odd weekend visit slip by because of all his duties at home and at church. And, as he said to his eldest son, 'You can always cycle to church and see me any weekend you like. It's just around the corner.'

But young boys who are used to being the center of attention don't like having to ride their bikes to see their Dads who are busy with something else. And young boys who have the power to throw energy have the potential to make anything they dislike feel very uncomfortable indeed.

Chapter Twenty One

One Friday evening, when it was John's turn to have Isaiah and the boy was sitting waiting in Venus's living room, ready to leave, there was a telephone call with vague apologies instead of a welcoming Dad. Then there was an irritated Mom because she had a date that night which she had to postpone and was running a one-day regression workshop at the house on the Saturday so having an ten-year-old around would be inconvenient to say the least. Isaiah, disappointed and hurt, had to cope with his mother's impatience and retaliated by being as obnoxious as he knew how to be all evening, gorging himself on the power of Venus's suppressed fury, eating sweets and watching television programs that he normally wouldn't bother with until he was hyperactive and over-tired and didn't go to bed until after midnight.

Venus had worked out what to do on the Saturday.

'You'll have to go and play with the Esparza kids next door,' she said. 'I'll ask their Mom to look out for you. You'll be all right; you've got your keys and you can come in and watch TV in my bedroom whenever you want. I'll be finished around six and you can find me if there are any problems — but try not to because I'm going to be real busy.'

Isaiah protested until he realized that he was shooting himself in the foot. Better to agree and make his own plans. So, he dutifully went next door after breakfast but, as soon as Venus had taken her eyes off him, he told the Esparzas he was going to play with some other friends, jumped on his bicycle and rode round to his father's. Ever since the inconclusive phone call he had had a deep inner conviction that it was all just a mistake: Mom had quarreled with Dad again and was punishing Dad by stopping Isaiah going over. Of course Dad wanted to see him!

He arrived to find the house empty, which was surprising. But it looked like there was going to be a party — there was loads of wonderful food on the dining room table and even more in the fridge and piles of prettily wrapped presents. Of course — it all made sense. It was Isaiah's birthday the following week and this would be a special party for him. Dad had just wanted it to be a surprise! He was probably driving over to Isaiah's home to pick him up right now.

He did try to wait until Dad and Stephanie got back but it was just too long for a little boy tempted by treats and gifts to do nothing. He had a couple of sandwiches from under the silver foil (they weren't very nice — no peanut butter or salmon) and he thought he'd just open one of his presents. After all, they were his and no one would notice just one.

The present was disappointing too. It was a pair of silver goblets. Isaiah turned them over in confusion. Why would someone give him two silver cups? Perplexed, he opened another present to find two fluffy teddy bears. Teddy bears? Isaiah had out-grown teddy bears! But this time, the message was very clear. Each teddy had a bib around its neck with a name embroidered on it. 'Evan' said one and 'Ada' the other.

In a rage of fury, Isaiah tore open all the other presents and then sat on the floor, howling with anguish in the wreckage. Not one of them was for him. The party wasn't for him. Even worse, the party was for his half-brother and -sister and no one had even invited Isaiah to come. He knew the word 'christening' which was on most of the presents; he had been to one christening with his father. Of course, he couldn't remember his own christening or that he had had quite as many presents, all he could feel was rejection. He hadn't even been asked.

By the time John, Stephanie and all the happy friends and family arrived, Isaiah had destroyed all the presents that were breakable, pulled all the food off the table and stamped it into the carpet and tipped all the contents of the fridge onto the floor.

He thought they would understand that he *had* to do that. He *had* to tell them how important he was and that they were wrong to fête the babies instead of him. He thought they would understand that he, Isaiah, was John's true son and these two, new children, were the interlopers.

But they did not.

When he ran, screaming, into the house where Venus was running her workshop, she heaved just one sigh and went out to him immediately, leaving the workshop participants to sort themselves out. Her reaction when she saw the stinging red mark of John's hand on her son's face was the moment that everything changed.

'He hit me! He hit me! Dad hit me!' wept the boy.

Venus didn't ask why; she just dialed 911 and reported John for child assault.

Many children have faced rejection and responded with lack of self-esteem, insecurity or maybe even bed-wetting. Isaiah stood up in court and accused his father of unprovoked assault. The poor man never knew what had made him slap his jealous, spoilt and destructive little brat — though he knew with bitter irony that no one had ever even criticized his own father for doing exactly the same to him thirty years before. John would never be able to explain what had made him snap and he could never know that it wasn't his head that had snapped but his son's. John didn't mean to hit Isaiah no matter how angry he was; Isaiah made him do it.

Once the boy knew that he was not understood; that his perfectly justifiable rampage of grief was being seen as a disaster; that he was being blamed for what he saw as being his right to protest; that he had been replaced by younger and inferior models, his heart broke and he offered his soul to any power that could give him revenge.

It was at that moment, when he saw the dark red flowing energy of his father's rage and how it wanted to attack but was being held back by the force of will, that he realized that he could reach out with his own energy and touch that rage, affect it and, maybe, even make it obey him.

Power: the greatest temptation of all. Isaiah's subconscious rage used it to make his father strike him on the face — where it would show. One thought was all it took and his father's reputation was ruined.

The satisfaction that Isaiah felt was almost enough to make up for the grief. Almost. He was too young to know what a bitter destiny he had embraced or that everything he saw through the filter of his own anger was a distortion of truth. He only saw that he could make people do what he wanted them to do. Very few grown people would reject that gift, let alone a spoilt child.

From that day on, Isaiah consciously read minds and, through the force of his will, he could change them. It was a kind of hypnosis but more than that; if he focused, he could actually feel the color of a thought's vibration and change it with a color of his own. That meant that, even though he couldn't put words into people's minds, he could change their emotions and lower their defenses. All he needed was their undivided attention for about five seconds.

Venus, fuelled by Isaiah's mind-manipulation, surrendered completely to her son. She pilloried his father mercilessly and instead of investigating her New Age calling sensibly as she had been doing before, she threw herself into the cult of victimhood. Soon she was practicing darker magic with varying results. She did have her own psychic power and she was delighted to observe the same in her son without realizing that it was his power that was influencing her own. Venus came to realize quite swiftly that her skill was nothing like as powerful as Isaiah's. As the cult of celebrity developed around them and the likes of David Blaine and Derren Brown became world-famous, she turned her attention to nurturing her son's gift full-time.

Isaiah, being spoilt, had been slightly unpopular at school but he now found that he could win most of the teachers and the other boys over with a new, consciously applied, incredible charm. He could also get revenge for any real or imagined slight with ease; he was always the other side of the classroom or playground when the other child hurt themselves or got into trouble. He could also get better marks by weaving a series of colors into his teacher's head rather than actually doing any work. Everything he tried, worked, and an addiction to control grew in him like a parasite. Where Venus at least tried to use her power to help people, Isaiah only wanted power for himself. His mother learnt to pretend that a lot of things were coincidences.

His skills made Isaiah very popular with the unintelligent and the weak who rather liked someone else to do their thinking for them. Those who had strong minds of their own and didn't succumb to his charm tended, instinctively, to keep away from him rather than confront him.

He also enjoyed becoming a conjuror and magician. Isaiah could keep people guessing with simple card games and hidden objects but nobody except his mother knew what he could really do and nobody would have believed it if they had known. As puberty approached, Isaiah's mind-bending power increased. He could get inside the head of nearly anyone younger or weaker than him and make them do whatever he wanted them to. And he enjoyed it. In his early teenage years he found, to his disgust, that hypnotic talent could not always overcome free will and inherent self-interest and that the smarter, more interesting girls would manage to resist him. The dumber ones, however, were fair game. He could think them into bed very, very easily. Sex was to be a very useful weapon.

What was silly about all this was that Isaiah was actually mind-blowingly beautiful and became even more so as he grew up. The nearest equivalent would be Brad Pitt meets Johnny Depp. And he had charm, too, so he simply didn't need to manipulate minds to get his own way or to get women into bed. The trouble was, he enjoyed the mind-bending far too much.

His mother admired him greatly and groomed him for celebrity telling him year in and year out that he would win *The Miracle Mile*. But his father was another matter. Once you have a conviction for assault against your son, you are going to find it hard to regain any position of authority. To do him justice, John tried. He wasn't allowed to spend time alone with Isaiah; there had to be a social worker present at all times unless they met in public. But he did visit and talk to his son and tried, with all his heart, to love him. But Isaiah could only see the greater love for Evan and Ada and, if he could not have all his father's love, he wanted none of it. His money was another matter; John paid regular maintenance until his son left school. Isaiah wasn't interested in college; he knew he was destined for better things.

John Delmar died in a traffic accident on the very same day as Gemma Goldstone. That accident too was inexplicable; he just walked out in front of a car in the middle of town for no reason that anyone could see. The poor man driving the Buick that killed him was totally exonerated by witnesses who said that he could have done nothing. One witness knew that even more than the others. Isaiah watched his father die with a strange feeling of tightness in his chest as though what had remained of his heart had finally turned to stone.

He had invited his father to come and have a coffee with him in town. John had come, against his better judgment and Isaiah waited for him with a strange pounding in his head.

He watched his father get out of the car across the road and felt aflame with excitement. He knew what he wanted — intended to do. He had been half-planning it for months. And now, the greatest choice of all had been made.

He exerted all of his power to bring destruction and the Universe obeyed. As angels lifted Josh Goldstone to safety, death claimed John Delmar and the darkness took possession of his son.

Isaiah didn't go to the funeral. He felt imbued with strength and power. Now was the time to take on the world.

'I've decided that I need a stage name,' said Isaiah to his mother as they headed for the stadium where *The Miracle Mile* auditions were taking place.

'Lucifer!' said Sam with interest as the exquisite young man walked into the room. 'Is that your real name?'

'Yes,' said the young man in a most charming and attractive voice. Deborah instantly decided (without knowing it) that he was through to the next round, whatever he did.

Gideon observed someone in his own line with what he thought was professional interest.

Josh closed his mind down fast.

He had felt something as soon as he got out of the car that morning, sensing dark, tense and powerful lines of energy coming from somewhere or someone nearby. Josh had kept very quiet that morning; he was aware of the flak that was generally being thrown at him, the hate mail and the death threats but they were all from the lower part of the human psyche — the inner demons that had attacked him in the desert. He wasn't afraid of them, come what may.

But this was a conscious mind, not an unconscious one. It knew how to feel what it wanted to feel rather than running on automated repetitive thought. This one was dangerous.

He took a few moments before even entering the building to ask for protection; not from the safety-disciples as they were now becoming known, but from the higher worlds. John noticed.

'What's going on?' he said quietly with a raised eyebrow. Josh had observed before that John was sensitive to atmospheres.

'Can't you feel it?' he said. 'Someone out there is a mind-bender.'

John concentrated. 'I can feel a stickiness in my head,' he admitted after a while. 'Is that it?'

'Could be,' said Josh. 'Stay close, if you would.'

John did stay close and was even in the audition room when Lucifer walked in.

Josh saw him wince as the boy's mind reached out to take power over those in the room. 'Ouch!' John mimed.

One side of Josh's mouth curved up. It looked like a smile but it didn't reach his eyes. He sat back in his chair, purposely looking very relaxed.

'What are you going to do for us?' Sam asked, smiling at the beautiful young man.

'Some magic,' said Lucifer with a delightful grin that lit his face up like an angel's. He knew that two of the minds in the room were closed to him — one more than the other — but three of the judges were open and three was enough. He could deal with the other one later.

He performed some simple but dramatic tricks with perfect timing and flair and, at the same time, his mind took strands of color and wove them into the minds of the three mesmerized judges. They would be able to do nothing but praise him and say 'yes'. To his delight, the fourth one — the mind that had been closed — suddenly opened in a great wave of silvery, creamy, luxurious color. It felt wonderful and it was much, much stronger than Lucifer's power.

Lucifer dropped a ball. He was too young not to let the anger show. He recovered in a second and smoothed over the judges' minds. They wouldn't even remember it in retrospect.

Josh's mind stayed clear, supple, open and totally unassailable, throughout the rest of Lucifer's session. The three other judges praised the boy; it was obvious that he would qualify whatever Josh thought. His vote came last and he knew he didn't want to contradict the others.

'I think, Lucifer, that you have quite a lot more to offer than you've shown us today,' he said. 'You're going to do very well. You are a stunningly good-looking young man with quite some talent. One word of warning: don't push it. It would be fair to say that you have quite a large ego and you think a lot of yourself — not so much egotistical as ego-testicle.' he said. Lucifer's face snapped closed and for a moment he looked almost murderous. The other judges, the spell broken, burst into laughter.

'I'm giving you two points,' said Josh. 'You're through to the next round. But remember if you have the power to bend minds — which you do — it comes with huge responsibility. Make sure you live up to that.'

Lucifer left with his piece of turquoise paper — the passport to Vegas — his face wreathed in careful smiles. It wasn't until he and

Venus were back home that he let any emotion but delight show — even to his mother. Even he couldn't work out exactly why he was so angry or why he hated Josh Goldstone so much. It wasn't until he took a gun into the woods and spent an hour shooting anything living that he could find, that he became calm enough for the fury to settle into anything he could identify. Then he knew that he was rabid with jealousy. Josh's silver-gold light was greater and more focused than any of Lucifer's powers and could inspire great love. This man was loved more than Lucifer was. That, thought Lucifer, stamping on the head of a rabbit he had winged but not killed, could not and would not be endured. Josh Goldstone had to be destroyed and Lucifer must become king of *The Miracle Mile.* Not just win it, but take it over completely. Nothing else would do.

'What was that?' asked John quietly when he and Josh had a few moments together at lunchtime on the day of Lucifer's audition. Josh waved him into his dressing room and shut the door. He looked suddenly very tired.

'That was the opposition,' he said.

'The opposition?' John's usually amiable full-moon face snapped shut. 'You've always said it didn't exist!'

'The devil doesn't exist — but human free will and temptation do. And those who have great powers get tempted early. That kid has incredible power.'

'Yes, I could feel him…bending minds?'

'Well it's a simple trick if you know how,' said Josh, rinsing his hands in the basin and reaching for a towel. 'The secret to all magic is to know how to do it and then *not* to do it. Otherwise you lose perspective and worse. This kid is going to use it all he can.'

'So he's bending the Universe?'

'Exactly! My will not Thy will.'

'It will snap back on him though. That's what you always tell us.'

'Oh yes — but he can probably hold it off for a while; he's young, strong and determined. You know I'd rather face a hundred Pastor

Jos than this kid.'

'Really?'

'Really. Oh well. It'll keep me on my toes.' Josh smiled, slapped John on the back and opened the dressing room door. 'Mary-Beth!' he called.

Mary-Beth, who lived on constant stand-by, ran into the room.

'Yes Josh?' her eyes were shining. John realized suddenly what nearly everyone else already knew: that the girl was crazy about her boss. He made a professional mental reference that she could no longer be trusted to use common sense in protecting him.

'Mary-Beth, there's a contestant called Lucifer who's just got through. I need you to find out his real name for me. And the names of any of his relatives that came with him or come with him to Vegas.'

'Yes Josh, I can do that.'

'Good girl,' he said, turning away, lost in his own thoughts. Mary-Beth hovered for a moment checking whether the mineral water, cookies and fruit on the table needed replenishing and then vanished. John followed her out; Josh had slipped into a world of his own.

'Lucifer in his own city,' Josh said to himself. 'I wasn't expecting that.'

Chapter Twenty Two

It was one of those hot drizzly evenings where the rain is particularly fine and depressingly damp without being cooling. Josh had felt restless all day; it was unusual for him to feel agitated and he wasn't sure what was causing it. Lucifer? Something else? Yes, there was *something* that felt out of kilter.

'Can we go out to eat tonight?' he asked Jude at the mid-afternoon break. She was very pleased with him. The 'ego-testicle' quip was the first one that would really put Josh on the judging map. It would have to be edited out of the Network recording of course but she thought she could push Josh into using it again live. And it was going to hit YouTube in a big way! It would follow Lucifer all the way to the finals if he got that far.

'Oh, he'll get that far,' said Josh when she mentioned it. 'No doubt about that.' He grimaced. 'I probably should have kept my mouth shut,' he said.

'Oh no,' said Jude. 'Open that cute mouth very, very wide!'

Josh looked at her quizzically. Cute? Did Jude think he was cute? He shook his head feeling that there was something slightly wrong with his judgment today. There was an unaccustomed buzzing energy somewhere. If it were the aftermath of Lucifer's audition, it would be understandable but he didn't think it was. It felt as though something, some Universal fabric, was changing. He couldn't explain it more than that but it felt as though he were being tugged at.

Food was always laid on for all the team 24/7 and often even Sam was too tired after a day's auditioning to want to hit the bright lights. Josh usually took a plate of food and vanished to his bedroom not to be seen again until the morning. Sometimes he didn't even answer the door or the phone if someone had a message for him which Simon tried to take him to task for; it being the security-disciples' job to keep him safe at all times.

'That means keeping in touch,' he said. 'I need to know exactly where you are. And if you don't answer, you could be under attack or even dead. We'd have to break the door down!'

Josh agreed amiably and went on behaving exactly the same as before. Simon felt like tearing his hair out when he discovered that Josh didn't even lock his door.

'That's so you don't have to break it down if you need to check on me,' said Josh with a smile.

Once, Mary-Beth, having no reply to her gentle knock, opened the door to see Josh curled up like a dormouse, fast asleep on the bed. She hovered by his side for a moment, then leant over and gently touched his hair. It was the first time she had physically touched him since they met. Josh sighed and stirred and Mary-Beth was infused with love and healing. She felt golden and glorious from crown to toes.

'I wasn't sure he was actually alive,' she confessed to Jude later. 'He was so still. And then there was such a strange, strong, warmth coming from him that I — well I *basked* in it for a few minutes. It was like a vertical aromatherapy massage. Does that make any sense?'

It did. Jude gave a tight smile. 'Did you touch him?'

Mary-Beth said nothing, slightly shame-faced.

'You touched him,' said Jude nodding. 'Walked into his halo. Yes, I know that one. It's better than Botox.'

Mary-Beth looked at the beautiful PR executive who rarely gave anything away and saw a rare touch of tenderness through the veneer and the Samurai sword. Somehow, Mary-Beth *got* Jude and didn't think her arrogant or cold. Jude couldn't work out whether that pleased or irritated her. She liked Mary-Beth too. The girl might look like a bag of worries on a stick but she could certainly organize.

But that night, Josh wanted to go out, so out they would all go together. It would be good to get out for once. By 8.30pm, Josh, Jude, Mary-Beth, Andrew and John were looking forward to what amounted to a party.

'No blow-fish,' chorused everyone. It was a silly joke that just meant 'No miracles this evening please Josh!'

Jude knew of a good but small Italian place and Mary-Beth had booked the whole of the upstairs section of the restaurant. The police-seconded extra security guys went on ahead to check it out and Jude thanked God for security gates and guards at the Miami complex entrance. There were crowds outside every day now asking for healing for themselves and their families. Josh had tried going out quietly with Andrew and John to see them in the evenings but was practically knocked off his feet into the bougainvillea that covered the outside walls by the pushing and almost deafened by the shouting. It wasn't even any use asking people to queue to see him. There were too many and it just took too long. In 21st century America, people didn't just come up and smile and shake hands and go away. They felt that they had touch you, be photographed with you and that they had an absolute right to tell you the life history of their illness and, in doing so, to hold onto the disease with unrelenting fervor so that very little could be done.

'And I'm not going to set up like some kind of guru, sitting in a temple and having people shuffling past,' said Josh firmly.

Jude instructed the driver and everyone crammed into the dark-windowed limo which shot out through the gates as security held back the crowds. The car ran smoothly into a less-popular part of town, the air-conditioning disguising the sultry damp heat of the night so that the girls were getting goose pimples on their bare arms.

'Is it safe?' asked Mary-Beth nervously. 'You hear a lot about Miami.'

'You're too young to remember Miami Vice,' said Josh. 'Even the movie.'

'I hear the news,' she said. 'Three killings yesterday.'

'It'll be fine,' said Jude impatiently.

But as the car turned into the brightly-lit street on the west side of town where the restaurant was located, it was clear to see that Jude was wrong. A small crowd of people was gathered behind a police cordon and half the street was blocked off. Two police cars and an ambulance were parked right outside the restaurant.

'Oh God!' said Mary-Beth as they saw the paramedics lift the stretcher with the body-bagged figure lying on it. Something – possibly blood – darkened the pavement but it could have been rain. It seemed that nobody else was hurt.

'Turn around,' said Jude curtly to the driver but, just as he began to maneuver, a woman raced up to the car. She was Italian, probably about forty years old and her face was blotched with tears.

'Mr. Goldstone! Mr. Goldstone! Help me!' she yelled, banging with her fists on the roof.

'How the hell does she know?' Jude's face was white. 'You didn't book in Josh's name did you?'

'Of course not,' yelped Mary-Beth (who had done just that but certainly never would again). 'The police must have told them.'

Andrew and John signaled to the driver who unlocked the doors. They slid out of the car, the doors locking automatically behind them.

'What do you want to do?' Jude said as the two men outside gently but firmly pulled the woman away from the vehicle.

'What I can,' said Josh. He was feeling a strange buzzing in his head and the restless feeling from earlier intensified by the second.

'He's dead,' said Jude. 'It will be her son, Francisco. He's pretty wild.'

'Right,' said Josh, relaxing. Okay, this was it; now he knew why. Somebody had died who shouldn't have died.

'Pete?' (Josh always knew the name of every driver, cleaner or security man). 'Unlock my door please.'

'Are you sure Sir?'

'Absolutely.'

'Right you are.'

Josh stepped out. Maria Passarelli was wailing like a banshee and beating her fists on John's calm, strong and slender chest as he held her round the waist. In the damp, darkness-stained night air she looked like a black crow fighting a silver statue.

'Let her go,' said Josh firmly. John hesitated and then obeyed. Andrew was now liaising with the police at the cordon. Maria threw herself at Josh screaming, 'Help me! Help me!'

'I will,' he said very firmly, taking her by the shoulders and giving her a little shake that miraculously calmed her down. 'Don't waste time. Take me to your son. Only you can get me to him.' He nodded at Andrew and the two policemen attached to his team. Something in his eyes stopped them from objecting. Instead, they lifted the tape of the cordon for Josh and Maria to climb underneath.

Maria stopped her wailing and pulled Josh by the hand, her face suddenly filled with hope.

'What was it? Gunshot?' said Josh as they turned towards the ambulance. She nodded, fresh tears springing to her eyes. 'Please help me,' she said again, like a mantra, but she was calmer now.

Josh nodded curtly and looked at the two paramedics and the three police officers at the back of the half-closed door of the ambulance.

'I want to see my son,' said Maria. 'And I want this man to see him.'

'I'm sorry Ma'am. There's nothing you can do,' said one of the paramedics gently. 'You can come with us to the hospital. The cops will bring you.'

'May I see him please?' said Josh. His voice was pretty much the same as always — not that good a voice; no timbre like Pastor Jo's; no depth or resonance like Sam's. It even sounded slightly tinny in that strange metallic air. But it was not so much a request as a command. And everyone there had heard about Josh…

The rain fell, gently washing the young man's blood into the gutter.

The paramedics and police exchanged glances. No one wanted to be the one to speak, do the wrong thing or get into trouble. But they didn't object as Josh simply walked through them and climbed into the ambulance.

He stood for a moment, looking down at the body bag, not sure what to do. Then Grady, one of the paramedics, slipped past him and unzipped the bag. Francesco Passarelli's blank, youthful face was white as chalk.

Josh stood silently with eyes closed for a moment, sensing the silver cord of Francesco's spirit still attached to the body and the agitation of the soul itself. There was a strange crackling sound.

'Put him on a drip,' Josh said. 'Do you have blood? He needs blood.'

There was no sense to it but Grady pulled out Francesco's dead, blood-covered arm and found a vein. Behind them, his colleague, Anna began to prepare a transfusion.

'Can you deal with the wound?' said Josh. 'He might start bleeding again at once. I don't know — I'm not quite sure how this goes.'

They nodded mutely. They hadn't expected a miracle-maker to be quite so practical. Afterwards, Grady said, it all seemed to make perfect sense at the time. If you're bringing someone back to life and they have a massive bullet wound then they will probably bleed again.

Josh took a deep breath and closed his eyes. He put both hands on Francesco's chest for a moment and then took a step back.

'Get up Francisco,' he said. 'And don't do it again.'

He turned away immediately and clambered out of the ambulance without looking back. Maria's (and Anna's) screams of disbelief and joy rang across the road behind him. Josh was grimacing as he looked at the blood on his hands and walking quickly back towards the car. Both John and Andrew were by his side in an instant.

'Go!' said Andrew as soon as they were in the car.

Francisco Passarelli sat up in the ambulance, clutched his stomach and then looked down, surprised. He was certainly covered in blood; he felt slightly dizzy but there was no wound. No wound at all. Both entrance and exit wounds had closed; his stomach had healed. There was nothing wrong at all.

Twenty-seven years later, Cardinal Francesco Passarelli, that former gang member and small-time thief, was elected Pope. He was an innovator, changing rules, allowing contraception, teaching tolerance, ending corruption and opening doors of understanding across the world. He was assassinated after seven years in office and, as he sensed the bullet coming, he fell on his knees in the street and thanked God — and his messenger — for the blessing of an extra thirty-four years of life.

Nobody said anything on the way back to the complex. Josh just looked out of the window. He kept his blood-covered hands cupped in his lap until Mary-Beth took them carefully into her own hands and wiped them gently clean with the scented wet-wipe tissues that she always kept in her bag.

As she bent over his hands, her long, golden-brown hair caressed Josh's arms and he closed his eyes, finding himself soothed by the loving touch. It was a long time since he had felt a woman's hair on his skin or the tenderness of love being ministered to him. It brought tears to his eyes; he missed Gemma so very much.

If you raise people from the dead in the modern world, you tend to confuse the police and the authorities, which is never a good idea. In this case, Miami police were searching the underworld for a murderer who had shot Francesco Passarelli dead. And suddenly, Francesco Passarelli wasn't dead. It wasn't that the paramedics made a mistake, just that Francesco wasn't *certified* dead in hospital and, in fact, didn't have a scratch on him.

The blood on the ground and on his clothes (and on the body bag) was definitely his blood. He was seen to have been shot by five independent witnesses inside the restaurant. He was seen to be dead — or at least horribly injured — by more than fifty passers-by plus police.

But he suddenly wasn't even hurt.

The bullets were real — three of them. Two were lodged in the doorframe of the Trattoria and one lay loose in the body bag. All of them were covered in Francesco's DNA. Obviously the usual suspects that the police had rounded up and now had in custody on suspicion of murder were denying it and, if the guy wasn't even dead, what could the cops do?

It was even more far-fetched than the last series of CSI Miami which had featured a possible vampire attack.

Luckily for Josh who, after a very thorough shower, a take-away pizza and an hour reading Terry Pratchett's *Small Gods,* had slept like a log, it didn't immediately filter through to the cops that they had a murder case with a body that was happily sitting up in a hospital bed (where he had, of course, been taken for observation), eating homemade muffins with his family who were proclaiming the miracle at the top of their voices.

Jude, on the other hand, was on the phone to Philippa the moment she was out of Josh's aura; they needed a council of war — and fast.

'This thing is going to hit the morning shows tomorrow like nothing you've ever experienced,' she said. 'We have to have a strategy.'

'Like what?' said Philippa helplessly. The phrase 'out of her depth' didn't even start to describe it.

'Stand by studio,'

'Five, four, three, two, one, go titles.'

'From the studios of *Fox News* in Los Angeles, breaking news with Alan Baylis and Susanna Doyle.'

'This morning, extraordinary claims from Miami, Florida. Did "The Miracle Man," Josh Goldstone raise a murder victim from the dead?'

'Twenty-year-old Francesco Passarelli and his family say it's true. Even the police say it looks like it's so.'

'In other news, tornados kill five in Kansas.'

'And violence in Tibet worsens. The Dalai Lama calls for peace.'

'But first, the story that has America on the edge of its seat. Josh

Goldstone, widowed husband of superstar Gemma Goldstone and judge on *The Miracle Mile* who has, apparently, been healing the sick wherever he goes, is now claimed to have raised a man from the dead.'

'Goldstone and his entourage came across what was believed to have been a fatal shooting in Miami, last night. Francesco Passarelli was shot outside his family's Italian restaurant in what appears to have been a drug-related attack. Witnesses — including police — say that Passarelli was killed. But after his family insisted that Goldstone was allowed to visit Passarelli's body in the ambulance, the young man emerged fully recovered with no wounds at all.'

'Unbelievable!'

'Maude-Lynn Sykes reports from the scene.'

'Run VT.'

'This is the Trattoria Italia in Miami's Surfside area. An unpretentious place where Josh Goldstone and his entourage were planning to eat last night. The Passarelli family had closed off an upstairs section to give the celebrities some privacy when, at 8.35 last night, 27-year-old Francesco Passarelli was shot by a gunman with a .22 Ruger revolver. His uncle, Paolo Passarelli saw the shooting.

(*Insert VT — Paolo Passarelli*)

'These guys came in to the restaurant and Francesco pushed them out. There was an argument and one of them shot him at close range. Here! You can see where two of the bullets went.'

'They didn't hit him?'

'These two went straight through him! Mama Mia he was dead! The men ran away and I saw he was dead; his eyes were open. It was terrible.'

(Jump-edit)

'The ambulance came. *They* said he was dead and wrapped him in a black shroud. My sister was crying; it was terrible. And then Mr. Goldstone came. My sister — Francesco's mother — ran over and got him from the car over here — and he went into the ambulance.

'Then Francesco was well! There were no holes in him and he was completely recovered.'

'Where is he now?'

'He is still in the hospital. They have him in observation and the police are with him. I saw him last night and this morning. We are all so very happy and grateful to Mr. Gol –'

'You say you believe that Josh Goldstone raised him from the dead?'

'Yes, yes we do. We are so grateful –'

(VT of hospital with Maude-Lynn voiceover)

'This is the hospital where Francesco Passarelli was brought at 9.30pm last night. Registrar Stephen Pole.'

(VT of Stephen Pole)

'At approximately half past nine last night a man was brought in after reports of a shooting. He was covered in blood and was suffering from loss of blood but, apart from what appeared to be dizziness conversant with loss of blood, he was fully conscious and apparently unharmed. There were no bullet wounds to any part of his body.'

(off-camera question)

'The blood on him. Could it have belonged to someone else?'

'No, it was his own blood but where it came from I can't tell. It's quite inexplicable.'

(VT, Maude-Lynn piece to camera)

'Police have arrested a man on what was originally a charge of murder and has now been changed to attempted murder.

'It's a complete mystery as to what really happened. Passarelli's family is adamant that Josh Goldstone raised Francesco from the dead. Police are now interviewing passers-by and local people to try and establish the facts. Earlier today Josh Goldstone's publicity manager Jude Isaacs issued a statement.'

(Insert VT Jude Isaacs)

'Last night Josh Goldstone, myself and some others visited an Italian restaurant in Washington Road, Surfside. When we arrived we found a shooting incident had taken place. Josh was asked by the victim's mother, Mrs. Passarelli to help her son who, it appeared was dead. He agreed and went into the ambulance with her. While he was there Francesco Passarelli recovered fully.'

'Jude you know that's impossible.'

'Obviously not. Josh Goldstone is a man with incredible healing ability. He has already helped hundreds of people.'

'Have the police interviewed him?'

'Yes, they interviewed Josh here this morning.'

'Is Josh available to speak with us?'

'No, Josh will be leaving for the next stage of judging of *The Miracle Mile* this morning.'

'The restaurant has claimed that they knew that Josh Goldstone was coming. Did you arrange this as a complex publicity stunt?'

'Josh Goldstone doesn't need publicity stunts.'

(Cue Studio)

'What do you make of that Susanna?'

'I don't know Alan. Do we have — I hesitate to say it — but do we have a new Messiah or an elaborate confidence-trickster?'

'Well Maude-Lynn Sykes is live in Miami right now. Maybe she has some ideas. Maude-Lynn?'

'Thank you Alan. I'm standing outside the gated complex where Josh Goldstone and his team are living while they film the Miami auditions for *The Miracle Mile.*

'What you can see, all around me, is crowds of people waiting to see Josh Goldstone. Many of them are sick and all of them are hoping for some kind of cure.

'With me is Sandra Barton. Sandra claims to have been a witness to the events in Surfside last night. Sandra, what did you see?'

'Oh my God! I saw a man shot dead. The sidewalk was just covered in blood. My husband was one of the people who called 911 — we were in the restaurant at the time. We saw the two men come in. They quarreled with one of the waiters and then, when he tried to make them leave, they shot him.

'It was awful. People were screaming; we didn't know what to do.

'I saw the guy on the ground and his stomach was — oh my God, it was just pulp. He wasn't breathing and his eyes were wide open. It was just *awful*!'

'And then?'

'Well we had to stay there for the police. Obviously, we couldn't eat a thing. We saw the CSI people and all that and police took our statements. Then, about an hour later, they put the body in the ambulance.'

'He was on the ground for an hour?'

'Oh yeah…he was dead. There's no doubt about that.

'We were being interviewed when this commotion happened and I saw him — with my own eyes — the guy who was shot — climb out of the ambulance — he was *covered* with blood — and hug his mother. People were hysterical.'

'Did you see Josh Goldstone?'

'Yes, I saw him getting into a car, just down the road.'

'Are you sure it was him?'

'Oh yeah.'

'And what are you doing here today?'

'I guess I just wanted to see him. I…I brought him some flowers. I just think he's amazing.'

'Thank you very much. So, Alan, Susanna, it appears that Josh Goldstone isn't coming out this morning so we can't ask him his views on what happened. It's not very clear what *did* happen but, certainly, something unusual did.

'For *Fox News,* this is Maude-Lynn Sykes outside the *Miracle Mile* compound in Miami.'

After the live feed had ended, Maude-Lynn stamped one immaculately shod foot with anger and frustration. 'It *can't* be true!' she said. 'It's *got* to be a trick.'

As she uttered a series of furious expletives, she heard her name called from the intercom on the side of the gates.

'Maude-Lynn Sykes?' it was Jude's voice.

'What?'

'Josh would like to meet you. Not the team. Not now. Just you.'

'Me?'

'For God's sake, go!' breathed the cameraman.

'Okay.'

She slipped through the tiny crack of door that was opened for her and took a deep breath as she walked up the rose-lined driveway to the cool, white building where the charlatan/Messiah awaited her.

Chapter Twenty Three

Mary-Beth opened the front door to Maude-Lynn in a slightly bristly manner. She knew perfectly well that this was the woman who had made a point of trying to bring Josh down. It wasn't as if Josh exactly belonged to Mary-Beth but it was getting to the point where an outsider might not have noticed the difference.

Maude-Lynn, who prided herself on being extremely observant, wondered if Mary-Beth were in love with her boss. Everybody else who came within ten meters of Mary-Beth was utterly certain that she was in love with her boss.

Jude — or as Maude-Lynn called her, 'the Ice Robot' — was waiting for them in the atrium, the two-story hexagonal center-piece of the complex with its own palm trees, exotic flowers and a fish pool containing enormous Koi carp. It exuded luxury, ease and (just slightly) ostentation. Maude-Lynn coveted it with a passion and felt an all-too-familiar cut of resentment and anger that others had what she had not.

Jude was standing up with the ubiquitous clipboard in her hand, her gray eyes expressionless. She nodded briskly in greeting to Maude-Lynn. Mary-Beth slipped away, un-noticed by either woman. 'You've got half an hour,' said Jude. 'It's totally off the record, do you understand?'

'No,' said Maude-Lynn baldly.

'Listen and hear!' said Jude. 'If you beh — if you are comfortable together — then we may be interested in arranging a one-to-one interview for you.'

Maude-Lynn looked as though she might be considering the offer. In fact she was ready to bite Jude's hand off.

'Okay,' she said after a moment. 'What's the deal?'

'We search you — there has to be strong security around Josh now. We're not looking for a gun but we will take away any recording equipment and give it back to you later. Andrew will do the search but I'll stay in the room while he does.'

'Very wise, in case I scream assault,' said Maude-Lynn.

'You'd be amazed,' said Jude, dry as dust.

'Oh I wouldn't.'

The two women looked at each other, each recognizing and disliking their mirror image.

Jude gave a tight nod and Maude-Lynn knew that the interview with her was over. Jude's mind was already working on the next phase.

Andrew frisked the reporter professionally. He was a good-looking man and Maude-Lynn rather enjoyed it.

'Through there,' he said non-committally. 'I'll keep your bag here.'

She nodded, suddenly nervous, and pushed the doors open.

The garden was small, walled, and consisted mostly of terrace and swimming pool surrounded by neat, almost Zen-like patches of gravel with pots of bright flowers. On the other side of the pool, beneath the bougainvillea-covered eight-foot wall was a strip of thick-bladed grass. Josh was crouching on it, looking intensely at something in the greenery on the lower part of the wall.

He didn't appear to notice Maude-Lynn at all and she felt time-agitated, conscious that she had just half an hour with him and that none of it should be wasted. She should have been past the handshake and into the usual courtesies now.

She could see that Josh was wearing a plain cream tee-shirt and blue jeans, nothing special about them. Maude-Lynn felt irritation at that realization. He was a celebrity, for God's sake — he should be wearing Ralph Lauren at the very least. Even Sam's trademark black tee-shirts were exclusive. Maude-Lynn wore designer shoes even if she couldn't afford them.

She began walking purposefully towards him, her turquoise Jimmy Choos clipping tightly on the terracing.

Josh didn't turn or look but he raised his left hand slowly and waved his fingers in greeting. Maude-Lynn knew that he was saying

'Hi! Come and look at this,' as though she were a friend. For a moment she preened herself, believing that he was recognizing her as an equal and regarding her as someone with whom he could be comfortable. Then habit over-ruled the moment's vanity and she sank back into the familiar feeling of being insulted. He couldn't even look at her, let alone come and shake hands!

Her high heels sank into the well-watered grass and it was impossible to walk to him with any kind of elegance. She stopped, overwhelmed with confusion and anger.

'Take them off,' he said quietly. It was a suggestion not an order. He still didn't look at her; his eyes were still focused on whatever was in the wall. She resisted but curiosity won over. She wanted to know what he was watching and she bent down to take the elegant shoes off and place them safely on the edge of the terracing.

She found herself almost tip-toeing over to him, the morning-watered grass squelchy and cold between her toes, and bending down to look at what he was seeing. There was absolutely nothing there but leaves. She squinted a little but saw nothing of interest.

Josh glanced up at her. 'Put your hand on my shoulder,' he said.

'What on earth for?' she started to say but bit her lip. She found that she wanted to obey. Hesitantly, she put out one small hand and touched him.

Instantly the world seemed to launch itself into rainbow colors. Maude-Lynn forgot to breathe for a moment, the sensation of wellbeing was so intense. She was already looking in the same direction as Josh was and now she could see a tiny pupa with a butterfly just beginning to work its way out. But it was not just that; she could see the very life force in the leaves and flowers around. She could sense waves of color everywhere, in Josh, in the flowers and leaves. It was a symphony of vibration.

She took her hand off his shoulder and almost shied away in horror at the blank grayness as her own world closed back in on her.

'Yes, of course,' he said to her unspoken question. Maude-Lynn put her hand on his shoulder again and knelt down on the grass beside him her heart filled with a love and joy that she had never imagined possible.

They stayed there for a full half-hour, though neither knew that, saying nothing but just watching together as the beautiful Miami Blue butterfly emerged and dried its iridescent wings. There were other pupa there too — and all sorts of other insects. A humming-bird hovered right by their faces for a few moments — all eternity, too, because Maude-Lynn could see every feather and every movement. At last the butterfly flew away.

Josh sighed with pleasure and turned to Maude-Lynn.

'Breakfast?' he said. 'I'm starving.'

He took her unresisting hand in his strong, warm one and led her past her forgotten shoes, past the pool and over to a table where pancakes, croissants and fresh fruit were being laid out by a young Mexican woman.

Before he let go of her hand, he said: 'Would you like to keep this?' and she knew he meant the colors and the glory.

'Yes — I don't know,' she said. 'Is it like this for you all the time?'

'Yes,' he said simply. 'Probably more so.'

Almost timidly, she took her hand away and sighed with relief when the colors and the brightness remained.

'Will it stay?' she asked.

'For a while,' he answered, sitting down and thanking the waitress who was pouring out freshly squeezed orange juice from a glass jug.

'While I'm with you?'

'Um…well I never really know,' he confessed. 'It might stick. It depends. It shouldn't ever go completely — unless you get into a real wave of negative thinking like hatred or anger. I think it would go then. Those are very boring energies; they don't *do* color.'

'Boring energies?'

'Yes, boring.' He smiled at her and offered her a plate of mixed fruits, beautifully prepared and arranged.

'I thought anger was red.' At the back of Maude-Lynn's mind she was shouting 'Stop talking such inanities! Ask the important questions!' but she ignored it.

'Good anger is,' he said, helping himself to Maple Syrup on his pancakes. 'The anger that changes things. But the hatred-filled anger is heavy and dark.'

'What color is the news?' she said suddenly.

He chuckled. 'You really, really don't want to know!'

It would be wrong to say that Maude-Lynn was in a dream state but that was the only way she could think of to describe it afterwards. It was more like what a drug-induced state *ought* to be with every awareness heightened.

As she ate the succulent fruits, she felt beautiful, powerful, elegant and whole…but slowly, even though Josh was still sitting next to her, peacefully eating pancakes (and feeding birds that flew down to his side of the table and took morsels from his fingers), she found herself moving away from that peacefulness back into the more familiar mottled tone of her own life.

She was realizing that she must have been in the compound for far too long already. Any second now someone would come and make her leave. She had to do something; make her mark; find out something real that wasn't just heightened awareness of colors. Find out details that she could report that couldn't be construed just as imagination.

She spotted her chance as Josh reached out with his right hand for a slice of passion fruit. A sharp fruit knife sat temptingly by her plate. Maude-Lynn snatched it up and stabbed it into Josh's hand below the second and third fingers, slamming the hand onto the table with the force of her thrust.

Blood shot up. Scarlet, living blood.

Josh gasped but didn't move his hand. Had he done so, the serrated edges of the fruit knife would have carved through a vein.

Maude-Lynn's heart pounded as she pulled the knife out. Her face reflected all her thoughts of horror: 'What have I done?' Satisfaction: 'Heal that in front of me and prove who you are!' And fear: 'They're going to have me arrested. I'll never work again.'

Josh took in a great gulp of air. He looked at Maude-Lynn but said nothing, just lifting his bloody hand and wrapping it carefully in a linen napkin. His face contracted with pain and scarlet blood began seeping through the white material.

Maude-Lynn just sat there, the bloody knife still in her hand, her eyes wide as her brain and heart fought a great battle for her soul.

'Heal it,' she said, in a rough, dark-stained voice. 'Heal it. Show me how you heal.'

'No,' said Josh. '*You* heal it.'

He unwrapped the wounded hand and laid it on the stained tablecloth in front of her.

Maude-Lynn looked down and saw, with horror, the serrated edges of the wound, bleeding more sluggishly now but gaping wide; it needed stitches, urgently.

'I…I can't,' she said. The words *sorry, sorry, so sorry!* were tumbling at the back of her mind.

'Yes you can,' he said. 'Put your hand over it.'

Revulsion and fear made her shake. She had always hated the sight of blood and the thought of actually touching the wound made her want to retch.

But whatever else she might be, Maude-Lynn was brave. She swallowed and looked up into Josh's brown eyes. That itself was an act of courage. There was no blame there and no anger. Perhaps even a little amusement.

'I don't understand,' she said.

'I know,' he said gently, one eyebrow raised slightly. 'Put your hand on mine.'

She did, her little copper-colored hand half the size of his lanky white one. Her raised palm didn't touch the wound itself but she could feel his warmth. Blood seeped between her fingers.

'What do I do?' she said.

'Pray,' he said.

'How?' Maude-Lynn had only hazy recollections of prayer.

'Just say, 'Thank you,' he said. 'That's all it takes really.'

'Thank you for what?'

'Anything. Thank you that I haven't thrown you into the swimming pool!'

Suddenly they were both laughing. He had every right to throw her into the swimming pool! She'd behaved outrageously appallingly and he was just so — so — bloody *nice!*

'There,' he said with a long breath. 'That's better!'

Hesitantly, Maude-Lynn moved her hand slightly. He nodded at her and she took it away.

Her face was a picture as he looked at the perfect skin beneath her hand. Yes, the blood was still there on the surface but there was no wound. None at all.

'Two,' he said softly. 'And probably three.'

She sat, slightly hunched and completely paralyzed. She wasn't sure if she was going to cry or be sick.

Josh rubbed his right hand with the other with a slightly wry smile, poured some water into a napkin and rubbed most of the blood off.

Then he got up and, in one smooth movement, grabbed hold of Maude-Lynn by the waist and threw her into the swimming pool.

'Four, five *and* six. Seven will probably sort itself out in its own time,' he said with great satisfaction, sitting down and pouring himself some more tea.

Chapter Twenty Four

What, only the day before, would have seemed to be the oddest of conferences took place on the flight from Miami to Denver for the next round of auditions. Maude-Lynn, her hair still slightly damp, sat side by side with Jude Isaacs on the private jet discussing their new TV project. Jude had suggested 'A Year in the Life of Josh Goldstone' with cameras following them around from the next set of auditions and Maude-Lynn presenting. The journalist could hardly stop her almond eyes from shining at the thought. This was her big break! Jude had already been approached by three Networks and the ubiquitous 'JoshTV' was updating itself almost daily across the Internet, increasing the need for something official to at least attempt to counter the more outrageous claims being made and insults being thrown. Both Jude and Josh were keen to go ahead with an authorized series. But, and it was a big but, it had to have the right presenter.

'But why me?' said Maude-Lynn. 'I've done nothing but hinder you.'

'Well you're the only person he's ever thrown into a swimming pool so there must be something good about you!' Jude was being unexpectedly light hearted. 'And you understand now, don't you?'
'I think I do. I just seem to see everything in different colors now.'

'Yes, it took us all like that.' Jude smiled and jabbed almost without thought at her state-of-the-art new Apple Organizer, bringing up the schedule for the next week together with the very latest news. It was invaluable for checking what stories were breaking when and kept her up-to-date on Josh's Google Alerts.

'By the way, you may have noticed, none of these things works within three yards of him.'

'What? I thought my battery had just died.'

'Oh no, it's his electro-magnetic field. It over-rules wireless — phones, the like. That's why we need you to do the program to be honest. We can't get a fair picture from outside sources because half the cameras break down when they're near him and the wireless and satellite transmissions don't work. So you'll have to use basic recording techniques and process them later.'

'What about other wireless stuff? Oh dear God! What about aircraft?'

'That seems to be okay — or we wouldn't be up here would we? It's all a bit confusing to us but I have a theory that basically what he wants to work does work and what he doesn't want to work doesn't.'

'He has that kind of power?'

'Maude-Lynn, he can raise people from the dead; he can heal long-standing chronic illness; he can make people happy. He can do pretty much what he likes. Not that he's manipulative. It's all real stuff — not trickery or mind-bending like that guy we've got on the show...what's his name?'

'Lucifer?' Maude-Lynn had seen the sneak preview of the magician on YouTube.

'Yeah, that's the one. He's young, handsome and sexy and you can enjoy his power because it's slightly wicked. But imagine what some kid like that would be like with Josh's power? He'd be a nightmare. With Josh it's all good. Just being with Josh makes you see things differently.'

'Was it sudden with you too?'

'No, it was kinda slower with me than with a lot of people and I guess I still resist it a bit. I don't make much of a song and a dance about things as you know. Control-freak meets tight-ass doesn't even touch it according to my partner, Charlie. But this guy is for real and you can't hang around him for long without taking some of it on too.'

Maude-Lynn stroked the smooth silk of her borrowed blouse; her own clothes were still damp and she was wearing a mixture of Jude's and Mary-Beth's wardrobes. Her own luggage was being packed up and sent on after — she had had to make the split second decision to leave with the *Gemstone Inc* plane or lose the momentum of that extraordinary day.

After spluttering, swearing and screaming at Josh for throwing her in the pool, she had capitulated, admitting that she deserved it.

'But what's with this ******* counting crap?' she yelled, treading water while he sat there laughing at her.

'Ah. Just the devils coming out,' he said.

'*Devils?*' Maude-Lynn lost her stroke and nearly choked.

'Old-fashioned word,' said Josh. 'Nowadays we'd call them habits, addictions, lack of self esteem, whatever. But devils is just as good a word. They're the nasty habits and thoughts inside that hurt and that stop us being happy.

'Are you coming out of there? Only we have a plane to catch and if you want to come with us and work out your new TV show, you'd better get dry. I don't suppose there's time to get your clothes from your hotel but I'm sure the girls can lend you something. We can buy you some new at the airport if you like.'

He held his hand out to help her out. Maude-Lynn considered pulling him in with her in retaliation but the hand he was holding out was the one she had stabbed. And she felt a sudden uncharacteristic shyness and a desire to hold that hand and be supported by it.

Josh had finally had to admit that when it came to getting the crew together and saving time, the private jet was a huge asset and he was glad he hadn't put his foot down totally (not that anyone would have noticed if he had, he thought wryly and inaccurately). Within an hour of the breakfast with Maude-Lynn they were taking off for Denver. He found himself wishing rather wistfully that there would be time to drive down to the *Sangre de Christo* Mountains and across to Durango. He had always loved the Rockies but that wasn't going to happen.

'That's not my life any more,' he said to himself, knowing that his ability to observe everything peacefully made what he did have infinitely more precious.

He could have joined Jude and Maude-Lynn to work out the

media schedule but they were quite capable of doing it all without him and he loved those quiet hours looking out of aircraft windows at the clouds and the landscape below. This would only be a four-hour flight but, even so, he gazed his fill before dozing, curled up on a leather sofa in what had once been his and Gemma's office/bedroom on the jet.

The sudden summer storm didn't wake him although it caused the jet to fall a thousand feet in just two seconds. The captain and his co-pilot had been warned of turbulence ahead but had no idea how bad it would be until it hit them.

Within seconds they were battling with a freak storm with frightening changes of pressure. Lightening forked repeatedly past the aircraft, far too close for comfort.

'What the hell is going on?' Max Jefferson, the captain was only just managing to keep the plane on a level let alone climb it to a safer altitude.

'I think we should get down as fast as we can,' he said to his colleague. 'Where is there?'

'Nowhere that I know of.'

'Well find somewhere. And fast.'

'Josh,' Mary-Beth, defying the flashing seat-belt sign, banged on the door of his cabin and, when there was no answer, opened the door. 'Josh?'

'Mmmm?'

'You're asleep?'

'Mmm…I was — wow, that's a bit bouncy!'

'Josh, everyone's scared. The weather's ridiculously bad and we're looking for somewhere to land. The captain's really concerned.'

'Oh, okay. Leave it to me.'

She nodded and shut the door behind her, leaning against the wall for support as the plane rocked again. For a moment, she closed her eyes and prayed that he could do what she believed he could do.

'Well darn it, what happened there?' Max Jefferson exhaled

sharply with relief as the aircraft shot out of the storm clouds into clear blue skies. The jet steadied immediately and the pilots craned their heads to see if they could see the extent of the storm to either side of them.

'No chance,' he said. 'It's way behind already. What the hell was it? I don't mind telling you that felt real bad. What's it like the rest of the way?'

It was calm the rest of the way. Jude went into Josh's cabin to thank him, but he was sleeping again. She looked down at his strangely vulnerable form, her gray eyes tender. 'Nothing's impossible now,' she whispered. 'Nothing at all.' It was a weird feeling to know that.

Josh would never look at the daily publicity digest that Jude's team put on his desk. He didn't care what was being said about him on TV, radio, in magazines or across the Internet. Simon, Andrew and James lapped it up and spent hours discussing what was posted on websites and blogs and squabbling with John who wasn't interested in hearing all the negative details.

Jude was the only one who really knew the extent of what was spreading across the world, varying from websites condemning Josh for not being vegetarian to those who believed he was Mahatma Gandhi reincarnated. This was true viral marketing. Officially she had done very little to support it apart from setting up Josh's own website, and his page on *The Miracle Mile* site alongside Deborah's, Sam's and Gideon's and, of course, his blog and Twitter. Unofficially, she had paid a couple of agencies to fuel the fires by blog bombing, raising questions on Evangelical Christian sites, on New Age sites and anywhere else that controversy could be provoked. She was a firm believer in the saying that there was no such thing as bad publicity. There were blogs everywhere discussing who or what Josh might be and what he had allegedly done or not done. There were YouTube videos; there were dozens of websites claiming that Josh was Christ come again and others claiming that he was the Anti-

Christ; there were assessments of videos of his body movements and hot debates on whether they were secret signs for the initiated to interpret or signals to his fellow extra-terrestrials.

The greatest outroar against him was for his celebrity lifestyle. If he were truly a good man, the commentators said, he would not be working on *The Miracle Mile,* not be based in Las Vegas and not be a part of a world where money and fame were gods and people were exploited by the media.

Once, Jude had questioned Josh about this.

'But where do you think I'm most needed?' he answered her. 'In a hallowed temple where my words are revered and my body is worshipped — or in the heart of the pain and misunderstanding of the ego? If the devil did exist, he would be in Las Vegas.'

'Which is why they say you're the anti-Christ,' she countered.

'They would always say that,' he said. 'But if I were the End of Days — which I am, emphatically, *not* — then I would have to face the darkness in its lair.'

'Surely the darkness would come to you,' she said.

'It already has,' he said. 'It's on its way to Vegas right now.'

Pastor Jo's team had been busy too. The faithful of Denver had plenty of notice that He-who-heralded-the-coming-of-the-Anti-Christ was on his way for the next round of *Miracle Mile* auditions. Fired-up with fury, faces distorted with the power of righteousness, they flocked to the airport with placards and banners. Two of them in particular, Francie and David Johnson, were almost howling with antagonism, overcome by the rapture of religious hatred.

The Goldstone team didn't advertise their time of arrival but Francie and David and their team of worshippers were happy to wait all day if needs be in the service of the Lord. As the black BMWs pulled up outside the arrivals entrance, they and their followers were there, shouting, 'Repent, repent for the Kingdom of God is at hand!' and 'You're not wanted, spawn of Satan' and 'We don't want your demonic powers here!'

'Good grief,' said Josh, hearing the cacophony and turning to Maude-Lynn who was just behind him. 'You were a piece of cake in comparison to that!'

She couldn't quite see the connection but John squeezed her hand and whispered 'Look *through* them not *at* them and watch carefully.'

Maude-Lynn frowned but was willing to try. She focused her eyes on a point beyond Francie and David and, to her amazement, saw flickering dark colors around them. She remembered Josh talking about the color of anger and realized that she was actually seeing it. Then, without consciously knowing how she perceived it, she could sense some kind of a force field emanating not from but through Josh towards them. Both the Johnsons seemed to convulse energetically and then the darkness shot from them to the area of the Denver cargo depot.

As the Goldstone team drove off, Francie and David lowered their placards.

'He doesn't seem such a bad guy,' said David cautiously. He never wanted to contradict his wife, especially not in public.

'Noooo,' said Francie, feeling slightly perplexed. 'But Pastor Jo said…' her voice tailed off. David took courage.

'You know, maybe we could look a bit more at turning the other cheek and trusting the Lord instead of just listening to others,' he said. 'If this guy is bad then the Lord will take care of it.'

The faithful behind them were silent. They too felt confused but strangely contented.

'Let's go get some coffee and muffins and go back to the church,' said Francie.

She sounded so peaceful and unlike her normal self. David tentatively took her hand, normally a pretty risky process. She smiled up at him.

'I feel really good,' she said. 'I'm not quite sure what's happened…are you?'

'What in tarnation has got into these darn hogs?' complained the cargo depot staff who were trying to load a pen-load of pigs suddenly gone so wild that you could have said they were possessed. 'I thought BSB was way over!'

In Denver, the Goldstone team had taken over an entire floor of their favorite hotel.

Simon, who was meeting them there, wasn't too happy about the security aspect as it was fairly well known that this was the place in Denver where the team had previously preferred to stay. Anyone targeting Josh would have researched that. And, Simon knew, they would have an easier job getting to him at an hotel than in a high-security housing area. Still, he was now in charge of a team of ten men and the relief of having a definite structure and enough manpower to offer quality security was palpable.

He, Andrew, John and James kept a watchful eye on the relatively small celebrity-hunter crowd outside the hotel doors where hotel security had roped off the entrance.

As Josh's car pulled up, a gaggle of autograph hunters began to wave their books.

'Extraordinary, isn't it?' said Jude to Mary-Beth as they climbed out of the second car and watched Josh signing his name and listening to people's commiserations and stories about Gemma. 'Here we have a *Bene Elohim* who can raise the dead and heal the infirm and they still just want his autograph because he's on the TV.'

'A what?' Mary-Beth had never heard the term *Bene Elohim*.

'Jewish. It means Son of God,' said Jude briefly. Her eyes narrowed; she had seen a commotion on the other side of the crowd at exactly the same time as Simon, James, Andrew and John did. The latter two smoothly moved Josh inside the hotel to the consternation of the last 20 autograph hunters while Simon moved like quicksilver to check out the possible threat.

As Josh was checking, Simon slipped into the space beside him and quietly asked him to have a word with an anxious-looking man standing, wringing his hands, on the other side of the reception area.

It was he and two others who had caused the commotion.

'His name's Jair Cohen,' he said. 'Rabbi at the Adonai Congregation — Reform. He was the reason we moved you in so fast; couldn't tell if he meant you good or harm at first. His 12-year-old daughter has acute meningitis. She's critically ill in ER at the local hospital. He's asking you to come and help.'

Josh stood for a moment turned within. Watching him do that was similar to watching a wild animal checking the air for danger but, in Josh's case, it was an internal re-tuning.

'Yes, that's okay,' said Josh turning round. 'I do have to go. Mary-Beth, can you take care of everything else here?'

'Yes of course,' said Mary-Beth.

'Can I come with you?' asked Maude-Lynn.

'Not this time,' said Josh with authority and, much to her surprise, Maude-Lynn didn't mind. She watched him walk over to the Rabbi and take the older man's hand, explaining that Simon was arranging for the car to come back round so they could go straight to the hospital together.

As the men were leaving, a large woman in her 40s dressed in sweatshirt and jeans slipped into the rotating doors behind them. She reached out and touched Josh's jacket with one hand and he turned, surprised, then smiled at her.

'Damn, that could have been trouble,' muttered Simon, kicking himself for not seeing the woman as a possible problem. Luckily she just seemed to be fan as she went off, down the street with a swing in her step.

The car reached University of Colorado Hospital in less than 15 minutes, Jair sitting silently, hunched in the seat. He kept trying to check his cell phone and grew increasingly more agitated that he couldn't get a signal. Just as they turned into the hospital entrance Josh, looking ahead, could see a woman equally frustrated holding a cell phone and standing at the curb. Her resemblance to Jair suggested a sister. Her face was white and tear-stained. From the way Jair's body slumped further down the seat when he saw her, it was obvious that she was the bearer of bad news.

The car stopped and Simon and Andrew stepped out. At once, it was surrounded by a small crowd of people with tear-filled faces.

'I'm so sorry, Jair,'

'Oh Jair,'

'Oh my dear…'

The Rabbi's face was ashen as he stepped out of the car, ahead of Josh.

'Too late?' he faltered.

His sister nodded and took his hand. 'Karen is still with her.'

'Take me up there,' said Josh quietly in Jair's ear. 'They are mistaken. Trust me.'

The older man hesitated. Then, hope springing again, he nodded. 'We're going up,' he said to his sister and walked on. Josh, Simon and Andrew walked with him.

No one said a word as they waited for the elevator, nor while they walked to the entrance to the emergency center.

The little girl was lying in a single room, watched over by her mother and younger brother. Already, the staff had taken away all the tubes and drips so that Sara's mother and father would be able to hold and kiss her until her body was taken away.

Jair opened the door and the raw agony in his wife's eyes as she looked up at him provoked a choke of grief that almost overcame him.

Josh slipped past as Jair lurched over to his wife and son and embraced them both tightly. The three, so immersed in each other, didn't hear what Josh did or said — and nor did Simon or Andrew who were warding off attention from outside.

Whatever it was, Sara's soul and spirit, hovering nearby, quivered between dimensions and returned to her plump little body. She gave a great sigh before beginning to breathe easily again.

By the time her parents registered the sound, her eyes were open.

'Where am I?' she said.

Josh slipped away, leaving the cries of exultation behind him.

'Is there a back way out?' he asked Simon. 'Quick. We need to go.'

'Stairs — over there.'

'Okay, let's go.'

Sixteen years later, Sara Cohen (by then Sara Langdon) finished her medical training and began her Nobel Prize-winning work on an effective vaccine against AIDS.

Josh, Simon and Andrew got hopelessly lost on the way back to the hospital entrance, to the surprised benefit of two male patients who had been brought across from the ophthalmology department to the main building for scans, and a man previously thought to have been suffering from advanced throat cancer who turned out to be perfectly okay.

Meanwhile, Maude-Lynn and Jude had been busy. It took a surprisingly short time to set up a deal with *Fox* that made Maude-Lynn gasp with wonder. A crew would be with them by morning and, for the next twelve months, she and the crew were assigned to record Josh's every move — and every miracle.

She wouldn't have been human if she hadn't resented missing out on the miracle of Sara's resurrection, but she was sensible enough to pour her energy into working out whether Josh and Pastor Jo should go head to head on Salema's show live or pre-recorded.

By the end of that evening, neither Maude-Lynn nor Jude could remember that they had ever been anything but friends. And that, as Josh reflected, was just as much a miracle as bringing back a little girl's soul.

Chapter Twenty Five

In Las Vegas everyone believes that they will get lucky. Las Vegas is where you get the chance to break the bank, collect your dues, outwit the system, and beat the odds. It is predicated on greed.

From the moment you arrive at the baggage collection section of the airport to the time when you leave the departures lounge, the slot machines tempt and entreat, calling to you again and again. '*This* one is the one. This coin will be the answer. There is always hope. Just one more. Just another dime. Just one last try…'

There is no such thing as false hope; hope by its very nature is hopeful as Josh's father, Joe, always said. But there is false belief: the belief in Mammon.

Webster's Dictionary describes Mammon as:

1. The false god of riches and avarice.

2. Riches regarded as an object of worship and greedy pursuit; wealth as an evil, more or less personified.

Mammon is not the god of Money as Josh would try to explain again and again. Money itself was neutral. Mammon, more like, is the anti-Christ of money. Not only does he inflame the loins of those who seek riches for their own sake or for financial superiority but he also entreats the holy to despise and hate money and to make it evil. Many a Christian has spat upon money itself and turned away from Divine abundance in order to be holy because of Mammon's temptation.

Simon could never quite understand Josh's meaning when he said that avarice extended to the hatred of money as well as the adoration of it. 'Too much attention to money is the problem, not the money itself,' Josh explained patiently while Simon fidgeted restlessly. 'Money is only a means of exchange; no more, no less. It is an energy form that can be used to make things fair, to enhance or to destroy. Money does nothing; it is humanity that fears it who makes it either bad or good.'

One of Mammon's favorite tricks is to misuse St. Paul's quotation, 'Money is the root of all evil.' Clever that one — the full quotation from 1 Timothy 6:10 is, 'For the love of money is the root of all evil: which while some coveted after, they have erred from the faith, and pierced themselves through with many sorrows.'

Josh, the ancient languages scholar, would laugh when someone quoted this to him and point out that the Greek word translated as 'evil' was *kakos* which had a totally different meaning.

'It means 'misuse money and your life is total crap,' he said. 'That truth can be seen in every person riveted into lack by debt or a hateful job that barely covers the ever-increasing bills or reeling from the gambling table. Avarice, whether we over-focus on money through poverty or through greed, brings sorrow and Mammon feeds on human pain.'

Whatever Josh might say, Mammon seems like a very powerful god in the modern world. And probably Mammon's greatest conquest is the city of Las Vegas, not only for the town itself but also for the condemnation and loathing that are focused on it by those who do not see that to condemn it is to add to its energy.

Mammon laughs loudest at those who throw rocks at him; he just eats their hatred and grows stronger.

Like the original Lucifer, the fallen angel who chose to rule in hell rather than serve in heaven, Mammon is beautiful — all the better to tempt us. He has so much to offer: bright lights, beautiful women and sexy men, free food and cheap lodging and machines, machines, machines, counting out, coughing out money, money, money.

Even the croupiers at Vegas have the virus of Mammon. Even the bar people. They all believe that one day their client will win and give them a massive tip of $100,000 that will change their life.

Las Vegas worships the mighty dollar. So does the rest of America; so does the rest of the world (remember that hating the dollar is still offering it energy, and energy to Mammon is worship). But Las Vegas is the best…

Josie Jones, Janice Colliver, Stuart White, Barbara Abbas, Colm

O'Reilly, Simon Libiyah and Lucifer arrived in Las Vegas on the same day as all the other quarter-finalists. They were met at the airport by cameras and entourages. Each one was a star for the duration, bringing fresh energy to feed the all-engulfing creature that is Las Vegas.

Each competitor had their own apartment in the vast *Miracle Mile* complex of hotel, studio, theatres, gardens, leisure facilities and audition center.

All the contestants under 21 were legally required to have an older person with them to be responsible for their charge not drinking alcohol — and (theoretically at least) to protect the contestant from any other trouble and *The Miracle Mile* from being sued.

Las Vegas has a motto: 'What happens in Vegas, stays in Vegas.' This is probably one of the sops that Mammon uses to ensure that people feel safe enough to go crazy — and to come back again and again. If no one lets on how badly you have behaved, with whom you have slept or exactly what you did to your hotel room, you can cover your tracks pretty well at home.

Those who took part in *The Miracle Mile,* however, had to sign half a dozen disclaimers and accept that whatever they said or did outside their bedroom door but within the compound was available for the whole world to see across the Internet on the daily *Miracle Mile* cable reality TV show. In theory, they could go out into the city and there the Las Vegas lore was valid. But as everything they needed was inside the compound and the vast majority of them wanted to hone and hone and hone their performances, there wasn't much bad behavior outside. Of course, the losing contestants did sometimes go off the rails before their plane, bus or car left town and that was, as a general rule, kept within the bounds of Vegas lore. The devil looks after his own.

This particular year, there was less temptation to go out on the town because of the rain. It had begun about six weeks earlier in Arizona and, combined with the unexpectedly early and heavy snows in the Rockies, had begun to re-fill Lake Powell on the Colorado River. Lake Powell in turn began to fill Lake Mead.

When Gemma died, Lake Mead, Las Vegas's reservoir, was 30% down and water was becoming almost as precious as gold. Already, it was back up to just 25% down and, as would be expected, everyone was incredibly pleased about that for about a week — and then they simply went back to complaining. Rain tends to be depressing unless you are British where, at least, the quality of rain changes every half hour and is a vital topic for conversation between strangers.

You might not think that the tourist industry of Las Vegas would depend in any way upon the weather — people could spend all week inside hotels that successfully pretended to be the great outdoors and get a far better tan in the fitness center than ever they would in the sun. But there is still some psychological urge even in the most spray-tanned, sun-bed-tanned and self-tanned of humanity that seeks real sunshine. Yes, the dedicated gamblers were still in the city, and those who had planned their trip for a long time still came, but the last-minute bookings were noticeably down. Tourism and income were badly affected.

The Valley of Fire had become damp and soggy; Mount Charleston and Red Rock Canyon were unseasonably cold with the tourist town of Bonnie Springs virtually washed out. Bryce Canyon, Zion Canyon and the Grand Canyon had tourist numbers almost halved (hail was afflicting the Grand Canyon specifically, stopping a lot of the scenic flights). The rides at Stratosphere Tower were almost empty and the water-efficient plants at the Desert Demonstration Gardens were gasping for breath from the continued onslaught of rain.

Only the indoor museums were doing reasonable business.

'It's you, isn't it?' said Jude to Josh, on the day they arrived in Vegas to a sky that looked like the inside of a Tupperware box. Drizzle fell depressingly in the deceptive way that it has, looking and feeling like nothing much but soaking you through in seconds.

'I've no idea,' he replied and, having been raised in England, he just put on a waterproof coat and found it all rather interesting.

It *was* him, of course. He could heal the land as easily as the people. The land needed water and it wasn't bothered about the tourist season or the American economy.

The *Miracle Mile* contestants didn't really care about the wet either. They were in Vegas in the proud hope that they would be the one to walk the city's own Miracle Mile at the head of the great parade held in their honor at the end of the contest. They were there to wow America (and the rest of the world *obviously* — where was that again?) and find fame, fortune, wealth and glory.

Mammon loved them and they loved him in return.

For Lucifer, Las Vegas was heaven. It was filled with so many minds that were cracked or lost; so much desire and hopelessness; so many broken dreams. He wandered down the Strip on the first night, hands deep in the pockets of his leather jacket, just observing. If you had asked him, he would have said he was listening to the colors; he felt the vibrations of color, sound, scent and taste. Where Josh would have felt compassion, Lucifer felt exultation. This was virgin ground for his extraordinary mind. Almost absent-mindedly, he placed a coin into a machine, engaged the gambler next to him with a greeting, twisted the desperate rope of the gambler's mind into believing that he had hit the jackpot and walked away, smiling while the delighted man's belief wore off in confusion and shame and he began struggle with two security men called to bring him to his senses.

'This is *fun,*' said Lucifer.

A great neon sign advertising *The Miracle Mile* with rotating holograms of Sam, Josh, Deborah and Gideon stopped him in his tracks. When it was Josh's turn to be displayed, Lucifer felt his energy deflate. He hissed like a snake. He had to make plans; that man had to be beaten.

The rain fell steadily as the beautiful man in leather stood silently on the Strip, his mind deep inside himself searching for an idea with which to destroy his antithesis.

The Miracle Mile conglomerate that was *Gemstone Inc, Sam Powell Inc., Gideon Jones Productions* and *Deforge Inc.* was very happy as it prepared for the quarter finals of the show in Las Vegas. There were forty-five contestants in each of the four categories — Singer, Dancer, Movement and Performance — and enough controversial footage of the auditions to send ratings through the roof. The first program went to air within 24 hours and the viewing levels of the 'unofficial excerpts' on YouTube promised a bumper season.

Mostly it was Sam who stole the live shows with his laconic criticisms delivered in an incredibly laid back style followed by wide-eyed amazement when his incisive comments caused outrage or offence. To do Sam justice, he was nearly always right; he could spot star quality if it were encased in concrete at the bottom of a swimming pool. He just didn't suffer from any false modesty about his talent, nor did he fail to play to his audience. He preferred the live shows in Las Vegas because of the feedback that groaned and shouted its way out to him from the darkness of the great auditorium but, actually, the auditions were where he really shone. His acerbic wit, deadpan delivery and caustic ability to pinpoint any point of weakness were justifiably legendary.

Sam always said he offered constructive criticism — and he was right; he just didn't offer a spoonful of sugar with the medicine. Gemma always had. She had sparkled while she criticized so that the person was both taken down and built up again and she offered witty, sage advice that people at home could nod wisely to and say, 'That lady; she knows a thing or two.'

Josh had done well in the auditions. The question was, could he do the same on live TV?

Well, yes he could. What a relief that was! In fact, Josh had quite a comic talent particularly when drawing on his love of the British author Terry Pratchett's work — the word 'charisntma' was one of the many Pratchettisms he used to great affect. He also understood that his English accent was an asset, so he was sometimes quite deliberately too highbrow; using words and constructs that the contestants (and the other judges for that matter) couldn't grasp. That became his signature so that he could be pilloried for being the lah-di-dah, upper class academic of the judges. By the time they had been live in Vegas for two shows, the cheerful roar of 'put that in plain English Josh!' would come from the audience as well as from his fellow judges.

In Denver, Gideon had started the game by bringing in a *Roget's Thesaurus* and an old copy of *Webster's Dictionary*, both of which he thumped down on the desk with a knowing look every time Josh opened his mouth. Occasionally, in breaks (which were filmed of course for *The Miracle Mile Extra* show), he would open the dictionary at random and get Josh to define a word.

Josh didn't mind. He would grin laconically and, if he didn't know the answer, make up something completely outrageous. On air, when both his fellow judges and the contestant wrinkled their foreheads in incomprehension he would enjoy using another equally convoluted but exact and articulate sentence. In the end, when they threw up their hands in despair, he would go 'good' or 'not good' and even the contestant would whoop and exclaim with relief that he had finally said something that someone could understand.

Gideon had always been the nicest one of the team. He had been a little concerned about Josh's advent as he didn't want his 'good-guy' status overtaken or outdone. He needn't have worried; the two men were excellent foils for each other as they enjoyed playing and having a good time. Gideon 'got' Josh and was surprised at how comfortable he was with the effect that his colleague had on contestants. So often, a word from Josh would calm them down and relax them (even if they didn't understand what it meant!) Sam and Deborah usually couldn't see what was going on at all.

Deborah, without Gemma there, was becoming a parody of a queen-bee bitch. It was probably fortunate for her that, when they were live, she was quite inarticulate which made her as amusing as she was vile. She seemed to have no ability to gather her words together without a re-take or a script and her phrasing was often so convoluted that she could start six consecutive sentences without getting anywhere. That alone made her a favorite with impersonators — though only one, that season, was stupid enough to imitate Deborah to her face on the show. She sat there, completely confused while the men fell about with laughter and, afterwards, confounded them further by asking in genuine bewilderment 'Who on Earth was that meant to be?'

'You, Deborah,' choked Sam.

'Don't be ridiculous!' And that was that. She could not be convinced.

Deborah hated talent in beautiful young women but always fluttered and admired beautiful young men. As she had no self-knowledge she never realized once that she felt threatened by female beauty or talent and repeatedly resisted Sam's attempts to inform her of her weakness as 'groin-led masculinity.' She was, of course, a gay-icon, and cross-dressers who could 'do a good Deborah' were about the only act more popular in Vegas than the winners of *The Miracle Mile.*

Apart from the Deborah Deforge impersonator, the other YouTube most-viewed clips before *The Miracle Mile* went to air were:

—Deborah yawning delicately as a young ballet dancer painstakingly wobbled her way through her routine, then sighing heavily as she said, 'You are so totally, like…You so…you…I don't know…without talent that I…don't…I can't…like…I think…suggest you get fat…fatter. Fat as fast as possible and go work somewhere, I don't know, in a diner.'

'Why?' the girl stared at her.

Luckily Deborah was now on a roll. She got better when she was on a roll.

'Because, like, a hundred pounds…on that already wobbling frame will, like, save…anyone from the risk of, like, believing your pathetic claims that you can dance.'

'Oh come on Deborah!' That was Sam. 'That's not fair. She only needs to gain fifty pounds to work in a diner.'

—Gideon, watching intently as a young contortionist wound her way into more knots than a kids' tie-the-balloons party and being hit in the eye when one of her silicone gel breast-enhancing shapes shot out of her bra.

—Josh calming down a young singer, hysterical with anger at not winning through, by ordering her to sit down and put her head between her knees and, when she wouldn't but continued screaming abuse, intoning 'Sit!' as though she were a dog. Totally startled by his authority, she sat and shut up instantly. Sam immediately went, 'Woof!'

—All four judges watching with horrified eyes as a totally atonal guy wrecked Dolly Parton's 'I Will Always Love You' and chorusing, 'Awful,' 'Dreadful,' 'Dire,' 'Appalling.' Whereupon the man burst into hysterical tears and dropped on the floor, flailing like a fish.

—The dog trainer whose German Shepherd hated Sam on sight and refused to obey, preferring to bark hysterically and back away. Sam even went over to try and make friends with the dog which then jumped into its owner's arms whimpering. Josh said, 'If you'd just told us it was a dog comedy act, you'd have got through on that alone.'

—The pair of street-wise break-dancers whose trousers split in the middle of their routine.

By the time they went live on air, Sam had more than 2,700,000 pages on Google, Josh 2,500,000, Deborah 1,807,000, and Gideon 1,300,000.

'Why has Josh got so many?' asked Bartos in amazement as Jude briefed the team on feedback so far. Seven faces looked at him in amazement. 'Is it because of Gemma?'

'Um, no,' said Jude with dangerous politeness. 'It's mostly because he is capable of doing miracles — you know, healing people.'

Bartos shrugged. That kind of thing was outside his mind's remit. 'Well that's cool, of course,' he said. 'But I wouldn't have thought it was that big a thing on the Internet.'

'Bartos, have you *seen* any of the churches in America?' asked Tadaeo. 'Like, about one every half mile! They all have something to say about a Jewish guy who can perform miracles.'

'Really?' Bartos didn't get the connection. 'Well that's great. Shall we move on?'

They moved on. Jude steamed quietly while, conversely, appearing colder than ice. It appeared that the show would be as successful as ever before with Josh filling Gemma's shoes quite well enough.

'Lucky really as he owns the majority of the company,' said Philippa dryly.

'Yes, but where is he?' asked Bartos.

'Well he's doing a TV head-to-head with some pastor and he says that the recording for the *Fox* show wears him out so he's gone to ground for a few days,' said Jude.

'The *Fox* show?' The ever-present image of Maude-Lynn and her team sticking like glue to Josh had gone right under Bartos's radar which, at least, demonstrated his ability to focus on his job. 'Yes, TV cameras following him around — like his own reality show.'

'That will piss the others off big-time,' commented Bartos.

'Not if they're on it!' said Jude.

'What's this religious thing? I don't want him doing religious stuff. That's really uncool.'

'You don't?'

'No!'

'I'll leave you to tell him yourself on that one.' Jude smiled sweetly. She would enjoy watching Bartos lose that fight.

Chapter Twenty Six

Marta Tecchio yawned delicately, one exquisitely-manicured, silver-nail-polished hand covering her pale, beautifully-painted mouth. Every man in the room hoped against hope that he wasn't the one who had bored her. Every woman wavered between admiration and loathing.

'Enough now,' she said in her delicately accented voice. 'I will leave the rest to you.' She nodded to the assembled group of personal assistants, executives and promotions people, stood up and floated elegantly out of the room. No one tried to stop her. Marta was a star and she could do pretty much what she wanted.

Fortunately, what Marta wanted now was to be the new host of *The Miracle Mile.* As the executives of the conglomerate had agreed that she was the only person who could possibly replace John Jordan, there were sharp exhalations of breath in relief when the negotiations were complete. Nobody quite knew why she had responded so well to their approach; she was riding high on a series of well-rated quiz shows and could have looked for even something higher. Okay, so *The Miracle Mile* was a ratings-beater but even so, it wasn't quite the star vehicle they would have thought Marta, at her peak at 25, would be seeking.

Marta's womanly backside, perfectly framed in white leather, swayed down the corridor, as she reached in her handbag for some nicotine gum. She often walked out on her team like this and they knew that it meant she needed a few moments on her own. If they waited for five minutes, she would be sweetness and light; if they followed her too soon they would be on the receiving end of a mouth as cold as it was beautiful.

Marta was not smart but she was street-wise and very well aware of her own strengths and weaknesses. That was what made her a good presenter — she never took on anything where she could not shine in the reflection of a great production team and a proven format.

Marta Tecchio was very, very afraid of appearing stupid. Perhaps it would have helped her fear if she had not colored her abundant hair but, physically, the gamble of joining the dumb-blonde brigade had been well worth taking. The contrast of the silvery mane with her smooth creamy skin and bright blue eyes was breathtaking. One man who saw her rounded feminine beauty and Jude Isaacs' stern magnificence walking together later that day was so overcome he had to go and have a little time to himself in the men's room.

In contrast with these two goddesses, Mary-Beth was looking even skinnier and plainer if that were possible. When Jude brought Marta to be formally introduced to him, Josh was leaning back in his chair, resting his head on Mary-Beth's bony chest as she gave him an Indian Head Massage. Marta's first thought was 'What on earth is *that*?' and Jude's 'Does he *still* not realize she's in love with him?'

Marta's attention left Mary-Beth to focus on Josh and her second thought was 'Yes, you'll do.' For Marta had a plan. She had no illusions about the length of tenure of a celebrity reality show hostess, particularly one who was not that intelligent. Marta wanted long-term security — but not the security of a life surrounded by sycophants and acolytes; she wanted marriage and children and, as the child of a devout Catholic family, she had no intention of wading through a series of men and marriages.

Marta's mother had married an older man, a widower, and that had worked well. With deep training in principles of family loyalty and duty and, especially, in this fragile, tear-apart world of fame, Marta too wanted someone proven to be reliable, faithful, loyal — and wealthy.

So she had joined *The Miracle* Mile with the full intention of becoming the second Mrs. Josh Goldstone.

Josh, she knew, was a quiet and undemanding man — and a good husband. She had seen him on TV and she had observed him in person before Gemma died (though at a distance) and had not found him repulsive. Her mother had taught her well — that outrageously good-looking men were only interested in themselves and sought new conquests to fuel their egos.

Josh was past his first months of grieving and would soon be ready to consider the future. Marta didn't care whether Josh were a miracle worker or a movie star; he was famous enough, wealthy enough and, slightly to her surprise, in the flesh, he was more than attractive enough.

'Hmmm,' she said, making her views apparent with the stance of her body, the curve of her mouth and the allure of those enormous sapphire eyes. '*You* must be Josh.'

Mary-Beth and Jude bristled simultaneously and Maude-Lynn, entering the room behind them at that exact moment also found herself instinctively reacting to the younger she-cat on heat.

'Oh my!' said Marta widening her eyes. 'You have a harem! How very exciting.'

She purred; she definitely purred and the other women's antagonism only served to emphasize her beauty.

'I haven't finished,' said Mary-Beth, flushing with heat but heading off the sexual charge with the brick wall of stubbornness. 'It's important that the whole therapy is experienced. If you'll just wait outside, Sally will get you a drink.'

Josh's mouth twitched. 'Better do as she tells you,' he said, closing his eyes again. 'I wouldn't want to meet you all unfinished.'

Jude's mouth twitched too. Marta almost flounced but thought the better of it. Maude-Lynn snorted quietly under her breath and Mary-Beth returned all her attention to Josh.

'Is…*that*…the girlfriend?' hissed Marta with horrified emphasis, once the door was shut behind them.

'Oh no,' Jude was now amused. 'The PA. By the way, this is Maude-Lynn Sykes who is producing and presenting the fly-on-the-wall documentary about Josh. Maude-Lynn this is Marta our new host.'

'Pleased to meet you,' said Maude-Lynn with deep dishonesty and curiosity swirled together with reluctant admiration. 'Jeez,' she thought, as Marta's elegant hand touched hers briefly and her nose picked up the siren's perfume-enhanced pheromones. 'This *is* going to be interesting.' Maude-Lynn didn't find Josh remotely sexually alluring but she did realize that she, Jude and Mary-Beth all thought he was their property in their own individual ways.

'Delighted,' said Marta realizing that Maude-Lynn might be worth charming. 'But I thought you were not a fan of Mr. Goldstone's?' She had a way of turning any sentence into a question which was utterly delightful when it didn't make you cringe.

'Times change,' said Maude-Lynn with a grin. 'Our Mr. Goldstone is worth changing your mind over.'

'Obviously.' Marta was intrigued. She decided to continue with the game. 'And *are* you his harem? If so, may I join?'

'I suppose we are,' said Jude. 'He spends more time with us than anyone else — apart from the disciples of course.'

'The disciples?'

'His minders. The security guys.'

'Well!' said Marta. It was another clever way of sounding engaged while saying absolutely nothing. 'Perhaps Josh's people could call my people and we could arrange a lunch when we both have time.' Her timing was perfect. Just as Josh came through the door, she walked away, fully aware of the effective sway of her perfect behind as she moved. She expected Josh to follow her. He didn't.

Mary-Beth, meanwhile, was bristling like a lavatory brush. Josh had let her finish the massage only in the hope that it would calm *her* down rather than him.

'Sit down Mary-Beth,' he said kindly once the office was empty but for the two of them. Mary-Beth was shuffling the interminable piles of correspondence on her desk.

She made a slightly distracted gesture to indicate that she was too busy for casual conversation.

'Sit,' he said, just as gently but with a note in it that no one, *no one,* would disobey.

Mary-Beth sat, her face gray.

'I'm not going to get into a relationship with Marta,' said Josh, sitting on the desk and taking one of her slender little hands in his.

'You don't know that,' she said shaking her head.

'And,' said Josh. 'I'm not going to get into a relationship with Jude.'

'Well of course not!' said Mary-Beth slightly shocked.

Josh grinned. 'And I'm not going to get into a relationship with Maude-Lynn.'

'I didn't really think so…'

'And I'm not going to get into a relationship with you…'

She looked up at him with pain in her eyes. 'I know,' she said. 'I know that. But Marta…Marta…' She shook her head. Marta was so beautiful, so transparent and so used to getting what she wanted.

'Mary-Beth,' said Josh. 'I'm going to tell you something. I want to trust you not to tell anyone else. Will you promise me?'

The sop of confidentiality lifted her sad little heart and she looked up at him eagerly. It was as though the light of dawn spread across the sky. If she couldn't be his love, she could be his confidante.

'I promise,' she said. 'I promise.'

For the next 48 hours, Mary-Beth Oliver walked around the building with damp, red-rimmed eyes but, if anyone had cared to notice (which they didn't), her posture seemed subtly different. She was more assertive with Sally and the post room staff and she had an extra little line in the center of her forehead which meant she was thinking a lot.

Once she had made her mind up and checked her savings account, she squared up her shoulders and went to see Colin and Chris in the makeover studios. Then she made some long-distance phone calls and submitted a leave form to her boss.

'You want four weeks off *now?*' Josh stared at a defiant Mary-Beth in genuine astonishment. It took a lot to ruffle Josh but this certainly took the biscuit. Literally. Without Mary-Beth he wouldn't get his morning chocolate digestive, imported all the way from

Britain. Part of him was deeply amused at what aspect of his irritation came up first.

'Mary-Beth, we're about to do the live show with Pastor Jo, then there's the start of the whittling-down process, to say nothing of all the correspondence. Or,' he added honestly, 'my chocolate biscuits. Why now?'

'Because it has to be now,' she said in her quiet, un-textured voice. 'Sally can take care of you.'

'Sally's not you!'

'*I'm* not me,' Mary-Beth thought to herself. 'That's the trouble.'

'You can have my resignation if you like,' she said out loud with the conscious cruelty of those who know they are indispensable but mean to have their own way.

Some of her hated herself for it; some of her was weeping (again) at the thought of not seeing Josh for a whole four weeks. Some of her was even more stupidly in love with him than she had been yesterday.

'Why do you need this time now?' Josh asked, knowing that it was probably none of his business.

'I'm going to Europe,' said Mary-Beth. 'I need a holiday.' She pursed her lips and, although it cost her dearly in self-control, would say no more.

'I'm British, Mary-Beth,' said Josh. 'Just "Europe" doesn't work with me. I actually know the different countries. Where in Europe?'

'I'm flying to Paris.' That was a lie; she was really quite surprised at how easy it was.

He knew it was a lie. The colors in the light around someone changed when they lied. The fact that she was lying to him was more shocking than anything else.

'Mary-Beth, you're not going to do something silly are you?' said Josh, the worry-lines of concern on his forehead touching her mangled little heart.

'It's my life,' she said. 'If I want to do something silly with it, I can. It's about time. I don't think I've *ever* done anything silly.'

She thought back to a childhood of poverty as the eldest of seven children with a wastrel father and an exhausted mother. Mary-Beth had coped; she always did cope. She never had time to grow pretty or witty or wise because she had the washing to do and her sisters to rear and a seven-day paper round.

'Well, please don't be too silly,' said Josh gently. 'You might not like it. But you're right; it's your life to do what you want with…and I've no right to ask you to do or not to do anything.'

'Then don't,' she said, head held high.

'When do you leave?'

'Tonight.'

'Tonight?'

'You can have my resignation —'

'—Oh for God's sake Mary-Beth, I don't want your resignation! You go with my blessing. But I will miss you.'

She went off to catch her flight with that little sentence held like sticking plaster over her frightened heart. Any other boss would have been furious (and rightly, she had to admit). He was just worried about her. She cried most of the way to Chicago but, when she boarded the 747 to Delhi, the immensity of what she was doing buoyed her up with hope that her life, at last, would truly change.

Meanwhile Josh was both intrigued and, it must be said, slightly amused that he had come nearer to getting upset over little Mary-Beth than over any of the insults, scurrilous claims or egotistical attacks that had come his way this last six months.

He didn't worry about who would take her place or how he would cope. He knew it always worked out. He was interested to observe that Maude-Lynn, Jude, John and Sally instantly formed an almost impenetrable team around him. Everything simply adjusted itself with the minimum of fuss.

And Sally was efficient even if she was a moaning Minnie.

'Why don't you take seven devils out of her?' asked Maude-Lynn as Sally went off grumbling to get some two per cent milk for Josh's tea.

'Haven't taken them out of you yet,' he said lazily.

'You have too!'

'Not seven. Seven is an awkward little devil. Six I'll admit to. Seven's waiting its time.'

'Seven deadly sins?' said John, drinking his own tea with half-and-half and grimacing. 'Which one is the seventh?'

'Lust, I expect,' said Maude-Lynn laughing. She rarely worried about anything much any more and was loving the feeling of healthy blood pressure, fragrant breath and fewer hangovers. She was also enjoying having her own assistant for the fly-on-the-wall documentary and found she was a natural boss. She didn't bully, she was happy to delegate and she could make clever, instant decisions. Life was very good.

'I don't think I want to give up lust just yet,' she said thoughtfully. 'Have you *seen* Simon Libiyah?'

Chapter Twenty Seven

Josie Jones, Janice Colliver, Stuart White, Barbara Abbas, Colm O'Reilly, Simon Libiyah, Melissa Brown and Lucifer were hot favorites for the finals and all but Melissa knew it. While Sam and Gemma had often bemoaned the fact that putting talent to a public vote often meant that cuteness and popularity would win out over real genius, they were prepared to play along with the crowd. Sam missed Gemma at this point; Josh was too darn relaxed about it all to agree with him that this year, the most talented were, fortunately for them, also the most attractive.

Janice was a leggy blonde as well as an extraordinarily talented musician who could play piano, flute, clarinet, guitar and violin and often did play most, if not all of them, in one piece of music. Josie and Barbara were singers — Josie a black soprano from Georgia who, amazingly, could sing Dolly Parton and do the expected pretty fair job on Whitney Houston. Barbara was a part-Iranian Harley-Davidson-riding rock-chick contralto from Los Angeles; Colm an Irish dancer from Pennsylvania; Stuart an All-American acrobat from Tulsa, Melissa had the voice of Aretha Franklin, Simon was a black break-dancer from Brooklyn and Lucifer was Lucifer.

At orientation, Lucifer marked out two pretty girls from a girl-band which, he correctly assessed, would be going home at the end of the first week. He loved preying on the weak, they gave him their energy so easily, and those who went home would not tell. These he could play with like a child pulling the wings off flies — not only did they go home unsuccessful but they had the added pain of watching him walk away from both them after he had got what he wanted and hating each other when they realized that they had both succumbed to the same man on successive nights. Later, Lucifer would turn his attention to anyone (man or woman — he didn't mind) who might be a professional threat. If he could get inside their body as well as their mind, then it was even easier to affect their performance the next day. This was *fun*.

It never occurred to Lucifer that he had the talent to win without manipulation and magic because manipulation and magic had become a part of who he was. He didn't just want to win, he needed to control it all. He must, must, *must* be loved more than Josh Goldstone, no matter how, no matter what.

While Lucifer was weaving his magic, his mother too had made a definite impression on the father of one of the contestants, much to the distress of the flattered man's wife. Venus was there, ostensibly, to chaperone her son but neither of them were willing to pay more than lip-service to that.

Lucifer and Mammon in Las Vegas was a match made in hell.

Deborah, Gideon, Sam and Marta had their own apartments or complexes in Las Vegas. Josh 'bunked', as he put it, together with the production team. It was safer (the death threats were still coming in) and more convenient for everyone.

So Jude didn't have far to go in order to wake Josh on the morning of the terrible news about John Jordan.

'Josh!' she banged on the door of his suite. 'Wake up! Code 54!'

Josh, wearing a toweling bathrobe, answered the door immediately. He was wide-awake and alert. He was used to having sensors — scanners or something like that — in his head and to receiving communications from different levels or vibrations and he knew even before he woke that morning that there had been a death close to him. But this time it was a death in its own time and not one that needed his help.

'Who died?' he asked, as he let Jude into the room.

'John Jordan.'

'No!'

'It appears that he was knifed by robbers right by his home.'

'It appears?'

'Details are sketchy at the moment.'

'Yes of course. Was he alone?'

'Yes. But there's talk that it was China.'

'China?'

'He was on a blacklist, Josh. He couldn't shut up about Tibet. We often had to tone him down when he was here.'

Josh sat down and gestured to Jude to do the same.

'When did you hear?'

'About 10 minutes ago. I've alerted the other PRs. You'll all be wanted to issue a tribute and do a news conference for tributes.'

'Yes of course — did John have anyone special in his life at the moment?'

'I don't think so.'

'Anything I should do?'

'No, just do the star bit — and go to the funeral.'

'Yes, of course. Parents?'

'Yes. Communication being arranged now.'

'Okay, had you better go organize or do you want to have breakfast with me?'

'I'd like that but I have to get on. Mary-Beth's cell phone is still off or out of signal by the way.'

'She ought to know though. I'll email her.'

He did but there was no response.

So that day was a day of comments to the press on the death of a friend and colleague. News came in pretty quickly that John had been receiving threats for his political activism and the massive police enquiry doubled.

John's murder made quite as many headlines around the world as Gemma's death had — maybe more because of the speculation about who would have wanted to kill him and why. And whether it was China or not, the assassination had only heightened the situation in Tibet.

Simon, Andrew, James and John had a council of war with Thomas, Philip, Bartholomew, Nico, Jodie and the others currently on the security team. Once one celebrity had been hit, the law of attraction encouraged other nutters — or assassins — to strike. Josh had specifically forbidden them to be armed but, as Simon said, circumstances altered cases. There was no need to tell Josh, after all.

John and James, who had no armaments training, and who were responsible for checking the mail and other communications, were exempted — but sworn to silence.

The funeral took place in Los Angeles with all the team attending including Marta. With consummate grace, she sat with Josh on the jet, taking Mary-Beth's vacant seat. Marta didn't gush or push herself. With Josh she was happy to sit and be peaceful (and alluring and gorgeous) as if she were already a comfortable and relaxed partner. She easily made friends with John, James and Sally and, when they got to Los Angeles, cuddled up to Josh's parents too. Maria and Joe had both known John Jordan and flying out for the funeral was a good opportunity both to pay their respects and to spend some time with their son. Marta strategically dripped the idea into Maria's head that it would be a good idea to stay on for a couple of weeks until Mary-Beth got back. Marta liked family, believed in family and was pleased to see that Josh was fond of his parents but not too tied to his mother. Mother-fixated men were somewhat of a challenge. However, building a relationship with her intended's family was crucial to her strategy.

Joe and Maria liked Marta. She was charming and genuine and perfectly open with them that she had what she carefully called 'a little crush' on Josh.

'Do you think...?' said Maria, on the morning of the funeral before she and her husband left their hotel room.

'No,' said Joe firmly.

Maria looked crestfallen. 'It *could* be part of the plan,' she said, rallying swiftly. 'You never know. And she's so...so different from Gemma but so similar in some ways. Shining — you know. He does like her; I know he does. She's like a moonbeam; she lights him up.'

'You never know,' said her husband lovingly — and tactfully. 'You look very nice my dear. Is my tie straight?'

The funeral Mass was held at the stunning if spiky ultra-modern Cathedral of Our Lady of the Angels in West Temple Street, Los

Angeles. John's body was to be interred there too, in the crypt, joining Gregory Peck and Jean Harlow ('Which just goes to show what counts for fame nowadays,' said Joe wryly). The plaza, gardens and the streets around the cathedral were crammed with onlookers, the police estimate being more than 5000 people. The cathedral café simply couldn't cope and, even before the funeral cortege arrived, people were wilting in the heat and complaining of hunger and thirst.

The stars of *American Idol* arrived first, then the judges from *America's Got Talent* and, finally, top of the bill, everyone from *The Miracle Mile.* Gideon walked with Deborah, Sam with Marta (as the most attractive couple they made all the front pages). Marta was angry to lose a publicity opportunity with Josh but her moody pout was breathtaking. Josh walked with Philippa and Bartos with Jude. The others, including past competitors on the show, walked behind them.

Josh stopped as they went into the cathedral and looked up at Robert Graham's eight-foot statue of *Our Lady of the Angels*. She was plain, with no figure — devoutly asexual — and, with the great halo of sky behind her, she looked extraordinarily innocent.

'Does she remind you of anyone?' asked Jude as his hesitation became slightly obvious.

'Yes, she does,' he said.

Jude squeezed his arm from behind and they walked on.

The Requiem Mass seemed, to most of the secular celebrities, to go on for hours. Josh sat and stood with everyone else, aware of the beauty of liturgy and music but completely unmoved by the service itself and perplexed by the crucifix and the need to depict Christ's suffering so profoundly instead of transmitting his joy throughout the world. He spoke a few times inside his head to the peaceful and awakened John Jordan who, as so many souls do, had turned up for his own funeral. Josh understood and stored peacefully in his heart (to be revealed to no one) the perfection of this death and its importance to his former friend's soul.

Gemma's essence was there too and that filled him with joy. She was such a delight; had always been a delight to him but now she was delicious in her perfection.

Afterwards, while the other guests moved into the conference center for the reception, Josh, accompanied by Simon, Jodie and Thomas, mingled with the crowds, shaking a hand here, healing unobtrusively with a touch where asked verbally or silently.

Where he went there was peace but in the other areas, hunger, thirst and irritation were rising. The crowd had wiped out all the food from surrounding shops that were open — and many had closed because of the tumult of people.

'It's their own fault; they should have brought food and drink. The police should send them home,' said Simon.

'Have you got anything?' said Josh. 'Any water?'

'Don't ask me,' said Simon. 'Does it look like I could fit a bottle in this suit? You're the manifester of smoked salmon bagels. Go to it!'

Josh just smiled and said hello to a group of children proffering autograph books. In a second he had vanished. He had melted into the crowd as they surged around him.

Simon swore and plunged after him. Jodie put a hand on Thomas's arm and said, 'Look!'

From nowhere, it seemed, dozens of fairground-like food vans appeared serving hot bagels and sandwiches, salads, smoothies, ice cream and drinks. Every one of them was *giving* food away.

'How the hell…?' Simon was amazed.

'It's Destriers!' said Jodie. Destrier were 'the new McDonald's' fighting to take their place in the major league of takeaway foods. What a publicity stunt it would be, thought their chairman to *give* food at a time when people were in need. And John Jordan's funeral, in Los Angeles, with huge media coverage was perfect. They couldn't be accused of disrespect — they were *giving* food. And John Jordan had always been great on charity fundraisers…

Someone passed Josh a carrot and apple juice as he mingled with the now happy crowds and he drank it with great enjoyment — to the utter horror of Simon who had just caught up with him.

'That could be poisoned!' he hissed.

'It wasn't,' said Josh, smiling.

'God, you make my job hard,' said Simon with feeling and, once they were back in the main building and Josh was fully covered, he went go off to have a quiet sulk with a cigarette.

'That was cheating,' he said to Andrew who wasn't above stealing a drag although he swore he didn't smoke. 'He should have manifested the food himself.'

'Modern times. The Holy One uses what there is I guess,' said Andrew lazily.

It was Deborah's evil genius that changed the mood. She was the first of the *Miracle Mile* judges to leave and, when she was getting into her limousine, someone asked her where Josh was. Immediately jealous that some other celebrity might be preferred to her, she said, 'Probably hiding somewhere so no one asks him how come he can't raise everyone from the dead.' To do her some credit, she realized as soon as the words were out of her mouth that they were both unwise and unhelpful to her image. So she added: 'But of course, he does a lot of good work.'

The effect of her words ran through the crowd as a frisson of resentment. Yes, why hadn't Josh raised John Jordan from the dead? The girls who were in love with the handsome TV host only needed a little push like this to head them into hysterical grief. Come to think of it, someone's Granddad had died the other week — not to mention that Orange County family who were reported to have died in a car crash the day before. So why were some favored people brought back to life and not others?

The mood rippled to start with, swelled and, by the time Josh, Sam and their respective teams came out to get into their cars and leave, there was a storm of fury ready to lash out both verbally and with missiles.

Angry people filled the road and the police, only just realizing that a peaceful crowd had suddenly gone on the rampage, were gearing up to get tough.

Luckily no one was carrying anything particularly dangerous but half-full water bottles are heavy and can hurt. Rubbish, bottles and handfuls of hastily grabbed earth from the cathedral gardens slammed into the car. One bottle hit Jodie and made her stagger. The security people closed ranks around Sam and Josh immediately. Hostility crackled in the air like heavy static.

'Why didn't you save John?'

'Why didn't you raise John?'

'Unfair!'

'We hate you Josh Goldstone!'

'In the car, quick,' hissed Simon, one part of his brain pleased to be proven right. He shielded Josh so that he could duck down into the back seat.

But Josh, seeing that there was currently no way that the car could pull out and that they needed a police escort, looked first to see if Jodie was all right and then slid out around both Simon and the car and vanished into the hostile crowd.

'Oh Christ!' muttered Simon, diving after him.

But the people parted as Josh walked peacefully into their midst. His calmness and gentle sorrow was balm to their unconscious souls. He walked out right into the heart of the anguish and hatred to where a young girl was sitting on the ground sobbing. The girl's friends fell back to let Josh past. He knelt on one knee and held his arms out to her. Josh looked at her with love and she, unquestioningly, threw herself into his arms.

The whole crowd fell silent, peace descending upon them.

That is, until Simon anxiously working his way through people who were standing like statues, pushed a little too hard and the frisson of anger raised its head again. Josh felt it and lifted his own head. He saw Simon almost engulfed in the masses and held out his hand. Instantly the people parted and Simon staggered through.

He had the wisdom not to say anything, just crouched beside Josh as he comforted the girl.

After a few minutes, Josh gently handed her into the care of her boyfriend and the two men walked peacefully together back to the car.

The crowds flowed away from the road and the cars drove off.

'I thought there was going to be a riot,' said Simon.

'Indeed there was,' said Josh. 'Simon?'

'Yes?'

'Get rid of the guns.'

'What guns?' Simon lied swiftly as his eyes flickered.

'Yours and the other security disciples. You can't spread peace while wearing a gun.'

'I beg to differ — and so would all the armies of the world. You *have* to be armed to enforce peace.'

Josh laughed. 'En-*force* peace?' he said. 'What a contradiction in terms. No. No guns Simon. Otherwise you might accidentally blow someone's ear off.'

'I wouldn't!' Simon was incensed. 'I'm an excellent shot.'

'Yes, and it's written all through your energy that you wouldn't mind giving it a go,' said Josh, suddenly stern. 'Don't you get it? It's not about enforcing peace. It's about *being* peace.'

'Tell that to the rest of the world,' muttered Simon resentfully.

'I am,' said Josh.

Chapter Twenty Eight

The long-awaited interview with Josh and Pastor Jo was to be recorded just five days after John Jordan's funeral. Maude-Lynn, who was organizing it, had wanted it to take place in Las Vegas but neither Salema nor Pastor Jo were willing to make the trip. The talk show hostess had too busy a schedule and Pastor Jo did not want to go to the City of Sin. However, he was perfectly happy to go to New York and then on to Chicago, home of the Christian *Total Living Network* and do some work with them after filming with Salema.

'I don't mind,' said Josh when Maude-Lynn fulminated about his seeming less important than the others by caving in to their desires and going where they wanted to go.

'Do you mind *anything?*' she said, hands on hips. Maude-Lynn was generally feeling very good about life but there were times she could have picked Josh up and shaken him.

Jude laughed out loud when the smaller woman stomped into her office to sound off. 'Now you know just how I feel,' she said. 'He has no pride, has he?'

'How do you persuade him to do things?' asked Maude-Lynn. 'I mean…how do you *make* him do things? He agrees to stuff and then it just doesn't happen if he doesn't want it to.'

'I think it's called the Law of Non-Resistance,' said Jude. 'At least he's stepping up to this interview. It should be good.'

'But he won't argue!' said Maude-Lynn. 'I need him to argue! I try him out with some of Pastor Jo's likely outbursts and he just smiles and says, 'You can think what you want.''

Jude saw Maude-Lynn's point. 'Maybe we should do a little more organizing. Maybe we should set something up that will make him speak out.'

'Do you know how?'

'No, but I bet you do. Can you find any dirt on Pastor Jo? You must have looked.'

'No, there's nothing...at least nothing I can find.'

'Well we don't have much time. Maybe we have to *make* something.'

'Make something? How on earth would we do that?'

Five minutes later, Jude walked into Lucifer quite accidentally, or so she thought. The young man, who was charming as always, walked down the corridor with her and flirted a little which made her laugh inside; Jude was sexually impervious to men and she was amused that a mind-reader didn't know that.

Lucifer loved it when a mind opened up to a slight feeling of superiority; it created a specific energy field that was so very accessible. As if he would actually flirt with a dyke! He smiled into Jude's eyes and engaged all his powers.

Pastor Jo was in heaven. His words were being listened to and he had an adversary who either couldn't or wouldn't speak up for himself in any way that the Christian community could relate to or understand. What's more, he had firm evidence of a precursor to the Anti-Christ so the End of Days *was* in sight.

All great Christian preachers (St. Paul included) have genuinely believed that Christ would return for the End of Days — and that these end times were coming within their own lifetime. Only then could you make people understand the importance of repentance *now.* For decades, the Evangelical Christians have been fully expecting what's known as 'the Rapture' where true believers will be lifted up into paradise, leaving the damned and the doomed behind to face their just desserts. Pastor Jo was certain of being in the front line of the saved.

The greatest problem for the Rapture-seekers is that the Jewish Temple in Jerusalem must be re-built before the End of Days which had led Evangelical Christians to support Zionists in the Holy Land in a rather strangely blinkered alliance.

But things were moving on, the Lord could act with devastating speed to sort the Israeli problem the moment He wanted to; the

Anti-Christ was here and Pastor Jo was handsome and charismatic. Christian America was poised for the debate of the century.

Jude, in the meantime, had had a brainwave and went to see Lucifer's mother. She knew what a risk she was taking but the worm will turn and Jude thought that she had been patient long enough. It never once occurred to her that the idea had never been hers but was bled into her mind by Lucifer. Maude-Lynn was right, she thought. It was time that Josh stopped being so laid back. Time to raise a sword. If he would not out-debate Pastor Jo, then either Pastor Jo had to be lamed so that Josh would be the winner whatever was said or, even better, Josh had to be provoked. And to provoke Josh would take some doing.

Of course Jude had been warned about Lucifer. She thought the boy was charming and enchanting and extraordinarily gifted and that Josh was almost certainly over-stating the case when he told her she should beware of him. Others maybe, but not Jude! And, anyway, she wasn't choosing to make Lucifer the agent of her plan. It was Venus who was the subject of her brainwave. Venus too was charming and courteous and she was probably open to the idea of a deal.

Venus and Jude made a striking couple as they sat having a drink in *Caesar's Palace*. Venus was luscious and dark and Jude elegant, cool and dark. Jude could tell that Venus had similar — if not so strong — powers as her son and also that her mother-love was deep and amoral.

Jude's offer was simple. She would make sure that Lucifer got his own show in Las Vegas whatever happened to him in *The Miracle Mile.* And she would soften his path through the competition as much as she could by giving him good promotional opportunities above and beyond the others. It wouldn't be difficult as Lucifer would shine anywhere.

'And in return, you want me to seduce this Pastor?' said Venus. 'That's amazing!'

'Well, he's a danger to the program and a danger to Josh — and frankly a danger to civilized people with his Evangelical ranting,' said Jude. 'However, he is a very attractive man physically.'

'Aren't you afraid that I'll turn you down and tell people what you asked me to do?' Venus was curious. She wasn't in her son's confidence and this seemed like a very big gamble to her. Not that Venus disliked gambles.

'No,' said Jude simply. 'I'm a good judge of character.'

'What if I'm identified?' Venus continued. 'What if it comes out?'

'Not much harm done if it does,' said Jude. 'So, we set you on him! If he falls for the honey-trap then he's still an adulterer and he loses his credibility and we are justified. Yes, we'd take a rap — I'd take the rap myself because Mr Goldstone doesn't know anything about it — and he would, frankly, seriously oppose it. But we'll just be the ones who set it up; not the ones who fell into it.'

'So how would I do it?' Venus was tempted.

'Lucifer — and some of the others perhaps — will come with us to New York, out of interest and support for Josh. Obviously you have to accompany your son. We'll just make sure you have some time with Pastor Jo and the rest is up to you.'

'What if he doesn't go for it?'

'Then he doesn't go for it but — with respect, Ms Delmar — you have mind-power like your son and Pastor Jo is all ego. Ego falls in front of mind-power doesn't it?'

Jude knew that she was playing with fire but she was arrogant enough — and sure enough that she had the best intentions — to give the plan a shot. Venus felt exactly the same. Apart from anything else, the Pastor was well fit.

'But what proof do I have that you'll keep your word?' she asked.

'I'll get a current star name to date Lucifer in New York,' Jude said. 'He'll get great publicity with an actress or a chart-topping singer on his arm. I've got one in mind right now. All you have to do is agree to go to New York and I'll have you meet her there.'

'Deal,' said Venus. Behind her, looking just like an ordinary tourist — as long as you didn't look too hard — Lucifer grinned as he fed money into a slot machine. It was all going to plan. The machine belched quarters — they often did for Lucifer — and he walked away leaving his winnings for somebody else to collect.

Joe Palmer thought it was his lucky day, standing next to the machine that won just as the player left. It was a sign; he knew it was a sign! He was so confident in his luck that evening that he bet far more on Blackjack than he had ever intended, waiting again and again for the luck to turn, and went home ruined instead of just broke. Mammon enjoyed that one.

Lucifer made headlines throughout the Entertainment News media appearing in New York with Melanie D'Angelo, the new Bond girl, smiling and waving to waiting crowds with her arm tucked firmly into his. Melanie, who was six years Lucifer's senior, was mesmerized by the young man's charm and pleased about the publicity. They slept together as a matter of course and began a kind of non-exclusive mutual grooming relationship that was, initially, to be of great assistance to both of them.

Venus was enjoying herself too. She had been made-over by Chris's team at Jude's behest and, with a smoothed brow, collagen lips and hair extensions she looked and felt magnificent. Her room at the Plaza was next to the one in which Pastor Jo and his wife were staying and, with all the socializing and press calls that were taking place and Jude's quiet authority arranging for Beulah to separated from her husband at all possible points, she found it easy to worm her way to his side at the special dinner being put on by *Fox* for all the participants in the debate and their hangers-on. She smiled at the pastor, shook his hand, admired his preaching and exerted her full charm.

And Pastor Jo *was* charmed. He sat with Venus, laughed with Venus and flirted with Venus. He thought she was the perfect woman.

His wife Beulah sat glumly at another table with people she didn't know and who didn't bother to engage her in conversation. For weeks now she had been feeling rather left behind and was trying not to resent Jo's fame and fortune. She felt middle-aged and rather chubby in the light of her husband's amazing catapult to fame.

Money had been flooding in to the Church's coffers and Beulah had new outfits for herself, for the choir and new pews for the church but for all that, she still felt lonely and lost. She faded to gray compared with a magnificent dark temptress and fell back into the shadows, her heart fading from self-hatred and neglect.

If Josh had been there he would, most likely, have seen what was happening. But Josh was not there. He didn't like celebrity dinners so Jude had arranged for him to visit the local hospice where, if he could not halt death he could at least bring peace. She laughed to herself as he trotted off like a lamb.

Beulah was a good woman — good in the sense of doing what she believed she ought to do and taking care of others. She didn't smoke and she didn't drink and she had never been sexually promiscuous. She wasn't that smart and not at all devious. In a nutshell she had no defenses.

Lucifer said goodbye to his girlfriend at the hotel's front door after dinner and floated into the elevator beside Beulah just after Pastor Jo and Venus went to look at the panoramic night view of New York from the top of the hotel.

Here, we must give Pastor Jo his due; he was not an adulterer and he was, at heart, an honest man. He preferred power to sex and, despite the mesmerizing allure of this woman who truly appeared to be a soul-mate, he was very, very aware that his behavior must be whiter than white. Not for a moment did he wonder if Venus's interest in him was a set-up. Fortunately for all, Pastor Jo did have an innate innocence alongside his arrogance and he couldn't believe anyone would actually do that. He had a wonderful time and flirted for sure, but no more than that. She tried all her wiles and every ounce of magic she could but although it could tempt the ego, it could not touch a strong heart — or a prideful one.

So Venus failed in her task. But Lucifer, catching Beulah in the midst of her pain and fear, carried out his real plan to perfection.

Although he couldn't directly affect Josh with his energies, he knew he could manipulate those around him. And he was quite skilled enough to hypnotise Beulah both into believing that he *was* Josh and that it was perfectly natural and justifiable to desire Josh. Lucifer had to grit his teeth to achieve his goal, but it was such a divinely wicked thing to do that he couldn't resist turning the tables on everyone — especially that cold bitch of a PR woman. He charmed Beulah, flattered her and made her see him as the perfect gift from God to make her feel whole again. She couldn't see Lucifer; she was drunk with his mind-melding and, had you asked her, she would have sworn that she was being seduced by Josh Goldstone. What she did know was that she walked into the lift a broken woman and came out infused with something that made her feel simultaneously extra-ordinary, beautiful and whole again.

Half an hour later, with clothes torn and covered with dust from — oh, the shame of it! — a cleaning cupboard, she stood, shaking from head to foot, outside her hotel room door, horrified, and paralyzed with guilt at what she had done.

She blundered into the room and, on a reflex turned on the TV just in time to see the local news programme broadcasting live from the hospice that the real Josh was visiting. Some reporter was talking about amazing healings and, just as Beulah began to say. "No…no…no!" in disbelief, Josh himself appeared on screen. Below the picture, the statement "Live" shocked itself into Beulah's soul and the last traces of the hypnotic link snapped.

Her world fell apart.

Lucifer didn't tell anyone — not even his mother. He didn't realise that his plan to incriminate Josh had fallen apart and slept the sleep of the satisfied. But Beulah, aghast with horror at herself, spent a sleepless, wretched night and then confessed to her husband that she had had sex with an unknown man in a broom cupboard while drunk. She made her confession while Pastor Jo was sitting in his dressing room at *Fox*, an hour-and-a-half before the all-important recording began.

Pastor Jo wasn't the kind of man to be able to see any personal responsibility in the situation in that he had flaunted another women in front of his already delicate, neglected wife. All he saw was his partner-in-Christ's weakness in comparison with his own strength; that she had let him down and shamed him at the most important juncture of his life. Beulah reeled out of the dressing room as his scathing condemnation tore her apart. She wept and pleaded but he cast her out (for the moment at least) and slammed the door on her to try and regain some equanimity before this all-important TV show.

Had Beulah still believed that her partner of the night before had been Josh, then all hell would have broken loose. But as it was, instead of firing the Pastor up with solid evidence of Josh's demonic presence, the news collapsed his ego into a spiral of horror.

Had it been a live broadcast, he might have been able to pull himself together more; it's amazing how you can rise to the occasion if there is no second chance to shine. But the Network had insisted that this was pre-recorded in order to be able to edit where necessary. If it all went horribly wrong, they had the chance to drop it entirely (although all the religious stations had already placed their orders for a copy).

Salema visited Pastor Jo in make-up just to take him through the running-order. The pastor was due to go on first, being interviewed, and then Josh would come on and the two were to be invited to debate with Salema holding the balance.

'What's wrong?' she said immediately. There was no doubt that this powerful man had received a body blow, no matter how he tried to hide it.

'Nothing,' he said bravely — and Salema could see that it was bravery. But she could also see that he had lost the plot. If he didn't pull himself together, the show could be in jeopardy.

'Wait here,' said Salema, unnecessarily because Pastor Jo was then under the complete power of Diane the Make-up Lady — and Attila the Hun would not have escaped her clutches.

The Sufi swept out of the room and round the corner to where Josh was being powdered.

'Come with me,' she said. It was a definite order and, as Josh was only with Diane's deputy, there was some chance that it could be obeyed. With a polite, 'Excuse me,' Josh got up and followed her to the doorway of the room where Pastor Jo sat slumped in his chair.

He stopped outside, sensing the man's deep distress, and touched Salema on the arm, shaking his head.

'He doesn't want my help,' he said. 'He won't let me heal him. If we're going to go ahead —?'

'We have to!' said Salema. 'The audience is in and the producers would go spare. And you can't quit just because he's already beaten.'

'Then we must make him fight,' said Josh. 'It has to be a fair fight. I can't go on with him like this. I'll go in...I'll...Well, I'll do something. You leave him to me, if you will.

Salema stood back and watched as Josh walked in to offer his hand to Pastor Jo. The older man's energy flared slightly but it was nothing to what it might have been.

Then Josh bent down and whispered something in the pastor's ear. To Salema who, it had to be admitted, was now peeping, it looked as though a balloon inflated itself. Whatever Josh had said was sufficient to out-weigh the pastor's own concerns. Pastor Jo took in a giant breath of air taking strength from outrage and color filled his face again. Ignoring Diana-the-Hun, he threw down the sheet covering the front of his suit, stood up to his full height and began to roar insult and condemnation.

'You spawn of Satan! Hypocrite! You will be damned to hell for what you just said!'

'I'll see you later, Sir,' said Josh, turning and leaving the room.

'What in God's name did you say?' said Salema, trotting after Josh as his long stride took him swiftly back to his dressing room.

'I told him that I was the Anointed Messiah for this generation,' said Josh grimly.

'But you don't tell lies!'

Josh turned to her and gave a tight smile. 'No, I don't, do I?' he said.

Chapter Twenty Nine

'What have you done? What have you *done?*'

Jude had never seen Josh angry before. Now, he was blazing. With only minutes to go before recording began, he had taken the stairs to the production gallery two at a time, caught Jude's arm and swung her out of the room, slamming the door behind them so that no one could overhear.

'I can see your fingerprints all over this,' he said, knowing he didn't have to explain what he was talking about. Her whole electro-magnetic field was radiating smugness.

'You've done *something.* Something dishonest and cruel — and you've hurt people who aren't smart enough to see you coming! God forgive you for what you've started!'

Jude bristled, about to defend herself.

'I don't have time for you now,' he said. 'I have a television program to do. But you will rue this day, believe me.'

She leant back against the wall, suddenly breathless as he raced away down the stairs. Part of her was shocked and upset but another part exhilarated. She had moved it all on! Perhaps Venus had broken Pastor Jo; perhaps something else had happened. But something had *happened.* Now it could be spun and worked so that the world knew who he was and what he could do.

And she — *she!* — was the one who was making it real.

'What on Earth was that about?' asked Philippa, who had been pacing anxiously in the observation gallery. She had always been uncertain about the wisdom of this show and she didn't like what she'd seen on Josh's face.

'Dynamite,' said Jude, quashing her qualms with the satisfaction of achievement. 'Josh is going to be the biggest star this celebrity-ruled world has ever seen.'

'Ah,' said Philippa. There wasn't very much else she could say. And the show was about to begin.

The TV show *was* dynamite. It did more to establish Salema as the best talk show host in the world than anything else could possibly have done. How she managed to hold a balance between Pastor Jo's roaring fury and fire and Josh's sure, certain and powerful calm she, herself, would never know. But her show had the exclusive of a man — a man *known* to be able to raise the dead — saying clearly and authoritatively that he was Anointed by God; that he was here with a message of love for *all* humanity, not just Christians or Jews and that he was here to help people to understand that they were themselves sons and daughters of God and that they could do all that he could do as soon as they could understand and realize that.

Pastor Jo threw thunderbolts and lightning at his opponent and Josh fielded every one. His knowledge of Scripture (and that included Hindu, Buddhist, Jain, Bahai, Muslim and Zoroastrian Scripture) out-quoted any Biblical weapon that Pastor Jo could throw at him. He refuted definitively that humanity was in its last days. 'We're children; barely school-age in our development!' he said. He refuted the idea that to be a *Bene Elohim* you had to be *The* Christ, explaining (when Salema found him space to do so) that there were always Sons and Daughters of God in the world — and one Anointed in particular at any given time.

No, he was not Jesus Christ — only Jesus Christ was Jesus Christ. But every generation there was one Anointed Messiah and yes, at this moment in time, he was the one.

But, he added, in any case, in the faith of his birth, Judaism, there was no 'savior' because we are already saved. The story of Exodus tells how God showed us the way out of slavery so we are free. An external savior is an idea that takes away personal responsibility. Christ is within *us* not to be projected onto others. *Bene Elohim* like himself just try and point that out — again and again and again.

Other *Bene Elohim*? Who knows — Gandhi possibly, Ibn Arabi possibly? Buddha almost certainly. Mostly they weren't famous people; they just did their job anonymously.

No, they did not have to be Christians — Jesus, just to make a point, was a Jew — it was St. Paul who invented Christianity. Incidentally, he had the utmost respect for Christians and Christianity.

No he, Josh, wasn't setting himself up for anything; he was just here to show people (if they wanted to know) how to find themselves. Not even how to find God because the Source is already in everyone, but to remember that they are not slaves, they are free. Once we find our own joy and inner light then we are aligned and can know for ourselves.

There was no virtue in believing in someone else's God, we have to walk the path ourselves and discover what we actually do believe. The Source can't come and find us — It is only and utterly joy. If we are in joy we experience it but if we are in anger or hatred or even criticism, It can't join us because it is none of those things. We have to turn to It. That's why — he guessed — God was pretty unpopular nowadays. It let us make the decisions instead of ordering our lives for us.

No, he wasn't the Anti-Christ — or even one of his heralds. Again, that day (if it were to happen like that which, personally, he doubted), it was a very long way off.

He didn't raise *all* the dead because he only could help the dead if they asked him to; if they had had the revelation that there was more to do in this life and they wanted to come back. It was the dead asking him to help — not the living.

As far as he was aware, global warming was more caused by humanity's unhappiness, inner pollution and self-hatred than flying Lear Jets or driving in BMWs.

The same with war — it would stop when we stop hating at all levels.

No, he couldn't stop the cruelty, badness, killing and pain — because it needed all human minds to be at peace for the world to stop reflecting what we feel within. And too many people benefited from the existence of war for it to be easily ended.

Did he care if he was mocked or reviled, called a liar etc. etc? No, not really. People had a right to think what they wanted to think.

What had he to say to the death threats? That he wasn't afraid of dying and would go home when his job was done.

Pastor Jo, apoplectic with fury, nearly shouted Salema down as she moved to wind up the show. Her incredible dignity stopped him in his tracks — which was quite a feat. Josh didn't turn a hair.

As she closed, Salema stood up and walked towards the camera, leaving her guests behind. 'I don't know what's true and what's not true,' she said. 'All I do know is that I suffered for many years from psoriasis and that when this man' (she gestured at Josh) 'touched me, the disease vanished. Whatever you may think or believe, I hope this program has made you think about *you* and how you relate to the world. If Pastor Joseph Sadd is right, then Josh Goldstone is an impostor and a charlatan. If Josh Goldstone is right, we all need to be peaceful and loving for our world to reflect that back to us. Even if Josh Goldstone *is* an impostor then I, for one, can't argue with the message he brings today.

'Thank you and goodbye.'

'*You* are going to hell!' said Pastor Jo to Josh as they walked off the set (Maude-Lynn's crew caught this neatly). The Pastor's face looked leaden; the adrenaline from the last hour was draining away as the world re-asserted itself.

'You are already there,' said Josh. 'You are in so much pain. And so is your wife.'

'Don't you talk to me about my wife!' Pastor Jo stopped dead in his tracks, a blue vein pulsing on his forehead. He was suddenly terrified that this magician might know what had happened to Beulah.

All Josh did know was that the colors and lines around Pastor Jo and his wife were wrong; distorted and warped and that Jude's energy (and another currently unidentifiable one) were in there too. As the Pastor stomped off, he hesitated, looking within himself and totally ignoring anyone around him. It was fortunate perhaps that there was such a strange light around him that no one knew what to say to him or how to approach him. Mary-Beth would have stood quietly, a gentle hand ready if required; Jude would have commented (derisively) on his performance but neither was present. Thomas, who was his current minder, didn't say a word. Maude-Lynn stepped forward, in front of her own camera and touched him on the arm. He looked at her, pulling himself back from wherever he'd been.

'Give me a moment, alone,' Josh said and turned away to take some time out in the men's restroom. There he sat quietly in one of the cubicles and unraveled his mind until he could see clearly again.

Ah, Lucifer, the mind-bender was here! That explained a lot. He had everything to do with this. But what in Heaven's name was he doing in New York? Was that what Jude had done…? Something to do with Joseph's wife? Dear God, the poor woman — and the poor man! And he, Josh, had walked right into it, reacting by giving Pastor Jo the only source of strength he could have taken in order for the show to be a fair fight.

'Oh well,' he said, startling the sound recordist in the next cubicle who had thought that the lavatories were empty. 'I suppose it had to happen. But now what?'

'Now what?' turned out to be finding the local Evangelical Church where Pastor Jo had been invited for a celebration service following the recording. Jude could wait; Lucifer could wait. Everybody else could wait.

Luckily, as Salema's program was pre-recorded, it didn't technically exist outside of the studio audience and the production team so, when Josh told Thomas he needed to get to where Pastor Jo had gone, the crowds outside were minimal.

'Just us,' said Josh to Thomas. 'Not Jude.'

'We'll be shadowed,' said Thomas, meaning Maude-Lynn's team.

'They won't get into the church,' said Josh.

'Yeah, but where are we going?'

'Oh God, I don't know. You get so helpless when there are people looking after you all the time,' said Josh, knowing that Jude or Mary-

Beth would have found out the name of the church in seconds. But even though he had been cosseted for months, he still had a brain.

'Follow me,' he said to Thomas.

'Er…yes!' said his minder. 'That's my job!'

They found the back door security easily enough and through the guard there contacted the department that arranged cars for guests. Yes, they had the address of where they had dropped off Pastor Jo and his wife and friends and it was only the work of minutes to get another car to take Josh to the same location.

'We should report in,' said Thomas. 'People will be expecting you in the Green Room.'

'Pastor Jo has bypassed that bit. So shall I,' said Josh. 'If you want to let Philippa know that I'm with you that's fine but no more than that.'

'Josh, is there a problem? If so, Simon or Jude are the ones I should call!'

'No — yes — no.' Josh got into the car, greeting the driver with a handshake and a smile. 'I don't want Jude to know where I'm going and Simon would try and stop me. Thomas, it's a bit complicated but the less anyone knows the better.'

'I'm only concerned that you're safe,' said Thomas. 'We'll be out of walkie-talkie range and you know my cell phone won't work. That's all. I don't pretend to understand anything; I just show up and do my job as far as I can. I'm getting Jodie to come with Maude-Lynn's car because if we're going anywhere with a crowd we could need backup. They'll be far enough back for Jodie's cell to work.'

'Fine,' said Josh, not really attending. He still didn't know exactly what was happening but he could feel Beulah's distress in his soul and he had to do something to make amends.

The Church was a modern one built on cheap land, just off the freeway, with a huge car park and spiky architecture topped by an agonized, crucified Christ. Josh winced as he looked at it.

Thomas got out ahead of Josh but no one was expecting them and there were no security people from the church at hand so there seemed to be nothing to worry about. They walked into the reception area and then hesitated, realizing that everyone was in the church itself. Josh cringed; the waves of unhappiness and anger were palpable.

'Oh well, in for a penny…' He said and opened the swing doors into the church.

'Darn saints,' muttered Thomas, following. Maude-Lynn's car with Jodie in it was just stopping outside the glass doors.

Inside the church there was standing room only and the atmosphere was electric.

'Oh you stupid, stupid man,' murmured Josh to himself as Pastor Jo's voice rose in a snarl that virtually flattened the hair of everyone there. The Pastor was venting his fury on his wife – in public.

'That den of vice; that place of unspeakable sin has corrupted my very own flesh!' he roared. 'My wife, my own wife has been beguiled by Satan!'

'Too right,' muttered Josh at the back.

Beulah stood, to her husband's right, looking wan and defeated. She didn't know what had happened or how it had happened to her; how she had found herself in such disgrace. The memory of the now unknown man's soft words and seeking hands seemed repulsive to her now. How could she have succumbed? She didn't know. And she felt the same revulsion towards herself as her husband obviously did.

'Whore of Babylon!' hissed Pastor Jo. The congregation, uncertain but eager to oppose the devil began to hiss too.

'Enough!' said Josh, speaking up loudly from the back of the church. He felt an aureole of power surrounding him as he walked up the aisle. The sun came out and shone down on him through the clear windows of the church and Josh walked like a king, so certain was he in himself.

Pastor Jo and the congregation fell silent with shock.

'Enough of this! Have you never sinned? Have you never made a mistake? Have you never been beguiled or tormented?

'Pastor, your wife needs mercy and forgiveness not your hatred. Marriage is about partnership not separation. If this has happened to *you* Pastor Jo, it is because of *your* relationship with your wife. In your hunt for fame and in your desire to condemn, you have cast her out of your heart.

'She was only seeking love. Yes, she made a mistake. But we all make mistakes. Isn't your Christ all about forgiveness? What would *he* have to say about the woman who committed adultery? And what would he have to say about your telling the world your own private business? Let he who is without sin cast the first stone!'

For a moment there was a stunned silence. The congregation couldn't have argued if it tried, for Jesus's own words about the woman taken in adultery rang across the aisles.

With a squeal, Beulah ran to Pastor Jo and wept, 'Forgive me, forgive me. I love you!' And because Josh, right then, was so filled with the Kingdom of God and shone so regally and so beneficially, the genuine heart of Pastor Jo, so hurt by betrayal, softened with love for his silly, erring wife. He put his arms around her. She leant into him, tears running down her cheeks.

Josh gave a great sigh, turned on his heel and marched out of the church. No one but Thomas followed him; the congregation sat, stunned, not sure what had happened or who it was who had harangued the pastor and made the world softer and more pleasant again.

It would be nice to be able to say that all would be well in Pastor Jo's and Beulah's marriage from then on and that both of them appreciated Josh's intervention in their affairs. It would be nice to say that Pastor Jo saw, finally, that Josh was a good man who meant well and who had done what he could to mend the evil that celebrity had brought through his entourage.

But it would not be true. And although the Pastor and his wife stayed together and even had several talks which could only be of assistance to their relationship, they had to blame something or someone for what had happened. And Josh was the appropriate, manifestly heretic target. Beulah never dared to tell that she thought her broom cupboard lover was Josh; that would have never have been forgiven. But she could believe that he was the source of the witchcraft that had beguiled her. The tool they could both most easily use to mend their relationship was abhorrence for a mutual enemy and both hated him with a burning fire that consumed everyone who came near them.

Lucifer was puzzled and then angry that his plan did not have the results he expected. He never considered that Grace could intervene to demonstrate Josh's innocence. Perplexed, he licked his wounds in silence and his soul too fed on hatred for the new Messiah.

Chapter Thirty

'You tried to set him up? You tried to trick him into cheating on his wife?' Josh was pacing round the room while Jude sat calm and, apparently, unruffled.

'What's wrong with that? If he'd gone for it we would have seen exactly what kind of man he was. And you would have had the full advantage.'

'Jude, do you *know* what happened because of your meddling?'

She bristled slightly at the word. It was a new experience for Jude to see Josh angry and it both fired her adrenaline and interested her greatly. This was how she got her kicks so she over-ruled her irritation.

'No,' she said shortly.

'Lucifer got to Pastor Jo's wife.'

'Lucifer?'

'Yes, Lucifer. He damn well nearly got into my mind and I'm damn certain he got into yours.' For Josh, who rarely swore, two damns in a sentence was going some.

'He did not get into my mind,' said Jude. 'It was my idea.'

'What was?'

'To ask Venus to stake out Pastor Jo.'

'Oh Jude…' Josh shook his head. 'Don't you see? Not only do we have to be whiter than white we have to be *seen* to be whiter than white. Just doing that makes us gray.'

'Makes me gray,' she said gruffly, her eyes flashing. 'You had nothing to do with it.'

'Any gray works its way through everywhere,' he said, brushing his hair back and making a face. 'Honestly Jude, you've heard of the good intentions that pave the way to hell haven't you?'

'It worked out!' said Jude. 'Okay, the Pastor was clean — but his wife wasn't.'

'Oh she was. She was innocent,' said Josh. 'She was tricked. That boy does magic — real magic. Just like the story of the serpent in the Garden of Eden. And it's the woman who's blamed! And now both he and his mother think that magic is the kind of thing we *approve of!*'

'No they don't,' said Jude. 'I told them you mustn't know — that you'd stop it if you did.'

Josh sighed.

'What did you promise them in return?' he asked.

'They've got it,' she answered evasively.

'Got what?' Josh was behind her now, leaning over her shoulder with his hands on the back of the chair. Jude felt a frisson of his power; it felt delicious. She closed her eyes and drank it in.

'Lucifer got a film star on his arm,' she said. 'That raises his profile and that's what he wants.

'He's already got his own website, MySpace and Facebook fan pages — and there's a lot of interest in him. He'll get his own show in Vegas whether he wins or not and I said I'd help with that too.'

'Oh dear God,' Josh put his hand to his mouth and blew on his fingers. Jude turned in her chair and looked up at him; she had never looked so sparkling or alive.

'Look,' she said. 'It's my *job!* People have got to know about you — you wouldn't be in this world if that wasn't true would you? And okay, what I did wasn't ethical or good but the end result was that you declared who you really are on the TV program. You wouldn't have done that otherwise would you?'

'Probably not,' he said, frowning. 'Jude, I daren't trust you any more.'

'Yes you can trust me,' she said reaching out and touching his arm. 'You can trust me more than anyone. I'll make sure your message gets out.'

'Pheeeeww,' Josh exhaled. 'What if I don't want it to get out?'

'Josh, you have to step up to this!' Jude got up and squared her shoulders. 'For God's sake, you're the Messiah of this generation. You can't hide your light under a bushel.'

'Et tu Brute…?' said Josh. He turned and left the room without another word.

Jude smiled. She felt amazing. 'I'll do my job,' she said to the ceiling. 'No one else could, but I can.'

Salema's show with Josh and Pastor Jo was not due to go to air until the day after the final of *The Miracle Mile*. Philippa had insisted that it did not go out beforehand. 'It would be a dreadful distraction,' she said. 'We need people to focus on the contestants, not on a weird judge.' She was deeply concerned about what she called 'this miracle *stuff*'. This season they'd probably be able to get away with it — and a certain amount of notoriety was good. But not *that* much. Once the interview with Salema went to air, the fat would be in the fire in a big way.

'The very least they're going to say is that he was abducted by aliens when he was lost after Gemma died,' she said to Bartos. 'Or that he's an alien himself. I'm taking a long holiday once this show's over.'

'He could be for real,' said Bartos slowly. He had watched the recording tensed from head to toe.

'Oh yeah, right,' said Philippa.

'He does heal things. We saw that bird with our own eyes.'

'It was just stunned,' said Philippa.

But watching Josh interacting with the other judges and seeing how he managed to draw the very best out of each and every contestant, she softened. 'I don't know or care who or what he is,' she said. 'He's good at what he does.'

It was time for the dramatic knock-out round in *The Miracle Mile*. At this point, the 5000-strong audience made the decision who stayed and who went but, in the end, the people of America decided. The rule was one vote from any given telephone only. Gemma had disliked the tradition of people voting a hundred times for their favorite contestant. The software had been tricky and very expensive but she said it made the contest much fairer. Of course, people could call from a number of different phones if they really worked at it but the favoritism aspect was nothing like as strong.

The contestants were being coached, styled, prompted and advised 24/7 by the teams brought in to ensure that every one of the final fifty were good enough to have their own show. All the coaches were spies for the casinos and their theatres for even the droppings from *The Miracle Mile* were worth catching in sensation-hungry Vegas.

In the knock-outs, over a period of ten days the contestants put on ten different variety shows, each participant having two spots in the same show. The audience simply voted, 'Yes' or 'No' to each performer at the end of the evening — and that was that. They were guided by the four judges who gave their often pithy reviews between acts and every now and then the unexpected happened.

Not so much this time however. All the contestants predicted to go through made it with ease and little Melissa Brown wowed everyone with her gutsy rendition of The Pointer Sisters' 'Fire' and an extraordinarily melodic version of 'McArthur Park.'

'Why choose such old songs?' Gideon wanted to know. 'You couldn't have been born when either of them was a hit.'

'My grandpa used to play them,' Melissa confessed.

'Oh dear God!' Deborah winced. She was always saying that the whole point of the show was to be contemporary.

Marta, supremely beautiful and elegant, dressed in shimmering silver, put her arm around Melissa. 'What a lovely thought,' she said in her deep and delicately accented voice. 'And is your grandfather here, Sweetheart?'

'Yes,' Melissa gestured to where her parents and grandfather were sitting, to a great round of applause.

'Well the songs worked wonderfully,' said Gideon. Deborah sighed.

'Whatever!' she said. 'Now, your image still needs a little work, Honey. The twee little girl look is as outdated as your songs. Your song choices are appalling.'

'I liked the image and the songs,' said Josh. 'You have a freshness and a love of what you're doing that shines. Don't let yourself get jaded or forced into spaces that don't fit you.'

'Jaded?' Deborah took that as a personal insult. 'It's not jaded to be contemporary and play to your strengths. Not that you would know anything about that!'

Josh smiled deliberately widely with his un-whitened teeth.

'Don't you snarl at me!' said Deborah.

'Now, now,' said Marta with her entrancing smile that somehow made you feel caressed and nurtured while you were told off. 'It's just a matter of taste and I think gentlemen feel differently from ladies in this respect.'

'*I* thought…' said Sam, who could always draw the attention with a simple *'I.'*

Melissa stood with her toes together and her eyes wide. Everyone knew that it was Sam's opinion that really counted.

'Melissa, *I* thought…it was just…brilliant!'

The audience erupted. Melissa burst into tears of joy.

Lucifer too brought the house down. No one even needed to listen to the judges; he was mesmerizing. The spotlight loved him and he interacted directly with the audience in the first few rows, demonstrating frighteningly accurate psychic abilities.

But surprisingly, Deborah was the only one of the judges who liked him. While they were live with an audience, they were working more consciously than in the auditions and Lucifer couldn't get through to the conscious mind as well as to the ego.

Deborah gushed over him, which didn't actually do him any good. Reluctantly, Gideon and Sam approved him — though Sam said, 'Frankly, what you are doing is manipulative, old hat and quite unpleasant. Unfortunately, you are very good at it and as this is the kind of trickery that appeals to the world today I suspect you will do very well.'

Lucifer stood there without a muscle of his face moving. But Sam had a headache for the rest of the evening.

Josh just said, 'I agree with Sam.' He didn't get a headache because he deflected the thought shot at him right back to Lucifer who really, really didn't like that.

Marta felt dizzy whenever she stood next to Lucifer which she found uncomfortable and inappropriate. It never occurred to her that the feelings weren't coming from her at all. Lucifer might have been very smart in many ways but he was also lazy in others. He misread Marta's energy, assuming that what she wanted from Josh was sex and assumed (as he couldn't get into Josh's mind) that Josh wanted the same from Marta. Well, he wouldn't get it while Lucifer was around…and if he, Lucifer, could get in there instead, that would be one small but important victory.

Simon Libiyah and Barbara Abbas were the other front-runners. Barbara was strongly political and had already used her small level of fame to run a powerful online blog about the situation in the Middle East — Barbara was a fundamentalist and wanted everyone to know it. The judges debated beforehand whether to warn her off the politics but decided that it was best to say nothing and hope that she got too busy selecting music and rehearsing to devote much more public time to her beliefs.

However, when she sang 'Let My People Go', there was a general round of sighing when it came to the time of judging. Sam was the only one who stepped out of the agreed line and, in his own inimitable style, squashed her with a succinct phrase.

'You know, Barbara,' we all think we know what's right and wrong in the world when we're young,' he said. 'But usually we are mistaken. In case you hadn't noticed, this is a talent show and if you keep choosing politically-motivated songs like that you will lose and deservedly so.'

Josh advised her to work on her breathing as the audible intakes of breath were affecting her performance. Gideon thought she still showed great promise (that one offended her more than the others!) and Deborah advised her to get her long, straight hair cut as she looked like a refugee from the lank plain 2000s look.

Again, Marta took the younger woman's side. 'It is very beautiful hair,' she said, aware that her own outshone it in every way.

Stuart White was simply breathtaking; supple, amusing and adept. All four judges were impressed and intrigued by the fact that an acrobat could also be such an amazing humorist.

'To call you a clown would be an insult,' said Gideon. 'You're not slapstick, you're witty, you're urbane, you're incredible!'

'A joy to watch. Your enthusiasm shines out of you,' said Josh.

'Most attractive,' purred Deborah.

'Amazingly, I agree,' said Sam. 'Not with Deborah obviously…'

'Now, now,' said Marta again, waving her finger and pouting. This was becoming her catchphrase echoed by the studio audience. They loved her beauty, her body, her accent, her talent and, particularly, the softness in her eyes when she looked at Josh. Already more than one magazine had postulated her suitability as someone to mend 'the broken heart of tragic Josh Goldstone' and there would be more press speculation to come. Sam thought it ridiculous but Marta wasn't Sam's type anyway; he preferred his women less emotional. Marta might be an angel on stage but in the dressing room she could weep like a teenager or sulk or have some completely unidentifiable mood at the drop of a hat. She would be all apologies and gifts afterwards saying she didn't know what had come over her. Even so, all her entourage walked carefully around her; they knew better than to question anything she said when she was in one of her states. Unless, that was, Josh Goldstone was on his way to see her. If that was the case she required advance warning and was suddenly wreathed in smiles with any previous upset completely forgotten.

As usual, the only one who didn't notice the feminine attention on him was Josh himself. Everyone has a fatal flaw.

Oddly enough, the relationship between Josh and Jude was not visibly damaged by the Pastor Jo incident after all. No one but those two knew exactly what had happened.

All that anyone nearby (which meant Maude-Lynn and her team) did know was that the two of them had a long talk in private which ended with Josh saying, 'I'm so sorry Jude; it's not going to be easy for you in the long run,' as he left her office.

But Joe and Maria, who were in Las Vegas both to over-nurture Josh while Mary-Beth was away and to have a well-deserved holiday themselves, were vaguely aware of something going on with Jude and Josh. They remembered the conversation that the three of them had had on the way into LA on the day Josh came back to them and Maria asked tentatively, 'You said Jude could be trusted up to a point. Have you reached that point yet?'

Josh considered. One of the things about him that drove people crazy was that he would never be pushed into a reaction. Live on air, he was crisp and precise but outside of the theatre or studio he considered everything deeply before replying. This was not very helpful for anyone in a hurry asking him what kind of sandwich he wanted for lunch.

'On reflection, no,' he said eventually.

There is honor among thieves and both Venus and Lucifer kept quiet about their end of the deal. All they really cared about was whether they were getting what they wanted. Venus saw nothing wrong with alliances that served all parties and Lucifer didn't want it getting out that he, who was beautiful, was willing to seduce unattractive women of a questionable age, especially when he had a hot, famous girlfriend *and* a chance with the glamorous new presenter.

Lucifer was actually feeling quite uncomfortable; in this world of celebrity, he was having more trouble getting control over people's minds than he had expected. The 5000-strong audience in the theatre was a piece of cake. Their votes for him were so overwhelming that he could afford to scale back his charm a little. But he couldn't do quite as well with the television audience as they were not within his own personal orbit and also were strongly influenced by the judges' views. Josh in particular repeatedly warned Lucifer publicly about arrogance — the 'Ego-testicle' remark had long topped Lucifer's ratings on YouTube and would follow him around for the rest of his performing career. Josh would say again and again, 'You are very talented but don't push for it; let it come to you.' As for Sam, the better Lucifer did, the more the older judge loathed him with every ounce of his own massive arrogance. Sam didn't have the self-knowledge to understand why the young man irritated him so very much but he knew that the hairs on the back of his neck stood up when Lucifer looked at him. Sam could hold onto his own mind but Lucifer could still send strands of color in there. The technique with everyone else was to weave color and feeling to make them release endorphins so they felt happy and fulfilled. They subconsciously associated those feelings with their source — Lucifer. Normally, if someone makes you feel loved, secure and happy, you like them — and you would vote for them. Ironically though, Lucifer's attempts to coerce Sam into feeling entertained, happy or satisfied backfired again and again.

The fact was that Sam only saw pleasure in self-attained achievement and in the prospect of new worlds to conquer not in peace or contentment. So Lucifer's attempts to interfere with Sam's mind threatened his mindset and so had the opposite effect from the one intended.

Lucifer was having to work hard and he didn't like that one bit. The odds on the official and unofficial websites were that he would come in second to Barbara Abbas. Second place, to Lucifer, meant nowhere. And he still had work to do in discrediting Josh. To a certain extent, the world was doing that for him — and when the TV interview with the pastor went out, Lucifer knew that the powers of hell would be unleashed against his adversary. But he was impatient; he wanted Josh to fall further and faster and sooner than that. Luckily for Josh, evil is naturally chaotic and undisciplined and, with all the effort he was having to make to win the competition, Lucifer was taking time to formulate a definite plan for his enemy's destruction. However, Josh was making other, even more powerful enemies every day.

Each evening, he defied police advice and went out with at least two of his minders and with Maude-Lynn and her team, to spend time with the people who had heard of him, believed in him, and hoped that he could heal them and their lives. Josh and the team had to drive away from the compound or they would never have got anywhere but this strategy worked well. Sometimes he just shook a hand in the street and sometimes he moved through an entire bar full of people just touching, saying a word or offering a smile. More and more, the people wanted to hear him speak and often he would sit in a pizza house or somewhere, surrounded by people all with a meal and a drink who were taking in everything he said about love and compassion and the importance of focusing the mind on good and not on bad. No one actually noticed that the staff turned off the generic Muzak but, almost always, they did.

What the people who wanted to listen to Josh didn't want to do was gamble. And when Josh was in or near a casino none of the wireless equipment worked which really made the owners angry — so much so that, once they had worked out what was happening, they began to ban him from their premises and even threatened to sue him for loss of earnings. Slowly, over the three months of the show, as the news got around about the miracles that were happening in Vegas, the motels began filling up with people who were coming for hope and salvation, not for Mammon. As the rain fell and fell and the drought receded, so did the gambling halls' profits. The healed did not drink or take drugs; they did not gamble or waste money; they just went home. The whole world had just recovered from a huge recession but now the recovery was being eroded and it was quite clear exactly who was the cause of the rot.

So far it was only a groundswell but economists began to wonder, to consider and to make sometimes rather disconcerting plans.

One evening, as *The Miracle Mile* was in full swing, a small figure walked off a plane from Chicago wearing a simple beige raincoat and dark shades despite the rain. Her hair was shaved almost to her head, and she walked with a strong, quiet confidence.

Everyone was expecting Mary-Beth to return with full breasts, a smaller nose, a bum tuck and liposuction at the very least. As she walked into the office in the morning, the gasps of surprise were palpable.

Josh unfolded himself from his comfortable leather chair and held his arms out to her and Mary-Beth walked straight into them. It was the hug of the best of friends, not of lovers, but it was a hug of two people in total accord. Sally saw it happened and the only word she could use to describe it was 'golden'.

'But…!' said Jude when she saw Mary-Beth.

'But…!' said Maude-Lynn when she saw Mary-Beth.

'Good God!' said Sam when he saw Mary-Beth.

'Oh my…!' said Deborah when she saw Mary-Beth.

'Way-to-go!' said Gideon when he saw Mary-Beth.

'Oh! Your beautiful hair!' said Marta.

'Oh my dear, I'm so glad!' said Mattie in genuine delight.

'Why is everyone so surprised?' asked Mary-Beth with a furrowed brow as she sorted out packets of genuine Darjeeling tea in Josh's office.

'I think people thought you had gone away to have surgery,' said Josh, meekly accepting a cup of black Darjeeling instead of his preferred *PG Tips*.

'Surgery? I wasn't ill!' said Mary-Beth. 'What are you laughing at?'

'You,' said Josh. 'You went to see Colin and Chris before you headed off for er — *Europe*.'

'So?'

'You dear, dim girl! Everyone thought you'd gone to have cosmetic surgery — to make yourself more beautiful.'

'What?' Mary-Beth stopped dead to consider. 'How very stupid! *You* didn't think that did you?'

He looked at her with a smile. Mary-Beth was standing completely in her own power. She looked taller; more spacious and true. And the *Stavros no. 1* haircut really suited her.

'No, Mary-Beth I didn't. I know how much you hate the ending to *Grease* when Sandy transforms herself,' said Josh gently.

'Too right!' said Mary-Beth, her eyes blazing. 'And those stupid people thought I'd gone off to get a new face and body to attract *you?*'

'I think they did,' nodded Josh.

'Dumb,' said Mary-Beth dismissively.

'So where *did* you go?' asked Josh curiously. 'Did you have a good holiday? You look like a Buddhist monk with your hair all cut.'

'Do you like it?' Mary-Beth was suddenly the little girl again instead of the spiky defensive Valkyrie.

'Yes I do.'

'I'm glad,' she said simply. 'Now, I need to have a serious talk with you. We've got a lot of work to do.'

'We have?' he said, amused. That week his image was on the front page of *Time* and *Newsweek* and, with leaks of the Salema show already on YouTube, he was probably one of the most famous people in the USA if not the Western World. Jude had been doing her job well of late. But he obviously didn't impress Mary-Beth.

'Yes,' said Mary-Beth. 'I went to see Colin and Chris because Chris's brother is a monk in India. He's pretty well connected, actually.'

She took a deep breath. 'I went to see the Dalai Lama…'

'Which is why you cut your hair? You've become a Buddhist nun?'

Mary-Beth snorted. 'You can't do that in four weeks. You know that! I shaved it because I was living in a dormitory and someone had lice.'

'Ah,' said Josh nodding and trying not to laugh at her solemn little face. 'And obviously the Dalai Lama did meet with you. How could he not?'

'Well he did,' said Mary-Beth seriously. 'It took about a week. But he's very interested in you.'

'He is?'

'Well yes — he's a *Bene Elohim* too isn't he? Anyway, we've agreed,' she continued. 'Once this show is over, you and I are going to India and then we're going to help him to liberate Tibet,'

That took the ticket. Josh just sat there with his mouth open.

'Josh, you've got to get moving,' said Mary-Beth drinking her own Darjeeling with commendable self-control. 'There's a whole world out there that needs you. We don't have much time.'

Chapter Thirty One

As far as the public was concerned, *The Miracle Mile* was doing very well indeed, with enough trauma and tantrums to make great TV. Ratings were up on last year. Some of that was the ghoulishness of wanting to see how they did without Gemma (there had been a long film tribute to her during the first live show); some was a sympathy vote for Josh; some was because people wanted to see the man who could do miracles; some was because Marta was so cool she was hot, hot, hot! But most of it was due to an engaging team and a winning format.

By now they were down to the final eight in each section and each one of them was a nationwide celebrity with their own websites, regular input on YouTube and other video sites, blogs and all kinds of unofficial comment sites. Their faces graced the front covers of a hundred magazines and they were golden-handcuffed to perform exclusively for *The Miracle Mile* in Vegas for the next full year. Josie Jones, Janice Colliver, Stuart White, Barbara Abbas, Colm O'Reilly, Simon Libiyah and Lucifer were all through and so was Melissa Brown. Melissa wasn't conventional star-material but somehow the US audience had taken to her youth and integrity. It became obvious too that she was hopelessly in love with Josh; she sang all her songs to him and, while this was thought charming to start with, it wasn't going to do her any good in the long run. Josh tried very hard to point out to Melissa that for her own sake, she should appear more detached.

Marta, on the other hand, encouraged Melissa's crush, commenting on it live on air and agreeing that the English Judge was all that was charming. Her radiant smile launched in Josh's direction was enough to encourage the already-growing speculation that they either were, or were going to be, an item.

This irritated Sam extremely even though he didn't want Marta for himself; he was used to being the star-candy and, let's face it, he kept in great shape, had regular Botox and wore designer outfits. It simply wasn't right that the most fêted woman in television had eyes only for the worn-out, lazy, would-never-have-made-it-if-his-wife-hadn't-died holy-moly loser. And that was his description on a good day.

On the show, however, he couldn't fault Josh's professional taste nor his comments. Sometimes Josh even said something incisive that threatened to change Sam's mind over a contestant's performance. What was also interesting was that the rejected contestants were still responding amazingly to Josh's final comments about what they should do next. Where Sam would say, 'Give up singing, you're just not good enough to make it,' Josh would say 'I think you've got just the voice for a career in animated films. Why don't you go and bang on the door at Pixar?' Where Sam would say, 'Lose the pretentiousness, darling, and get yourself a job. You might be able to perform your act at the country fair each summer,' Josh would say, 'You've done your best; now you can give it up and do what you really, in your heart wanted to do. You only really wanted to be a star to show others what you could do — and you've done that. So decide where you want to live, move away from home and start living your own life.'

Perhaps the saddest elimination was David, a 25-year-old blind man who sang like an angel but had a podgy face and rocked back and forwards like Stevie Wonder on speed while making flailing gestures with his arms. Had David been cute, he would have got through to the final and, if he'd not been blind from birth, he might have been able to understand how other people moved and gestured.

Simon and James used to imitate David's jerks and arythmical movements. It wasn't meant to be malicious or mocking; it was just horribly funny. The trouble was that they weren't the only people doing that and, in the end, celebrity in the modern competitive world has to have some relationship to glamour. David could never have glamour.

Andrew, who had been impressed by what both John Jordan and Mary-Beth told him about Buddhism and who was now deeply interested in the idea of Karma, asked Josh whether being born blind was David's Karma from a previous life (had he put out the eyes of someone else?) or was it something that his parents had done to have deserved the difficulty of raising a disabled child.

'Probably neither,' said Josh pragmatically. 'I expect something went wrong with the baby's growth in the womb and the souls concerned decided to go ahead with the birth anyway. Or maybe David would never have discovered his voice if he'd had sight. Or maybe he would have been an air force pilot killed in Iraq when he needs to live a long life and to be the father to some sacred child.'

'Blimey, that's a bit complex,' said Andrew.

'Well life is complicated in that respect,' said Josh. 'Everyone has their own story. You've got to be careful with Karma because the truth is that you'll never know. And mostly it's not your business.'

'Are you going to heal him?' asked John.

'Only if he wants me to,' said Josh. 'He hasn't so far. I can understand that; it might be really hard becoming sighted after a lifetime of using other skills.'

But David did want to be healed. He had just thought, erroneously as it turned out, that he had a better chance in the contest with a disability. The morning after he was eliminated, he asked one of Jude's staff if he could have a moment alone with Josh. Jude herself asked on his behalf and Mary-Beth came to fetch David from the reception area.

'Why do you want to see?' asked Josh, who never beat about the bush.

David didn't react the way a sighted person would — as in, 'Of course I want to see!' He said, 'So I can learn how to become a better singer.'

'But you're an excellent singer.'

'I lost because I can't see,' said David. 'But I love to sing and I'd like to have a career as a singer so I'd like to do my best. I'd like to be independent. And I'd like to marry and see my wife and my child.'

'Okay,' said Josh. 'But think about it before you make the final decision. Close your eyes; I'm going to touch you now so don't be afraid.'

He touched the young man on his closed eyelids and David felt a frisson of light pour through him.

'Go back to your room for a while and bathe your eyes,' said Josh. 'You'll be able to see for a couple of hours. If you like it and want it to be permanent, just say so and it will be. If you don't, just bathe your eyes again and the sight will go.'

David nodded and stood up.

'Thanks,' he said. 'I will want to see.'

But an hour later, he wasn't quite so sure. The complexity of sight, the distractions, the brightness, the contrast and movement were all extraordinarily frightening. David couldn't balance himself correctly or relate to perspective. His reflection in the mirror horrified him as did the discontent and sadness he saw on people's faces outside his room. After an hour had passed he had a headache from stress. If Mary-Beth hadn't knocked on his door at one hour 55 minutes, he might well have washed the sight away again.

As it was, Josh sat with him for the rest of the day, discussing his reaction. He explained very gently about the brain's reticular activating system that filters images and sounds. David's had never had to work with sight and was seriously overloaded which made it want to reject the new gift and return to the safety of nothingness. In addition, he had suddenly realized that he would have to give back his seeing-dog Rifka, whom he loved with a passion.

No one knew how they worked it out but David went home with just a nominal amount of sight which still meant he could be registered as blind. Over the next three years, his eyes recovered completely — by which time Rifka was too old to be re-assigned. A quiet miracle but a perfect one.

So, *The Miracle Mile* was a huge success. But Las Vegas itself wasn't happy.

People were still flocking to the town: that wasn't the problem. In the past they had flocked there to see *The Miracle Mile* and the other shows and to play the machines and the tables at the same time. Now, it was a different demographic of audience who were certainly very happy to move into the cheap hotel rooms and eat the free or cheap food — but who avoided the slot machines. The campsites were full too with people traveling long distances to see the miracle healer. The problem to the economy was growing.

Having now been banned from the pizza places by both their and his security people, most afternoons, from 2pm to 3pm, Josh would give a talk for free in the big gathering area outside the *Miracle Mile* auditorium and from 3pm to 3.30pm he walked in the crowd talking and healing. This was still the bane of the security people's life — and a complete anathema to all the production staff — but Josh was insistent despite the continuing wet weather.

'Better that it's wet, then only the people who want to come will come,' he said.

There were still many hundreds — if not thousands — of people who wanted Josh to come to them. They couldn't get to Las Vegas or they couldn't leave their hotel and they shouted very loudly for his attention in the media, on the telephone and via the Internet. But most people with a genuine need could and did get to Vegas.

'It's part of the test of faith,' said Josh. 'It's their faith that heals them, not me. So if they're not prepared to ask for the first miracle that would enable them to show up I couldn't do anything for them anyway.'

While what happens in Vegas stays in Vegas, you can't tell that to the international press and several reporters managed to sneak in to do 'exposés' or criticisms. Maude-Lynn threw them out cheerfully when she could identify them but a couple of reports got through. The first was of Josh eating a cheap hamburger with screaming headlines of how an alleged healer shouldn't eat rubbish food or give the impression that such food was good for others who would surely imitate him.

For that one, Jude just re-issued an old quotation from Jesus that nothing that goes into someone can defile them, it's what comes out.

The second news item was angrier and lasted longer. A wealthy family from Saudi Arabia brought their daughter to Josh asking for healing from leukemia. They could afford a private jet to Las Vegas, a suite at the most expensive hotel and an entourage to take themselves and their child to the afternoon meeting. The little girl was so sick she had her own ambulance which tried to make its way through the intensely irritated crowd.

Even Josh hesitated for there were so many of his own countrymen and women who were asking him for help and, the first day, the Saudis did not get into the compound. But, on the second day, the child's mother, in full Burkha, queued from dawn and begged a minute of Josh's time. He called her in and she fell at his feet saying she knew she was the daughter of his traditional enemy and that fundamentalists of her Islamic faith had hurt people of the United States but, please, to spare some of his great love for her child for she could see he had enough for the whole world.

Josh raised her up with tears in his eyes and agreed to see her daughter privately that night after the show. The next day, the Saudis left just as they had come but with a much smaller medical entourage.

The press went crazy. Josh was pilloried across the world for giving precedence to wealthy foreigners — and Muslims at that. Pastor Jo roared defiance and several religious groups were quoted as saying it was 'not tactful' to put foreigners before local people.

Jude was amazed to find that she actually got a quote from Josh about that one! He said simply that the world had no borders if you looked at it from space and that one sick child was as worthy as any other whatever her religion. It wasn't enough for the press, of course, but it was sufficient for them to chew on for another few days until the next celebrity mishap.

The daily meetings continued. Simon and several of his team

muttered and complained and criticized but Andrew, John and Jodie listened spellbound to Josh's talks every day. Jude, Mattie and Mary-Beth too would make time to come down and listen and Maude-Lynn filmed every single afternoon. She was thoroughly enjoying life at last, loving having a real purpose and, together with Jude, Jon Taylor and his IT team, she had revamped Josh's website to reflect his teachings, posting a new video every day. She made sure, at Josh's request, that the recordings on the net did not show the individual healings although she did film those — the most dramatic being the healing of a deaf boy with a cleft palate and the people who simply got up from their wheelchairs and walked. Within two weeks of the improved site's being up they had four million subscribers and had to hire doctors to proffer general medical advice (without diagnosis) and discussion board moderators.

Mattie and Josh still had lunch and supper regularly, somewhat to Marta's disgust. The beautiful presenter believed that she was about to hunt down her quarry. He obviously enjoyed her company and was very happy to be her escort to all kinds of celebrity functions where film stars, rock stars and the very, very rich of all persuasions put up with the fact that their cell phones wouldn't work for a couple of hours. They looked wonderful together — like a king and queen she thought — but Marta couldn't comprehend his fondness for the frumpy women around him. Mary-Beth might look better with the crazy hair style but, let's face it, she was a no one and it could only be his immense kindness that meant that he voluntarily spent time talking to her. Jude, she could understand, for the woman was elegant and proud, but she was spoken for and, once Marta found out about her relationship with Charlie, she could relax on that front.

Maude-Lynn was assessed as a possible threat but only in a cursory way; she appeared tarnished and used in Marta's eyes even though the journalist had regained much of her youthful vibrancy.

'It's not that I'm *trying* to cut back on the bad stuff,' Maude-Lynn explained to Jude who had complimented her, one day, on the healthy glow of her skin. 'It's just that I *can't* drink much any more. It makes me feel ill.'

'Something about raising vibrational levels, I suppose,' said Jude, who'd been very interested in that day's talk about resonance and how the world reflected back the individual's own vibrational frequency.

Marta listened to Josh's talks politely when she had the time. She had no problem with her boyfriends having a hobby or an obsessive lifestyle – she had briefly dated a top NASCAR driver who was fanatical about his work and about cars in general. As a Catholic she gently disapproved of Josh's Judaism and graciously perceived that his talks were essentially interdenominational. Her own knowledge of her faith was basic so when Josh spoke of the Ten Commandments and loving one's neighbor as one's self (no more and no less) and of aligning with the Source Energy she felt that, despite the slight strangeness of the context he wasn't doing anything that actually was wrong.

And he made her feel so good! When Marta was with Josh she walked differently, she laughed more, she felt intelligent. He was somehow reflected in her. But although he would hold her hand when they walked along a red carpet and put his arm around her shoulder in public, he only kissed her as a friend not as a lover and she simply couldn't get time with him alone. Her complaints about the others who were willing to share him where she was not did not endear her to any of Josh's team.

She was coming to realize that she might have miscalculated: perhaps it was still early days after his bereavement. More and more she knew that Josh was the man for her and she could be the patient hunter, casting silver cobweb-like nets that he would barely feel. She was certain she would win in the end. After all, she only had to look in the mirror to know that she was irresistible.

Jude and Maude-Lynn tried to warn Josh that he might be getting into hot water with Marta but he laughed and said that destiny had other plans.

'Perhaps you should tell her that before she really falls in love with you,' said Jude.

'You can't stop people falling in love,' said Josh.

'Have you any idea how callous you are?' said Jude, provoked beyond her usual detachment.

'Yes,' he said. 'But you know there's so much to deal with and think about that I really do have to let most of it sort itself out. If I try to interfere then I'll just make a hash of it. All I can really do is try to be myself and try to teach others to be themselves.'

Jude softened at once. She, of all people, knew the energetic pressures on Josh. She didn't exactly shield him from the oceans of publicity, criticism, condemnation, adoration and inaccuracy about him that flooded the world media but she didn't push his nose into it either. He trusted her to do what she could, when she could and, she had to admit, Maude-Lynn was a complete gem in helping her and her team to do just that.

'Marta wants marriage,' was all that she said.

'And she has every right to,' replied Josh smiling. 'But it won't be with me.'

He sighed. 'You're right; I must say something to her about that.' But *Bene Elohim* though he might be on some level, he was also a man and somehow he didn't get around to it.

Chapter Thirty Two

Mary-Beth, meanwhile, organized and organized. She had Josh's schedule for the next year worked out already, including a visit to St James's Palace in London, England, an audience with the Pope in Rome and four months laid on one side for a very specific purpose where all participants were sworn to secrecy and, surprisingly enough, actually kept silent.

She managed to set up a regular Skype link between Josh and the Dalai Lama which both men found uncomfortable at first but then, realizing that they had found in the other a powerful kindred spirit, found that they could surrender to each other's mind and soul and began to speak in total harmony. The Dalai Lama's end was set up by his assistant, Eleazer, formerly a Christian monk who had converted to Buddhism and who was now Mary-Beth's alter-ego in Dharamsala. This Eleazer had been a friend of John Jordan and was also the brother of Chris, the *Gemstone Inc* makeover guy. It was he who had agreed to try somehow to grease the wheels for Mary-Beth to meet His Holiness without having to book an appointment months in advance. However, when the small, focused dynamo on a stick arrived in Dharamsala, the sheer force of her energy was enough to make the air crackle with intent. There had been no problem in finding some time for her.

Eleazer and Mary-Beth too talked via Skype making plans and building hopes and bringing in a Vajrayana monk in the tiny English-speaking kingdom of Sikkim, on the other side of Nepal. Chandaka could only speak to them from an Internet café in the capital of Gangtok; his own monastery was close to the Nathu La Pass from Tibet to China but he made the 54-kilometre journey once a week to consult with a sense of wonder with those the other side of the planet.

'Are we being very stupid?' Josh asked the Dalai Lama once as they began to discuss Mary-Beth's audacious plan.

'Almost certainly,' was the reply. 'But if we are not angels, we may, at least, be fools.'

The Miracle Mile moved on to its conclusion with several surprise eliminations — Janice Colliver, the multi-talented musician, and Josie Jones the glorious singer were voted out but rock-chick Barbara Abbas, tenor Buddy Williamson, choirboy Alex Higgins and sweet Melissa Brown stayed in as the four finalists in the Singing category. The Performance Group included Lucifer by the skin of his teeth — he had slept with one ex-contestant too many and she spoke out publicly. Lucifer's trophy girlfriend dumped him and it was a close thing between being considered a stud and a love-rat. For two shows running Lucifer was in the bottom three in his section and he didn't like that one bit. To his horror, he was struggling just to keep going and he didn't have the time or energy to plot against Josh. His rival finalists were a juggling act, a female comedian and, to add insult to injury, another magician.

The top sixteen contestants were now mega-stars across America and it was the final week of the competition. While each section would have its own champion, the overall winner was the one who would really, really count. Simon Libiyah was thought sexy enough to win the Dance Section over Irish dancer Colm O'Reilly, a brother-and-sister duo aged 14 and a ballerina and, in Movement, Stuart White, the acrobat, and Maureen Wang, the contortionist were joint-favorites over a trapeze troupe and a mime artist.

The revenue from the phone calls was enough to finance four major health initiatives in the USA, UK, India and Africa as well as enhancing the shareholders profits. The prestigious *Miracle of Miracles, Gemstone Inc's* contribution to the great American tradition of fundraising telethons, incestuously linked to the personal charities of major celebrities, brought in stars such as Arianna Bel and Marco Montbretia and — somewhat to everyone (except Mary-Beth)'s surprise — every single existing or still-living past United Nations Goodwill Ambassador. Marta herself had just been invited to become one of that elite and, not to be outdone by her and Josh's obvious altruistic work, Sam donated more than he was actually comfortable with to build an orphanage in Saigon. Gideon provided his usual solid and reliable support and Deborah had to overcome the humiliation of being overheard criticizing the program as 'too concerned with black babies'. She issued an immediate and gushing denial and sacked the employee who had leaked the quotation (who was himself black). Philippa and the team made the final decision that this was to be Deborah's last year on *The Miracle Mile* and began considering who else could be brought in. In one of those wonderful synchronicities, Deborah was almost immediately approached to co-host a daytime chat show so both parties wasted a lot of time trying to work out how Deborah could leave without breaching her contract.

The consortium had mixed feelings about Josh continuing with the show too. He was becoming such a big star — but partly in such an unfortunate way — that it was perplexing. They didn't need a hero or a healer for their show; they needed a celebrity and frankly the less concerned with other things the better.

'I'd let things take their course,' said Mattie wisely at one of the habitual directors' meetings called by Philippa. 'It will either all come to a head, in which case he'll leave anyway, or it will all die down and you can see what happens next season.'

'What do we do if he marries Marta?' said Bartos who was torn between admiration and jealousy for Josh's ability to attract the gorgeous presenter.

'He won't,' said Mattie.

'Actually, that could be the answer,' said Philippa thoughtfully. 'He could be persuaded to leave as it would be unethical for them both to work on the show.'

'And go back into the background as with Gemma,' said Jo.

'He'll never be in the background now,' said Tadaeo.

'What do we do when this program with the pastor airs?' asked Jamie.

'It'll sort itself out,' said Mattie. 'People like Josh don't last very long. Their light shines very brightly and then burns itself out.' She felt a lump in her throat as she said that. Mattie wasn't stupid and she knew that the others would take her remark differently from the way she meant it, but that was all to the good.

'Well I guess that's true enough,' said Tadaeo thoughtfully.

They let the matter pass for the moment; there were enough ordinary decisions to make to let the extraordinary one take care of itself for the moment at least.

The last night of the show was almost upon them now with the eight ultimate finalists facing the deciding votes — Barbara Abbas, Melissa Brown, Stuart White, contortionist Amy Willow, Simon Libiyah, Colm O'Reilly, comedian Sara Black and Lucifer. This last night was a marathon of TV — eight hours long in total with both the section finals and the ultimate winner. At the end of it came the party of all parties and the carnival parade along the whole of the Las Vegas Miracle Mile. Dozens of celebrities vied to hold the party of the evening with Elton John currently maintaining the crown with celebrity couple Arianna and Marco's extravaganza a close second.

Both Lucifer and Marta had plans for that last night. Marta was hoping to turn Josh's heart and mind completely towards her and get some kind of a public declaration at the *Miracle Mile's* own party afterwards. Lucifer, having realized rather too late that with the wider public he didn't have as much power as he thought, was not so much planning to win as planning on assisting the others to lose. Once he had done that, he thought, he could turn his attention big-time to deposing Josh Goldstone.

His thinking was, on the surface, uncomplicated but Lucifer had a habit of over-simplifying. He thought no further than hypnotizing all the other contestants into performing at less than their usual standard. He had studied their strengths and weaknesses with as much discipline as he could muster and he knew that this was only something that he would be able to get away with on the last night. If he had tried it before, there would have been too many people for even his talented mind to control at any one time. One-offs were easy and he was confident that he had disposed of several strong rivals, including both Janice and Josie. It wasn't hard; all he had to do was find the strands of energy that represented their fear of failure (or conversely their fear of success) and add reinforcement to them with his own strength.

Sara Black was the obvious first target; she *had* to be eliminated for Lucifer to win his section and go through to the ultimate final at the end of the show. Sara was gay and although Lucifer knew he could still entrance her himself, nowadays he was a little wary of being observed. For some days he had been working on weaving illusions of doubt and betrayal between Sara and her partner, Katie. By the morning of the final, he had them both suspecting infidelity and gearing up for an explosive row. Add to that a little hypnotism for Sara's coach and a family member of Katie's to stir the pot — and Sara was strained to breaking point.

Brilliant!

Melissa was next. She was the most susceptible to any outside influences; the girl couldn't even watch the news without crying. The only reason that Lucifer hadn't tried anything with her before was that he'd assumed that her own nervous disposition and lack of star quality would eliminate her without his help. She was also the most likely of the finalists to succumb to an irrational fear and fall apart on stage. But somehow neither had happened — yet. Her innocence had won everyone over and she was far more likely to win her section than the deep-voiced Barbara with her loud political bias. Melissa definitely needed a Lucific nudge. However, she was surrounded by family members when Lucifer went to find her so he had to change his plans. Instead he went to see Stuart, the favorite in the Movement Section, who was warming up for a final rehearsal. Lucifer sat in the wings and watched, biding his time.

It was quite simple to disorientate Stuart at one vital moment. The acrobat never knew why, but as he came to the star moment of his act, he lost focus for just one moment and slipped and fell awkwardly on one ankle, twisting it sharply.

Lucifer wasn't stupid; he wasn't trying to get Stuart to sprain or break his leg and so go out of the competition altogether. He wanted him just sore and unbalanced enough to perform off-peak but quite well enough to go on stage and hope for a return to strength.

As Stuart swore and rubbed his leg and the medical staff raced to help, Lucifer slipped invisibly away. He wandered down the corridor past the dressing rooms, whistling softly to himself and noting that Melissa was still surrounded by her protective cocoon. Instead, he found Colm in his dressing room. For a few minutes, he leant against the door and, under the pretext of mutual nervousness, he chatted with the dancer until his carefully chosen words had made the other feel quite unsettled enough for Lucifer to focus just the right amount of energy to his already existent feeling that he wasn't quite good enough to be where he was. Colm actually burst into tears and Lucifer's anxious comfort only increased the flow. He knew full well that Colm's face would swell up with the emotion. He might be able to get the swollen lids down by the time he went on stage but he would worry all afternoon — it would just look so bad that a man had been crying with nerves.

There was a slight swagger in Lucifer's step as he returned to his original prey. Melissa was still not quite alone; she was singing quietly to one of *The Miracle Mile's* voice coaches as she prepared for her final rehearsal. But Lucifer was impatient now. He told the coach that Barbara Abbas was asking for her, trusting correctly that Melissa would urge her to go immediately to help a fellow contestant. Somewhat to his irritation, Melissa got up to walk with the coach towards the stage and Lucifer had to follow, chatting amiably along the way. He didn't dare do anything until he had Melissa alone; the coach was also a psychologist (one of a number trained to help the contestants with their emotions when they were eliminated) and she didn't like Lucifer at all.

The older woman turned off down the corridor to the rehearsal room that Barbara used and Lucifer walked on with Melissa towards the stage. Carefully, he probed her mind with his own, seeking for the perfect point of attack. Melissa was already embarrassed that the handsome and magnetic magician was choosing to spend time with her. Just as they reached the wings, Lucifer found the perfect point of weakness, her fear that her epilepsy might return, and, without hesitation, he launched his dominant intent at it.

At that same split second, Melissa saw Josh and Sam standing in one of the boxes above the stage, discussing the final rehearsals. She lifted her head and her heart opened fully with total, unconditional love. She never expected anything from Josh; she just adored him and whenever she saw him she experienced unreserved delight.

Josh saw her too and smiled, creating a powerful energetic link between them. As Lucifer attacked, Josh's own defense systems felt the change in Melissa and responded instantaneously. A great flood of protective love surged into the teenager, love so powerful that it overwhelmed Lucifer's own mind.

Lucifer did not understand unconditional love. All he knew was power, control and sex. Momentarily lifted out of his mind with an unrecognized emotion, his brain translated it into lust and he grabbed Melissa, without thought, crushing her against him and kissing her fiercely.

She yelped, pushed back and, as she managed to tear her mouth away, screamed. Maddened by the uncontrolled energy, Lucifer grabbed the back of her head, twisting her to his will. Blood surged into his penis, disorienting his head even further and he lost control completely.

Melissa went limp in his arms, fainting clean away just as Sam yelled, 'Leave her alone!' with all the strength of his lungs. 'Cut it out, you bastard!'

The mystical charm was broken leaving only the agony of the fall from Grace. Lucifer's face as he looked up at Josh and Sam was demonic, inhuman, possessed; all his beauty temporarily destroyed. Perceiving vaguely that he had fought with Josh for the girl's soul and lost, he threw Melissa's unresisting body to the floor and ran away.

Sam got to Melissa first, noting the twisted lie of her arm. Josh was one step behind him, bending down to the innocence crumpled on the wood of the floor.

'Don't you bloody well dare!' said Sam as Josh's hand automatically went out towards the broken arm. 'You can damn well fix it once it's been diagnosed as broken. We need the evidence.'

Josh nodded and went to call for the medics.

Chapter Thirty Three

Five hours later, when *The Miracle Mile* finalists took to the stage, Lucifer was missing. Formally disqualified from the competition for assaulting a fellow competitor, he and Venus were already on their way home to Florida. Josh made sure they had a chartered flight at his expense if only to make sure that the minimum of people were affected by Lucifer's rage.

He took it on himself to tell Lucifer — and Venus — the executives' decision. Gideon, who was technically Lucifer's mentor, would have done it but instinct told Josh that the boy's behavior had been personal and Gideon was perfectly willing to have the load taken off his back.

Josh didn't like to talk to the others about evil but he knew that the Universe continually strove to find balance and, if there were a *Bene Elohim* then there would also be enough of a build up of energy to offer opposition. John came with him and Maude-Lynn trailed behind with her video camera. John was the person who had first sensed something in Lucifer and the only one Josh felt comfortable talking to on the subject of evil.

'Look at the name he chose!' he said as the two men strode down the corridor to the room that was known as 'quarantine' where troublesome contestants and families were sent when an issue got out of hand. They would be met at the door by two members of the *Goldstone Inc.* legal team and by one of the psychologists who would counsel Lucifer and Venus if required. Everything in and around 'quarantine' was on CCTV.

'Lucifer, the name of the angel who preferred to rule in hell than serve in heaven,' said John.

'Absolutely. The boy just opened himself up to negative power. He's used everything he could to manipulate others — and he's got a great gift. It could be used for good.'

'Okay, so why does evil even exist?' asked John. 'Everyone wants to know that one. If God is all good and all powerful, what's with evil at all?'

'Evil is purely the misuse of human free will,' said Josh shortly. 'We have free will to do what we want. It's our choice.'

'But God could intervene and stop it!'

'Then it wouldn't be free will would it? Look —' Josh stopped dead and turned to look into John's eyes. Brown met blue, clearly. 'We are the children of God. We are creative powers in our own right. Everything we ask for, do or say, is obeyed by the forces of the Universe. That's our right as divine children. That's *everything* we ask for, John. Not just the things we think we are asking for consciously but *every thought we think.* We create evil through negative thoughts, anger, hate and fear and all those thoughts combine and create what seems to be an external, evil force. But it's *not* external; it's just us. Just thank God the energies take time to build up otherwise a single thought of 'I hate you' would be enough to cause physical hurt.'

'What about earthquakes, floods, natural disasters that kill thousands?' said John.

'That's not evil; that's a planet sneezing,' said Josh. 'We live on a living, breathing angelic being called Earth. She's still growing and moving and sometimes her plates move. You know the real problem with that?'

'Obviously not!' said John with a smile.

'We don't spot the signs any more,' said Josh. 'Animals know when an earthquake is coming. They'd tell us if we'd listen and observe. And we'd know if we weren't so interested in our own little worlds instead of the wider picture. We'd move.'

'But that would mean losing everything — home, job and all that.'

'Those can be rebuilt.'

'That's rather harsh.'

'Yes, I know. The truth is rather harsh. Or rather it's very simple. Be awake and aware and you will see what's coming. Be asleep and you'll get hit unawares. And don't let your possessions possess you so that you can't see the signs and move with them.'

'What's going on right now then? With this Lucifer guy?'

'A build-up of power of any kind can be harnessed,' said Josh. 'This show is a melting pot of ego and feeling. Lucifer's been riding on it; surfing it if you like. How he's going to react now he's been shown up is anyone's guess. Try and feel the energy. Then you can be prepared without defending.'

'Without defending? Dear God, is this the whole 'turn the other cheek' thing?' said John.

'Absolutely. Whatever anyone says or does to you is their business. If you take it on board and defend it, then you make it your business. Defense is the first act of war. Lucifer and Venus will be building huge defenses right now.'

'Defense is...?' But there was no time for John to continue questioning. They were outside 'quarantine.'

'Just notice what you feel and let it slide through you,' said Josh and he turned to greet the waiting lawyers and psychologist. 'Are we ready? Let's go.' He shook his head at Maude-Lynn who sighed and stopped recording. She would not be allowed inside but, at least, she would get access to the CCTV later.

Inside, in a comfortable cool-colored room with soft seating, food, drink and a wooden coffee table, Venus sat poised on the edge of a chair; a fiery ball of resentment, anger and justification on behalf of her son. She exclaimed, she defended, she shouted, walking up and down and gesturing wildly. Lucifer sat silent in an armchair. John felt darkness and winced.

Josh waited until Venus had run out of steam and then turned to Lucifer. He said all the correct formal things about 'actions inappropriate with the ethics of *The Miracle Mile* forcing us to terminate your contract with immediate effect', but knew full well that Lucifer wasn't listening. Josh remained standing until the correct procedures had been completed and Venus's protests and objections had been dealt with by the psychology and legal team. Then, just as everyone else was prepared to go, he sat down on the opposite side of the coffee table from Lucifer.

'Isaiah,' he said.

The boy raised his head, his dark eyes filled with hatred.

'My name is Lucifer,' he said. John winced as he felt the power of the boy's enmity.

'Tell me,' said Josh gently.

'What?'

'Why you feel as you do about me.'

'I feel nothing for you,' said the boy furiously. 'You're a nothing, a nobody. It's me that's great, not you.'

Everyone took a step back; even the most insensitive realized that this felt bad.

'I am you,' said Josh. 'And you are me. You are loved as much as I am.'

Unexpected tears sprang into Lucifer's eyes. 'That's not true,' he said, bowing his head.

'It is,' said Josh. 'Whatever you do, whoever you are, you are loved as much as me. You *are* me. You are the beloved son. You can choose that any time you like.'

Lucifer leapt. In one split second, he was across the coffee table and had Josh slammed against the wall, one arm across his neck and the other punching wildly at his face. John knocked the boy down with a sideways elbow-blow to the cheek. Lucifer fell like a stone, then rolled and leapt up ('I swear he was hissing like a snake,' John said afterwards). Before anyone could move, the door was thrown open and both Simon and Andrew were inside, grabbing Lucifer and holding him by both arms.

'Are you okay?' John turned to Josh and blanched. For a fraction of a second, his mind's eye saw Josh totally destroyed, his face smashed and his body shattered — and then there was just a man who seemed perfectly calm and unhurt.

'Josh?' he said urgently.

'I'm fine. Really.' Josh reached out and touched his friend

reassuringly on the arm.

'Do you want to file charges for assault Mr. Goldstone?' asked one of the lawyers.

'No, let him go. It never happened.'

'The most unkindest cut of all,' murmured John, quoting Shakespeare as he followed Josh out of the room and Maude-Lynn switched on her camera.

'What, not acknowledging it? Yes, I suppose so. But non-resistance is very powerful.'

'Josh...I saw...for a moment...'

'Yes,' said Josh crisply. 'You saw everything. And now we move on.'

There would be huge fall-out in the press the next day but, in the meantime, it was showtime. Josh, Sam, Gideon, Marta and Deborah posed for the cameras outside the great theatre and gave the appropriate sound bytes for the press gathered around the red carpet. Josh never liked wearing full evening dress but his cream tuxedo suited his lanky frame — even with the ubiquitous cowboy boots. Marta, in a shimmering silvery-blue strapless dress, looked incredibly beautiful and managed to brush up against Josh just enough to get him to laugh and kiss her hand. Deborah was, as usual, slightly too fussily dressed in several different shades of greens. Gideon wore a purple and silver waistcoat that stole the show. Sam was just seamlessly elegant in black as always.

In the retrospective, mutual grooming part of the live show where all the judges praised each other and the production team, Sam offered a toast of champagne to both Marta and Josh who had had to step into shoes much loved, and much mourned. 'The Golden Couple' as he called them were applauded onto the stage together and millions of the romantically hearted, watching on live TV, hoped that the announcement of an engagement was imminent. It would just be so nice to have a show business happy ending. Marta beamed up at Josh who smiled at her affectionately before introducing a tribute VT to Gemma. As it was running, he slipped off the stage and back to his place with the other judges so Marta had to announce the separate tribute to John Jordan on her own.

Then it was time for the retrospectives of all the finalists. Marta spoke to each judge in turn about their mentored favorites (although the mentoring was in name only — teams of professionals did the actual work). Josh praised Melissa who, he said, had had an unfortunate accident but who was still going to perform and Gideon said something tactful about Lucifer having to withdraw in unforeseen circumstances, knowing full well that the story would be all over the press within minutes. He wasn't looking forward to the press interviews afterwards.

Melissa, her arm in plaster, performed bravely but falteringly, not winning enough of the sympathy vote to beat Barbara Abbas. Sara Black was automatically given the best Performer title by default with no Lucifer to contest her. Simon Libiyah won the Dance Section and Stuart White, to his surprise, the Movement. None of them ever knew that Josh had quietly sat in on the last-minute dress rehearsals noting and unraveling the threads of Lucifer he found in their heads and healing Stuart's ankle. Sara and Katie made up five minutes before rehearsals, both realizing that they had been mistaken.

In the end, Stuart was fourth, Sara third, and Simon an honorable second but Barbara Abbas was a worthy winner. With a timely letting go of her rock-chick image, she sat peacefully at the piano and gave such a beautiful and poignant rendition of 'The Rose' that many of the audience members found themselves in tears. The judges heaved a sigh of relief. That performance was unbeatable no matter how good anyone else might have been.

'Order wins, chaos loses,' murmured Josh to himself as Marta announced Barbara's name to tumultuous applause.

Three hours later, Jude, Maude-Lynn, Mary-Beth, Andrew, John, Simon, James and Josh were on a scheduled plane to London. They missed the after-show party and the triumphant procession along the Miracle Mile with Barbara Abbas hailed as a princess to the accompaniment of a band, dancing, fireworks and the magnificent street party followed by the private celebrity bashes. The winner was grinning from ear to ear — no wonder as she now had a multi-million-dollar recording contract and a number-one single and album predicted within a month.

The lack of Josh's presence at the *Miracle Mile* after-show party was a great sadness to Melissa, Gideon and Mattie, an extreme irritation to Philippa and a delight to Sam and Deborah who had more of the limelight to themselves.

Mary-Beth, with innate tact, had ensured that Marta received the most beautiful bouquet from Josh, giving his apologies and excuses for not being there but, even so, Marta, in her exquisite Donna Karan gown of watered silk, felt betrayed, publicly shamed and humiliated as she posed for film and TV with the others. She knew for sure that the lack of Josh by her side would be registered all around the world. One minute they were the Golden Couple and the next she was ostentatiously alone. He had chosen and he had not chosen her.

Chapter Thirty Four

The next night, Salema's interview with Josh and Pastor Jo went to air and what Jude called 'the serious doo-doo' hit the fan. For Jude herself, the media frenzy that followed was paradise. Forgetting completely that she and Charlie had an annual agreement to go on holiday at the end of each *Miracle Mile,* she and her staff moved straight into full-time publicity back-up, fielding the fall-out from the new Messiah, giving quotes, slapping people down for being really *too* stupid and getting the best adrenaline high in the business. She flew back and forwards from London; now that Josh had left the US, she didn't need to spend time in Vegas and Jude liked London's style.

When Charlie complained, she was quite short with her.

'This is a one-time opportunity,' she said. 'I wouldn't get in the way of your career. You know that.'

Charlie took it – this time – and went on holiday with a friend instead.

Jude even hired a full-time London-based assistant to help handle Josh's Public Relations – Joanna Duvalier, an Afro-Caribbean who was as short as Jude was tall and as round as Jude was slender. They soon became known as 'the long and the short of it' though Simon, in a bad mood could expand that to 'the thin and the fat of it.' Joanna was a terrier; deeply scary, and just what Jude needed for the tabloids. She was also a Church-going Christian which, at first sight, seemed to be a real no-no. Luckily, Joanna had an open mind and a modern outlook. She took a long look at Josh on the Salema interview, listened properly, and pronounced him 'the Man'. From then onwards she was unswerving in her loyalty.

'That was lucky,' said Susannah, who liked Jo but found her a bit overwhelming. Susannah could have been excused for feeling rather put out. She had had to face up to Jude's moving in and taking over, big time.

'Luck has very little to do with it,' said Jude absently, reading through a press release. 'This is very good Susannah. You are a superb writer.'

Some inner part of Susannah appreciated how Jude managed not to make her feel any the lesser for the new appointment. Jude was turning out to be as good a boss as Gemma had been but, even so, Susannah was getting quite nervous at the way things were going.

'It's all getting too big,' she confided to Mattie on the phone. 'I'm scared. Aren't you?'

'Yes,' said Mattie.

There was very little positive press coverage but, as Jude said to anyone who would listen, 'the only bad publicity is no publicity'.

Probably the most benign of all the coverage the day after the TV show aired was the front of *USA Today* which had a half-page Photoshop-enhanced picture of Josh's head superimposed on a kitschy picture of Jesus as the Sacred Heart with his arms out. It was topped by the headline, 'The Man Who Thinks He's The Messiah'. The rest of the press proffered coverage of various degrees of vitriol or thought the whole thing was ludicrous enough to be funny.

For an ordinary man, the craziness would have been disturbing, perhaps even shaming. But, as Josh was exactly who he said he was, he didn't mind. It wasn't his business if people chose to misunderstand what he had said. All he felt was a little impatience about how difficult it was to try and go out without being besieged by press, people wanting healing and, now, people yelling insults. During his brief period back in London, a quiet stroll on his own was completely impossible. He couldn't even stay in his own home.

Mary-Beth minded — and so did Mattie who talked to Josh often via phone and Skype. And so did Fred and Sarah Dawes in the house in Dartmouth Park which was the primary location for the press and for the outraged to gather and throw stones, either physical or metaphorical. The front of the house was daubed with the word 'Blasphemer' in black paint and a petrol bomb was thrown through the Dawes's own basement front window.

Josh apologized to Mr and Mrs Dawes for the inconvenience, felt sorry that the beautiful wisteria vine had been damaged, arranged for a clean up of the stone front of the house and helped Mary-Beth find somewhere else for the Dawes's to stay in the meantime. Fred Dawes, however, had to leave his job at the local pub because he couldn't bear being besieged by the press. He lost his rag on his last day at work and was quoted in the *Evening Standard* saying that Josh was nice enough but all this show business stuff had gone to his head. Messiah indeed! Fred thought that Gemma would be ashamed of him.

Sarah Dawes was terrified that Josh would abandon them for that piece of disloyalty. She thought he must have gone crazy too but was too concerned with having a roof over her head to be willing to say that in public. But Josh didn't bear grudges — as Jude was the first to attest — and the Dawes's were kept safe until things got better and then moved back home.

Josh, in the meantime, got on with a lot of what were, essentially, secret meetings with celebrities and dignitaries while Jude, Susannah, Mary-Beth, Simon, John and the others dealt with all the fall-out as much as they could.

The meetings included sessions with the Prince of Wales, the Prime Minister of Great Britain, several movie and rock stars, the Archbishops of Canterbury and York, the Chief Rabbi of the United Kingdom and the Aga Khan. And that was just in the first week. The Pope in Vatican City had to wait until the following week.

What was surprising — and quite heart-warming — was that after meeting Josh, both the Pope and the Prince of Wales spoke publicly of their belief in his integrity. Not that he was *the* Messiah (obviously) but that he was a truly holy man with great gifts. Both of them took the time to emphasize that Josh had not, at any point said or even implied that he *was* the Messiah and, whether or not they believed in the Jewish mystical concept of a Messianic figure living in every age, if it *were* the case, then Josh could well fit that bill.

The Chief Rabbi of the UK, meanwhile, lay low and said nothing apart from a brief statement that anything to do with Messiahs returning was a matter for the Christians not the Jews, given that what was generally termed as 'The Messianic Age' had not yet come. This, as both he and Josh agreed, was probably the most sensible stance for him to take.

'The Pope!' said Jude, her eyes shining with the glory of the meeting at the Vatican where Pious VIII's kindness had moved the hearts of all the team. The Pope's public approval was truly a miracle — as was the Pontiff's complete and obvious recovery from a chronic and worrying disease from the moment that Josh kissed the Papal ring. This Pope might not approve of what was happening but he knew a truly spiritual soul when he met one and he was prepared to say so.

The Prince of Wales was not quite such a coup; he was known to be a spiritual rather than a religious man with advisors who had great mystical knowledge. But it was still good.

The doo-doo was still in circulation when Josh, John, Maude-Lynn and Mary-Beth left for Dharamsala and the others returned from Rome to London. Their first standoff was Philippa, on behalf of *Gemstone Inc,* calling into question Jude's own loyalty and telling her that she was supposed to be their PR, not Josh's.

'Don't you think it's a bit late for that point of view?' Jude asked. (She had an enviable talent for being able to think things through on her feet and argue with clarity even when hit by a bolt from the blue). 'You were perfectly willing to let me do all the work for Josh up until now. And up until now all the other PR work has been more than satisfactorily handled by my staff. And, anyway, Josh is major shareholder of *Gemstone Inc*. Whether or not you are the boss, he's the big cheese.

'If you want to fire me right now, go ahead. Josh will hire me as an individual.'

No, Philippa did not want to fire her. But she did want this furor to end.

'It has completely overshadowed the show,' she said.

'Nonsense,' said Jude crisply. 'The show is over. And anyway, every single report refers to *The Miracle Mile.*'

'That's what I meant,' said Philippa. 'It's bringing it into disrepute.'

For a second, Jude had to choke down laughter at the idea that a miracle healer with a plan to help the world one step further towards peace could bring into disrepute a talent show for wannabes based in Las Vegas.

'I disagree,' she said crisply. 'All publicity is good publicity. Anyway, it's a nine-day wonder. Everything is. And we can come up with all kinds of promotional opportunities for Barbara and the other contestants at the same time.

'If Sam, Gideon and Deborah are complaining at you, just refer them to their own PR people. It's not my fault if they can't come up with a story to beat this one.'

Philippa snorted. But she knew Jude had her beaten, for the moment at least.

Salema's interview with Josh and the Pastor was only broadcast in full in the USA but within hours it was all over YouTube, the most hits being on the tiny section where Pastor Jo accused Josh of being the Anti-Christ. The same 65-second clip had been on nearly every single news broadcast around the entire world. This is how it went.

Pastor Jo: 'You are a blasphemer and an agent of Satan. No one else would claim to be the Christ. You can't deny it; you said to me yourself that you are Jesus Christ.'

Josh: 'No, I didn't say that.'

Pastor Jo: 'Liar! Hypocrite! Do you now deny it?'

Josh: 'I would never say I was Jesus Christ because I'm not. Only Jesus could be Jesus. I'm…'

Pastor Jo (interrupting): 'You said you are Christ! I put it to you that you are the Anti-Christ. *Satan!*'

Salema: 'Let Josh finish, Pastor.'

Pastor Jo: 'I don't want to hear any of his blasphemy!'

(The Pastor was on the edge of his seat, his face contorted and a blue vein pulsing in his forehead. Josh meanwhile was sitting back, looking relaxed, one leg crossed over the other and with his hands loosely clasped in his lap).

Salema: 'Please be quiet and let Josh answer. Josh?'

Josh: 'I said to the Pastor that I was the Axis of the Age. A Maitreya, not *the* Maitreya. There is always one of us alive in the world. We're not here to be a religious leader, nor to found a new religion, but to be a teacher and guide for people of every religion and those of no religion. We are here to help the world find its peace. Mostly we are very private, hidden people. I just happened to get the job of doing this in public.'

Pastor Jo: 'You are the Anti-Christ. Satan himself!'

Salema: 'Josh, you believe you are *a* Maitreya. Have you always believed that?'

Josh: 'Oh goodness, no. This only happened to me when the previous one died — less than a year ago.'

Salema: 'When you came out of the desert?'

Josh: 'Yes.'

Salema: 'Did you know the previous one?'

Josh: 'No. It doesn't work like that.'

Pastor Jo: 'Don't listen to him! He is the Anti-Christ!'

Opinion remained divided. Opinion that had actually *listened* to what was being said and which was open to the idea of there actually being people who were representatives of God, the Source, the Creator or whatever you'd like to call it, thought that Josh was probably a good egg. After all, there was now plenty of evidence of miracles. However, the fundamentalists and those who liked having a whipping boy, pointed out that magic was the only option (look at Derren Brown and David Blaine let alone David Copperfield or that guy on Josh's own show, Lucifer).

The second most-watched excerpt was a very short one where Pastor Jo said scathingly that anyone who was setting themselves up as holy would not be concerned with ego-based talent shows in the capital city of sin, Las Vegas. To which, Josh replied with a smile, 'Where else would someone setting themselves up as holy be more needed?'

Salema asked, 'Is that why you were there — because Las Vegas needed you?'

'Actually, it was more me who needed the training,' said Josh laughing at himself.

Those around him, who knew him well realized that was the truth. Since leaving Las Vegas, Josh appeared to have grown both physically and in beauty (Las Vegas itself, by the way, was not yet showing any inclination to returning to being hot, dry and full of people eager to gamble — that would take a little time).

'Beauty is the right word,' said Maude-Lynn to Jude as they had lunch together before the party split in two. 'As are kingship, and power, and…and *wisdom*. Have you seen his eyes? They just glow.'

'Can't miss them,' said Jude, enjoying her forest fruits ice cream. 'There's something inside them nowadays that is indescribable. A glory, I think. Aren't we lucky to be living now, here and with him?'

'How are you getting on with your healing practice?' asked Maude-Lynn, dodging answering. While she was incredibly happy both being with Josh and filming him, she didn't want to make too much of it in case it was suddenly taken away. She'd been reading up on past holy men, especially Gandhi, and she knew how short their lifespan could be. If she got too involved or too close, she could get horribly hurt.

The healing was a moot point. Josh had been teaching all those close to him how to center and balance themselves so that they too could be a channel of healing for others. John was quite good at it and Andrew reasonable. Simon was hopeless and impatient with himself for being so ('And that's *why* you can't do it!' said Josh). The girls were able to do it when they concentrated hard on *not* concentrating — and Maude-Lynn had experienced the wide-eyed amazement of one of the Pope's entourage who accidentally brushed up against her and felt the alleviation of some persistent back pain that he had been feeling. The trouble was that it was not constant. 'But even mine's not always constant!' said Josh. 'You can't expect it to be. People have to *want* to align through your channel. You can't *make* them heal.'

He couldn't *make* people rise from the dead either; only a few whose souls were still attached to the body by what Josh called 'the silver thread'.

'They're the ones who have died out of turn or who have something more to do here,' he reminded them. 'Most people die in perfect time — when their souls want to go. I wouldn't even try to bring them back. It would be disrespectful even if it were possible.'

'But what about the people grieving for them?' asked Mary-Beth.

Josh's eyes flashed. 'No!' he said. 'So much harm is caused by our wanting other people to behave in a way that suits us. And death is included in that. Do you think I wanted Gemma to die? No. But Gemma's soul knew that it was time. And it *was* time. We know so little down here on the Earth. We think we know better than the great Cosmic Forces. If we had our way we'd impede the very turning of the Earth because we saw a gnat in its way!'

'But people get so hurt by premature deaths,' said Andrew.

Josh looked at him, one eyebrow raised. 'I know…' he said.

'Is it only because we don't understand?' asked John.

'No, we do get sadness even if we do understand,' said Josh. 'I understand about Gemma but I still miss holding her in my arms. Living on a physical world means you will have to experience loss.'

'But why?' Simon always wanted Utopia.

'It's to do with living in a finite world of duality — up-down, in-out, light-dark, male-female, good-bad, life-death,' said Josh. 'We have choices and all choices have consequences. And we place value judgments on the consequences. And we get emotionally tied up with other people and the other people leave or die. That's the deal. But it doesn't hurt as much if you understand that this is not all there is; that we are all connected to the glory of the Source and that we live on when we die. Only the physical world dies.'

'But I didn't choose to be born,' said Simon.

'I think we all chose to be born,' said Josh. 'At least the first time we did. Maybe with further lives our choices were limited, maybe not. But there was a choice at the beginning.'

'How do you know that?'

'Good question. I just do — in fact I think I can remember it — but that doesn't mean you have to believe me. In fact, the last thing you should do is believe me. The last thing anyone else should do is believe me!'

'What?'

'You have to decide for yourself otherwise you're just not making your own choices. Not making your own choices is why people get into a mess.'

'I don't get it,' said Simon.

'You will,' said Josh.

'Now you sound like my mother!'

'Perish the thought!'

'So do we choose to die?'

'Yes.'

'So how can some deaths be a mistake and others not?'

'Another good question. People do make mistakes and wrong decisions that are so against the life plan that they are trying to follow that they can accidentally die. Then there's usually some re-orientating process — or miracle — that brings them back. People come back from the dead a lot more often than we think.

'But for most people even a tragic death can be plotted in a gradual downswing of life-force or a death-wish or a lack of care about life that doesn't see the warnings.'

'Warnings?'

'Yes, we usually get three warnings if we are going in a destructive direction. The question is whether we see them.'

'What about Gemma?'

'She had done her job. Better to go swiftly like that than to die of some disease.'

'Yet others die of terrible diseases and they're not bad people.'

'No, they're not. But what happens to them is their story; we can't expect to understand it.'

'What are these warnings like?'

'They all differ according to the person. Feelings; overheard phrases; brick walls. Continuing to live in a situation that hurts you or that you know in your heart is wrong. Physical disease always follows psychological issues.'

'What about cancer?'

'As I just said, every story is the individual's own story. But as a general principle, cancer is a loss of self-identity; a life lived more for others than for the self.'

'You mean people should be selfish?'

'People are happiest being themselves – their true selves – rather than aborting their own life in order to fit into the boxes that others want them to fit. When people are happy in themselves, they are an inspiration to the world. When they run around doing what others want – while denying what they want – they are not living the life they came to live. Sickness is a warning. Sometimes people decide that they'd rather go home and start again.'

'Home?'

'Yes, home. We're here for quite a short time and the physical world is not our real home.'

'Which is?'

'Indescribable,' said Josh. 'But you could start with Helen Graves' book *Testimony of Light*. My mum bought me a copy of that when my grandmother died. It was amazing.

'You see, as long as we think that our physical bodies are the most important thing, we can't truly be happy. If we can live in our souls, our true selves, then the world works; miracles happen; people are healed because we've got the connection then; the connection home.

'It *is* about self. Self-responsibility. Because of the nature of our minds, our eyes, ears and senses can only respond to what is already inside us. If it is totally alien we don't even see it. There's some story about the people in the Caribbean who couldn't even see Columbus's ships because they had no concept of big ships existing so their eyes couldn't translate the images to their brain.'

'So I can't see something good or bad unless that thing is already in me?'

'*Exactly.* We see and create wars because we are filled with war ourselves — against family, colleagues, the world at large. If we made peace with ourselves, war would stop.'

'Someone shot Gandhi,' said Simon. 'He was full of peace.'

'Maybe it was his time to go and the easiest way for him,' said Josh.

'That doesn't mean what the killer did was good,' argued Simon.

'No, but it's not for us to judge,' said Josh. 'We don't know; we weren't there. We didn't see it; we weren't a part of it. It's what we see and understand *now* that is in us.

'Consider — it's all about what people call the Law of Attraction. Where you put your attention you extend energy. So what do you think people are doing when they launch a war on terror or a war on a certain disease?'

'They're trying to help.'

'Yes, but they are putting more attention on the problem — giving it energy, adding to the pain. Mother Theresa had it right; she said she would never march against war but she would march for peace.'

'Okay,' said Simon slowly. 'I think I get that. You're saying that if we focus on the negative, we create more negative and if we focus on the positive, we get more positive. But that's just basic positive thinking.'

'That's the start of it, certainly. But it's more than that. It's about understanding that whatever is *in* you is a part of you as well as external to you. So if *you* heal *you* then you also heal the world.'

'Sorry?'

'If I see war then it means that I contain war. If I heal war inside of me so that there is only peace then war *cannot exist where I am*. So if there is no war around me and I can teach others to find peace so that there is no war around them, then war must recede on the Earth.

'That's what the Christians actually mean when they say that Jesus took on the sins of the world in order to heal them.'

'Oh no it's not!'

Josh laughed. 'Well, it's what they originally believed. That is what it was all about. It's not about worshipping Jesus, it's about understanding that he healed whatever was in him in order that it should be healed around him.'

'And they nailed him to a tree! He cried out that the Lord had betrayed him!'

'Yes — because of the level of pain that he felt. *Then* he healed it within himself and said 'Father, forgive them, they don't know what they are doing' and *then* he said 'Thy will be done; it is finished.' Actually I think that all the way, he was reciting the 22nd psalm because all those elements were in it — but I digress. The point is that he experienced that humiliation and pain in order to heal the emotions that appeared to be in the outside world but were actually in himself. And in doing that, he healed the world.'

'So much so that Christianity has made war everywhere and people have been mass-murdered in his name,' said Simon.

'Well maybe it's just time to do it again in the hope that people will get the point this time,' said Josh.

'So you're going to sort out the conflict over Tibet then?' said Simon. Everyone took in a sharp breath. Now they were at the nub of it.

'What conflict?' said Josh.

Simon was always okay as long as he had Josh to ask about things but when Josh went away, he doubted terribly and he didn't know how to explain Josh's teachings to others. He knew that, if all went well, they'd all be going to Tibet in a few weeks' time and, as long as Josh was with them, that was okay too. But once he was still in London and Josh and the others had left for India, it wasn't okay at all. Fortunately he had Jude to talk to (although he drove her crazy with his questions).

'So what is the point of contacting all these people?' he asked. 'Are we really asking them to risk their lives for a principle?'

'That's exactly what we are asking them to do,' said Jude. 'The price of celebrity just went through the roof.'

Chapter Thirty Five

Just occasionally, events can be organized on the grapevine without the media discovering them. Mostly these are events that would have no intrinsic news value and feature nobody in whom the press (or public) would be interested. But this time, there must have been Grace because, right up to the time where it mattered, nobody actually spotted what was going on. The timing was also a very helpful factor — his Holiness the Dalai Lama always offered a week of teachings for the public in the early spring and there was nothing particularly odd about more people than usual going along or the idea that there was going to be some sort of extension — a peace meditation or some such thing; it wasn't exactly clear.

This year a small Exodus of famous people from all walks of life (and their friends and contacts) were taking or planning trips to India for the Spring Teachings. Obviously, celebrity Buddhists like Angelina Jolie, Orlando Bloom, Tina Turner, Allen Ginsberg, Phil Jackson, Richard Gere, Keanu Reeves, Sting, Sharon Stone and Steve Jobs were bound to visit Dharamsala once in a while as were celebrity spiritual authors and mentors like Deepak Chopra, Salema, Oprah, Eckhart Tolle, Jerry and Esther Hicks so, although the press planned to be there for the event itself, there was no particular interest beforehand.

When the celebrities found out the reason behind why they had been invited to this particular event, some of them went straight back home again. Some went home and came back later when they'd thought it through (or seen which of their rivals had stayed). Some went into hiding or found pre-existing contracts that they couldn't escape. Some regrettably did have pre-existing contracts that they couldn't change. But nearly a hundred of them stayed in Dharamsala and they invited friends along too. Once the hotels were full, a lot of very posh tents — palaces rather — began to be set up around His Holiness's residence.

Next came the not-so famous spiritual people from all different walks of life, all of whom had been approached individually and all of whom understood that this was a once-in-a-lifetime opportunity to support peace.

After them came the not-so-spiritual but definitely seeking *something* celebrities. The boy and girl band stars, the people who had realized that fame didn't bring them everything, the philanthropists. And most of the winning contestants on *The Miracle Mile* for the last five years.

Lucifer was not invited. In fact, he was proving very useful as a distraction for the media as both he and Venus had worked out that they now had nothing to lose and everything to gain in coming out against Josh and accusing him of both corruption and of magic.

They went to the press to accuse Jude, and through her, Josh, of setting them against Pastor Jo and his wife. Venus disliked having to assert that she had tried and failed to seduce the Pastor and Lucifer had to overcome his revulsion at the thought of Beulah being shown up as someone with whom he could have sex — but they both enjoyed the flush of fame and they wanted Jude to hold good to her promise that Lucifer would work in Las Vegas.

The fact that Melissa had refused to press charges for sexual assault on Lucifer was an asset to their case. Jude, when approached, had no problems simply telling the truth in that she had, indeed set Venus on Pastor Jo to test his integrity but that she had not set Lucifer on Beulah — and that Josh had no foreknowledge of what she did and, when he discovered it, had threatened to fire her.

'He was horrified at what I had done,' she said in a live press conference from London, having already explained that Josh was out of the country and out of contact 'on a retreat' and therefore couldn't possibly comment on this or anything else.

'I thought it was fair to see if the Pastor was a good man — which he proved himself to be. I also think that Lucifer did a seriously unethical thing especially as he was already in a relationship at the time. Given what we believe to be the situation concerning one of the *Miracle Mile* contestants for which Lucifer was disqualified, my heart goes out to Mrs. Sadd and I unreservedly offer her and her husband my apologies and condolences on behalf of *The Miracle Mile* for what may have happened to her.'

Wonderfully loaded words! Jude was, immediately, fired by Philippa to disassociate the rest of *Gemstone Inc* from the scandal. But, as the next thing Jude did, in her new role as Josh's private Public Relations Officer, was announce (with his permission) Josh's retirement from *The Miracle Mile* and intention to reconsider his position over *Gemstone Inc,* she wasn't the slightest bit concerned. Jude had the bit well and truly between her teeth. There was plenty for the media — and the consortium — to chew over in that news. Philippa and the others were terrified. Since Gemma's death, Josh owned the name of the show and the rights. Without Josh's backing there could be one big implosion on the way. Sam and Gideon were also scared and angry (Deborah didn't give a rap) — and Marta was furious. Josh had invited them all to the Spring Teachings in India (without saying why) and they were all relieved that they couldn't go, all having other shows to work on and other contracts to fulfill. Marta too stayed in the USA. Again, she reasoned, that she had been premature and under-estimated the time it would take for Josh's heart to mend. One week before the Spring Teachings was the first anniversary of Gemma's death. Perhaps that would be the time for Josh to move on. In fact, Marta, justified to herself, it had been silly for her to expect anything earlier. A year was the appropriate time for mourning. She hoped that Josh hadn't done anything silly with his hair — like Mary-Beth — although she had no particular problem with his obviously-developing Buddhist tendencies.

Meanwhile, poor Pastor Jo was right back in the spotlight for all the wrong reasons. Being basically a good man if somewhat shortsighted and fanatical, he had, eventually, made his peace with his wife. But now the whole shebang was all over the media, you could not blame him for being riled and, of course, Josh was right in the firing line for all his anger.

Beulah thought she would be totally humiliated but, instead, she was offered a place on a TV makeover show. She hesitated but then, driven by the desire to find herself in some way, she allowed herself to be transformed. When she emerged, Botoxed and restyled, Beulah became a middle-aged woman's icon of elegance and beauty.

So that was a happy ending for her and Pastor Jo got a beautiful wife who was never quite as subservient again.

What he also got, to his deep discomfort, was a publicly repentant Lucifer in his church, complete with television cameras. Joseph Sadd was justly hoist with his own petard for he could not refuse Lucifer's sudden decision to convert to Evangelical Christianity; could not deny his fervently-expressed wish for forgiveness and, let's face it, he could not dispute Lucifer's claim that Josh was evil personified.

The Pastor, to do him justice, tried to disassociate himself from Lucifer as much as he could but the media loved the link between the two. For a start they were both such handsome men and such good speakers. Together they fanned the flames against Josh adding weight to the general mish-mash of invective, insults, offence, fury, revelation, silliness, copy-cat antics, conspiracy theories and accusations that were being hurled in Josh's direction every day.

You can't be different — especially if you are holy and different — without causing a major reaction in the hearts and minds of those who come into contact with you. Josh, being a miracle man who was, albeit technically, Jewish, seemed to have no particular religion. Perhaps it would not have been so hard if he had aligned himself with his Jewish faith (of which, it must be said, he was very respectful although he preferred the mystical aspect rather than the letter of the law). Or if he had pronounced himself a convert to Christianity or Islam — or Paganism or Wicca. Or even Hinduism, Buddhism or Jainism or Bahai-ism. All the organized faiths felt left out in the cold — particularly Judaism which was his hometown as it were.

Josh's *Google*-search quotient was up to seven million pages by the time he had left London. Interestingly, no one who was not officially in the know, realized where he had gone. He was now adept at the art of invisibility.

Fortunately, Gemma had ensured that every appropriate Internet URL for their names and all their derivatives had been bought up by *Gemstone Inc* a long time ago, together with all the possible versions of her own name. The show's name, *The Miracle Mile* had offered some resistance, having been bought up long before she thought of it but once Gemma searched for her own personal number plate for her car and found that M1RACLE would do just as well, she made that the show's trademark.

Josh's own websites were still flooded with prayers and requests but Jude had put a stop to Maude-Lynn's regular updated reports on what Josh was doing and where he was going to be. Until now, Josh's own words had been transcribed and available for people to read and, when he could, Josh had spent a couple of hours each week reading through the prayers and requests and helping those he could help, but now it seemed as though he had simply vanished. Some people wondered if he had ascended; others thought he had run away. The press certainly looked for him but, just as a tree could hide in a forest, Josh was strangely safe amongst the celebrities at the Dalai Lama's Spring Teaching.

His websites, meanwhile, were linked with many similar teachers worldwide who supported what Josh taught and believed and who took strength from his miracles and his quiet knowledge of Divine Love. In their way, they helped to spread his message far better than Josh did himself, teaching that the Universe was fundamentally benign; that we are children of the Source and co-creators of all we survey; that we have one hundred per cent responsibility for our own life and can change it with our thoughts and feelings whenever we choose to do so; that war and hatred in the external world are just reflections of the war and hatred within us. If we heal ourselves and seek joy — then all else is added unto us.

Groups of modern-day Essenes, Mary Magdalene Energy teachers and followers of the Ascended Masters, ranging from the basically sensible to the seriously weird, either supported Josh or denied him. But they all got a few more clients and a lot more interest because of his advent. There had certainly been a swelling interest in the Law of Attraction teachings and interfaith movements, churches and trainings which concurred whole-heartedly with Josh's own beliefs.

Much more widespread, and with a lot more hits, were the more basic celebrity-oriented blogs which discussed Josh — and the religious sites which (mostly) condemned him or at least denied him.

For what else could the organized religions do? Until now, the 'New Age' teachers had been deniable — kooks or illusionists or deluded people who were trying to water down the message of God's supremacy and His Divine Right to call to account his children for bad behavior or disbelief.

Catholics the world over had been stunned when the Pope came out in support of Josh and the Pontiff was pressurized into issuing a virtual denial the following week, emphasizing his own commitment to Catholicism but re-asserting his recognition of those with differing beliefs who were still valid and good.

Ultra-Orthodox groups such as Opus Dei and the Jesuits were publicly silent and the Archbishop of Canterbury, too, initially kept mum on his meeting with Josh, having been burnt black by previous statements on interfaith that had been howled down by the press. Under pressure, he took the premise of 'wait and see' as his official comment.

Ultra-orthodox Judaism, which — to put it tactfully — wasn't entirely sure that the Chief Rabbi should be regarded as their spokesman, was understandably dismissive on the idea of a present-day Anointed of God. Liberal and Reform Judaism leaders remained interested but politely sitting on the fence.

Islam however was openly paying attention to Josh. While the far right of course was locked in its own invective, the more moderate and the Sufis were fascinated. As long as Josh didn't claim to be *the* Messiah or an incarnation of the Prophet Mohammad but a *Bene Elohim* who appeared to be working within Islamic principles, he was generally accepted as being 'a good thing'. Certainly those Muslims who had been healed by him or heard him speak were impressed. The mystics were openly excited, wondering whether Josh might be a new Mohammad Ibn Arabi, the great Spanish mystic of the twelfth century who wove together many faiths within his own Islamic belief.

The detractors soon had grist for their mill when it was trumpeted across the media that some of Josh's miracles were not necessarily long-lasting let alone permanent. 'Victims' of the short-term benefits were encouraged to parade their anger. The media proclaimed that Josh's work *must* be magic or a temporary hypnotism. With wonderful irony, one of the major television Networks hired Lucifer to demonstrate how magic could trick people into believing they were better. Lucifer was delighted to oblige.

Josh taught his close followers that the truth about the healing was more complex, It wasn't the healing itself that wore off but, if the person's lifestyle, thought patterns or emotional distress that had caused the physical disease in the first place were still being practiced in exactly the same way as before, then their body would become re-affected. Josh could only help people re-align themselves and heal themselves; he couldn't stop them going back to old patterns and habits which caused the sickness in the first place.

But a short-term miracle looks like evidence of trickery and, even though Pastor Jo had the complex problem of a Lucific figure hanging round his neck, he was still the main man when it came to slagging off Josh Goldstone. On *Fox News* and syndicated around the world he lambasted the 'fake and cruel temporary illusions of healing' that Josh had perpetrated.

In fact there were only fifty or sixty cases out of tens of thousands which had reverted, and it should be of no surprise to note that these were the people who most complained about everything in their life anyway. They now had yet more about which to complain which, had Josh been involved in the debate, he might have said was a perfect example of the Law of Attraction working.

He had already tried to explain the concept of free will — where humans can choose what they think, say or do rather than reacting from old habits. But as he pointed out, free will requires effort and can often be uncomfortable to apply to a lifetime of custom and familiar demons. It's easier to slip back into the old routine and throw rocks.

'This man is evil personified,' said Pastor Jo on Network TV. The Pastor was getting canny. 'I realize that not everyone listening shares my belief in the Second Coming of the Lord Jesus and that Josh Goldstone's signs and wonders appear to do good in the world but I say to you 'by their fruits shall ye know them', the words of Jesus Christ himself. And Josh Goldstone's fruits are young men hypnotized into sexual depravity; innocent women beguiled by the serpent of sex and the false hope of miracles followed by the despair of betrayal.

'The Bible is clear that before the End Days, the Anti-Christ and his messengers will come, appearing to make signs and wonders and fooling the unwise. I say to you all, this man must be stopped; he must be exorcised; he must be called to account for his actions.

'Where is he? He has gone into hiding. He does not even answer our criticisms — because he cannot. He is a servant of Satan and he cannot come out into the light.'

'A statement would be good,' said Jude via Skype to Josh, Maude-Lynn and John in India.

'Saying what?' asked Josh who was relaxed, scruffy and happy and just back from a leisurely ramble to St John's church en route to which he'd seen at least two different types of ibex, a porcupine and a Himalayan fly-catcher. 'We've already apologized for Venus and Lucifer's behavior. What has Venus got to say by the way?'

'She's undertaking a retreat at a Carmelite monastery,' said Jude in a deliberately non-committal way.

There was a moment's silence as they all took in the value of this impressive piece of public relations. And then a series of snorts of laughter that only subsided into giggles a full minute later.

'We could release some footage of Josh here,' said Maude-Lynn, wiping her eyes. 'It's almost the same thing.'

'No,' said Jude. 'He's not even officially there. Best to keep him out of what's happening in India as long as possible.'

'I'm practicing being invisible,' said Josh apparently *à propos* of nothing.

'Successfully, I gather,' said Jude dryly. 'The world has noticed.'

'It's amazingly effective,' said Maude-Lynn. 'People just don't see him unless he wants them to. Even if he's right in front of them.'

'I could do with some of that,' said Jude with feeling.

'Think gray and fade,' said Josh, doing just that.

'Stop it!' said Maude-Lynn elbowing him in the stomach. 'We need a strategy.'

'We always do,' he said.

'There's the bit from John Jordan's funeral where he's telling that girl how sorry he is that he can't raise John from the dead. You know, where he says that he can only assist people in doing what they are willing to do themselves and that he's a catalyst rather than the instigator of the miracle,' suggested Maude-Lynn. 'We could put that out.'

'No, say nothing. It will only fuel it,' said Josh.

'Josh you really don't care, do you?' Jude was indignant. 'Jo, Susannah and I are fielding so much stuff here — you've no idea! There's so much hostility.'

'Then we don't fuel it,' said Josh. 'Are *you* safe?'

'Yes, we've got protection — Simon's organized us some security-disciples of our own. And people know that you're not here so we're not actually surrounded by hecklers.'

'Is Charlie with you?' Josh knew how little time Jude and her partner had been spending together lately.

'No. It's a busy time at work in California,' said Jude. 'It's okay. We both knew what we were taking on.' She was lying and Josh knew it.

'Why don't you take a week's leave — both you and the rest of the team — and go visit with family,' said Josh. 'Yes, that's the thing to do. Just go on expenses. Let it all have time to die down. There's no need to fuel the fire.'

'What, now?'

'Now — before the next stage. Then you really will be busy. If I can vanish, you can vanish. Give the rest of the world a chance to look at some other news for a change.'

'Okay,' said Jude. 'But be aware that the lizard from outer space theory is gaining ground!'

'Doesn't that put me in with Bill Gates and most of the British Royal Family?' said Josh with a chuckle.

'It does indeed.'

'Takes a lizard to see a lizard I suppose,' said Josh. 'They're only projecting their own lower animal nature.'

'Don't you ever get riled?' asked Jude. It was a common question that she put to Josh.

'Do you?' he countered.

'Yes, but I guess you're right; it's only reaction. Once I take some time out it doesn't seem so important.

'So, how are things going in India?'

'Well I've never before met Buddhists so furious they could squash a bug,' said Josh. 'To be fair, Mary-Beth's idea has been a very difficult concept for them to take on. Some of them think it's mad; others think it's evil; some think it's just stupid. They, quite understandably, say it means condoning all the deaths at the hands of the Chinese over the last 60 years. But they do understand that to forgive is not to condone and that if they don't hand out respect they can't receive respect in return. I have to hand it to them, they're all coming round. It must have been really hard especially with a Yid from the UK trying to persuade them.'

'Watch the self-deprecating Jewish stuff Josh,' warned Jude though she was pleased by the content of what he said. 'You really can't afford people thinking you're bringing Judaism into disrepute.'

'Now you're sounding like Simon!' said Josh. 'Go and take a break now — we're ready to announce in ten days time after the Dalai Lama's Spring Teachings so that's when I'm going to need you refreshed and ready.'

That week was wonderful — for Josh at least. The invisibility technique that he seemed to have perfected (probably through the focus of meditating and praying with the Dalai Lama) meant that he could wander for hours along pathways and roads, observing without being noticed. He was definitely there but just as a rather peaceful space rather than as an intrusive human. Animals and birds noticed him but they found him unthreatening and let him wander among them. However, if Josh wanted to interact with them, he stayed visible. His heart sang the first time he held his hand out to a pine-martin and it sniffed it, unfazed, and then licked the salt off his skin.

Each day, after meeting with the Dalai Lama, his friend and co-mentor, he would walk and walk and walk through oak and rhododendron groves, under pines and cedars, brushing his hand among the scented herbs. He learnt to recognize several different kinds of deer and goats through describing them to Eleazer afterwards and, one day, even sat for a magical hour watching two young snow leopards playing.

On the day before the anniversary of Gemma's death, he donned his favorite walking anorak and went hiking with a backpack containing a tiny tent and enough food for three days. He knew that pretty soon all the entourage would be arriving, and he would be surrounded by strangers and he was firm with everyone that he needed some time on his own.

Eleazer offered to drive him into the hills where he could get far away from the commerce and everyday life that had spread so far around the city. Mary-Beth lovingly tucked a packet of chocolate digestives into his rucksack without his noticing and remembered not to wave him off in case it looked horribly needy — and in case Josh didn't turn round and wave back to her. She had been wrong in hoping that she would be over him by now but at least the love she felt for him was enjoyable nowadays rather than the cause of a deep inner ache — and she adored all the organizing and liaising she was doing with Eleazer and the others. Chris's brother was a sweetheart and sometimes she felt like a tiny Queen Bee in a hive of attentive helpers. After all, it wasn't as if *she* had time to swan off into the bushes and meditate!

Josh spent three whole days in the hills, wandering and meditating in the spring sunshine and watching the Dhauladhar peaks, the sky, the animals and plants. He marveled in the agility of the monkeys and langoors that played overhead and the bright and beautiful birds — even including peacocks and peahens that carped at him from low branches. A brown bear grunted and stood up on its hind legs when he came upon it unannounced. Josh stood stock-still, holding his breath in wonder. He didn't feel fear; he knew now that no animal would hurt him. Slowly, he reached into his bag and offered the bear one of his chocolate biscuits and it sat down suddenly on its haunches, perplexed at this unexpected event in its life. The biscuit smelt good, so he took it gently from Josh's hand and sat down again to sniff at it. Yes, it was good but not good enough to hold the bear's attention for long and, after eating it with what appeared to be elegant politeness, it grunted and wandered away.

Josh discovered that he had only to hold his hand out to a ring-dove and the bird would fly down onto it and coo while he stroked its soft head and neck. He found he could meld with the trees and the rocks and feel their own slow and powerful life force. He could understand the meaning behind the birdcalls — the urgency of the spring and the mating season and the passion that was eggs! He could lie in the grass and become one with the Earth and hear the music of the spheres again.

He knew that he was very, very blessed. On the third night, he reviewed the last twelve months, realizing that he could have practiced invisibility much sooner — but then, maybe he had needed to be visible. It had been a good and sound training for the next stage of the work. He eschewed the tent and lay immune to the night-cold watching the stars for hours, just as he had done a full year before in the desert. One day, soon, he would be going home to the stars and that would be good too. But there was work to do first. In the morning, he bade Gemma's spirit a final and loving farewell, sighed deeply, got up, dusted down his scruffy jeans and wandered back to the dirt track where Eleazer had left him and where they had agreed to meet on the fourth morning.

Chapter Thirty Six

There was no one there.

Oh well, perhaps he was early. Josh ate his last chocolate digestive as he walked peacefully down the track — he had been saving it for Eleazer but it was too good to resist. After another half hour, he found himself wandering along the road that led to and from the distant concrete mass that was Lower Dharamsala. He walked slowly towards the town and kept going. Eleazer would see him as he drove along. After another hour, he was able to hitch a ride in the back of a Toyota Hylux but now he was concerned. He could feel Eleazer around him — no doubt about that. But Eleazer himself had not shown up.

By the time the truck was winding its way through the outskirts of the city, honking at the scooters and negotiating itself around the sacred cows, tourists and overspills of market produce in the streets, he knew for certain that Eleazer was dead — but that his spirit had not gone. Josh was surprised — Eleazer, surely, was essential to their plans. But once he had cleared his mind and listened to the spirit, he understood. It was a little dramatic for his personal taste but he could see the sense in it.

So when the truck dropped him at the Lower Dharamsala bus station and he thanked the driver for his kindness, he wasn't surprised to be met by the whirlwind of hiccupping tears that was Mary-Beth and was ready to pick her up in a great embrace of love and dusty anorak and hold her tightly saying over and over, 'It's okay Mary-Beth. I know all about it. It's okay. We can sort this. It's okay.'

For Mary-Beth it was a curdling of emotions: fear, loss, anger, love and delight all trying and failing to mix themselves together.

'Why weren't you here?' was all she could say. 'He wouldn't have died if you were here. And now it's too late. Oh why Josh? Why?'

'When did it happen?' he asked, lifting her off her feet and carrying her out of the way of the other traffic to the safety of what passed for a pavement. She was light as a feather and so tiny. Surely she didn't eat enough?

'As soon as he got back from taking you into the hills,' she said, rubbing at her tear-streaked eyes with her fingers as he put her down behind a suitable sacred cow. Josh looked into those swollen eyes in the blotched face and knew she had been frantic for all that time.

'I didn't know how to find you,' she accused. 'And now he's really, *really* dead!'

'Where is he? Have they had the funeral?'

'No, it's today. It's later today. He's at the palace. I wouldn't let them take him to the morgue.'

'You wouldn't *let* them?' he wondered at this tiny ball of fire who could boss around the Dalai Lama and his entourage.

'No, there are rats at the morgue. They eat the bodies,' she said pathetically.

Josh took this statement with a pinch of salt but if Eleazer's body was at the palace it was all to the good.

'They don't take the internal organs out or anything odd like that do they?' he said deliberately to spark her indignation. He knew perfectly well that Buddhists didn't but he wanted Mary-Beth back from her dismals.

'Of course not!' she said, taking the bait and firing up immediately.

He squeezed her affectionately with one arm while hailing a taxi with the other.

'It's still the first Bardo, Mary-Beth. Eleazer isn't gone yet. There's still hope.'

'But his eyes are all sunk,' she said still caught between emotions – misery, hope and indignation that he obviously knew perfectly well about Tibetan Buddhist death rituals. 'What do you know about the Bardos?'

'I saw a very good video with a commentary by Leonard Cohen once,' said Josh as the taxi pulled up next to them. 'Have you got any money?'

The Tibetan Buddhists believe in three Bardos or states following death. At the moment of transition, the personality of the dead person goes into a state of trance for four days where they don't realize that they are dead. During this First Bardo, monks say special verses and prayers in order to reach the dead person to help them to see and not fear the brilliant light that shines on them to call them to the Divine at the end of this Bardo. If the soul can comprehend and love the light, then it will pass through to the higher realms; if not, it will flee from the light.

The person then becomes conscious of death and the Second Bardo begins. The person sees every action and thought that they experienced while alive passing in front of them. This can be a time of great terror if the life was what Buddhists tactfully call an unskillful human. Then comes the Third Bardo, which is the state of seeking another birth. All previous thoughts and actions direct the person to choose new parents, who will give them their next body and the lessons they need to move on in the great wheel of Samsara.

Josh and Mary-Beth were driven upwards through the tangle of buildings with its mesh of telegraph wires above street level, past precariously-balanced yellow and white apartments and multi-colored hovels garnished with corrugated iron. Josh asked the cab driver to stop at a café and, with Mary-Beth's money, bought them a paper plateful of hot dumplings. She ate two to please him and was amazed at how much better she felt for the food.

'You forgot to eat didn't you?' said Josh. She nodded.

'The benefits of a good Jewish upbringing — eat, eat!' he laughed, enjoying one of the dumplings. Part of her wondered at his callousness but she knew too that he must be hungry — and that it was only sensible to eat. Tenaciously, she reached out and took the last dumpling and his face, humorously indignant nearly made her choke on the food.

They stopped again for a second plate of dumplings and shared it between them as the taxi wove its way past dogs and cows and monks and arguing women (Josh had already noted that half the population seemed to wear bobble hats). Roadside shops were awash with prayer scarves, holistic centers offering massage and Reiki healing, stall after stall of postcards and images of the Dalai Lama — and nearly everything in English, the 'official' language of the town.

At the gates to the Dalai Lama's palace, the taxi man dropped them off, asking them anxiously to ask his Holiness for prayers for his mother who was sick.

'Don't worry, she's well,' said Josh, almost absently, touching the man briefly on the shoulder as Mary-Beth counted out notes.

They nodded at the gate attendants who bowed in the Namaste and Mary-Beth led Josh through a side door and turned towards the room where Eleazer lay. Josh could have found it simply by following the waft of incense that filled the air.

He didn't go in but he could see the monk's body lay on a bed on the floor covered in white prayer shawls. Around him incense sticks burned and there were offerings of barley and butter. One Lama sat cross-legged by the body, reading the great ancient texts of the Bardo and others prayed silently.

'Can you get them out of there?' Josh whispered to Mary-Beth.

She looked up at him, her face suddenly alive with hope.

'You can do something? Even now?'

'Yes, he hasn't gone,' said Josh. 'In fact, he's nagging me pretty hard!'

'But the body…' faltered Mary-Beth.

'This is a very fragile reality,' said Josh with a smile. 'It's subject to higher worlds; to a higher order. But I think it would be too frightening if he just sat up while they were there don't you?'

'What is this, what is this?' a voice behind them spoke. The Dalai Lama himself had come up behind them silently. 'You are back. This is good. But here is much sadness as well. Have you come to pray with me for our friend?'

'Your Holiness,' both Josh and Mary-Beth bowed in the Namaste.

'Come in, come in,' said His Holiness but as his eyes met Josh's an understanding spread between the two.

'So you want to be alone with him, eh?' said the Dalai Lama. 'Well I believe you know what you are doing.'

He put his hand on Josh's shoulder and called gently to the Lama and the monks in the room to come out for a moment. They did, with the utmost reluctance, filing out with perplexed faces.

'We will be over here,' His Holiness nodded to Josh and to Mary-Beth. She backed away, suddenly frightened, leaving Josh standing alone at the doorway. She didn't know what he was going to do but she didn't really believe that he could do anything. Mary-Beth had bathed the already atrophying body of her friend the previous day. He was too far gone for any help no matter what Josh might believe.

She went and stood with the monks, incongruous next to their maroon and saffron in her jeans and sweatshirt. As if he read her mind, the Dalai Lama whispered (to help her feel more comfortable): 'You would look very nice in Indian clothing. Perhaps you should buy some. The bright colors would suit you, you know.'

She smiled up at him shyly. She had got to know this great man quite well and loved him deeply. He patted her shoulder and whispered, 'We shall pray together.'

She closed her eyes tightly and automatically slipped into the 23rd psalm, a memory from childhood. As she whispered, 'Though I walk through the valley of the shadow of death…' she opened her eyes to peep briefly.

Josh was still just standing at the door of the room, doing nothing. Mary-Beth's heart sank. Bravely, although she could feel tears forming behind her eyelids, she finished the psalm and then, like the innocent and courageous child that she was, she turned to the Dalai Lama and leant forwards to be embraced. He, somewhat surprised, but nonetheless touched, wrapped his arms around her.

'Eleazer!' It was Josh's voice, strong and loud. 'Get up. Come out.'

The Dalai Lama and Mary-Beth both stiffened slightly. Mary-

Beth opened her eyes and turned her head in time to see Josh walking over to stand by them, his face slightly clouded as though he had made some great effort.

Behind him, there was movement. One of the monks must have stayed behind in the room and was just leaving. Mary-Beth couldn't see clearly; Josh was in the way. And it didn't matter. He hadn't gone in; he hadn't touched Eleazer. It was all for nothing.

And then the Dalai Lama almost pushed her away as he moved forwards.

'Eleazer!' he said. Just that one word.

Leaning against the door of the room, certainly pale, definitely weak and actually rather frightened, stood the dead monk.

He strengthened visibly as they all stared at him, seeming to grow taller. As he stood up straight, two of the white prayer shawls fell from his shoulders, sliding gently to the ground.

The Dalai Lama stood before his friend, his arms held out in wonder. Mary-Beth fell to her knees and wept as she had never wept before. Three of the monks ran away in terror, the others began to pray in equal terror. Eleazer walked forwards taking deep breaths.

'Life is good,' he said. 'Your Holiness, we must talk!'

'Would you like some tea?' asked the Dalai Lama. He had to say something and this really was a very new situation.

'Yes, indeed, I would!' said Eleazer.

'Tea!' said one of the monks who had remained, transfixed. 'Yes. Tea. I will arrange tea.' He and his companions hurried away, aware that they had the biggest news to spread in the whole wide world. Only the Lama, holding the written Bardo, was left standing, his mouth still open.

'Josh?' the Dalai Lama turned but Josh was nowhere to be seen. There was just Mary-Beth now up and hopping from one foot to another in her tearful excitement but not wanting to crowd Eleazer or get in His Holiness's way.

'Come here child,' said the Dalai Lama and the strangest three-way-hug in modern history took place in a sea of delight and tears.

Chapter Thirty Seven

It was time.

It would be fair to say that His Holiness knew that the announcement he was about to make would be seen by campaigners and Buddhists as a betrayal of all those who had fought for Tibetan independence for more than half a century. He knew that it would call into question his authority and he knew that it would change the future forever. Both he and Josh had already faced initial outrage and horror from the Tibetan Government in Exile and the Office of Tibet in London but, as they explained again and again, nothing else had worked; nothing would continue to work if they didn't change their plan. Frankly, his Holiness wasn't getting any younger and they had to do something different if they wanted to resolve the problem.

Mary-Beth's plan was an incredible turn-around that could only be seen by those who didn't understand as an horrific disloyalty. Even worse, if it didn't work then *all* would be lost.

'But all has been lost for a very long time and none of the resistance or believing that the situation is wrong has helped to make it right,' Josh had said gently when the two men first discussed the extraordinary venture for liberating Tibet. 'This way, at least, we allow the Source to act through us, aligning with peace instead of resisting the bad that has come. You can't create peace when you are in vibrational harmony with conflict.'

The Dalai Lama had sighed. He was the epitome of love and simultaneously tired of a lifetime of fighting. He knew that what Josh said made sense and, also, that if something were not done in his lifetime, his next reincarnation would be harder. He was already nearly eighty and not as strong as he had been.

'Good is not easy,' he said. 'But at least I believe that I will reap what I sow.' His beautiful, serene face lit up with humor. 'And I cannot hurt the next Dalai Lama without his permission!'

Both men laughed, they had had a wonderful accord, each recognizing himself in the other. It was easier for Josh to see the peaceful outcome of ceasing to resist the Chinese rule because he wasn't personally involved in this conflict. Had it been the Middle East, he confessed, he would have found it harder.

'So I must do that one for you next lifetime!' said the Dalai Lama.

'Yes please,' said Josh, and he meant it.

Mary-Beth's idea was simple (but not easy). After all, she said, China got possession of Tibet through calling its 1951 invasion 'the Peaceful Liberation' and China genuinely believed that Tibet belonged to the Chinese. So, she reasoned, if that was a happy belief, then it must be in vibrational harmony with Source Energy, even if the rest of the world disagreed. Because the desire was strong and the vibration was in alignment, Chinese rule of Tibet was bound to happen. And the condemnation of the rest of the world strengthened the situation by giving it energy rather than taking away from it.

The main problem, she summarized, was that before 'liberation,' Tibet had been ruled by a theocratic feudal government where the life of the people had not necessarily been good. Nearly 95 percent of Tibetans were illiterate and the same percentage of the population were serfs born into slavery — owned by monasteries and nobles — without any possibility of bettering or freeing themselves. They understandably wanted a better life — and the power of their desire grew. But the old Tibetan government was not willing to change so change had to come from somewhere else.

'It was a very backwards society,' she said. 'Of course *we* think it would have been better if they could have liberated themselves but, if they hadn't and Tibet was still ruled the way it was before 1951, we'd now be attacking the Tibetans for Human Rights abuses instead of supporting their desire for freedom.

'Yes I know the Dalai Lama isn't like that — but he was born for a reason; to be the one who not only helps his people come into the 20th — and 21st centuries — but also to be bigger than the Chinese; bigger than his predecessors, more spiritual, even more holy, and to see the wider picture.

'There's no way that China will give power back to Tibet. It has to be earned back because it was only lost because there were abuses in the old system. That's how Karma works isn't it? Tibet drew the invasion for two reasons, power was being abused — a noble could cut the head off a slave any time he liked — and because the serfs themselves wanted a better life. They wanted it — and frankly they got it! Their life expectancy is much higher now; they have education, better farming techniques and a certain freedom to worship. They just don't have it the way they think they want it. And of course, they believe they are oppressed so they create evidence of oppression.'

'So why do anything?' asked Josh, amused at her fervor and wanting to act as devil's advocate.

'To show the world what Gandhi showed it and what Jesus showed it — that the way forward is through non-violence; through peace. Through surrender if you like.

'Look at me and you — for example. I fell in love with you and it was hopeless because you were never going to love me. And I *wasn't* me, I was resentful and unfulfilled and upset — just like the Tibetans are now and actually how they were with the old regime before China took over.'

'I don't think I ever invaded you,' said Josh, thoughtfully.

Mary-Beth hit him on the shoulder.

'Ouch!' he said.

'Listen!' she said.

'Okay, okay...'

'You *did* actually invade — in that you arrived out of nowhere, transformed and updated if you like. You took over. Every single part of *Gemstone Inc* was changed when you came.'

'I was invited,' said Josh mildly.

'Only because you'd been an unacknowledged part of it before. You knew it belonged to you — it was yours automatically anyway on Gemma's death. So actually you, just like China, thought you owned it. It was just whether you chose to come in or to walk away.'

'I can see that,' he acknowledged.

'So, having been 'peacefully liberated,' some of us changed and some of us felt resentful and I fell in love with you. And the only way to solve the pain I felt that you didn't love me was to do something to develop me. There was no point in whining about not being loved or that you weren't doing what I wanted or calling for you to leave or do what I wanted you to do was there?'

'No...'

'So I stopped resisting it. I accepted that you didn't love me — and went to find peace and a way forward. And in finding peace, I found something for you too — a path — which has brought us together as friends (I won't say equals) and transformed our relationship so I don't need to be soppy over you and actually have a much better relationship than we did before.

'And if I can do it, Tibet can.'

She sat down with a thump, satisfied at her logic.

Josh sat in silence for a moment, thinking

'Okay, go on,' he said.

'Go on?'

'Yes, what do you want me to do; what do you want the Dalai Lama to do?' His face twitched with amusement. 'Presumably you've already talked this over with him.'

'Yes of course I have,' said that totally amazing woman that Mary-Beth was becoming. 'He's got his doubts but he wants to talk to you.'

'You didn't tell him it was my idea did you?'

'No, but I told him you were the one to help him do it.'

'Any particular reason?'

'Yes of course. Because if we peacefully liberate Tibet — by walking in over the border with a hundred major celebrities — '

'A hundred celebrities?'

'Yes, and cameras so the Chinese daren't shoot them.'

'I see. Go on.'

'So if the Chinese *do* get silly for a moment and shoot someone —'

'Yes?'

'You can raise them from the dead and it will all be all right,' said Mary-Beth triumphantly.

'So, basically, she just wants me there as a kind of hospital unit in case anything goes wrong.' Josh said to the Dalai Lama as they sat drinking tea together before the Spring Teachings.

The old man's face lit up with his brilliant smile.

'Well we can see for ourselves that you are certainly useful in this manner,' he said. 'I like this! We should all have our uses in life!'

They both chuckled.

'She is quite the brave soul, that little one,' said his Holiness. 'Do you think that she is right?'

Josh sighed. 'Yes, I do,' he said. 'Forgive me if this is not respectful but the Spirit doesn't need to be recognized. It's our egos that need to be recognized. It doesn't truly, in the great scheme of things, matter if a country is ruled by one State or another as long as there is peace. And it doesn't matter whether China recognizes this Dalai or Panchen Lama or that one. The souls of the people will know. And if you hold the Spirit of your people — as you do — then you don't *need* to be recognized by China.'

'I may not need it, but the people need someone to hold a focus for them.'

'Maybe they do and maybe they don't. I don't know. What I do know is that you've said, on record, that you will be reincarnated next time in a free country. Why not make that free country Tibet? You can make it free by not resisting the idea that it is anything else right now.'

'But the Chinese have invaded.'

'And as long as we believe that, they will have control. If we truly — *truly* — believe that Tibet is free and act as we would act in a free country then, by the Law of Attraction — by Karmic Law — then Tibet must *be* free. You don't have to kick the Chinese out, you have to make them a non-problem. Then they will either cease to be what Tibetans — and the rest of the world — consider to be bad and either become good or leave.

'It's a fundamental law of the Universe — if you change then others must either change too or move away. You can't make anyone else change, you can only change yourself.'

'Do you want me to recognize the Chinese Panchen Lama instead of the Panchen Lama that I know is the true one?'

'I'm sorry but only the Source knows who is the true Panchen Lama,' said Josh. 'In the Jewish mystical tradition I learnt in London when I was younger, we were taught that there are three people aligned on Earth for each great task that needs to be accomplished. If the first does not or cannot fulfill the task, then it passes to the second and then, perhaps, to the third.

'I know you have a different belief — that it is just one soul that is the right soul — whereas I believe that we come from a soul *group* where we can even mingle and merge after death and before life. I have no doubt that you did recognize the soul of the true Panchen Lama. And then, when it was made impossible, I suspect the mantle was assumed by another from the same soul group. It may well be that the second soul is the man who is the Chinese choice or, if it is not, if we move peacefully, then it will appear naturally who it is and the Chinese Panchen Lama will give up that mantle.'

His Holiness considered.

'There is one other matter,' he said. 'It is the Panchen Lama who must recognize me as the Dalai Lama when I am reborn. What if this young Chinese choice does not recognize me?'

'The world has changed,' said Josh. 'We live in a media fishbowl now. So when you are reborn even if the Panchen Lama doesn't recognize you, you can still be who you are and the world will see that. I didn't have to be born of a virgin in a cave surrounded by shepherds, did I? And neither did Gandhi or Buddha. After all, the whole situation depends on your being enlightened — so you *choose* to incarnate rather than *having* to incarnate. So if you have that power, you certainly have the power to create your own reality next time. My goodness, everyone can choose their own reality — you should find it pretty easy! And as you said before, you can't hurt the next Dalai Lama without his permission. Could the next life be harder than this one? I don't think so.'

The Dalai Lama sat, peacefully, in silence and Josh knew that it was time to leave his friend to consider. He had said enough.

As with most politics, the situation in Tibet was not as clear-cut as it might have seemed. The tendency was to see China as 'bad' and Tibet as 'good' but, as Mary-Beth had discovered Tibet had had its negative points too.

It would appear that until the European 20th century concept of sovereignty, China and Tibet had a non-specific friendly relationship where Buddhist Chinese Emperors relied on advice from Tibetan Lamas particularly in efforts to pacify the Buddhist Mongols. The relationship was really that of patron and priest with both religious and symbolic content. No one used absolute terms of who owned where or who was beholden to whom. China was — and still is — full of different ethnicities including Han, Hui (used for all Muslims), Yi, Manchu and Mongol. Tibetan was considered one of the ethnicities and as long as everyone was getting on perfectly well together, the question of exactly who ruled whom simply didn't arise.

But with 20th century British, Japanese and American imperialism, the annexing and then liberation of the British colonies — particularly India — and the rise of nationalism and the coming of communist rule to China, it all changed. The British had left India two years before the communist government was established in China and India was feeling, understandably, somewhat anti-imperialistic and pro-nationalistic. The British had been keen to help Tibet assert its independence in a world where 'sovereignty' had become an issue, because supporting Tibet was strategically helpful for Britain. India was happy to assert that Tibet was a part of China and China thought that Communism was the great panacea. For

China, the assumption of Tibet could only be good for a country run on such outdated principles; for Tibet it was a betrayal of a 'gentleman's agreement'. Never the twain would meet — unless someone backed down and refused to fight.

Perhaps now was the time of the great backing down…

On the last day of the Spring Teachings, with some of his advisors still doubtful or even opposed to the move, his Holiness the Dalai Lama made a public announcement that he accepted the Chinese Panchen Lama as the true Panchen Lama and that he appreciated the modern development of investment that China had made in Tibet. He added that he acknowledged that the old Tibetan regime of his childhood had become untenable; that education and freedom were very important for the people of Tibet and that without China's help the country might have found it much harder to move into the second half of the 20th century.

He sent greetings of peace and fellowship to Beijing; thanked them for allowing Buddhist worship in Tibet despite their own communist convictions; forgave them for any and all human rights abuses or deaths and asked forgiveness for any deaths or injuries at the hands of the people of Tibet. He re-committed himself to peace and said he was very much looking forward to going home to Lhasa and living in joyful harmony with his own people and with the Chinese.

Chapter Thirty Eight

Well! What headlines that made around the world! People were queuing up to give their reactions. Beijing was a little cautious, not to mention suspicious, and Buddhists all over the world were divided as to whether they had just seen a living saint in action or whether it was a complete betrayal of everything they had been fighting over for more than 60 years.

'But I do not wish to fight,' said his Holiness. 'Whatever has happened in the past, we must have peace in our hearts now.'

It was a bitter pill to swallow for those who had spent so long fighting injustice and Chinese rule in Tibet. Human beings take on causes with great passion and don't realize that they are giving energy to the problem if they focus on it or they fight it. It seems so *right* to fight sickness, injustice and poverty. Otherwise, surely you are condoning it? But all the spiritual teachers of the modern world say that the external is a reflection of us so we must heal the hatred, diseased thought and anger within ourselves in order to see a change in the outside world.

The massed celebrities in Dharamsala were a huge help. They all had immense respect for the Dalai Lama and Arianna Bel and Marco Montbretia, the man and the woman voted the world's most beautiful actor and actress, spoke out strongly and supportively about a new age; a time of moving on and closing the door on the past. Pictured standing one each side of the Dalai Lama, with their brood of children, both blood-born and adopted, their images shot around the world, creating front cover photographs that stirred a secret hope in the hearts of many.

But of course there were more than enough detractors; those who, if this ended the conflict, thought that they had wasted 30, 40, 50 years of their lives; those who recognized or had personally experienced human rights violations in China and those who thought that the Dalai Lama was mad — or senile.

That Josh was in Dharamsala and in some way involved was mentioned here and there but his profile still remained surprisingly low. Some detractors tried to say that Josh's evil influence had corrupted the Dalai Lama and although his Holiness's words were so obviously of conciliation and peace some judged them to be foolish and harmful to the cause. But no one really thought that his Holiness the Dalai Lama would be tricked by some American would-be Messiah.

Barbara Abbas made some headlines by saying that Josh, being a Jew, should focus on trying to create peace in the Middle East rather than interfering with Buddhist issues but, as there were plenty of other Arabic celebrities in Dharamsala and as Barbara was known as a strong advocate against the Israeli state, her views were a one-day wonder.

'If we had said 'no' what would you have done?' Eleazer asked Josh on the day of the announcement. They were standing outside the palace, looking at the clouds over the mountains and sharing a companionable cigarette. Josh didn't smoke but he knew the value of a peace-pipe and when Eleazer offered a puff on one of his hand-rolled cigarettes it was a gesture that it would be churlish to refuse.

Eleazer sighed while he awaited the answer. Life was very good — how well he realized that! And even more, his savior never once suggested that smoking was bad for his health.

'I don't know,' said Josh, watching a moving dot that might be a tawny eagle circling high in the sky. 'I was sure that you would. It's one of those Divine timing things. It could never have been done before today; absolutely not. But today is the right day.'

'I repeat my question,' said Eleazer with both respect and interest.

'Gone somewhere else, I guess,' said Josh. 'I go where God sends me.'

'This belief in an external God is still strange to me,' said Eleazer, carefully placing his cigarette butt in the portable closable ashtray that he hid among his robes. 'You talk almost as a Buddhist would —

that it is our task to be enlightened and spread peace — and then you speak of a Higher Being like the Jews, Muslims and Christians.'

'Ah I could talk about that for hours!' said Josh. 'I find it so fascinating. I think, in a nutshell, we are all children of the Source Energy; all fully responsible for our lives and, when we link together in love, we form great collective consciousness that can move mountains — think of the Maharishi and how his world-wide peace meditation helped heal the Soviet stand-off over Cuba. But I also believe that we are all one drop in an ocean which includes many parts that we can't see and cannot conceive of — and I know that when I ask for help or guidance that it comes through Grace. And that Grace is both external and internal simultaneously. Perhaps it's easier to call it God; I don't have a problem with the idea of God. But many people do so that's why I call It the Source. It's a consciousness — but far and beyond what I can understand and therefore feels more than me and, in a way, external to me while still being the essence of my heart and soul.'

'Some say you are the devil or the Anti-Christ,' said Eleazer.

'To them, maybe I am,' said Josh. 'People see what they choose to see. We none of us see the total truth.'

'So you could be wrong?'

'*I* can be wrong, of course!' said Josh. 'But the great Consciousness isn't wrong and I can feel it in me. The great Consciousness is Now. It is always perfect in the Now.'

Four days later, unsuspecting border guards at the Nathu La border crossing between India and Tibet, were completely overwhelmed by an influx of more than five hundred people who calmly and assertively walked, cycled or rode mules along the narrow road to the border. Not one of them had the requisite papers; not one displayed a visa but not one of them intended to stop and explain why they were there.

Within the throng, surrounded by Josh's security-disciples and his own entourage of monks, his Holiness the Dalai Lama rode in a carriage pulled by a donkey. Right at the head of the cavalcade walked Josh Goldstone together with seven instantly-recognizable movie stars, two of the world's most famous international footballers, sixteen rock and pop stars, four super-models, twelve noted religious and spiritual figures (in full, ceremonial robes where appropriate) and many others whose faces were known to everyone in the world who had a television a newspaper or an Internet connection.

Wrong-footed, flustered and uncertain — and aware that even if they were ordered to shoot, they would run out of bullets before they ran out of people crossing the border — the guards tried to call for orders but none of their communication equipment would work. This was the most dangerous moment as far as the peaceful invading army was concerned. Those who had agreed to walk in front or to flank the more vulnerable could be excused for feeling very frightened indeed but the calmness and confidence of both Josh and the Dalai Lama were both palpable and comforting. Mary-Beth, walking behind Josh, was right. Someone who can raise you from the dead is very comforting to have around when there are guns being thrust in your face. Some members of the peaceful army almost lost their bottle at the border itself with guards lining up in front of them and firing warning shots into the air but the swell of people approaching from behind meant that they simply *couldn't* stop and had to go over, under, through or round the barricades and meet the soldiers face-on.

Then one of the guardsmen lost his head and fired into the crowd. The bullets hit Arianna Bel in the stomach and legs and she fell gasping back into Josh's waiting arms. Next to her, Marco Montbretia shouted out defiance. Josh, now down on his knees put out one hand to calm him and Mary-Beth too, put a hand on his arm. Marco stood, his chest heaving and tears in his eyes watching as Josh returned his attention to Arianna. She buckled backwards, choked slightly and recovered consciousness. As Marco took her hand, she stood up again, her eyes wide in amazement at the damage to her designer dungarees and the spent bullets that fell with a soft thud to the ground below her.

The horror of what had been done to her — and her immediate recovery — were enough to vanquish the guards and they fell back in disarray.

'Thank you,' said Josh softly to the actress. 'You have just liberated Tibet on your own.'

'Thank *you*' said Arianna, still breathless from what had happened to her.

Maude-Lynn Sykes, almost choking with excitement, was right at the forefront, filming carefully with a miniature camera. Later that day, the images of Arianna, Marco and Josh, sent around the world by satellite, knocked everything else off the world news. The actress — with two Oscars and three husbands — was clearly seen to have been shot by the Chinese guard. And her recovery was just as visible. It was a sensation.

Maude-Lynn was traveling with her small but highly efficient film crew carrying everything they would need to record and then transmit their amazing images to all the major Networks. Joshua, the cameraman, was filming openly with the help of his assistant, Ben, but a mixture of modern technology and *Gemstone Inc's* indefatigable IT guy, Jon Taylor, made it quite possible for Maude-Lynn to carry secret cameras herself in order to continue the incredible video diary of Josh's life without it being immediately apparent that she was doing anything of the sort. She had to record to a mini-disk and transfer the tape onto digital later, but she'd got used to that!

Arianna gave a short interview later in the day, again recorded, transferred and finally transmitted by satellite, talking of how she had felt when she was shot and how important it was to make this peaceful march to Lhasa to take the Dalai Lama home.

'This is an amazing moment,' she said. 'We are making history; making peace. I implore China to be our friend and help us bring the Dalai Lama home. I know that I and all my colleagues here —' she waved her hand at several multi-millionaire eye-candy stars — 'Are willing to risk our lives for this mission. This is the *good* that we can do in the world today and we are proud to show up and take our place in this great march for peace.'

There were other film crews present too – international television companies had been briefed just before the cavalcade began its 300-mile journey to Lhasa. Maude-Lynn herself had done the briefing – Jude was still in London. The one-time embittered, alcohol-sodden reporter was in her element. She thoroughly enjoyed seeing the complete amazement on the fellow journalists' and film crews' faces as they realized that they were in the right place at the right time to record a piece of history in the making.

'You mean they think they are all just going to walk to Lhasa and move in without a shot being fired?' asked the Sky News reporter in disbelief. 'The Chinese will destroy them!'

'I don't think so,' said Maude-Lynn. 'China doesn't want the kind of negative publicity that comes from shooting or even arresting a hundred of the most famous people in the world for just taking a walk without a visa.'

'My God, it's going to be a massacre,' said the woman.

'Again, I don't think so. There are 24 places on a bus to the border which is leaving in five minutes. Are you coming or not? We'll be walking the first 20 miles into Tibet, camping overnight and then buses from within Tibet will pick us up and drive us all to Lhasa. It's no place for sissies and if you're too scared to come, we won't argue. But believe me, the Chinese do not need the kind of negative publicity this plan going wrong could give them.'

Maude-Lynn was right and Josh was right. From the moment that the images of the shooting and healing of the incredibly courageous actress sped around the world, the journey was almost a formality. There was very little that China could do to stop it and, anyway, his Holiness had already given them what they wanted.

Even so, nobody knew how long the cavalcade was expected to take, winding its way through the high passes and across the barren Tibetan lands and, within hours of the news breaking, hundreds more people were already trying to join it — some flew in from the furthest reaches of the world and others traveled from parts of Tibet itself.

To start with, everyone was gung-ho with delight at the initial success. But mobile phone masts were somewhat lacking near the border which made keeping up with the global news pretty difficult and those who lived their lives in the spotlight found it very frustrating not to have any contact with the outside world or to know directly what the reaction to their bravery was. But here, in the desert, with the wide spaces, the strange, still lakes and the odd, passing yak, the outside world didn't seem so very important any more. Occasionally, vultures circled overhead but most people mistook them for eagles and, as the cavalcade wasn't dropping litter or leaving food behind (celebrities who take on great causes are very environmentally-conscious), they weren't seen close up for what they really were.

The Dalai Lama's team knew that they needed to get to Lhasa pretty swiftly before China had time to over-rule the publicity and think up any reason or opposing force to stop them. Most of the people walking had, initially, been enthusiastic about a three-week hike (romantic but unrealistic) but Mary-Beth, Eleazer and their team had been a lot more practical.

As it was, only a few of what was to be called the 'Peaceful Liberation' had come properly prepared for even one night. They probably assumed there would be roadside diners and motels as there were at home. Instead, it was a long and hard walk through barren, rocky land (with incredible views of the Himalayas) on just that one day. And by the evening, those celebrities who were not super-fit had more than had enough. While they didn't actually regret what they were doing they wanted their luxury back.

In the last mile before camp, Simon's painful feet even pushed him into trying to argue with Josh over what business he had to interfere with Tibet in the first place.

'You're a Jew,' he said. 'Your responsibility is towards us Jews. Yes of course the rest of the world matters; yes of course it's a Global Community but this just isn't our business. Overcoming anti-Semitism is our business; clearing up the war in the Middle East is our business; getting the Palestinians out of Jerusalem is our business.'

Josh stopped dead and turned to Simon with a flash of light in his eyes.

'I'm here because I can be detached,' he said. 'Because detachment is what's needed in issues like this. I'm here because it's the right time and it's the right Dalai Lama at the right point of his incarnation to get this problem sorted. It's also the right Chinese officials in the right places at the right time. This is not about me!'

'Yes, the Middle East is a Jewish problem; that's why I'm *not* there. There's too much emotion tied up in it. And if you even start saying we've got to get the Palestinians out then you're incapable of detachment towards the situation.

'I wouldn't dare try liberating the Middle East from any religious faction with you there Simon! You are so certain what is right and what is wrong and I tell you that there *is* no right or wrong; there's just love and fear; that's all. Where there is fear there can be no love and where there is love there can be no fear.

'The Middle East isn't ready until all three religions are willing to settle their differences.'

'But what about anti-Semitism?' asked Simon doggedly. 'Shouldn't you be doing something about that?'

'No,' said Josh. 'That's your job. Now quit hassling me and get on with it.'

For once, Simon was silenced. Later, you could hear him saying, 'What did he *mean?*' to everyone who would listen to him.

'Manna from Heaven?' Mary-Beth asked Josh as everyone sitting down for supper around a series of campfires found a woven basket of bread, cheese, figs and olives together with a bottle of water beside them.

'Well it is an Exodus,' he replied, smiling. 'They'll just think it's catering.'

As the multitude ate, the Dalai Lama talked, sitting in his donkey cart so that all could see him. He talked of reality and non-reality, of compassion for all living beings and of a great hope. He had probably never had quite such a standing ovation in his lifetime.

In the middle of the talk, Josh went missing from his place at the campfire. He hadn't just gone invisible, half seen, half not-seen in the flickering light. Maude-Lynn, John and Mary-Beth could usually spot him when he did that nowadays. He must have wandered away; he had had a tendency to drift away from the crowd a little during the day and everyone respected that he liked his space.

'Though it's not actually space; it's full of *something*' John said. 'Something with bright colors,' he added, quietly, to Mary-Beth. She nodded. It was very clear that something progressive was happening to Josh; something that lifted him up in an inexplicable way.

'I actually crouched down to see if his feet were touching the ground when he walked this afternoon,' confessed John. 'I couldn't see any footprints. I know it sounds strange.'

'No it doesn't,' said Mary-Beth. 'And were there?'

'I'm not sure!' said John. 'I felt too much of a prat staying down so I couldn't really tell. It's not like he prays…well not the way you expect people to pray. And he never talks of the Lord the way religious people do —'

'He *is* praying,' interrupted Mary-Beth. 'Every breath is a prayer. Every moment of his life is some kind of prayer. It's not the kind of 'please forgive me, please look after me' kind of prayer, it's like total acknowledgment of the glory of life. Even in a bug, he sees the glory of life. I think that's why he's so happy. And why we feel happy around him. And why this is working. It couldn't work if he weren't here — even with the Dalai Lama.'

'It's getting bigger too,' said John and Mary-Beth knew just what he meant.

Quietly, they set out to see where Josh had got to. It wasn't likely that there was a pack of wolves nearby but even so, when it was obvious that he wasn't anywhere in the camp, John alerted Simon and James and they formed a small posse just to check without interfering in case Josh was having some private conversation.

It *was* a private conversation. All three men came back to camp, shaken. When the girls asked them if Josh was okay they said 'Yep.'

'Absolutely.'

'Fine.'

And seemed loath to say more. After some vigorous tickling from Maude-Lynn however they said that Josh had been meeting some people — but not people from this world.

Wide-eyed, the girls demanded more. All three men were embarrassed.

'Bible people,' muttered Simon.

'I saw Jesus — or at least an image that looked like Jesus,' said John, sheepishly.

'You mean like the usual pictures of Jesus — long brown hair, beard and a kind of rough toga?' Maude-Lynn was very skeptical.

'No, very dark haired, short; couldn't see much more — there was this big ivory-emerald-*purple* light. But Josh was certainly talking to people who weren't physically there. The thing is...' John hesitated.

'What?' said the girls, their antennae alerted.

'Did you ever read *The Lion, the Witch and the Wardrobe?*'

'Yes,' said Maude-Lynn while the others said, 'No, but we saw the movie.'

'It was like the picture in the book of Aslan walking with the White Witch before he was sacrificed — oh, I'm not saying the people he was with were bad or anything like that, it was all too bright and glorious for that, but it sort of looked like some kind of a deal was being made.'

'Oh,' said Maude-Lynn. Nothing else could be said.

When Josh came back into the camp, he went straight to see his Holiness, so no one asked him anything.

That night, Mary-Beth cried herself to sleep.

The next day, a fleet of buses arrived, more than 30 of them, appearing first as clouds of dust across the red-gray barren landscape. Some came from India and some from within Tibet itself. All of them were driven by supporters of the Dalai Lama who were absolutely delighted to have the opportunity to help bring him and his entourage home. Most of the buses were pretty knackered but they were quite capable of getting the peaceful liberators to Lhasa within the day. They even came complete with local people who were willing to take care of the animals — mules, donkeys and a couple of ponies — which had been used by those who couldn't walk very far. And they were loaded down with food and supplies.

Marta arrived with them together with a *Fox* film crew. She had decided not to participate in the walk itself but to be filmed arriving with the buses as if they had been partially her idea (her people had arranged her a visa so she had no trouble crossing the border legally). She was beautifully dressed in designer jeans and a v-necked cashmere sweater in soft blue with a lapis lazuli necklace that cleverly matched the one that Josh usually wore (but which he had actually left behind in Vegas). Her wonderful silvery hair was encased in a workman-like, neat French pleat that snaked down her back and she glowed with cleanliness and exfoliated health that made the marching celebrities grit their teeth and feel very aware of how scruffy they must be looking. Most of them had set out without consciously carrying their egos and had been prepared to face discomfort, dust and a significant lack of bathrooms in order to do a higher good but Marta's reflected glory, somehow, brought those tired and uncommonly-challenged egos home to roost.

She carried an elegant rucksack filled with light accessories — and was accompanied by two members of her entourage with pull-along suitcases of clothes and make-up. She hadn't done any walking at all — but she would be in at the end of the journey which was what really mattered.

Fox caught her emotional reunion with Josh, the genuine tears in her eyes and his affectionate hug. Maude-Lynn, with instinctive journalistic savvy, aimed her own camera at Simon, John and Mary-Beth as Marta began a rather girly-run towards Josh, her feet feeling strange in her new designer trainers. The team's faces were carefully schooled to be impassive but there was just a suggestion of a snort from Mary-Beth as she turned away to get on with something more important.

The *Fox* crew brought news that China had publicly sanctioned the peaceful invasion — possibly helped by a little amiable pressure from the British Royal Family, six Presidents and two Prime Ministers. The Chinese authorities looked forward to a profitable and enduring friendship with the Dalai Lama and a peaceful co-assumption of power. Everyone from Presidents to anti-China campaigners were totally amazed — including the Chinese themselves — and there were suddenly all sorts of celebrities explaining in public how much they had wanted to be there had it not been for work/family commitments.

Maude-Lynn was in her element. Everything she, Joshua and Ben shot, she transferred from tape and then downloaded into her tiny notebook computer and emailed via satellite to Jude in London. Jude, meanwhile, had created a temporary office in Josh's Dartmouth Park House together with Joanna and they worked flat out handling enquiries and doing what they could to keep their end of the spin on the Peaceful Liberation of Tibet positive. Jude enjoyed liaising with her fellow PRs although she found most of them pretty inefficient when cut came to thrust. Now it was turning out to be a safe(ish) venture they were relaxing a little but, as they, themselves, had never been in direct contact with Josh, none of his spirit, courtesy or comfortableness had been able to rub off on them.

Maude-Lynn was incredibly nervous about the reception they would get in Lhasa and she knew that she wasn't the only one. There had been helicopters hovering overhead at least three times that morning and everyone knew about satellite surveillance. China knew absolutely everything that was going on.

Fortunately, China had decided that the Dalai Lama's arrival in Lhasa could be a PR coup for them. Officials were hurried there in force to welcome his Holiness home and officials hastened to deck the city for a major celebration. As the buses came to a halt at the base of the Potala Palace, the Dalai Lama and his entourage were feted and cheered by thousands of waiting Tibetans. His Holiness, almost overcome with emotion, kissed the ground beneath his feet. He was too frail to make the traditional pilgrim's journey of kneeling, prostrating, kneeling, standing, praying and repeating the movements but nothing would stop him from slowly, slowly, slowly climbing the sacred steps up to the Palace. It had long been transformed into a museum but was now filled with Chinese and Tibetans waiting for this historic sight. The very air sang with joy. Maude-Lynn, Andrew, John and Mary Beth caught their breath trying not to cry at a sight that no one had previously believed was possible in their lifetime. The palace, they thought, was incredibly impressive even though it had been built from mud, straw and tree trunks almost 1400 years before.

Slowly and carefully, his Holiness climbed the central staircase — which no other personage was allowed to do — his progress recorded by a barrage of cameras. He then called on all his people to ensure that they kept the peace even if the next few weeks were difficult for them. He spoke gravely of forgiveness and letting go of the past. There must be no more blame; no vendettas; a new start for all. Many people were in tears and Josh's team gave up any pretence of being cool.

Maude-Lynn was two streets away, engrossed in supervising the filming of this incredible historic event when the Chinese police came for Josh. They were so smart, so clever that no one realized what was happening until there was one circle of armed Chinese guards around Josh and another round Mary-Beth, Marta, Simon, John and Andrew. Simon darted forward, one hand inside his jacket, intending to pull a knife but Josh caught his arm to stop him. 'Let it be,' he said, as Simon was manhandled back into the second circle. 'It's part of the process. There has to be accountability and this is it.'

Marta began to scream.

Chapter Thirty Nine

Maude-Lynn felt as though she were living in a riot of bright shades of light. Even though the Dalai Lama's impending arrival had only been a rumor to the majority of the people of Lhasa — and his Holiness had come days before he was expected — the people put on their festival clothes and sang, danced and cheered in the streets. Beaming women crowned with multi-colored striped felt hats dangling with what appeared to be white locks of hair made from wool and wearing vermillion and brown kimono-type dresses with multi-colored, textured aprons and sashes and ornate necklaces of coral and turquoise, mingled with monks in maroon with ornately embroidered tabards and sashes of daffodil yellow. Other, older women in pillbox hats carried tiny prayer-wheels that they span as they sang in cracked voices. Multi-colored prayer flags waved and wafted everywhere in a haze of dancing light. Maude-Lynn saw young and old Chinese people dancing with the ethnically-dressed Tibetans. There was color, joy and delight everywhere.

Tones of red, blue, emerald and orange adorned the houses and buildings from the old, almost wattle-and-daub homes to the great concrete lumps on the main streets. There were murals everywhere, high-up balconies flowing with flags, banners and pennants, doorways painted and varnished in blue, vermillion, crimson, gold, green, turquoise and orange. Here and there, images of blue-faced gods, golden Buddhas, dragons and flames leaped out from the walls glimpsed between the carousing locals. Drums, trumpets, cymbals and a great hum of voices thronged the air. Her nose twitched, unconsciously, registering the unknown essences of yak-butter, lamp oil, juniper incense, waxy-rank Tibetan clothes and sweaty bodies,

A small part of her wondered how come the adventure had all gone so easily. Yes, the most famous people in the world were there — and she nudged Joshua the cameraman to indicate a tranche of

Miracle Mile winners and finalists, including Simon Libiyah and Colm O'Reilly. They were dancing as though inspired alongside a group of Tibetans down a road lined with market stalls, brilliant-colored fruits and vegetables, sacks of gingery, maroon, vermillion, yellow, brown and green spices.

Surely, she thought, there must be some opposition? Could China transform so completely? Even if the top people were in agreement, what about the middlemen, the petty officials, the rebels who were dedicated to fighting, the soldiers and police, so used to oppressing?

Just as her brow crinkled with concern and she wondered if she should go and look for some trouble — after all, there must be some, somewhere — a just discernable echo of a scream resonated through the music and laughter.

Instinctively, she knew that she must go alone. With a quick word, she left Joshua and Ben recording the joy and delight and wormed her way through the crowds in the direction from which she heard the noise. More screams greeted her and some kind of inner knowledge confirmed that it was Marta's voice. She began to run. Her almond-shaped eyes took in the whole situation in a second and she had her mobile phone video camera aimed at the arrest almost before she thought. She could get enough, surely, before she got close enough for the wireless to fail?

That was her undoing for there were plenty of other police present and they did not want some Westerner interfering. They had already winded Simon with a blow to the stomach and pushed Marta to the ground where she yelled her head off until one of them pointed his gun at her head, gesticulating quite clearly that she was required to shut up. Then the TV presenter gulped and stayed silent through sheer terror. The Chinese were nervous, hissing commands to each other and holding John, Andrew, Mary-Beth and the wheezing Simon at gunpoint while two others put handcuffs on Josh. One of the guards on the periphery knocked the cell phone out of Maude-Lynn's hand and stamped on it. As Maude-Lynn gasped, she was grabbed from behind and handcuffed. Her yelp of shock was cut off by a hand clamped over her mouth and, in seconds, both she and Josh had been bundled into a small van and driven away.

Marta, staggering up, her hair in disarray, was in hysterics. 'They'll kill him, they'll kill him,' she wept. Mary-Beth, with tears flooding down her own face considered slapping her to calm her down but was relieved when John took Marta by the shoulders and shook her gently to bring her back to the moment. Mary-Beth was grimly aware that a slapping on her part, at that point, would have been personal.

A young man from the crowd came up and started talking to Simon in accented Mandarin but Simon didn't know what to do or say; he was in shock, aware that he had let Josh down completely. When Joshua and Ben arrived through the watching crowds, the Tibetan gabbled at them instead, taking out a cell phone and indicating that he had filmed what had just happened.

'Maude-Lynn and Josh have been arrested,' said John gruffly to the film team. 'If you can get the images of the arrest off this guy's phone and send them, please do. And meet us at the gates of the Potala Palace.'

Joshua nodded and gestured to Ben and the Chinese with the cell phone to follow him. They vanished into the rapidly-dispersing crowd aware that they should get away as soon as possible to where no one would be interested what they were doing.

John was still holding the shuddering Marta in his arms, calming her down. Andrew was comforting Mary-Beth who stood still, holding his hand tightly trying to control herself. There was never such a contrast between women, he thought. Mary-Beth's eyes were swollen with the swift onslaught of tears but she looked golden compared with the broken, hysterical Marta.

'What do we do now?' the two men mouthed to each other. Simon seemed to have vanished into the crowd.

'He'll need some time. Hurt pride,' said John. Andrew nodded. They were both aware of their friend's volatility and, let's face it, they knew how he felt. They *had* failed. But what could you do against official police?

'Call Jude?' said Andrew.

'I guess so. And regroup.' John sighed and patted Marta's back gently. She was calming down now and he was holding her like a child.

'I didn't see this coming, did you?'

'No but I think we ought to have. As Josh said, they would need some kind of accountability; some statement that said you can't just walk over the border like this and totally get away with it.'

'What do you think they'll do?'

'No idea. Look, you get the girls up to the Potala and see if you can get anywhere near his Holiness and I'll let Jude know.'

'Right.'

'Are you okay?' asked Josh as Maude-Lynn recovered consciousness. She had hit her head hard as the guards threw her into the van. She groaned and struggled with the handcuffs. God, she felt dreadful! This was worse than a hangover. Everything hurt, particularly her head and she had a raging thirst.

For a moment she didn't answer, taking stock with a kind of dumb despair. It was so horrible that her mind found it hard to conceive that this could be reality. Surely, this kind of thing only happened in movies?

The two armed guards gestured at their two captives vigorously with their guns to encourage them to shut up but Josh gave them his relaxed, courteous smile and, for some unaccountable reason, they both felt slightly better about themselves.

'Are you okay? Do those cuffs hurt?' Josh asked Maude-Lynn. She was through despair now and feeling a mixture of fury and terror. How on earth had this happened?

'I guess,' she muttered. 'God, Josh…'

'It's okay,' he said reassuringly. 'They would have to arrest someone. Any government would! We have to go through the process.'

'But we could go to jail; we could be executed!'

'Not executed,' said Josh. 'And if it's jail I expect it will only be me.'

'Only you! But you can't rot in a Chinese jail! You're...you're...'

'Shhh,' he said, noting that her words were agitating their guards. 'Just trust, if you can. I don't have a bad feeling about this; it was bound to happen. An eye for an eye and all that kind of stuff, you know?

'Come and lean up against me; that way we'll be buffers for each other and the jolting won't be so bad.'

She shuffled herself painfully over the hard rubber-laid floor and leant against him while the Chinese watched her nervously. The back of the van had no windows and it was too dark to make out much but the metal walls and some seating which certainly wasn't being offered to the two people huddled on the floor. She became aware of impending cramp in her right foot and wriggled uncomfortably to try and stave it off.

'Where are they taking us?' she asked after a while of trying and failing to control her feelings of panic. As soon as she spoke she felt stupid. As if he would know!

'Probably Beijing,' he replied. 'We'll be taken to the airport most likely. Maude-Lynn, could you calm down? I need to give you a message and you need to take it in.'

'But I'm arrested like you!'

'Shhhh,' he said softly. 'Close your eyes and listen.'

Reluctantly, she obeyed him. Very gently he talked to her about nothing in particular, just that he knew she would be safe and that all was well. She felt comfort seeping into her.

'This is the message,' he said when he knew she could listen properly. 'It's very, very important. When I've finished, I want you to repeat it back to me word for word. Can you do that?'

'Yes,' she whispered.

'Tell his Holiness that he must *not* intervene. He must not make any calls for my release or insist that China lets me go. To do so would put him and the Peaceful Liberation in jeopardy and that would make it all pointless. Now repeat that back.'

'His Holiness not to do anything; not to intervene or call for your release — but Josh —'

'Shhh,' he said again, but lovingly.

'There has to be accountability. There has to be a fair exchange of energy,' he continued. 'Tibet for me. That's the deal, okay? You don't need to worry about me; I'll be fine. Really. This is what I'm here for. The atonement. This is my job. Now repeat it all back to me.'

Maude-Lynn gulped; she was moments away from tears.

'His Holiness not to intervene; not to call for your release as it would jeopardize the peace in Tibet,' she managed. 'It would make it all null and void. You are the cosmic exchange for peace — the atonement. You're okay with that and don't want anyone to interfere.'

'I couldn't have put it better myself!' said Josh admiringly. 'That's it. Now remember it and tell *everyone.*'

'They won't listen,' said Maude-Lynn opening her eyes.

'They will,' said Josh. 'The important ones will. The Dalai Lama and I have already discussed it. He just needs reminding.'

He leant sideways, awkwardly.

'He's going to kiss me!' thought Maude-Lynn in a sudden wild panic. She didn't know whether to agree or pull back. Instinct made her close her eyes and raise her mouth.

It was the gentlest, most innocent of kisses but right on the lips. Maude-Lynn felt power and light surge through her. She opened her eyes, startled, seeing color everywhere in the darkness.

The van stopped, the door jerked open immediately, and they stumbled out into the dusk of the airfield, to find themselves surrounded by Chinese guards.

At once, they were separated — Maude-Lynn was superfluous to requirements and there were only so many seats on the plane.

'Don't take illegal photographs!' an officer said to her threateningly in accented English. He unlocked her handcuffs and pushed her roughly down onto her knees. She thought she was going to be shot. Maude-Lynn knelt, her head low, saying nothing. To her perfect amazement she felt no anger, no hatred and no fear.

As they bundled Josh onto the small military aircraft, she risked looking up. He was looking back over his shoulder to check that she was okay. She smiled, love flooding through her.

As he took his last look at her, Josh smiled with great warmth. 'Seven,' he said to himself almost inaudibly.

Five minutes later, Maude-Lynn was alone just outside Lhasa airport, a hundred kilometers from the city with no money, no telephone and no idea whatsoever what to do next. Her passport was in a bag being carried by Ben back in the city, which was a small comfort because her bum-bag containing personal stuff including make-up, handkerchiefs and some cash was probably still in the military van that was just driving away. Above her, the aircraft taking Josh to Beijing twinkled its lights in the gloaming and, involuntarily, she waved. It was a silly childish reaction but maybe he could see it?

The airport was closed to civilians. Probably it was a security measure because of the Dalai Lama's return. There were a few security people and soldiers around and they kept a watchful eye on her as she skirted what she could of the terminus building, just to see if she could get in to use the lavatory at least. She found herself staggering slightly because her legs were not feeling anything like themselves and rubbing her wrists where the handcuffs had chafed. She was so very thirsty…

Maude-Lynn was nothing if not resilient. She might have no money, no way of contacting the others, but she was free and she had a message to deliver. But there were no buses today, even if she had the money for the fare and the taxi rank was ostentatiously empty.

She contemplated beginning to walk back to Lhasa and maybe hitching a ride on the way but it grew darker by the minute. The great mountain peaks now loomed vaguely instead of raising their heads proudly above the airport and a flock of bar-headed geese startled her with their honks as they flew overhead seeking their night roost.

'What I could really do with now is a miracle,' she said out loud. In reply, her inner voice said 'Well ask for one then!'

Now Maude-Lynn may have believed totally in Josh's divinity and she knew that when she was with him, she too could channel healing power. But never until this moment had she sent up a true prayer acknowledging a Higher Source and asking for help. Josh had told her, repeatedly, how important it was to ask and then let go of the worry and fuss and accept that the answer was coming. Now, she was so tired and so helpless that she did just that: she gave in.

She never knew how long she sat on the concrete just outside the driveway entrance to the airport; she thought she would probably have to sit there until dawn. She daren't sleep in case she missed a passing car — and anyway, how could she sleep when she was so uncomfortable? She had relieved herself behind a tree, grimacing at the harshness of the dry leaves that were her only available tissues but that was scant comfort in the face of the raging thirst that seemed to consume her. She knew she should focus but she couldn't gather enough thoughts to do anything and wondered vaguely if she were what was technically called 'in shock.'

The streetlights above hurt her eyes and made her head ache. The evening was growing steadily colder and she had no jacket but somehow it was too much effort to get up and walk in order to keep herself warm. But when a giant cockroach started climbing onto her left foot, it was the last straw. She leapt up, kicked it away, stamped on it and burst into tears, her body shaking with grief and trepidation.

Chapter Forty

Way before dusk in the city of Lhasa, the joyful people were lighting torches and preparing for a night of celebration. Impromptu dances and songs sprang up from nowhere, the inhabitants filled with the need to express their delight. So far, the Dalai Lama and his entourage's urging for peaceful celebrations were being honored and both Chinese and Tibetans were enjoying themselves.

In the Potala, the initial greeting ceremonies and polite preliminaries were also going well. Many of the Dalai Lama's entourage had to keep mentally pinching themselves that they were talking and listening peacefully to the Chinese who were, seemingly, perfectly happy that they were there.

'It's called forgiveness,' his Holiness said, nodding happily, whenever anyone mentioned it to him. 'Forgiveness is letting go of the past. It does not mean we condone; we just release what has gone before and walk on in peace.'

He noticed the absence of Josh however. And he knew that his friend had left Lhasa; he could feel it in his bones and despite his happiness, he felt an echo of loss.

'Now it is up to us,' he said to Eleazer. 'We have had Grace to bring us here; now we have to use our own wisdom.'

He was tired; he had to admit it to himself — and after all, he was a good age! He was permitted to be tired. But he must spend the whole evening alert and willing to be pleased by both his own people and the Chinese as well.

There were two major outstanding issues to be overcome; firstly the negotiations for the 150,000 Tibetans still living in exile in India to be able to come home — they would need accommodation, jobs and money. The second, his Holiness viewed as far more of an ordeal: the Chinese Panchen Lama was apparently going to arrive this very night and he had to publicly accept someone whom he still, at heart, thought of as an impostor.

He kept his spirits up by walking outside every hour to wave and speak to the people of Lhasa and, when he did that, he remembered anew that this was a dream come true for all of them. But he ached to pray and give thanks alone and just have a little time to rest. He didn't mind that the Chinese had fitted out rooms for him in the red palace, nor that they had selected where the first public worship would take place and he calmed the slight indignation of some of his followers.

'Resistance means suffering,' he said. 'We do not resist. We are here; it is a great healing; we do not resist.'

He was grateful that the Chinese had appreciated his age and vegetarian diet and had provided a simple meal for this evening — the multi-course elaborate banquets would begin tomorrow. The food was absolutely delicious after the long journey and refreshed him greatly but he wished that Josh were there.

Messages had been brought to him by now from Mary-Beth and John.

Poor things, he thought. They didn't know...and he wished that he could go to them and comfort them. Instead he sent Eleazer, with careful instructions.

The monk held his arms out to Mary-Beth as he was shown into the room where she, John, Simon, Andrew and Marta waited. She ran to him like a little girl and hiccupped out some tears as he held her tightly, feeling a deep and compassionate love for the instigator of all that had happened on this amazing day.

Tea had already been provided and Eleazer asked for food.

'We cannot eat!' said Marta dramatically.

'You must,' said Eleazer gently. 'Strength is vital now.'

He listened carefully to their accounts of what had happened. Marta kept demanding to see the Dalai Lama himself until Simon threatened her with physical violence if she didn't shut up. Thereafter, she kept a sulky silence

When they had all finished, Eleazer bowed his head and spoke:

'Josh and his Holiness agreed that this was a possible outcome,' he said. 'It may not be easy for you to understand but it is, in its own way, measure for measure. I know that will not make it easier for you. But we must agree that we have all committed visa violations! We have broken the law. Two people's arrest is mild compared with what could have happened in retribution.'

'Does that mean you're not going to do anything?' Simon was on his feet, volatile as usual and almost purple in the face with indignation.

'No,' said Eleazer. 'But that we understand that there is nothing we can do right now. The negotiations must go ahead before anything else.'

'Are they going to kill him?' asked Mary-Beth in a small voice. She was still holding onto Eleazer's hand like a child.

Eleazer looked down at and smiled. 'I doubt it,' he said. 'That would be foolish of them. They need some kind of a ringleader to hold up to justice but they will do it fairly so the world cannot condemn them. I expect he will be sent to jail.'

'Jail! For how long?' Andrew and Marta's faces were white.

'It could be years,' said Simon grimly.

'I doubt it,' said Eleazer firmly. 'There will be huge international representations. It will probably be an elaborate charade and China will hand him over to some envoy after, say three months, and then it will all be done.'

'And what about Maude-Lynn?' asked John but he wasn't expecting any answer because there could be none. They would have to wait and see.

John was feeling less nervy than the others and, having spoken to Jude, was somewhat forewarned. She had been her usual matter-of-fact self when he telephoned her.

As he called, John had had one of those lucid moments of watching himself from outside as though he was seeing himself in a movie. Never, once in his life had he ever considered that he would be in Lhasa, looking out over great stretches of water flocked with birds and surrounded by great snow-capped mountains, let alone standing there with the streets alive with celebration and a party to the liberation of a country. And there he was telling someone the other side of the planet — someone sitting in a suburb of London — that their boss had been arrested by the Chinese.

Jude had been silent for a moment and then she sighed.

'Well, I suppose it was only to be expected,' she said.

'Was it?'

'I guess so. You can't just walk into China with impunity can you?'

John had rather thought that you could. But he wasn't up to discussing it. Jude was always so utterly practical.

'But what do we do in the meantime?' he asked, feeling out of his depth on every level.

Jude sighed again and thought for a moment.

'Well, I'll go and look in the folder on his desk that says, 'Open this if I don't come back'' she said. 'That may help.'

'There's a folder saying that?'

'Yes John there is.'

'And you haven't read it?'

There was amusement in Jude's voice when she replied, 'No, I haven't read it.'

'Okay. But what about Maude-Lynn?'

'Realistically John, is there anything you *can* do?'

'I don't think so.'

'Then do nothing. Trust.'

Maude-Lynn spent the night in a Tibetan yurt having been carried there in a kind of daze on the back of a yak. She must have dozed off in a crumpled little heap by the side of the road after the scare with the cockroach — or maybe she just passed out? Whatever it was, being awoken by a hairy nose snorting in her face was not exactly helpful to her nervous system and she shrieked out loud. But the yak, one of several in a small herd, was stoical and snuffled at her again, being joined by two of its friends who wanted to know what was so very interesting and whether it involved food.

The cowherd loomed up behind them looking to see what was concerning his beasts. Understandably, seeing Maude-Lynn's oriental face, he spoke to her first in Tibetan and then in apologetically clumsy Mandarin. She turned a face of total incomprehension to him but had the presence of mind to realize that she had found help — or more accurately that help had found her.

She pointed at her mouth, sticking her tongue out, miming thirst. The man grinned and made the thumbs-up sign and unwound a glass jam-jar half filled with tealeaves that was hanging from string around his neck. He unscrewed the top and handed it to her. Any other time, Maude-Lynn would have rejected this offering out of hand, not only for the taste (extremely stewed) but also the hygienic aspect. As it was, she gulped down all four precious inches of cold tea and felt immediately better.

The man — she could see now that he was very young, probably early twenties — looked her over and made a 'tsh-tsh' noise as he noticed a nasty graze on her left arm. Matter-of-factly, he tipped up the jar so that damp tealeaves fell into the palm of his hand. He slapped them onto the wound and tied them on with a strip of rag that probably doubled as a handkerchief.

Maude-Lynn stood up shakily and thanked him. The young man looked around him at the now darkened, deserted airport, blew out through his cheeks and said he supposed that she had better come with him then... That much was very clear no matter what language he was using.

'Shere-shere,' Maude-Lynn thanked him rather pathetically and with the worst Chinese accent in the world. She nearly baulked when the boy indicated that he would give her a leg up onto the back of one of his creatures but sense prevailed. She didn't know what distance they were going and she certainly couldn't walk very far.

On top of the coal-black beast, she was half repulsed and half soothed by its beefy, rancid, warmth and scent. As it walked, it swayed heavily from side to side and she had to hold tightly to the almost dreadlocked thick hair. Until that time, she hadn't known that you could ride on a yak and doze at the same time.

She awoke with a start as they arrived at a small cluster of what looked, to Maude-Lynn's exhausted eyes, like square white tents. The cowherd exhorted her to get down by a series of clicks and clucks which were intended to reassure her and, strangely enough, did. He ushered her through the yak-skin doorway into a smoky, smelly but beautifully-warm dark room where two women crouching on three-legged stools looked up and, seeing the state of her, jumped up and came forward, holding out rough, striped, woolen blankets.

Half delirious with the scents and totally exhausted, Maude-Lynn allowed herself to be wrapped in the wool and to sink down by the fire. She accepted a bowl of hot, fragrant yak-butter tea. It tasted like nothing she had ever had before and she knew, dimly, that it was really quite disgusting. But the needs of her body over-ruled her too-pretentious senses and she had drunk it to the dregs before her outraged taste buds had made their objections fully felt.

She didn't remember much more; in fact she keeled over and, once they had rolled her as politely as possible to one side of the yurt, she slept deeply (with some fairly impressive snoring too) for five full hours.

Dawn and the family's bustle woke her to a painful stiffness, bemused recollection and a mouth that felt as though it had been used for shoveling gravel.

She staggered out of the yurt, wondering with great urgency what these people did for a lavatory. Not a lot, was the answer and whatever personal dignity she might have still possessed was lost when the younger of the two women smiled at her and pointed to a stinking half-full bucket behind back of the yurt. There was some Chinese newspaper next to it, thank God.

Christ, she was dirty! Not to mention smelly. God knows what her hair and face looked like. And where the hell was she? How would she get back to Lhasa? She remembered Josh's message with a sick-feeling thump in her stomach. What if the others were activating? What if it all went wrong? Oh crap!

The woman gave her a damp rag on which to wipe her hands. Maude-Lynn thanked her and wondered how many more lethal bacteria it had incubated. She was suddenly shocked at the poverty she saw around her and realized that these people had taken her, a stranger, in with no questions and were sharing with her everything they possessed.

The older woman gestured her to come back into the yurt — there was no sign of the man — and handed her a bowl of some kind of meat soup. Oh, how good it smelled and how very, very good it tasted! She drank straight from the bowl with the two women nodding and smiling and handing her some flat bread to wipe the dregs. They didn't eat and she wondered if they had eaten earlier or whether she had deprived them of their own breakfast.

She thanked them again and again, this time remembering the Tibetan word pronounced 'Thug-je-che' and aware all the time that she might have insulted the man the previous night with her Mandarin. Vaguely, she was aware that she had to leave; she must contact the others somehow but there was nothing she could do.

Outside, the day was warm and sunny with a refreshingly cool wind. All around her the land looked sparse and dry just as it had been for most of the trip. The magnificence of the mountains all around had already become almost commonplace in Maude-Lynn's mind. But even so, she stood looking appreciatively at the landscape, suddenly realizing how incredibly lucky she was to be here and not in some Beijing prison.

'Thank you,' she said in English to the great un-nameable deity of creation. 'Thank you very much.'

When the young cowherd arrived a half hour later, greeted her and handed her a battered but fully-serviceable cell phone, she practically snatched it out of his hand.

Chapter Forty One

It had been an unusual night for everyone. The Dalai Lama got to his bed incredibly late (even he was amazed at his own stamina, given his age and the journey he had undertaken). It was hard to sleep even so; there was much to think about, especially the meeting with the Panchen Lama.

He had, understandably, dreaded it and, although he recognized a spiritual logic in what Josh had suggested about more than one soul being capable of a certain destiny, it went against centuries of Tibetan Buddhist teaching and his own deep, inner, personal belief. Not only that, but acknowledging the Chinese Lama would make it appear that his previous selection of the Panchen Lama might have been wrong — which cast doubts on his own ability at a time where unity among Tibetans would be vital. He may have been one of the most enlightened beings on Earth but he was also human and such thoughts were troubling.

The Panchen Lama too had been dreading the meeting. He had spent years knowing that he was regarded as an impostor. He was utterly certain that the Dalai Lama would never, ever accept him. The mantle of his role had grown on the Chinese Lama rather than being with him from his birth. The latter had always been the case before (or so he had been taught) — but once the die was cast and he had been chosen by the Chinese, his spiritual guidance, both incarnate and discarnate, had not let him down: the young man's soul was strong and true and well developed. Now he was in his mid 20s and he was very capable of dealing with the secular, politics and everyday life. He had always hoped against hope that there could be some resolution over Tibet but had privately doubted it. He could see both great good and great error in both sides of the equation but had felt helpless to resolve it.

There was also the thorny issue of the 'real' Panchen Lama who was approximately the same age and who lived in quiet retirement somewhere in Tibet. If there were to be any kind of resolution, at some point, they would have to meet — and then what?

The Panchen Lama too was tired when he arrived in Lhasa, having been hurried there at the last minute. Once the authorities had realized what was happening and that the event had a momentum that even they could not stop (and which, for some reason, that they didn't understand, they did not want to stop), the plan was that the Panchen Lama should be in Lhasa before the Dalai Lama. That would demonstrate that China still intended to have things its own way.

But the liberators arrived in Lhasa an hour before the Panchen Lama's plane was due to land and Meng Tie-Ping, the Tibet Autonomous Regional Government chairman — who was certainly having one hell of a week — decided that they simply had to be flexible. They couldn't wait for the Panchen Lama before going ahead with the welcoming ceremony. It wasn't a popular decision in Beijing, and several officials commented that Meng had been the wrong choice for the position in the first place, but an immediate decision had been required by the man on the spot. And it might be unacknowledged in their hearts, but the Chinese knew that this was their only chance to dissolve the decades of trouble and take a huge step forward in their relationship with the Western World. It was all contrary to their natural Imperial and warrior inclinations but trade had certainly suffered since the furor over Tibet over the last few years and their young people had become steadily more unreliable over Chinese Imperial Rights now they had access to the Internet.

So the Panchen Lama came to meet his fellow leader as the supplicant rather than the iconic presence he was intended to be. That was fortunate because it helped to soften the outside world's view of these incredible events in Tibet.

It was frightening for the Panchen Lama to approach the Dalai Lama but, once the two men's eyes met, it was blessedly easy for him to drop at the Dalai Lama's feet in reverence, whether or not this offended his Chinese mentors. His heart was filled with awe as he finally saw the great warrior priest whom he had been taught not to venerate but did, most deeply revere, with every fiber of his being.

There was room for one more miracle in this time of wonders: the Dalai Lama saw a respectful and loving son and the Panchen Lama saw a wise and powerful father. They loved and recognized each other on sight.

How the Universe had worked it out, no one would ever know but worked it out, the Universe had.

Yes, they could work together! Yes, they could guide their people together. Yes, they could bring peace. Yes, they could ensure the future of Tibet. After an hour of relief, discussion and growing bonds of friendship mixed in with all the official formalities that had to be observed, both men went to bed amazed and, after counting their blessings, slept the true sleep of the just. Whatever happened from now on, they knew that they could be one unit for good.

Meng watched with cautious approval. The Tibet Autonomous Regional Government chairman might look like a politician but he was every inch the warrior. He was tall for a Chinese and powerfully built with slightly aggressive-looking spiky hair, strong but well-manicured hands and deep-set dark eyes. He marched rather than walked through the streets of Lhasa as if he were commander of the Imperial guard of the First Emperor. One look at his naturally fierce face was enough to convince most people that he should be allowed his own way in pretty much anything but, actually, Meng was very good at listening and even better at making fair decisions. His height and frowning brow concealed a peaceful heart.

Meng had lived and worked in Tibet for just two years, having come from a similar position in Mongolia (and those who met his cool and courteous wife were sure that such an elegant woman must despair of ever living well in Shanghai or Beijing). In those two years, Meng had come to view the Tibetan land and its people with a deep and loyal regard. He had alleviated the aggression of his predecessor; calmed the fervor of the police and soldiers; handed out justice as opposed to rule and done all he could to give Tibet the opportunity to calm down after a decade of virtual revolt. He understood that these measures took time to take effect and had managed to reassure Beijing that the recent scuffles were just the old habits wearing themselves out.

Of course there had been blips in his peaceful plan but he knew that this was par for the course. He bided his time, said and did just enough of the right things to keep Beijing happy and his influence had steadily begun to calm years of rioting in the capital city. No one could actually put their finger on why, but there was an undercurrent of knowledge that when Meng made an official visit to one of the temples, he actually participated in the services and the people who spoke to him felt that he had heard them.

That night after an exhausting series of events, meetings and organization, sank into bed with his wife, Ning Fang who asked him politely if he felt the day went well.

'It went very well,' he said. 'And there have been no comments and no complaints and there is nothing reported on the news either.'

She knew he was referring to Josh's arrest. It was of great concern to her because she knew that Meng had acted unilaterally of Beijing. As a general rule in China it was not wise to act first and apologize later but, if it were done carefully — and presented as Beijing's own idea — it just might work. The central government had its whipping-boy; the ringleader and Meng, now, had just a little time to see if all this could be pulled together.

'I am pleased,' she said with a little nod.

Meng lay back into his pillows wishing, for the thousandth time, that his wife were just a little less cold. He had no cause for actual complaint but sometimes he just wanted to be closer. She saw no sense in that whatsoever. They were an excellent team and there was no need for any of that sentimental stuff.

Simon didn't sleep a wink (or at least, so he said). As with most people who say they didn't sleep, he did get several hours-worth of poor-quality dozing but, as it was haunted by anxiety dreams, it was hardly refreshing. It wasn't helped by the fact that so many people in Lhasa needed accommodation so Josh's team were sleeping on the floor of one of the rooms of the Potala. They had been given simple monks' mattresses and blankets but they seemed uncomfortable and smelly and they all longed for a hot shower or bath. More than that, now it was all over, they were experiencing a huge anti-climax (tinged with fear) and they just wanted to go home.

But of course, they couldn't. Simon was torn with guilt at not stopping Josh's arrest and fury at his own helplessness. Logic (and the others) told him that no one could have stopped the Chinese government if they wanted to arrest someone. And he also knew that the last thing the Peaceful Liberation needed was a focus on Josh's arrest. But he also felt resentful that the Dalai Lama hadn't done something immediately. And it was just as bad that the old man hadn't invited them all in to his meetings or publicly thanked them either. Not to mention the fact that he'd hoped to be able to go straight home and now, he'd probably have to go to Beijing.

Poor Simon, he could never make sense of things without Josh. It was Simon who had researched his namesake, Simon Peter, in the Gospels and, with Josh's linguistic help, had realized that *that* Simon never got it either. There were whole tracts in the Gospels where the original Greek made it clear that Peter was on a completely different page from Jesus. The modern Simon, when he read Jesus' quotation of 'this is the rock on which I shall build my Church' understood it in a very Jewish way as '*this* is the rock on which I shall build my Church?' The rock did not get it; the rock was flawed. That had, at least, helped Simon forgive a lot of Christianity. That and understanding that it was a religion based on St. Paul's teachings rather than those of Jesus.

One other thing haunted him. As he had wandered, confused and angry in the crowd just after Josh was taken, a Chinese army officer had come up to him and asked to see his passport. Knowing full well that it did not have the correct entry permits, Simon lied, saying it was at his hotel. He named the Sheraton in a wild bid for respectability.

'And how did you get here?' said the officer.

'Flew in last week,' lied Simon. 'With a tour from London.' He winced inside, knowing that he could easily be found out.

'Aren't you with the Dalai Lama's people?'

'No. No I'm not.'

'The American people from India?'

'No. *No!*'

The officer nodded and turned away. Simon walked on, hastily, his hands in his pockets, his shoulders hunched, feeling as though he had denied everything they had come there for in order to save his own skin.

Marta did stay at the Sheraton. A room became available at the last minute (as they so often do when celebrity PAs start pushing) and all the hotels in Lhasa had opened their doors wide for visiting superstars. In one way, she would have liked to have remained with Josh's team but she had to think of her entourage and, anyway, having been traveling for more than 24 hours, she was not going to go anywhere else without a hot shower and a face-pack. She also had a sneaking and accurate perception that she wasn't exactly welcome in Lhasa. She put that down to jealousy. In the meantime, she was outraged that her two assistants had to share rooms with other celebrity assistants but never once thought of offering to share her own room with them.

Of course she was worried about Josh. How could she not be? But she had listened to Marco and Arianna's reassuring words about diplomacy and the United Nations and realized that it was all a bit of a storm in a teacup. Of course the Chinese wouldn't execute him! He might go on trial but nothing more than that. And Marta could get wonderful publicity while campaigning for his release. She sank into sleep with a vision of herself on the front cover of *Time* as the brave and loyal woman who brought her fiancé home.

To be fair to Marta, she did love Josh as much as she was capable of loving anyone other than herself and, had he been so inclined and had he been planning a life of continued celebrity, Marta could well have made him the perfect wife.

Mary-Beth slept fitfully, trying hard not to worry. She was technically more concerned for Maude-Lynn than for Josh although her heart told her quite clearly that she was just as much in love with her boss as she had ever been.

'Stop interfering, damn you!' she said to it. 'I have to think clearly.'

But her sentimental self berated her for putting Josh into such danger while her head exclaimed that this line of thinking was pretty rich given the global consequences of what they were doing.

Josh would cope; she knew that. He would be okay. But part of her was scared that he would die, either at the hands of the Chinese or for some other strange reason. After all, he would have come to Earth to do some great Messianic task and, let's face it, he'd just done it.

'He told me once that he wasn't going to be on Earth for long,' she had said to John in a very little voice. 'That's why I set this up. I forgot about afterwards. In all the excitement I never thought about afterwards,'

'We don't,' he replied. 'Otherwise we'd probably never do anything!'

Mary-Beth knew that, once she had established what had happened to Maude-Lynn as well as to Josh, first thing in the morning, then she would do anything she could to get to Beijing as soon as possible. They might let her see him; she might be able to help in some way. Her busy mind worked anxiously at how to get the permits required and she finally dropped off to sleep thanking God for Eleazer.

Josh slept on the aircraft for most of the way to Beijing. He had always been one of those enviable people who can sleep sitting up and, even if he had grown rather too used to first class and was completely surprised by the tiny seat and lack of leg room on the military plane, he could deal with it quite easily by dropping off.

He felt fine. There was just a moment's concern about whether his Holiness would remember their pact in the heat of the moment; whether his own team would be able to stand back but, after all, he had done his part and he simply had to let the others do what they had to do. There was little point in worrying about it.

He wasn't concerned for his own fate either. With the spiritual maturity that had developed further in him every day since leaving Las Vegas, he knew that, now his great job on Earth was done, every extra day was a bonus. He might be taken home to the higher worlds at any point and he had nothing to complain about if that were to be the case.

And if he were jailed, well what was that to someone who could call the birds of the air to him and listen to their song? What was that to someone could close his eyes and listen to the music of the spheres and the songs of angels? What was that when there was the opportunity to learn a new language and to understand a whole new nation? What was that with a whole jail of unhappy men to help and heal?

No, Josh was very satisfied with things whichever way they might go. But he was both interested and, in some way amused, at how much he realized he was going to miss Mary-Beth. Not just for her chocolate biscuits and tea or her subtle nagging or her determination but just for her presence alone.

No, she wasn't Gemma; she could never be Gemma and she never should be Gemma. But slowly and surely Mary-Beth had wound her own way into Josh's heart. He said a prayer for her just before he fell asleep. Mary-Beth would understand, but it would not be easy for her and he was sorry for that and sorry, too, that he could not have been more for her when they had been together.

Chapter Forty Two

Of course, in the modern world, everything is on speed-dial so it is one thing to have a cell phone and another to know what number you want to call. But the ever-practical Mary-Beth had foreseen the running out of batteries and the losing of cell phones before Josh's team left India and had had dinned into absolutely everyone on their team the utmost importance of memorizing the number of Jude's cell phone back in England. She had even written it in indelible ink on the forearm of everyone who would let her.

'This way you have a contact point no matter what happens to your own phone,' she said. Maude-Lynn thanked God that she had allowed the fussy PA to write on her arm. And even though the Tibetan phone in her hand was almost certainly on a pay-as-you-go tariff, she thought there should be enough credit to send a text to Jude with this cell phone's number on it and wait for her to call.

Except, of course, the characters were in Chinese.

She managed to ask the cowherd — whose name was Anil — in mime, what was the number of his phone and he wrote it out for her on the back of a scrap of paper.

With her heart in her mouth, she punched in Jude's number and panicked when she got the answer phone. But no, as long as the credit lasted that was better as it would save time on questions.

'Maude-Lynn. Tibetan cell phone 878 443 9172' she almost barked at the tone. 'Urgent. Urgent. Call me, for God's sake!'

She practically went down on her knees with gratitude when the phone rang less than ten minutes later but, when she grabbed it before Anil could answer, instead of Jude's crisp tones, she heard a male voice speaking to her in Tibetan. Sick with disappointment, she passed the phone back to its owner and sat down heavily on the ground feeling very lonely and willing him to get off the phone as soon as possible so that Jude could get through.

Oh God, what if she had given out the number incorrectly?

Then some instinct made her realize that the phone call was about her. Anil was waving his left arm around and speaking animatedly while both smiling and nodding at her. He handed the telephone back.

'Maude-Lynn? Are you okay?' said John's voice.

For a moment, she couldn't answer; the tears of relief flooded into her eyes and fell in what seemed like cascades.

'Yes,' she said in a kind of hiccup.

'I gather Josh isn't with you?'

'No, he's gone to Beijing.'

'But he's alive?'

Of course! She remembered that the others had no idea what had happened. They must have been worried sick.

'Yes, as far as I know,' she said. 'He was fine when the aircraft took off last night. They left me behind,' she added, rather unnecessarily.

'Okay. Well we're coming to pick you up in a car. Eleazer's coming too. He's the one who speaks Tibetan.'

'Did Jude call you?'

'Yep. Must go. We're on our way. Take care.'

The line went dead and Maude-Lynn thanked God for Jude's incredible efficiency.

She was picked up nearly two hours later after a long walk with Anil and two of the yaks. He mimed to her that they were pack-animals and that he was expecting her rescuers to bring some grain in return for looking after her. That was pleasing as she had been wondering how to thank him.

The yaks were smelly and ponderous but quite pretty in a surprising if rather grubby way. Unlike the black one she had ridden the previous night, both these had a white face, belly and legs that contrasted strongly with their heavy black pelt.

With the relief of incipient rescue, she could let her mind relax and wander a little and she was amused to find that part of her felt slightly disappointed that Anil wore Western clothes. His mother and wife had made some concession towards the local costume (and Maude-Lynn's fastidious nose wondered if they ever changed clothing or got the opportunity for a bath. It wasn't BO exactly, more like an all-pervading musty smell). But Anil wore a short navy jacket, blue jeans, trainers and a bobble hat. His face, however, like the women's, was burnt dark by a lifetime in the sun. He had one front tooth missing and the rest were very yellow and his smile was taut as though he didn't often have occasion to use it.

The slow yak-train wound its way to the appointed spot and waited. It was bleak and dry, the ground around the road rugged. They could hear the sound of aircraft and see planes rising from and falling towards the re-opened airport to the West.

After half an hour with a desultory trickle of traffic passing by, a yellow truck appeared in the distance, wobbling in the dust of a mirage. It was obviously coming at some speed and Anil, who had been crouching flat-footed on the ground, lost in some inner reverie, looked up, grinned and leapt to his feet. The yaks, awoken from their own contemplation, jumped and pulled back on the ropes with a series of offended grunts.

As the truck came closer, both Maude-Lynn and Anil shaded their eyes to try and work out who was in it and what it carried. There was obviously a man — and possibly two — in the back as well as a driver and two passengers in the cab.

'That can't be it,' said Maude-Lynn out loud. But it was. A hand — it turned out to be John's — waved frantically out of the passenger window and the noisy, battered machine, revving constantly, pulled up on the side of the road in front of them.

John and Eleazer jumped out and John and Maude-Lynn raced to each other embracing as though they were long-lost siblings. The shock and emotion of the last 24 hours engulfed them both for a precious moment of companionship and safety before they pulled back, pretended not to notice each other wiping away a tear and were able to give their full attention to thanking Anil.

There was no need; Anil was ecstatic. In the back of the truck were two young pitch-black yak calves, lying on their sides with their legs tied and a Tibetan boy sitting on each of them to stop them struggling. As soon as the truck stopped, the boys began to maneuver them with their feet (while still sitting on them) towards the end of the truck so they could be lifted down in a kind of canvas sacking arrangement. Both yaks began to struggle and bellow indignantly. Eleazer, the driver, the two men and Anil, managed to get them down onto the ground and untied the ropes. Then, as Anil danced with joy at the abundance of the gift, the two yak-sitters loaded three bags of rice and buckwheat onto the back of the big, benignly uninterested full-grown black and white yaks.

'They're cows,' whispered John to Maude-Lynn. 'There's a very high calf mortality rate apparently. So we brought two female yearlings. They're worth their weight in gold.'

'How did you pay for them?' asked Maude-Lynn, aware that credit cards weren't the best of currency for yak farmers.

'The Dalai Lama paid,' said John. 'He said to tell you that he's waiting for you and he thought you ought to know that you are worth ten times your weight in yaks.'

The small joke made them both laugh out loud.

'He'll be able to do something about Josh,' said John making Maude-Lynn's face snap shut as she remembered.

'He mustn't!' she said. 'Oh John, get me there quickly. I've got a really important message for him from Josh.'

In the Potala Palace, Meng and the Dalai Lama sat together with the Panchen Lama, effectively holding court together. Once the two Buddhist monks had finished their morning prayers and meditation, several hours had been filled with courtesies, discussions and photo-shoots. The world's press had descended on Lhasa with the dawn re-opening of the airport together with several officials from Beijing. Nothing had been said about Josh publicly and, although there was a rumor floating around, his friends were keeping quiet until they had Maude-Lynn back. Jude, in London, was also waiting for the journalist's return before reading them the 'living will' that Josh had left containing precise instructions.

Jude's call about Maude-Lynn had been relayed via Eleazer to his Holiness. He was relieved that she was safe; he had no doubts about Josh. Meng and he had already discussed the matter with what Meng thought was commendable restraint on the part of the Dalai Lama.

To his surprise, Meng had not needed to explain the necessity for Josh's arrest. He still had done so, formally, that morning because once you've rehearsed a speech it aches to come out whether or not it is required. But the Dalai Lama had listened politely and said all the right things without implying anything about saving face. And then he had said something totally unexpected.

'It is his law. An eye for an eye; a life for a life. He will be at peace with this. I await his instructions.'

The Dalai Lama awaited the instructions of some jumped-up Jewish millionaire from a television program that corrupted the morals of masses? Meng felt disappointment mingled with a feeling of 'I told you so.' He had very little faith in religion or the people who practiced it. But the Dalai Lama should know better.

His Holiness could read his mind. Bending forward a little, he said kindly, 'There is much in heaven and earth that we do not understand. And the strangest people can be the most wise or the most holy. It is not just we leaders who know what is right.'

As he spoke, there was a small kafuffle at the entrance to the old stateroom. Meng barked a command to the guards at the entrance but the Panchen Lama, whose eyes were sharper than his father and teacher's, spoke swiftly.

'It is the American girl with Eleazer and two other Americans,' he said.

The Dalai Lama bowed to Meng and reluctantly the Chinese politician gestured that they should be allowed in.

This was the crunch point. Although there were no cameras actually in the room and no other press had been allowed in either, the media would have been able to see Maude-Lynn arriving. They knew that she was attached like a burr to Josh and it was obvious that the link between them had been broken. While Josh might have the oddest way of just vanishing when he was right in front of people, there was something wrong when the person who had raised the world's most famous actress from the dead didn't show up for the press conference where she had been talking about it.

So there was a little agitation going on. There's a human trait to think that things can be too good to be true and, if anything had happened to Josh (and rumor said that it had) then all this could still come crashing down.

Both the Dalai Lama and Meng knew this. The Dalai Lama would not have been who he was without an inner belief that this crusade (as he called it privately) was destined and would work but, even so, there could still be skirmishes, difficulties and egos to get in its way and make things hard.

This phase of the process all rested on this one, small woman. A journalist, no less, who was trained to make the best story. And she had the scoop of a lifetime. What was she going to do with it?

Meng did not want this fragile peace to founder. His unilateral rule was already precariously-balanced and if he had made the wrong decisions both his and Tibet's future would be in doubt. He too knew that Maude-Lynn was a journalist and cursed the ill luck that had made the soldiers arrest her too. He was ready to hate this little upstart of a media person who would, he was sure, make a scene and start the process of destroying what had been achieved.

And then Grace took a hand in the oddest of ways. Maude-Lynn, still dirty and rather disheveled in combat trousers and a reddish-orange tee-shirt, her rather lank black hair tied back in a simple pony tail and wearing no make up whatsoever walked in and looked up. Both Meng Tie-Ping and the Panchen Lama fell instantly in love with her.

It wasn't entirely surprising, Maude-Lynn might be grubby but she was glowing with an inner light that lit her skin to pure copper and touched everyone in the room. But it was at the Dalai Lama, Meng and the Panchen Lama that she looked with those dark, almond-shaped eyes now clear of all the old angers and resentments. 'Aphrodite!' thought the Dalai Lama as he observed her and the other two, consciously knowing that *something* had connected between these people. He would watch with interest he thought, smiling happily to himself.

It wasn't sexual love that Meng and the Panchen Lama felt — or so they both justified to themselves later. Meng loved his wife; the Panchen Lama had eschewed all sexuality. And they might have been right: Divine love or ecstasy can often be mistaken for sexual desire. But whatever it was, or whatever they thought it was, a bond of understanding was forged between Maude-Lynn and each one of them.

Maude-Lynn felt it too. Subconsciously she knew that she was deeply drawn to the tall Chinese in the dark suit who was looking at her so curiously and she felt a great warmth towards the young unknown Lama. But, as the seventh demon had left her with Josh's kiss, she felt no need to succumb to lust. She had a job to do and by God, she was going to do it!

Hardly realizing what she was doing, she bowed first to the Dalai Lama. He, in return made the gesture of the Namaste.

'You are well? You have been taken care of?' he asked.

'Thank you, yes. The yaks and the food were much appreciated.'

'And you have a message for me?'

'I think it is for you in private,' said Maude-Lynn slightly nervously, looking around at what must have been a hundred people gathered in the room.

'Hmmm,' the Dalai Lama rubbed his chin thoughtfully. 'I think that we are all friends here.'

Several of his monks and most of the Chinese gasped, if not audibly certainly energetically. While everything had been going very well, there was still a fine balance to maintain and this was quite a statement to make!

'As you wish,' said Maude-Lynn. Her nerves had vanished with the Dalai Lama's words and she felt incredibly calm. Some part of her was experiencing a great sense of *deja-vu*, as though she had stood here a thousand years before, five hundred years before, forever before and, every time, passed on a great message. Whether it would be heard, she did not know; it was only her job to pass it on. She felt quite floaty and vague. It wasn't unpleasant.

She closed her eyes and spoke carefully, aware that her words were being translated by interpreters into both Chinese and Tibetan.

'This is the message,' she said. 'It's from Josh Goldstone to his Holiness the Dalai Lama and it's very, very important.

'Tell his Holiness that he must *not* intervene; he must not make any calls for Josh's release or insist that China let him go. To do so would put the Tibet accord in jeopardy and that would make it all pointless.

'There has to be accountability; there has to be a fair exchange of energy. Josh is the cosmic exchange for peace — the atonement,' she stumbled slightly over the word, then went on without opening her eyes.

'That's the deal. You don't need to worry about Josh. This is what he is here for. This is his job. This is how it's meant to be. No one must interfere. It's okay.'

She stopped, sighed and, to her own subsequent and everyone else's immediate consternation, dropped in a dead faint on the floor.

Chapter Forty Three

It has to be said that Jude Isaacs was feeling rather disappointed. She sat, leaning back in a chair in Josh's office in Dartmouth Park, looking out over the blossom-filled roadway and tapping her perfect teeth with a pen. Joanna was talking on her cell phone next door — calls and press enquiries were coming in non-stop but, even so, it wasn't quite what Jude had hoped would happen.

She had tried to keep her mind open as to the possible outcome of the Peaceful Liberation but she had to admit to herself, if to nobody else, that she had, all along, anticipated some kind of publicly-observed execution for Josh. That was how the story went wasn't it? As a natural fundamentalist without a religion, Jude had locked into Josh's mission with a passion. The almost sexual excitement of it ensured that she was on the adrenaline high of a lifetime. She had genuinely thought that she, Jude Isaacs, would be the one to present the news of a man coming back from the dead! And now, if Josh were in Beijing already, then no one would ever know whether he had been killed or not and the whole point was lost. The Chinese were unlikely to offer any footage if it did happen.

Jude had no doubts as to Josh's power. He was the Messiah of this age and therefore, would be able to rise from the dead. It couldn't be much harder than raising others from the dead after all, could it? She could kick herself for not going to Tibet to organize it all. She could see so clearly in hindsight that the liberation of Lhasa was the parallel to Jesus' riding on a donkey into Jerusalem but nobody in the team had even thought of a donkey at the Lhasa end despite the totally obvious symbolism.

Okay, Josh might say he wasn't Jesus but Jude had been doing a lot of reading these past few weeks and, even if Josh hadn't intended it, he had lived the events of the Gospels chronologically, event by event. He did acknowledge that he was the Anointed of the time so a death and resurrection scene was obviously one of the cards that was available for him to play. He just hadn't done it — probably because he had no one on hand with the courage to orchestrate it for him.

Jude had also been doing a lot of research into how, where and when Jesus had met his death. She had to admit that she was extremely impressed with how Judas had sorted it all.

Quietly, she sang Tim Rice's lyrics to *Jesus Christ Superstar*:

'Why'd you choose such a backward time in such a strange land? If you'd come today you could have reached a whole nation. Israel in 4 BC had no mass communication.'

The lyrics were so wrong! Jerusalem had been the center of a great trade route in 4 BC — a part of the Roman Empire — and Jesus had been crucified in public in Jerusalem at the time of Passover when absolutely *everyone* was present. You couldn't have missed it as an event. Without the palms and the hosannas and the entrance to Jerusalem and the timing, it would have been perfectly easy for someone who objected to Jesus and his teaching to have stabbed him quietly in a back street — and then, who would have believed in a resurrection? And if his death had happened somewhere huge like Rome then it could have been covered up — look at St. Peter's death and St. Paul's death, both shrouded in mystery. No, the crucifixion in Jerusalem was a brilliant, not to say inspired plan. And Jesus had known full well what was happening — didn't he say to Judas 'Go, do what you must?' and hang around waiting for it in Gethsemane? Yes, he knew — and he knew that it had to be done in public. 'Done and seen to be done,' she said to herself quietly. 'I've screwed up here haven't I? I should have done some organizing.'

Well, there was nothing to be salvaged right now apart from getting on a plane back to Los Angeles with Josh's folder and ensuring that his wishes for *Gemstone Inc* and all his staff were carried out to the letter.

Or was there? She felt in her gut that Josh was alive; that the Chinese were just saber-rattling to show that they didn't let people get away with Peaceful Liberations that easily. They just needed to make the point that you can't just walk across borders with impunity — and who could blame them? Perhaps she wasn't too late after all? What she really needed was to get Josh out and get him to some important public event in the States.

Jude swung round, feet back on the ground, and focused on her Apple notebook. When was the Superbowl next year? She Googled the date and location and sat back, enjoying the connections that her fast-moving mind was now making. Planning was Jude's greatest joy. And this was a good scheme. All it needed was Barbara Abbas to have two number one hits this year; for Josh to stay safely in jail in China for — how long? Say six months? During that time there would need to be a carefully engineered public and emotional campaign to get him back — she could already see the candles outside the White House and public appeals to China all perfectly timed to allow the Chinese to appear to be gracious but still just. Marta would be the ideal person to head the campaign. She was already a United Nations Goodwill ambassador which was just perfect...she was crazy about Josh...and then Josh could get back to a blaze of publicity and, of course, he would be the perfect person to introduce Barbara at the Superbowl.

Yes, that would do it. In fact it was perfect, even better than a shooting in Tibet would have been. In six months without Josh, the Las Vegas economy would recover; people would return to consumerism, the world economic recovery would continue — and his return would spark fear and terror in the political world. It would be easy enough to see who was the most threatened by another potential economic meltdown through the auspices of a returned Messiah who had liberated a nation. Imagine Josh Goldstone around for years and millions of people healed so that they didn't need alcohol, medicines, shopping or the politics of fear? The world economy simply couldn't take it. Something would have to be done.

And she, Jude, would have the PR scoop of the millennium.

Okay, what first? She snapped shut the notebook and called to Joanna.

'We need to get back to the States ASAP. And see if you can get hold of Marta will you?'

Josh, meanwhile, had slept quite peacefully in the aircraft on the way to Beijing. The guards accompanying him had intended a little verbal and emotional abuse for his colossal cheek in bringing shame on their country — but for some reason they couldn't focus on him and kept forgetting that he was even there. So they left him alone and, apart from some hunger and quite a lot of thirst, he arrived at his destination totally unscathed.

Josh knew all about the Scapegoat — a real goat that used to have the sins of the people laid symbolically on its head by the High Priest of Israel and which was then let loose in the wilderness once a year. So, now he was the Scapegoat and, as he was unburdened by resentment, he would be very interested to see how things panned out.

Like Jude, he had been aware that his death was a possibility. What had been more worrying was whether anyone else was hurt or killed during his arrest. And he was pretty sure that nobody had been.

His passport had been removed from the pocket of his jacket as soon as he got on the plane, together with all his other personal possessions. They would be able to see that he had a perfectly valid Chinese visa and a Tibet visa too (God bless Mary-Beth's foresight — and she'd have a photocopy of it too) but it just wasn't stamped on the entry to Tibet. Hardly a capital offence in itself but that might not be a logical line of thought to follow. However, he thought he was probably more use alive than dead — to the Chinese at least. And in the meantime? Josh wasn't exactly sure what conditions in a Chinese jail were like although he had read the odd story on the Internet of political prisoners who were physically and psychologically tortured or put in solitary confinement for months on end.

One story, he did remember, was of a man who had to assemble leaves for Christmas trees and who was hit repeatedly for every leaf that failed to pass the quality inspection test and then hit again for forgetting to thank his assailant for hitting him. Oh well, he thought. I'm pretty resilient and, if the worst comes to the worst, perfectly capable of sleeping on concrete or even while sitting up. The physical body whined and whinged — as was its right — but it was very comforting to know of a reality beyond it where you could go to alleviate pain or discomfort.

On arrival in Beijing, he was manhandled into what looked, from the brief time he was able to see it, like an armored truck and, together with two guards, driven for about an hour. At the end of the journey, he felt tired and stiff but still in fairly good spirits. As he clambered down out of the van into a uniformly concrete yard surrounded by concrete buildings, he smiled. There was work for him to do here.

In Tibet, Maude-Lynn had assumed a kind of command of Josh's friends and colleagues. Eleazer had arranged for her and Mary-Beth to have some time alone with the Dalai Lama where they had talked at some length about what to do and what not to do next.

While they were still in Lhasa they were all under less pressure from the media than they would be when they returned either to London or the USA but they could not stay there indefinitely. Obviously the Dalai Lama's place was in Tibet — but the complications of moving everything and everyone from Dharamsala were fairly daunting let alone the idea of government itself. It had to be that way for the success of the plan but His Holiness did not have very much time to offer to his new friends much as his heart might bleed for them — and for Josh.

The world's press was now running with the news of Josh's arrest — they were also calling it 'disappearance' in a way that felt quite ominous.

'But that's in order to use it as a stick with which to beat China,' said John. He was right. Those who had lived for 50 years or so in the belief that they had to fight in order to get Tibet back were more than willing to take up and wave that particular weapon.

Marta wasn't helping. She was talking to everyone who would listen about the unfairness of Josh's being taken away. Luckily her voice wasn't very loud as yet and she wasn't officially any kind of girlfriend so her credibility wasn't all that high. But she was completely incapable of understanding that Josh himself would want her to be silent. Jude hadn't been able to get through to her yet so Marta was still acting as a loose cannon.

'But he's been taken away!' she said repeatedly. 'It's not fair. It's not right. Of course I must speak out! What do I care about the situation in Tibet? I care about Josh's welfare and you should do too. You are being completely heartless. Me, I have a heart!'

'What do I care about the situation in Tibet?' echoed John helplessly. 'What in God's name does the silly bitch think this was all about?'

He did, on the other hand, think that Mary-Beth was being incredibly brave. Although she often shed a silent tear, she never said a word about trying to get Josh back. She didn't need to — Simon said all that everyone felt inside about not being there to stop the arrest and wanting desperately to know that Josh was all right.

After twenty-four hours of celebrations — and rather too many cockroaches scuttling in the rooms of the less salacious hotels — the celebrities, spiritual mentors and others now wanted to leave for their other commitments. Maude-Lynn thought that it would be best for everyone to go but there was the small problem of how to get out of Tibet when you weren't supposed to be there in the first place.

'Did you think that far ahead?' she asked the arch-organizer Mary-Beth.

'Well yes, for all of us when we first went to India. We've all got Chinese visas and Tibetan visas,' said Mary-Beth. 'But they haven't been stamped so they're hardly valid. And I don't think any of the celebrities have got them. I didn't check. Believe me, there was quite enough to think about!'

'I can imagine. But it's something that's got to be sorted now I think. I had better go and see Meng.'

'What a very good idea,' said Mary-Beth with a twinkle. She had seen how Meng Tie-Ping looked at Maude-Lynn even though he pretended not to. Maude-Lynn twinkled back. She might be fresh out of demons but she knew how to use her charms and prepared to be quite ruthless where she needed to be. Besides, she found Meng attractive and she might as well enjoy herself while she was sorting things out.

She asked Eleazer if he could arrange a meeting for her — and went shopping on the basis that she might as well find something pretty to wear. When, later that day, she was ushered into one of the ubiquitous white-chaired meeting rooms in Meng's own governmental offices, she was pleasantly surprised to find that the two of them were left alone together. Fortunately Meng's English was superb.

They stood, facing each other as the door was closed behind her. Meng was wearing a dark gray suit and tie which, she automatically noted, both added to his authority and complemented his coloring. Probably chosen by his wife, she thought. This was not the kind of man who worried about his clothes. But she was glad that she had made an effort.

Automatically, Meng invited Maude-Lynn to sit and she walked — or to his eyes floated — across the floor to the chair on the other side of the thermos flask of hot water that was traditionally placed there for their tea. Maude-Lynn had chosen simply and well and was wearing a traditional Chinese cheongsam in pale green with matching slightly-heeled slippers. She would no more have appeared in flat shoes than she would walk to the Moon. The figure-hugging silk was elegant, sensual and respectful of tradition — quite a combination even without Maude-Lynn's curvy figure, light copper skin and lovely dark eyes. She had left her hair loose and, although in her view, it was too long and slightly out of style, in Meng's, it was simply feminine. He smiled at her with both mouth and eyes as she sat down carefully, adjusting to the narrowness of the skirt, and accepted his offer to pour her some tea.

'That is a very lovely dress,' he said in his heavily accented but pleasingly deep voice.

'I hoped you would like it,' she replied simply. 'It is good to look and feel like a woman again. I have been in trousers for too long.'

Meng nodded. She was playing by the rules of etiquette but adding a little gentle seductiveness. This was acceptable to him because it was a game of flattery that underlay a mutual attraction. He was pleased that she had taken trouble to please him.

Meng knew perfectly well that Maude-Lynn needed a favor and he was pretty sure that he knew what it was: the question of how to get more than 150 major and minor celebrities, their entourages and hundreds of hangers-on out of Tibet without visas. It had been interesting him as well.

But tradition required more courtesies before they addressed any business.

Maude-Lynn lifted her mug of tea and drank. As she did so, he noticed the down of hair on her cheek, the curve of her neck and a slight scent of Jasmine. His skin tingled.

'Was your journey here pleasant?' he asked. It was the daftest question possible considering the nature of their business but uncharacteristically he was floundering.

'It was most interesting,' she replied. 'Warm in the day and cold at night. The mountains are, of course, magnificent. There were carpets of blue and white flowers everywhere. Do you know what they are called?'

'No.' She was wrong-footing him delightfully. 'I know nothing of flowers but their scent. You smell of Jasmine, I believe.'

'Yes, I bought some Jasmine oil this morning. I'm glad you like it.'

They locked eyes for a full second before Maude-Lynn dropped hers. She liked him! She really liked him. Meng was enchanted. And it was true; she did.

'Would you like to walk in the garden with me,' he said, surprised at the hoarseness in his own voice.

'Careful,' warned Maude-Lynn's head. 'Careful,' warned her

heart. 'This is not lust,' said both.

'Yes, I'd like that,' she answered in all truth. She was feeling that strange emotion of timelessness again, feeling extraordinarily feminine and both powerful and vulnerable. She sent up a brief prayer for protection and that she might do and say the right thing and then placed her fingers in Meng's proffered hand as she stood up. He led her out of the room into a place of light and glorious scent.

Chapter Forty Four

In the concrete jungle lined with brightly-colored prayer scarves that was Lhasa, a garden filled with pastel colors, pale blue harebells and trees awash with cherry and orange blossom was both surprising and pleasantly subtle on the eye. A gentle breeze shimmered through the flowers throwing dappled shadow on the over-long grass as Meng and Maude-Lynn walked without touching along a paved pathway. Their hands had parted by mutual agreement as they stepped outside but both hands now felt strangely empty.

They made somewhat banal comments about the warmth of the spring sun, the prettiness of the flowers and then turned to sit on a very hard concrete bench that faced the way they had come. They did not touch but the electricity between them shimmered.

Maude-Lynn couldn't help smiling at the incongruity of such a hopelessly romantic situation with the man who had had Josh arrested and who could at any moment arrest her too.

'This is a set-up,' she said to herself. 'A Universal set-up!'

'What did you want to ask me?' said Meng, aware that he did not want to talk business at all. 'Please be aware that we will be alone a very short time. It is customary for me to have staff with me for meetings such as this.'

She understood — and was grateful — that he had manipulated time in case she had a private concern. And also flattered that he had wanted to be alone with her.

'Thank you,' she said, placing her small and slender hand very fleetingly onto his strong but well-manicured one. He appeared to flinch but Maude-Lynn had been a siren long enough to know that it was not revulsion that he felt.

She folded her hands in her lap demurely half-aware that one second longer and he would have lifted her fingers to his lips.

'I wanted to talk about how all the celebrities and the others who came into Tibet without visas can leave Tibet without visas. I don't know exactly what to ask.'

'Ah yes, it is an interesting problem, that,' Meng was able to regain full possession of himself although he had treasured that brief moment of intimacy. He watched the pathway to the bench carefully to ensure that they were not being overheard.

'However I am sure that something can be arranged. I shall have them deported to India I think. That would do it without more trouble. Then they can make their own way home from there.'

'Will India agree?' Maude-Lynn was aware that India had sent some pretty comprehensive messages to China about its lack of knowledge, responsibility or participation in what had happened across its borders. The Indian government was obviously fearful of a backlash from China.

'I think that they will agree with anything that China suggests right now,' said Meng.

'And *you* are China?' she asked.

What a pointed question, he thought appreciatively. No, he was not China but while he had autonomy in Tibet he could do this. The question was whether he would continue to have autonomy in Tibet if he continued quite the liberal line that he was intending. Meng's English wasn't quite good enough to explain that so he just said, 'Today, yes, I am China. Tomorrow, who knows?'

'Then they must leave today,' said Maude-Lynn firmly.

'She is an Empress!' he thought in amazement unaware that he too was acting as Emperor.

'Do you love him?' he said. The question was totally out of the blue. Meng looked straight ahead as he spoke — or more accurately blurted it out. Maude-Lynn knew exactly whom he meant and why he was asking her and her healed heart melted with compassion.

'Mary-Beth is the one who loves him,' she said. 'But I am his friend and I am very fond of him. He is a man who inspires love. If he were here, you could feel only happiness in his presence. If he had stayed here, there would be lasting peace in Lhasa. He heals things. Not just people but places too.'

'While I am here, there will be lasting peace in Lhasa,' the Emperor interrupted.

'I am glad to hear that,' said the Empress, somewhat unimpressed.

At that moment Meng spotted the officials who were due to meet with them peering around the door into the garden at the other end of the path. He was both disappointed and relieved.

In less than a minute, they were joined by three rather perplexed Chinese officials who had been expecting this meeting to start inside and 15 minutes later. Introductions were made and folding chairs brought out by hovering staff after Meng indicated that, as it was a beautiful spring day, it would be preferable to enjoy the sunshine.

He knew that the issue of Josh was what his colleagues would wish to be able to report back to Beijing. They were not there to participate, rather to observe. He was quite used to that.

'You are concerned to know about your employer?' he asked Maude-Lynn. *I am so glad you do not love him.*

'I am sure that China will treat him well. But I and my colleagues would certainly appreciate knowing what is likely to happen to him,' said Maude-Lynn with admirable diplomacy. *I do love him but not in that way.*

'He will be tried for visa violations I believe,' said Meng. *I will do all that I can to help if it pleases you.*

'But he has a Chinese visa,' said Maude-Lynn. 'His assistant made sure we all have Chinese-Tibetan visas.'

'It was not verified at the border,' said Meng. They both knew this perfectly well but the game had to be played. 'As you will appreciate one person must stand trial as…as…' he struggled for a word.

'Scapegoat,' said Maude-Lynn clearly.

Meng did not know the word. He bowed. 'Example,' he offered. *You have no idea how much worse it could have been.*

'Yes, we understand that. And so would Mr. Goldstone. We are grateful that we have not all been arrested.' *And very grateful that it is you that we are dealing with, not these stuffed shirts. So how do we get out of Tibet?*

'I would suggest that all those of you who do have visas present your passports to my office today and we will have them stamped. Then you can leave as normal tourists when it suits you as opposed to being deported.' *Perhaps you, yourself might stay a little longer?*

The Chinese observers raised mental eyebrows at this and noted that Meng was really rather *too* liberal. All the invaders should be deported to their mind — apart from the Dalai Lama and his entourage; they would have to be tolerated. It was too important a coup for the rest of the World to see to have that interfered with.

'This deportation — will you fly the celebrities to your chosen destination in one of China's aircraft or can their own aircraft come and fetch them?' *They'd just love to fly Economy!* She smiled to herself.

'We will fly them. And I will send word to all the hotels and hostels that they must leave tonight or face arrest.' *The sooner they are gone the safer you will be, believe me.*

The other officials pricked up their ears. This was more like it! Meng was having the guts to throw the visa violators out without any ado at all.

'And how long will it take to legalize our visas?'

'A day perhaps.' *But surely you don't have to leave that soon.*

'That's wonderful.' *I don't have to leave that soon.*

He nodded at her as a kind of 'then the meeting is over,' gesture. It was reluctant but he thought they could go nowhere else in this conversation. But Maude-Lynn hadn't finished yet.

'I would like you to meet Mary-Beth,' she said. 'She is Mr. Goldstone's assistant and the one who is the most concerned with his welfare.'

'Why?'

'Because I think it would be a good idea. You may get the impression that Marta is more — um — involved with Mr. Goldstone but it is not true.' *I don't want you getting rattled by anything that Marta says or does.*

'I will remember that. Thank you. Miss Tecchio will be leaving tonight.' *Visa or no visa. Don't worry, I could see through that little*

Prima-Donna with one look.

Maude-Lynn stood up. The attendant men shuffled upwards in a ragged line, somewhat outraged that she had been the one to close the meeting. She shook hands with them all and walked, with Meng, to the door of the office building.

'I would like to see you again,' he said very softly.

'That's entirely up to you. I have no power in the matter,' she said matter-of-factly but looked up at him with a smile that said 'Yes.'

That evening, two hundred and four celebrities and followers with emotions ranging from bemused to outraged were politely escorted to Lhasa airport on a series of buses and loaded, like luggage onto two 757s for Delhi. Another four hundred people who were less famous were herded in their turn onto a series of smaller airbuses also heading for Delhi. The film crews who all had visas were permitted to stay if they wanted but the majority of them preferred to be where the stars were and only the hardened news teams remained behind.

Marta was not as outraged as many; she had several messages from Jude on her cell phone and knew that once they met up in Los Angeles they could make some important plans. Jude had explained that Josh had left clear instructions that all his staff were to be kept on and paid and that she herself would focus on helping Marta work to get him released.

Josh's team, slightly confused and in several cases, seriously wanting to go home, remained in Lhasa for the moment at least. There were, now, rooms available in the local hotels so they could at least relax and have a bath. Maude-Lynn and John made sure that Mary-Beth had flowers and chocolates in her room to say thank you for her foresight and organizational abilities in getting them all visas. She had done it quite simply by booking them all on a tour of China and Tibet that automatically dispensed the appropriate paperwork. Of course, there was now some poor tour guide somewhere with more than a dozen spare spaces on her trip; but they had been paid for so all that really meant was more room to spread out for the others.

Mary-Beth was doing surprisingly well. She said very simply, when questioned, 'But I knew he'd get into trouble. He knew he'd get into trouble. There's no use in being upset when you know it's coming.' And she didn't cry. Much. And that was mostly in private.

'What's Jude up to?' John asked Simon the next day as they, Andrew and James walked down one of Lhasa's sloping streets to their hotel, having been acting as tourists for a surprisingly pleasant morning.

Jude had emailed them all a scan of the documents that Josh had left behind, stating that if he were alive, everyone was to be paid full wages from *Gemstone Inc* until his release (unless of course they wanted to leave the company) and that they were to focus on whatever they could do to promote the peace in Tibet or any other form of healing work. The security-disciples, he said, should keep the others safe in difficult circumstances but everyone should be entitled to take up to three months' fully-paid leave to do whatever they wanted.

If he were dead, he wrote, then he left 20% of his shares in *Gemstone Inc* to Mary-Beth Oliver, 21% to Mattie Jones and 20% to Jude Isaacs and, if he were alive, they were to hold that balance of power for him and recommend to the rest of the board what they thought he was most likely to want.

If he *were* dead then everyone else was free to go and everyone got six months pay full stop.

It was fully legally written and witnessed so perfectly sound and indisputable.

'Jude's going to deal with the *Gemstone* people,' said Simon. 'Technically Mary-Beth should go with her but when I told her that she had 20% of the shares to look after she did her stunned rabbit in headlights act.'

'Not surprising,' said Andrew. 'If anyone needs a holiday that girl does.'

'But what do we *do?*' said Simon, still smarting that Josh had been arrested while in his care.

'We go home and wait,' said James. 'Jude says that Marta's going to mount a 'get Josh home' campaign so that can focus the attention on her — and it also shows that we're not just doing nothing.'

'But Josh didn't want a campaign,' Simon kicked the toes of his shoes in the dust like a sulky boy.

'No, but there has to be one!' said James. 'The world would really come down on all our heads — and Marta's — and *Gemstone Inc*'s — if we weren't at least seen to protest, even if Josh didn't want it.

'Jude says that if Marta does it, then it will be fairly ineffective and that will kill two birds with one stone — it won't offend the Chinese so it won't hurt Josh and it will show that we all care.'

'Jude says!' said Simon with a snort.

'Well I think she's got a point,' said John mildly. 'The Chinese will probably let Josh go when they think enough time has passed but they can pretend it's because of Marta's campaigning.'

'And Marta will then marry Josh!' said Simon, who was renowned for his lack of observation.

'I think the problem will be that Marta *won't* marry Josh,' said Andrew. 'But we can deal with that another day.'

'But what do *we* do,' said Simon again.

'Go home to our families. Take a holiday. Wait,' said James. 'The Dalai Lama doesn't need us. The Chinese certainly don't want us here.'

'The Dalai Lama's been very appreciative,' said John fairly. 'But you're right. We're somewhat surplus to requirements now.'

'It's all over then, really,' said Andrew.

'I don't know,' John was thoughtful. 'I don't know. I don't think there's anything any of us can do now — except Maude-Lynn. She can put together that fly-on-the-wall documentary thing. The rest of us simply do have to wait and see what transpires.'

'Bit of a bloody anti-climax,' grumbled James.

John laughed out loud. 'We did liberate Tibet!' he said. 'I think practically anything would be an anti-climax after that!'

Meng Tie-Ping did meet with Mary-Beth before they left. He was interested in this small, spiky, wiry little creature with unintentional big hair (Mary-Beth's previously-shaved head was now looking distinctly bush-like). No one would ever have thought that this funny little thing could be the actual instigator of the liberation of Tibet — unless they sat down with her and took her seriously.

Maude-Lynn was at the meeting too — as were the ubiquitous other Chinese officials — but Meng made sure that Maude-Lynn understood that a ritual exchange of gifts was to be made and that she should take charge of that part of it with an interpreter which would give him a chance to say a few words to Mary-Beth in semi-private.

He did this because he wanted to understand the power of a small, shy adversary who had, effectively, vanquished his country.

He asked her some unexpected but pertinent questions about her childhood and found that they had much in common. She was a survivor, a slow developer with incredible tenacity. And in her eyes he saw the valor of a hero.

'Why do this for Tibet?' he asked. 'Your employer is Jewish. He is American. There are many more causes more appropriate.'

'Because I knew that was what needed to be done,' said Mary-Beth simply. She looked embarrassed. 'I'm sure you're not a religious person — and neither am I really — but there is a kind of inspiration that you just can't ignore. A once-in-a-lifetime driving force from something bigger than you. That was all.

'And there was Josh himself, of course,' she added proudly. Meng noted the affection in that. 'He has such powers of healing and love — it seemed stupid not to use them.'

'So you used him to get your way?' said Meng.

Mary-Beth laughed out loud, her face opening up with mirth, her mouth surprisingly wide and laughter-lines crinkling her gray eyes.

'I'm sorry,' she said, wiping away a tear of laughter. 'You've never met Josh have you? You really wouldn't say that if you had!'

'I think I should meet him,' said Meng thoughtfully. 'If he is holier than you.'

'Holier?' Mary-Beth bristled. 'I'm not holy!'

'Well, as you say, I have no religion,' said Meng. 'But I can recognize the blessed all the same.

'I asked you here because I will go and see your Josh in Beijing sometime in the next month. Do you have a message for him that I can take?'

'Thank you, no,' said Mary-Beth surprisingly. 'He will be busy and there is no need to remind him of me.'

'He will be busy?' Meng was genuinely astonished.

'Yes,' said Mary-Beth in all seriousness. 'He'll be healing China.'

Chapter Forty Five

'He's not dead. I know he's not dead. I would just *know,'* Maria Gardener de-headed daffodils ferociously in her London garden and, with the accomplished hand of a practiced gardener, tied their leaves in a knot so they would rot down tidily. There wasn't much room in the couple's neat and orderly yard and overflowing daffodils would make that worse. Joe sat hunched in a green plastic garden chair, a copy of *The Times* resting on the table in front of him.

'I'd *know,'* his wife said again. 'Have I ever been wrong?'

Joe sighed. No, she had never been wrong, not when it was serious — as it was again today. She had been quite right when Gemma died, against all the odds. But surely, his more rational mind reasoned, there would come one day when Josh *would* be taken down and Maria was quite capable of going straight into denial. And this was political; this was China, not some freak accident. Logic told him that the most sensible outcome for the Chinese would be for The Miracle Man's body to be found, conveniently, in a ditch somewhere. They hadn't even confirmed that they were holding him yet despite the unofficial reports of his arrest. If he showed up, dead, somewhere in the back streets of Lhasa, or even Beijing, what could anyone do?

'It would have been nice if he'd told us what he was up to,' he said mildly. 'It's really embarrassing at the snooker club. People keep saying, 'Didn't you even know he was in Tibet?' and I have to say I didn't.'

Maria nodded as she dead-headed the last daffodil. She looked up and saw her husband looking searchingly at her. She sat back on her heels.

'What is it?'

'It's not today,' he said. 'We haven't lost Josh yesterday, today and probably tomorrow. But there will come a day when we *do* lose him.'

'Oh don't,' she said. 'It might not happen like that this time. It might all be okay. He might get to live a long and happy life. He might even marry again.'

'Sufficient unto the day...?' said her husband, ignoring the bit about marrying again. Not likely, he thought.

'Yes, live each day in hope and knowledge that he is all right,' said Maria. 'And that the Lord will bring him home safely. He will, I know he will.'

'Bless you,' said Joe. 'What would I do without you?'

'Well you wouldn't have had such an amazing son for a start!' said Maria.

'Or you as much pain,' he answered softly.

The table in the interview room had come from the Children's Palace just down the road. It was painted pale blue and, even though it had been used by the elite of Beijing's children, it had not escaped the ravages of graffiti or the idle carvings of a bored student. It stood incongruously in the center of the bleak, gray concrete room with a gray metal partially-padded chair on each side.

The Axis of the Age and the, as yet unwitting, future president of the People's Republic of China regarded each other cautiously across the table. Meng had felt uncharacteristically nervous about this interview and had found it hard to explain to himself why. It wasn't that it would be reported on; that was normal. He was quite aware that the four guards standing at each corner of the room would both be fluent in English and under orders to recount every word that was spoken to add to the evidence of the CCTV camera.

He considered the man in front of him in silence. Apart from the rather too short gray prison trousers and shirt and the past-its-best cream tee-shirt underneath Josh didn't look much different from the man Meng had viewed in the series of Internet clips his secretary had assembled for him. A little thinner perhaps but these tall, lanky Western men tended to be spare anyway.

'Are you well?' he asked politely.

Josh chuckled. 'Yes, I'm well, thank you.'

There was silence. Meng was perplexed. He had expected questions about friends and family; about why Josh was there. Something other than a constant quiet amusement which was what he felt coming from the man in front of him.'

'Don't you want to know why I'm here?'

'I'm sure you'll tell me just as soon as you've worked out whether or not I am who you want me to be. If I'm not, then you'll make some polite excuse and leave.'

Suddenly, both men smiled, each recognizing in the other a formidable opponent — or ally.

'Nobody is meant to know that you are here; nobody *does* know that you are here. And yet, there are queues of sick, disabled and crippled outside the jail,' said Meng. 'This is — how shall I say it? — embarrassing to the authorities.'

Josh leant back in his chair and nodded. 'They do tend to turn up when I'm around,' he agreed. 'I'm not really sure what to suggest.'

'I gather that your presence appears to be having a positive effect on the other inmates as well. This is somewhat awkward for the authorities too.'

'You mean that everybody has got better? Yes, I guess they have. It's a knack that I've got. Goes with the job.'

'The job?'

'Yes, it's a vibrational thing. Some people's vibration is a — a catalyst — for other people's vibration. When they come in contact with it their own vibration is raised and their minds and bodies recover from disease.'

'I thought it was something to do with being the Son of God?'

Josh shrugged. 'We're all sons of God,' he said.

He looked at the Chinese, his face totally open and clear. Meng's scorn dissipated, rather to his chagrin. He sighed, without realizing it and then got a grip on himself. He had a job to do.

'Josh,' Meng leant forward. 'May I call you Josh?'

'Of course.'

'You've spent three full months in what was supposed to be

solitary confinement. As far as we know, you've not had any contact with anyone in the outside world and yet *there are queues of people outside wanting to be healed.*'

'Well I guess word does spread from the warders,' said Josh.

'The warders have been bringing people to you haven't they?' said Meng. 'Sick people, dying people.'

'Aren't they supposed to?' asked Josh evasively.

Meng sighed. 'No one knows what to do with you,' he said. 'You're a phenomenon.'

'I'm sure there's a plan,' said Josh. 'And, as I gather from my guards that you are the Government's representative in Tibet, I presume that it involves you.'

'It involves quite a lot of people,' said Meng. 'There is quite a campaign for your release.'

'Who is campaigning?'

'Marta Tecchio.'

'Not the Dalai Lama?'

'No.'

'Good. And is all well in Tibet?'

'Surprisingly so.'

'I'm glad,' said Josh simply. 'I landed you with quite a problem there. It was easy enough to get people in and change the system but maintaining that change is the real task. I'm sorry that it must have made life very difficult for you.'

Meng blew out his breath in a long hiss. 'You are a most unusual man,' he said. 'You are right; it has taken a lot of work and it will take a great deal more. I did wonder if you had considered that.'

'Well this is where we get back to God,' said Josh jovially. 'There is always a plan; the right people are always in the right place; they just have to step up to the task. None of it could have happened if you hadn't been in charge. None of it.'

Despite himself, Meng was flattered.

'But you didn't know me,' he said.

'No, but God does. Whatever you may conceive God to be. Your vibration was right, if you prefer.'

'And if it hadn't been?'

'That would have been a completely different story. But there's no point wasting energy on what isn't, is there?'

At that moment the men were interrupted by the arrival of tea. Meng knew that this was unusual in itself. Hot water in a thermos flask could be a painful weapon if used by a desperate criminal. But by the way Josh thanked the warders carefully in Mandarin and through their acknowledging smiles, Meng understood that this man was known and trusted.

'He's a king!' he thought suddenly and felt humbled despite himself.

'I have some messages for you,' he said.

'Oh!' Josh brightened immediately. 'Mary-Beth?'

'Aha!' thought Meng to himself. Baldly, he replied, 'No, I asked her if she had a message and she said 'No, he'll be too busy healing China.''

Josh chuckled. 'Isn't that just like her?' he said. 'It was all her idea, you know.'

'Invading Tibet, yes — Maude-Lynn told me.'

Josh looked at Meng through narrowed eyes for a moment and the older man felt that his soul had been downloaded, digested and understood. 'Maude-Lynn,' he said. 'Is she okay?'

'Yes, she is very well. She has been editing the series of documentaries about you which will start being broadcast next week.'

'Ah,' said Josh. 'Then I expect I need to vanish even more, don't I? Is there a plan?'

'There is.' Meng was impressed with Josh's understanding of the situation. 'I wanted to discuss it with you.'

'That's unusual,' said Josh. 'I wasn't expecting consultation.'

Meng ignored the remark. Josh could have no idea just how very unusual it was — nor how much persuasion it had taken.

'There is a town on the borderlands with Tibet. It's called Xining. It has a jail where the worst of people are sent and a hospital which people do not leave because of the sickness of their minds rather than their bodies.'

'And you are going to send me there.' Josh was matter-of-fact.

'Yes, we want to use your talents while you are here in China. We may not understand them but we are a practical people. And Xining is both accessible and sufficiently off the beaten track for it to be a little more invisible without isolating you completely.'

'So you want me to heal the jail...and be a kind of performing healer for the rich and privileged that you will bring to me there?'

'Yes.'

'And in return?'

'Why should there be a return?'

'There's always a return,' said Josh smiling. 'You know that!'

'In return, we will release you one full month before we tell the public that you are free. And you can live a life of freedom in China — or Tibet — for that time before you return home to America to a life that will probably be cut short quite swiftly. You do realize your extreme unpopularity within the economic sector of the United States? You are too dangerous to be allowed to live Mr. Goldstone.'

Josh nodded.

'And?' he said.

Meng smiled. 'And during that free time in China, you can do what you want and you can have whatever company you like,' he said. 'It might be difficult but I'm sure we could arrange something.'

Josh nodded. 'That would be acceptable,' he said.

Chapter Forty Six

The Peaceful Liberation of Tibet was just another nine-days' wonder in the annals of a world addicted to crises. Peace, like good people, is ultimately uninteresting and goes mostly unreported. Of course there were condemnations of the Dalai Lama's stance, accusations that he had sold out and a new kind of 'Make the Dalai Lama change his mind and then we'll accept the Liberation' anti-Tibet movement.

There was also a rash of celebrity stories about the stars' part in the Peaceful Liberation — and a short run on Hollywood adoption of Tibetan babies. Arianna and Marco became official Buddhists and Arianna spoke often about her death experience on the India-Tibet border but this was in a world that had long accepted TV shows where people could resurrect, be healed and act as heroes. For the younger generation at least, it all became par for the course.

The Dalai and Panchen Lamas, together with Meng Tie-Ping ruled Tibet wisely and well. The Lamas prayed every day for Josh and gave thanks for his help. And they discussed the future. The Dalai Lama now was confident that the Panchen Lama would recognize his soul in a new body after his death. Both men agreed that it was very good to know that the impossible *was* possible through totally unexpected channels.

Josh Goldstone remained in jail in China for just over eight months, almost as Jude had predicted. While also promoting her own career, which went from strength to strength, Marta lobbied regularly for his release. She and her team of advisors and PR experts based their campaign on that of Jill Morrell, the former girlfriend of British journalist John McCarthy, who was imprisoned in Beirut back in the early 1990s. Jill's story was more appropriate than Marta was willing to admit. Both Jude and Mattie pointed out to her carefully that John McCarthy and Jill Morrell did not end up being together but Marta had such a blind spot when it came to Josh that no one could get through to her. She was addicted to the idea of a celebrity happy ending and she was too attached to that outcome to look reality in the face. And the media was perfectly ready to support her in her delusion, calling her Josh's girlfriend more often than not.

Maria and Joe Gardener spent some time in Los Angeles, helping and supporting Marta in her campaign. They also cautioned her against assuming that Josh would settle down with her when he came back (Joe's fear that he would be executed had faded as the weeks went past) but they were grateful for her efforts on behalf of their remarkable but often inscrutable son.

The Gardeners also traveled to Beijing to try and see Josh — in the company of a British delegation to China. It was an entirely understandable request but they were told that it would not be possible.

'In that case, I want proof of life,' said Joe, who was feeling his age and willing to be awkward. After all, he had very little to lose. It was a reasonable demand, all things considered, and the Chinese offered it perfectly happily — an Internet web camera video release showing Josh in some kind of library, sending his love to his parents and friends and saying that he was enjoying learning Mandarin. He seemed quite willing to say what date it was and held up a copy of *USA Today* with that day's date and headlines as evidence.

The Chinese also gave Joe and Maria a two-week free holiday and guided them round all the important sites. They wondered if it would be politic to refuse but when someone in Xian slipped them a hand-written note from their son confirming that he was fine and telling them that he was needed in China, didn't even consider himself to be in prison and would be freed after the appropriate time, they relaxed and had a surprisingly good and well-earned break.

Maude-Lynn did indeed get on with editing the fly-on-the-wall documentary and did some quiet liaising work with, and for, Meng at the same time. Ning Fang noticed their level of contact over telephone and Internet but did not concern herself with it. She was traveling a great deal and frequently made the front page of

European magazines with her work with Tibetan orphans. She wasn't the slightest bit alarmed. Meng and Maude-Lynn did not have an affair — but they did remain in love.

Maude-Lynn shared her knowledge of Meng's meeting with Josh with Mary-Beth but apart from that she kept very quiet, not even including Jude in the loop as to where Josh might be or what he was doing.

Jude was liaising with Marta and working to consolidate all the website content about Josh to ensure that his presence was constant and that foundations, support groups, interfaith discussions and all kinds of appropriate services and events were staffed, funded and overseen. She was quietly confident that her plan would work — she was powerful enough to see that Barbara Abbas had the pick of the best songs and the young rock star duly had her two number one hits and was booked to sing at the January Superbowl. At the end of that year, Jude had been voted the most powerful public relations officer on the planet. She had features about her, not just her clients, in the glossy magazines. Charlie found it amusing at first and then slightly irritating. They had talked, just before Tibet, about adopting a baby or maybe two and Charlie was quite happy to be the one to stay home to take care of the children — but that had all gone rather by the wayside. Again. Charlie's fears about their relationship being used by the fundamentalists as another brick to throw, had proved to be unfounded. 'I guess there's too much flak to throw everywhere else,' she said. Jude smiled; it wasn't a nice smile and Charlie winced. There was some unacknowledged change in her partner that couldn't be identified but it made Charlie uncomfortable. She did say that they needed to talk about the future, whether there would ever be time again for the two of them and whether they would have children.

Charlie was no longer sure that she wanted to give up work to have a child if her partner was going to be absent so often. That matter was going to need some sorting out in the near future — and Jude knew it too. She too was uncomfortable but said, brightly, that there was just a little too much to do right now to focus on the relationship. She did tell Charlie that she was quite confident that it would all peak at the beginning of next year and then, after that, things would get back to normal. Charlie wasn't convinced but gave Jude the benefit of the doubt — again — for now at least.

Philippa and the others at *The Miracle Mile* were relieved that Mattie, Mary-Beth and Jude had no intention of ganging up on them or trying to change anything apart from imposing Josh's decision that all his employees should receive their full salaries. They decided in an unofficial meeting to get some kind of legal ruling to put them firmly back in charge if Josh didn't return in six months but, in the meantime, there was a show to organize. They ran another season of *The Miracle Mile* with Marta now as a judge rather than presenter. Her replacement was an up-and-coming young man with great ambition.

Her replacement was Lucifer.

How he did it, no one but Lucifer himself knew. But his rehabilitation through Pastor Jo's church and his beauty and ability to mesmerize were powerful factors. Perhaps, had Mattie and Mary-Beth been more observant shareholders, they might have raised an objection. As it was Mattie was quite distressed when she heard the news. But it was too late by then.

Jude had kept her word to Lucifer and, if truth be known, had rather enjoyed her frequent contact with him. She found him amusing and, as she was obviously immune to his powers, where was the harm? He was offered his own show in Las Vegas as soon as a suitable amount of time had passed following his tumultuous exit from the previous year's *Miracle Mile*. It was a small show admittedly, but it was greatly to Lucifer's advantage to be in Vegas where *The Miracle Mile* had its home.

Lucifer's fury when Josh was a part of the Peaceful Liberation of Tibet was incalculable. Again, the chosen son had triumphed and achieved glory. Again, Josh had won the love of millions. It was a bitter pill to swallow.

But this time he could regain the ground by finding his way into the Usurper's kingdom. Lucifer reckoned that if he were an integral part of *The Miracle Mile* then he could take Josh down from within. What a coup it would be for him to return and find Lucifer with his feet firmly under the table! It never crossed the boy's mind that Josh would not come back; in his own way he was just as capable as Maria in telling whether or not his enemy were alive or dead. But he could change a lot of things while Josh was away and the hero would come home to something that was already under Lucifer's control.

It was simple enough to place himself within the electromagnetic fields of people like Philippa and Bartos and, once he was sitting at the next table or standing in the same elevator, all he had to do was breathe a different color into their minds.

'My goodness, you again! What synchronicity!' said Philippa for three days in a row as she found herself standing next to the attractive young man who had (she now thought) been so unfortunate at the end of the last run. She found herself going to see Lucifer's own show — although she couldn't quite work out why. It was very good; you might almost say mesmerizing. The thought occurred that he would bring a breath of fresh air to the compère's job, which was now open by Marta's becoming a judge to replace Deborah and Josh. Just think, she thought, Lucifer could do some simple but impressive magical tricks as he linked the different performers. That would brighten things up a little — and perhaps he could take Sam down a peg or too as well. And he was utterly gorgeous so hundreds of thousands of girls would tune in just to see him. The appointment was sorted before she had even thought it through and she never told anyone about the one-night stand after Lucifer's show that clinched it. Philippa was married — and intended to stay that way — but this time she couldn't resist... She was just so grateful that the beautiful young man who had made her feel twenty years old (and a size six) again was so kind and tactful — telling her that he found her dynamic and deeply attractive but that he knew they had done wrong, that although he could never be sorry for what had happened, he was very uncomfortable at the idea of her suffering for it. She must stay with her good and loyal husband and they must, in future, keep their very real affection under wraps. It was very convincing.

So, *The Miracle Mile* had a new start with an intriguing star who was both gorgeous and known to be dangerous. And, on air, he was obviously angling after the beautiful Marta who was visibly pining for the less charismatic and very absent Josh (though not so much that it affected her beauty, obviously). The world's celebrity media sighed with joy and Philippa covered her jealousy with pragmatism.

The security-disciples went home to England for three months — and decided to stay there pending Josh's return at least. There was plenty of work available for people who had had such high-profile employment with an almost-unprotectable celebrity. Simon, however, did not continue to work in security. Instead, he worked in conjunction with Josh's websites on interfaith and healing. Mattie very cleverly kept him on the payroll so he could do it from London while supporting his family.

Mattie had quite a challenging time, being the one deputed to deal with Paul Goldstone's unexpected and quite rabid submission to *Goldstone Inc.* that Josh was not the person who had been judging *The Miracle Mile* and that he was actually dead and always had been. His place, Paul said, had been taken by a look-alike who was obviously mentally unstable. As this person had now vanished, Paul wanted his rightful shares handed over.

He didn't have a legal leg to stand on, but it was still a time-consuming and unpleasant case to deal with. She did have a couple of inconclusive meetings with Paul's lawyers in London and Los Angeles. They seemed to think that there was some DNA evidence that Josh was not Josh but she was able to disabuse them of that quite easily once she had spoken to Jude about it. The extraordinary PR guru chuckled out loud and pointed Mattie to a Las Vegas pharmacy which had been storing regular deposits of Josh's DNA which she had ensured had been gathered every month since he returned from the desert. Also stored was DNA evidence from Gemma's cars, which had all been sold, and Josh's clothes from his wardrobe in the Las Vegas house — to which he never returned after the accident.

'How...? What...? Who authorized you to do that?' spluttered Mattie.

Jude could easily have said that Josh had but she was rarely anything but brutally honest.

'No one,' she said. 'But aren't you glad I did?'

Mattie was glad but she was pretty indignant at the same time.

The lawyers droned on and on, but Mattie ignored them as much as was reasonable. Eventually, she figured, Josh would come back and then the rest of it would go away.

Jude based her work from her office-at-home in Los Angeles, telling herself that it would help with her relationship with Charlie and be the place to which Josh would most probably return when he was released. She was busy — coordinating Marta's work as well as the campaign for Josh's return. But she was also rather bored.

Lucifer, however, was enjoying life as a celebrity. He could have anything (and anyone) he wanted with hardly any effort. After the failure of his bid to hypnotise Beulah into believing he was Josh, he had lost confidence but, even so, his heart burned with the desire to destroy the absent king when he returned. He cultivated Jude and credited himself with creating the darkening patch in her heart that also wanted to destroy Josh. He didn't care about her reasons or even remember the story of resurrection; he only recognised the darkness. It was perfect. All he had to do was help her on the way and vengeance would be his with no blame attached.

For Marta, the step up to judge on *The Miracle Mile* was a superb career move. She was much better with a script or short bursts of information. As a presenter she had had a tendency to ask the same question several times because she couldn't think of anything else.

Marta had to admit that she had wilted a little after the Tibetan miracle and Josh's arrest. She had been thwarted again but at least this time she couldn't blame herself or Josh. Fortunately, she had an army of attendants to ensure that no personal upset would actually show on that perfect face and figure. Jude and her PR people, working with the UN arranged for her to raise awareness of Josh's capture; including three trips to Beijing for a series of pointless but well-televised appeals to the Chinese government. *US Weekly* magazine did two features on her, firstly a Mass and night vigil at St Patrick's Cathedral, New York where hundreds of people placed candles at a shrine outside for Josh (which was maintained throughout his captivity) and secondly a home-feature when she was appointed judge on *The Miracle Mile*. Two of the pictures of Marta in that featured silver-framed photographs of Josh and her together and she was quoted saying shyly that she was 'very fond' of him and that she sent him regular letters and gifts and hoped that the Chinese authorities let them through (they didn't).

When Lucifer joined *The Miracle Mile* and began to flirt publicly with Marta she was, at first, outraged. The man was six years her junior and even if she weren't obviously linked to Josh, she had no need to seek out a toy-boy. Leave that to the 40-year-olds! However, Philippa persuaded her that she could look upon Lucifer as a younger male friend who made a good escort while her true love was absent. No one would think they were a couple, they said, but it would be good PR. So Marta and Lucifer became a show-item if not a real one. And Lucifer behaved himself. He certainly had a vested interest in Marta, wanting to turn her attention from Josh to him. It would be a small victory to steal Marta right out from under Josh's nose but amusing nonetheless. It never occurred to him that Josh's interest might lie elsewhere — why would it? The egoic mind cannot see past physical beauty to the inner kind and it was obvious that Marta was the only suitable goal.

This year, the producers decided that it was vital that no singer should win the finals of *The Miracle Mile* — that had happened two years running now and, even if there were four category winners, the outright champion was the one who made the celebrity A-list. Non-singers were beginning to complain and say it wasn't worth entering and, as singers made up the bulk of the auditionees, that was likely to become a bit of a problem with the selection process. As a result, rather too many not-very-talented non-singers got through this year.

Obviously, nothing could be *seen* to be done to rig the competition and luckily there was one phenomenal talent in comedian Russell Connelly. But there were also rather a lot of very good singers including three youngsters with extraordinary operatic voices. Philippa and Bartos thought long and hard before approaching Lucifer to see what could be done. Their scruples were hardly honest ones, rather more 'scared-of-being-found-out' ones. The best way around it, they thought, was to drop a few heavy hints and say that his contract for the next year would be assured only if Russell won. If another singer won, they said mournfully, the Network might pull the plug.

It was about as subtle as a brick but it suited Lucifer to plot and to manipulate so he helped them out in his own particular hypnotic way restoring much of his own confidence in his ability at the same time.

Gideon was always prone to voting up the non-singers, Marta was happy to be guided by her scriptwriters but Sam was primarily a businessman. Without Josh or Gemma there, he had realized that, whether it had been his plan or not, he couldn't really avoid taking more of an interest in production. His company quietly began to expand and, as he was by far the most charismatic of the judges and he had decided that he wanted to be the one to contract the next winner of the program, he thought a young operatic-style singer might be just the kick-off point that was required. And Sam's mind was strengthening against Lucifer's. That alone stopped the ratings falling as much as they might have done without Gemma, Josh or Deborah because the two men hated each other with a venom that showed in nearly every edition of the show. Lucifer wasn't as smart as Sam but he could ensure that Sam's favourites did lack-lustre performances.. And Lucifer could encourage voting with what seemed like romantic, elegant and (to Sam) soppy comments which softened the hearts of the audience in the best magical way. So, although Sam was as witty, urbane, cutting and scathing as ever, Lucifer's charm became steadily stronger and more powerful and Russell was on course for winning the competition.

Just two nights before the live shows went to air, Marta made the headlines because she thought she had seen the ghost of Josh Goldstone outside her dressing room. She fainted, of course, and images of her being rushed to hospital for a check-up made the news with a bullet.

'He was standing at the door, smiling at me just the way he used to do,' she told the press afterwards. 'He was as solid as you are; he even looked slightly younger. I spoke his name and jumped up but it was all too much and I fainted.'

Obviously, Marta's emotions had overcome her but it was still a lovely story — and to her delight and relief, Lucifer backed it up, saying publicly that he too thought he had seen Josh several times. It had been Lucifer, of course, just trying out his hypnotism again now his confidence was growing.

Both stars put out a plea to China to hear that their friend was still alive — to no answer — and several celebrity mediums tried to contact Josh through the psychic realms. One authority on Angels declared that he was dead and sending them all messages of joy and peace; another stated that he was alive and well in Shangri La, that part of Tibet that inspired Dennis Wheatley's old book of the same name. One of them was pretty near the mark.

Mary-Beth Oliver, meanwhile, had just faded out of the picture. She took a long holiday, apparently in Europe, and then resigned as a PA for *Gemstone Inc.* In theory she should have been able to keep in touch with everyone via Skype, telephone and email, but apart from Maude-Lynn, very few people heard from her at all.

But it just so happened that a school in Xining needed a teacher of English in a foreign language and was able to hire an inconspicuous American woman who had spent four months ferociously studying just enough Mandarin to be able to get by. The visa was sorted very easily and a small, reasonably elegant and warm apartment was arranged. So when Josh Goldstone came out of jail, into a China that the world had already noted was remarkably more open, relaxed, prosperous and willing to share its resources, he had a home to go to and arms to hold him for the last, treasured month of his life.

Chapter Forty Seven

It was one of those hoar-filled winter mornings when your eyelashes ice up, hats are essential, breath freezes, the very air seems white and dogs' paws stick on the pavements. On the outskirts of Xining a tall man with Western features, all muffled up in a military greatcoat was saying goodbye on a doorstep to a small, slight figure wrapped in a quilted anorak.

'Are you quite sure you won't come?' he asked. 'If not, this is the real goodbye, right now.'

'I've made it quite difficult enough for you as it is,' she replied. 'I've been totally selfish about this. If it weren't for me you'd go to the States perfectly happily.'

He smiled and touched her face with his hand. 'I'm very glad for this happiness,' he said. 'Now it *is* hard but you know me well enough to know that I'll just focus on the job in hand. It has to be done. I can't say I wouldn't like you there — but we both know what's going to happen. Do you think it would hurt you more if you came?'

'I'll be better here,' she replied. 'Term's not over and there's work to be done. I don't have anything to do in the States and I'd get in the way.'

'All right.' He kissed her lovingly and turned away to get into the official black car that would take him to the helicopter.

'I love you,' she said quietly as he blew her a kiss through the half-frosted window and he mimed back his own favorite endearment so she would always have those cherished last words.

Then she walked back into the tiny ground-floor apartment and shut the door behind her with a hiss of outgoing breath. She needed to get ready for school. Once again, she didn't have time to cry.

The Chinese officially announced the release of Josh Goldstone in time for midnight (US time) on New Year's Eve. Meng Tie-Ping and the Dalai Lama were in Beijing together to supervise the release and accompany Josh to the airport where he was to fly first class to Los Angeles on a scheduled China Airways flight.

Maude-Lynn, who was tipped for an Emmy nomination for her documentary series about Josh, was able to give Jude 48 hours advance warning (under strict embargo) and quietly told Joe and Maria as well.

'Yesss!' said Jude punching the air when Maude-Lynn told her. 'Perfect, perfect, perfect!'

'It's good,' said Maude-Lynn. 'But why perfect?'

'Because he can introduce Barbara Abbas at the Superbowl,' said Jude.

'Isn't Lucifer doing that?'

'Not now!' said Jude. 'Not now.'

Jude came alive again after months of frustration. Maude-Lynn's six documentaries about Josh had kept her busy for a while — there had been a huge Evangelical back-lash about it with Pastor Jo magnificently at the forefront accusing the film-makers of trickery and delusion and official denials of Josh as the Axis of the Age from Islamic, Jewish, Hindu and Christian leaders (surprisingly *not* including the Pope). The documentaries also pointed out what a threat Josh could be to other institutions. Although their reactions were much quieter, certain governments and corporations were making preparations, just in case...

America's economic leaders and the world's religious leaders — and the drug dealers too — had been much happier with Josh safely in prison in China. If he hadn't been arrested, one Las Vegas hotel magnate was overheard to say, somebody would have had to have taken him out.

Consider: if Josh could heal people — and teach others to heal people — no one would need *Medicare*. Or medicine. Or therapy. Or drugs.

If that healing extended to psychological healing (which it appeared to do), then there would be no court cases and no need for police. No need for alcohol. No need for mood-enhancers. No need for smack or cocaine or heroin.

If that healing extended to money, there would be no debt and no gambling.

If that healing extended to the planet, it would make all the charities and anti-global warning campaigns redundant.

If that healing made people feel good about themselves without depending on their looks, there would be no Botox. No plastic surgery. No anti-wrinkle creams. No glossy magazines telling us how we should look and be. No cult of celebrity. No fashion industry.

If that healing meant you were directly in contact with God yourself and you could understand how life was meant to be lived without priests, there would be no religion, which meant no control, no need for churches, synagogues, temples. No need for war. And if there were no need for war, there would be no need for governments to prevent or wage war. And no need for the multi-billion-dollar weapons industry.

Being healed would destroy the economy, *the economy*. THE ECONOMY!

In just a year, Josh Goldstone had already healed upwards of half a million people who no longer gambled, took drugs, committed offences, needed medical help, worried about money, thought that their appearance was the most important thing or followed a specific religion.

If they did have a religion, that religion was Josh — someone who repeatedly told them that they needed to go within themselves for their own relationship to God and that they didn't need him.

Some of those he had healed *were* healing others. *Medicare* and the other health schemes actually had noticed a drop in profits. The casinos in Vegas had dropped income by 20 per cent even though many of the clients had come back when Josh left. Religious centers were facing unpleasant questions about outdated doctrines.

In just a year, Josh Goldstone had frightened nearly every single multi-million-dollar business in the world.

It was still a small groundswell while Josh was judging on *The Miracle Mile*, small enough to be discounted as a blip. But even so, Las Vegas was watched carefully by concerned businesspeople as the celebrities who used to drop $100,000 on Blackjack when they came to a *Miracle Mile* party stopped gambling. The Ferrari dealership at the Wynn complex reported falling sales, as did all the great designer shops. People certainly flooded to Vegas but they came to see Josh, to touch Josh, to feel better — for good and for free.

The conglomerates held out some hope when Pastor Jo came on the scene. He showed them the way to denigrate The Miracle Man. He must be denied; he must be degraded; he must be shown up as a fraud.

The trouble was that as long as he was alive and in America it was quite evident that he was not a fraud.

And when he helped the Dalai Lama regain Tibet, Jews, Muslims, Hindus, governments, war lords and economists held their breath in horror. What if they were next? What if this damn *spiritual* leader tried to force them to climb down from their long-held views on what was right? For God's sake, the Dalai Lama had done a complete U-turn. He had *allowed* China to be right! He had stopped fighting! Of course everyone wanted peace — *everyone* wants peace! But everyone wants peace on their own terms. You have to be right and prove the other person, country or religion wrong in order to have peace. Everybody knows that!

If Josh had come directly home from the liberation of Tibet, he would, almost certainly, have had to have died, quietly, at some assassin's hand in some dark alleyway and a lot of very wealthy people would have heaved a sigh of relief and quietly covered up if they knew who had done it, or ordered it done. And when China arrested him, the economic and religious world put their hands together in a prayer of gratitude to Mammon. Some quiet lobbying was done behind the scenes to point out that no one would object if Josh didn't come home at all — and to be fair, China was tempted. Not to kill him (he was far too useful) but to keep him there for longer. But there was just too much good PR in the human rights field to be gained by letting him go — and they didn't want him destroying their own economy after all — so they simply had to release him after eight months.

However, in the time that Josh was not there to prove himself, the denigrators could gain momentum. Video footage could be edited, angry people who were not healed could be found — or people who had been healed but who had lost their livelihood through it. Josh's philosophy could be pulled to pieces by organized religions. The non-religious could remind people that religion — and that amorphous load of rubbish called *spirituality* — were ways of giving false hope to the desperate. That anything other than practical, sensible, provable reality was just imagination, suitable only for children.

The New Age gurus who supported Josh found their lives, visas and workshop locations all became a little more challenging. They had been tolerated because they filled hotels and hadn't yet affected the world enough to make an economic difference. However, those teachers who sold lots of very expensive products to enhance what they taught were still fairly welcome.

Jude had watched all this with increasing irritation. She believed in Josh — she *knew* Josh was the real thing but it was so easy to denigrate when he was not there. More and more she realized that she was right; it had to be proven to people once and for all who he really was. Then, they couldn't deny him. *Then* the world would be healed and changed. Yes it would be dramatic and a lot of people would lose vast amounts of money but, if they came into direct contact with Josh, they'd understand that that just wasn't a problem. It wasn't as though Josh promoted poverty — some of those who tried to put him down cited the fact that he was wealthy as proof that he couldn't be holy. They ignored the fact that Josh gave away two-thirds of his income and *still* drew more to him through his own natural abundance. Mattie had often despaired at his virtually non-existent expenses — people just fed him or bought him meals or offered to ferry him around at no cost. It was all perfectly above board and it didn't cost the company anything. If Josh were understood to be who he truly was then *everyone* could have enough. It could be a world Utopia. And Jude could help it to happen!

Jude had done plenty of plotting, finding out who had a serious axe to grind and who was ruthless enough to use it and, as Josh's official representative, she had sat in on many a business meeting where executives had explained their issues to her and she had been — they thought — interestingly forthcoming in return. But it all depended on the timing. The last eight weeks had been serious nail-biting time. The time had to be right. And the timing *was* just right.

As soon as Maude-Lynn called her, Jude swung into action, liaising, setting up, promoting — and liaising with *The Miracle Mile's* PR staff. The president of *Gemstone Inc* was grateful to have been given the heads-up on Josh's return 24 hours before it was announced. Now they would be able to sort the company's future out — and hopefully get Josh to sell off his shares. He might have been a media phenomenon but the season of *The Miracle Mile* without him had been a lot more peaceful. Gambling had returned to Las Vegas and the pressure from their fellow conglomerates had eased off. Of course, he must come to Vegas and meet this year's winners and be paraded in the streets but, after that, they would be able to get back to business. Whatever happened, he mustn't be allowed back on the show.

Jude also called Marta who was totally wrong-footed by the news and furious that she had not been the first to know. 'The United Nations should have told me!' she wailed plaintively to her staff as they frantically made arrangements for her hair and clothing so she could be elegant and coolly beautiful at Los Angeles International Airport. Several of them thanked God that she was in Las Vegas and not on the other side of the world. That would have been a disaster.

New Year is usually quiet for media stories and the release of The Miracle Man was perfect for a feel-good-news start to the year. Los

Angeles International was packed with press and Jude had pleased all-comers by setting up a press conference for Josh as soon as he arrived.

They had spoken while he was on the plane and she was surprised at how emotional she had felt to hear his voice again. 'I need to talk to you in private,' she said excitedly.

'Yes, I know you do,' he replied. 'That's fine. Give me 24 hours for the media-frenzy and the family.'

'I'll set something up,' she said. 'Now, what are you wearing? I've got a selection of clothes for the press conference. Have you lost weight? Do you need a haircut and a shave or are you presentable…?'

'From the studios of *Fox News* it's breaking news with Alan Baylis and Susanna Doyle.'

'Josh Goldstone, political prisoner for eight months, is freed by China.'

'Emotional scenes as The Miracle Man arrives home'

'The Dalai Lama has expressed his country's joy at the liberation of the man he calls 'Our eternal friend.'

'Good morning, the news today is dominated by the announcement by China that Josh Goldstone has been freed from prison. And Josh himself has just arrived at Los Angeles International Airport.'

'Apparently he will be speaking to the press live in a few minutes time.'

'We're delighted to say that reporting for *Fox News* at the airport today is Emmy-nominated documentary producer Maude-Lynn Sykes. Maude-Lynn, over to you...'

It was a strange sensation of deja-vu as Maude-Lynn presented a series of interviews and VT clips of comments from Josh's parents and colleagues: the official announcement from Beijing and the film of Josh emerging from the aircraft half an hour earlier (Jude had arranged for steps up to the aircraft so there could be the classic shots of Josh waving from the plane itself). Then it was over, live, to the press conference where Josh, a little thinner in the face but looking surprisingly well and dressed in a royal blue shirt, jeans and the traditional cowboy boots was blinking slightly at the blinding level of lights. His parents were standing behind him, both beaming and he gladly took their hands to pose for the cameras, thanking them for their continuing love and support.

He fielded all the questions easily, implying nothing whatsoever negative about China, rather saying that everyone had been most reasonable; he'd enjoyed learning Mandarin and Tai Chi and that he was delighted to hear that all was well in Tibet; that Barbara Abbas was doing so well and that, actually, being out of touch with the news for a full eight months hadn't been a bad thing at all!

It was when Judith Lucas from the *Los Angeles Times* asked 'Where is Marta?' that he put his foot in it. It wasn't entirely his fault — no one had told him about Marta's campaign or even that she was now a judge on *The Miracle Mile*, let alone setting herself up to be his girlfriend.

'Marta? Marta Tecchio? I've no idea,' he said. 'Should she be anywhere in particular?'

At that exact moment, Marta was standing in the airport Press Office demanding to be taken to Josh. When his words, transmitted live to the television over her head, broke into her consciousness, she stood stunned for a moment. There was just time for her personal assistant to find her prescription mood-calmers before she exploded into furious hysterics and collapsed sobbing on the floor.

'Hell hath no fury...' said one of the Press Officers wryly.

'Marta shunned by Josh' and '*Miracle Mile* judge's heartbreak' would be all over the gossip press tomorrow and Marta would need someone to blame.

'Oh good,' said Lucifer when he read the scandal sheets.

Maria, Joe, Josh and Jude hid in the Beverley Wilshire just as they had less than two years before. Again, Josh was subjected to a physical check-up — 'That's what's expected,' said Jude although this time it was a new, younger doctor who was quite excited by it all and got Josh's autograph for her mother.

'We've got a couple of days until the pleas for healing mount up,' said Jude, effectively calling a council of war. 'Maude-Lynn's documentaries didn't make the blogs on the websites go through the roof while you were away simply because there wasn't all that much point in people asking for your help if you weren't available. But it's all going to get pretty frantic very soon. The documentaries will be shown again in a one-night extravaganza tomorrow — and from then on it will be worse than it was before you went to Tibet. We need a plan.'

'Mum, Dad, would you mind giving Jude and me a few minutes?' asked Josh. 'After that, I would like some real quality time with you but I need to brief Jude so she can leave us in peace.'

They couldn't argue with that so went off to their own room to watch the TV coverage and have some much-needed breakfast.

'Did you think it would be like this?' asked Joe, patting his wife on the shoulder as she wept some tears of emotional release.

'No,' she said. 'How could I? When we were young the media weren't this bad. I know people thought it ate Princess Diana alive all those years ago but it's so much worse now. God knows what it will do to Josh.'

'He'll get to help a lot more people,' said Joe.

'But he'll be like a performing seal!' Maria complained. 'He will have to hide to get any privacy at all.'

'I guess that's the deal' said Joe. 'We'll just have to help Jude find a hideaway and meet up with him when we can.'

'I've been living in a fantasy land,' said Maria. 'I thought we could have him back without all of this media stuff. I thought he might stay abroad or something and we could go out to him. At this rate, he'll be nothing but a target.'

Her husband took her hand lovingly. 'We've lost him twice now,' he said. 'And he came back. You're probably right. You always are right. But I do hope you're wrong this time.'

It would be fair to say that Josh was pretty tired and, later on, Jude was to wonder if he had understood her properly. At the time she was certain that he did. But later — well, later, was a whole new ball game and hindsight is often cruel.

When they were alone in the suite at the Beverley Wilshire and Josh was enjoying a pastrami and Brie sandwich on rye, she took a long draught of mineral water and geared herself up for what she had to say.

'Isn't that the same dress as you wore when I came back from the desert?' asked Josh conversationally just as she was about to open her mouth and disarming her completely. 'I remember my mother saying that you were the only woman she had ever met who could wear blue and orange together and make them work.'

'Um...yes I think it is,' she said, looking down at the soft woolen dress. 'I'll never live that down — being seen in the same outfit in public more than once!'

'Jude,' said Josh.

'Yes Josh,' said Jude.

'You didn't do anything wrong about Tibet. I had some work to do in China.'

'Oh. Right. Thanks.'

'But I am living on borrowed time nonetheless. And it's not even a matter of months, just weeks now. That's just the way it is. I think you know that.'

'Yes.' Oh wow, he was making this so much easier for her!

'I've read the Gospels — I know what's supposed to happen,' she ventured.

'Well it isn't exactly like that — that was then and this is now — but you just do what you have to do, okay? You don't have to tell me anything. I'm fine with it. It's all part of the process. Just do it from you and don't get influenced by anyone else. That's important.'

And that was it. He nodded to her, got up and wandered across the suite to his parents' room to ask them what they'd like to do next.

Obviously, Jude couldn't tell anyone what she was planning. Not even Charlie. And unlike her Biblical namesake she *knew* that Josh would come back and that there was no shame in facilitating something that had to happen publicly rather than clandestinely. She also knew that this would be the biggest PR coup of two millennia. People would respect Josh then instead of all this carping and denying. And what a story it would be!

Obviously it did have to be done very carefully. Jude had thought long and hard about that. She waited until she got final approval for Josh to appear at the Superbowl before she picked up her cell phone and made a couple of calls to interested parties in the government. Officially this public appearance was to be kept a secret with Josh appearing unannounced on the day. The stadium said it could not be responsible for the security if Josh's attendance was generally known and Philippa agreed that it was too dangerous with advanced publicity. A file full of fresh death-threats gave weight to both views.

Alerting certain parties was all that she could do and all that she needed to do. You could often protect a client from the people who made the visible death threats but the powerful adversaries were usually invisible. What they did was up to them but the level of fear was high enough for it to be intentionally terminal.

She called the security-disciples too and arranged for them to come and protect Josh on a temporary basis at least — John, Andrew and James were champing at the bit (though their families were not). Simon wavered for a moment but then agreed to return to his original work. Of all of them, he had always loved Josh the most. In the meantime, the *Gemstone Inc* security staff were doing as good a job as Josh would let them but it was important that Josh's own people should be over here as witnesses if nothing else.

When Jude rang Lucifer to break the news to him that he would not be headlining at the Superbowl. Lucifer told her that he was very, very disappointed and, quite easily, got inside her head so that she told him that it would be Josh replacing him without her even knowing that she had done it.

Lucifer was not at all disappointed. In fact he was very, very interested. It was time and he knew exactly what he wanted to do — and exactly what he was capable of doing.

Chapter Forty Eight

Marta's villa just outside Las Vegas was wired up for security by the best in the business. Her entourage lived there too and you had to jump through hoops to get to Marta herself unless you were family — or Josh Goldstone.

When her security guard paged through to Marta's personal assistant at 10.30pm two nights before the Superbowl saying that Mr. Goldstone was outside and asking to see her privately, everyone within hearing distance held their breath. They had never publicly doubted Marta's certainty that Josh belonged to her but this was a surprise indeed.

It was an odd time for him to call — and lucky too, for Marta was out most nights at some celebrity party or other. Josh hadn't turned up at any of those parties, in fact he was generally assumed to be in LA. He certainly hadn't visited the Vegas complex or *Gemstone Inc* since he got back.

'Are you sure it's him?' Stacy asked doubtfully. She couldn't quite go so far as to ask whether the visitor had ID.

Oddly enough though, on this particular evening, the CCTV had broken down so she couldn't check for herself.

'Yes Ma'am,' said the doorkeeper.

Stacy had the foresight to say that Marta wouldn't be available right now but that if Mr. Goldstone would come in, she would see what she could do. She knew full well that Marta would go into a frenzy of confusion about what to wear and what to do with her hair.

'And it's probably just some charity presentation he wants her to do with him — or something to do with the Superbowl,' she said to Camilla, her second-in-command.

Camilla was the lucky one who actually got to inform Marta that Josh was there. She said later that seeing Marta's face light up with relief made up for all the backstage tantrums and 'poor me' howling fits that she had had to contend with over the last nine months.

Luckily, Marta was feeling particularly pretty. Coincidentally, Lucifer had encouraged her to have a facial and massage that afternoon as they had a couple of days off and he had a slot booked that he didn't want. She'd had her hair cut and styled as well and it didn't take even Marta half an hour to find a suitable outfit to wear. So she was walking elegantly, but with a racing heart, down to the entrance conservatory-atrium within 15 minutes of Josh's arrival.

He had brought her flowers — her favorites, white lilies. That in itself was uncharacteristic, for Josh was more of a bloke than he looked and his idea of romance was to tell someone they looked quite nice. But she was mesmerized; it was like the perfect dream; it was wonderful and magical, that is until the door of her private apartment was closed and she saw not Josh but Lucifer.

'What are you doing? How did you get here?' she gasped, almost hysterical with anger and realising that she and all her entourage had been duped.

Her hand went out to the panic-button but Lucifer threw a bomb of submission at her mind and she hesitated.

'Just listen to me please,' he said. 'We have all been duped. I need your help to set things straight.'

He proffered the flowers again with a supplicant's smile and Marta remembered that this kid adored her. He would never mean her harm. And Josh…well Josh had not even remembered her when it most mattered.

Lucifer sat humbly on a chair and confessed to her that he had often impersonated Josh — at Josh's own request — when the presenter had not wanted to take on some of the obligations of fame. He had only done it now to show her exactly what had been going on because he knew he could trust her. He was very sorry to have to tell her that Josh was a cocaine addict and he, Lucifer, had helped him cover up his habit.

Marta listened open-mouthed. The sensible part of her brain cried 'no!' but her hurt ego and her pride were easy targets for Lucifer's mind-weaving tactics. What he said made terrible sense.

'I was framed at the end of *The Miracle Mile,*' said Lucifer. 'He didn't need me any more so he needed to discredit me in case I spoke out. He has no heart; he's only interested in fame and in magic,' he added.

'Not true, not true!' cried Marta's heart.

'He didn't love *you,*' said her pride softly.

Now Josh was back, it had all started again, Lucifer said sadly. He had refused to help this time but he didn't feel he could let it go on. Particularly, he couldn't let Marta continue to be fooled and hurt.

'But I have a plan,' he said. 'He must be exposed for the fraud that he is. And you must be the one who saw through him first. We must do it at the Superbowl. You're going to introduce Josh and with your help I'll be able to make the world see what an imposter he is. Will you help me?'

Marta wondered why she had never seen before how attractive and gentle this young boy was. He just wanted to please her! He had been abused by someone they had all thought was good but was only power-crazy. And she had been fooled. No more!

'Yes, I'll help you,' she said.

The day of the Superbowl dawned bright and sunny with no sign of Seattle's legendary rain. Everyone in the know was ready, bright and early and waiting for Josh in the Executive Club at the *Safeco* Stadium. Barbara Abbas's sound crew were there at dawn, checking the levels out on the podium on the pitch.

Jude seemed uncharacteristically nervous, Simon was very frustrated because the stadium's own security firm was trying to over-rule him and his team and changing their method of operation and he couldn't get hold of John and Andrew who were supposed to be with Josh. They were meant to have called in by now — and he'd rung both their cell phones to no effect. When Jude raised an eyebrow at him he explained rather sheepishly that if anything awful had happened to Josh, their phones would work. She nodded with a sudden smile; there was some logic there.

John and Andrew would be accompanying Josh; they had all

stayed overnight with him in a small hotel the other end of town that had been cleared of all other guests. It was all very low key — deliberately so. To take Josh anywhere publicly now would just be too overwhelming — and dangerous. Complicated code-names had been invented and whether the local police should be told had formed quite a fierce debate. Jude said no, in case the police had been infiltrated. Simon, John, Andrew and Philip were rather horrified at her level of paranoia.

'Though I suppose it's possible — the police themselves seem to be uneasy about protecting him,' said Andrew. 'There's definitely something in the air. Can you feel it?'

John could, and Philip. Until Tibet, Josh could have been seen as a passing show. But now the odds were far too high. Simon never could feel these things but he worried as much as if he did.

The crowd thronged the car park and the stadium filled up steadily with fans and celebrity-seekers. In the executive suite, the caterers brought out the sushi and nibbles and opened bottles of sparkling water, champagne, red and white wine. Jude took a glass of the red, which was unusual for her; normally she never drank on duty.

Marta and her entourage arrived with Lucifer, to everyone's added discomfort.

'I wanted him to come,' she said airily. 'I have the entitlement to invite any guest I choose.'

Simon muttered angrily but she was right. After staking her claim, Marta was strangely silent, speaking to no one, let alone to her special guest. She looked fragile and there was a slight strain in her eyes. Lucifer, unusually, just sat in a corner and observed. He was exultant; all he had to do now was lock into all the energies in the room and he would get to walk out onto the pitch as though he were Josh. They would believe him and it didn't matter that once he was in the stadium the spell would be broken. By then he would have the microphone and be telling the world, on live television, the sordid truth about Josh Goldstone.

The camera crews were aware of a tension in the air and sussed that some extra, major celebrity was coming. The time began to get worryingly short if that was the case.

Just ten minutes before the opening ceremony was about to start, Josh arrived seemingly out of nowhere to Simon's complete consternation. Something was horribly wrong.

'Where are Andrew and John? Why didn't you get in touch earlier?' he hissed as he escorted Josh through the doors. He felt strangely unfocused.

'Bit of a problem at the hotel. They'll report in as soon as they can,' Josh said easily. 'Nothing to worry about. Sorry if I'm late.'

'You're not late,' said Simon, blinking slightly, checking his watch and calling in on his walkie-talkie. From then on it was just routine; the usual well-oiled machine (apart from those officious new security people) and it all went like clockwork as far as Simon was concerned. He and the others escorted Josh to the executive club. It was just a few steps from there to the carefully examined pathway to the center of the Astroturf where a group of local schoolchildren were holding up banners to depict the American Flag. Servicemen and women were marching out to stand in line for the special salute to be followed by a flyover by Super Hornets from the VFA 122 Flying Eagles. The excitement was tangible.

Josh greeted Marta with an affectionate kiss on both cheeks and she smiled up at him with the slightly nervous look of a child. He and Jude didn't greet each other; there wasn't time — so many hands to shake and delighted exclamations to field from people who were amazed to see him. Everyone who had any connection with the stadium at all was there, all dressed in their best. Once they had greeted the stars they would move up to the viewing rooms so as to be able to see the game itself but the celebrity greeting was part of the deal.

Josh was charm personified. Much more charming than usual.

'Time!' the producer said to Marta. She nodded, swallowed her nerves and, to the sound of the announcer's voice, stepped out into the open air. The crowd went ballistic.

Barbara was to go out after Josh. She stood, chewing her lip slightly, hiding her own nerves, in a world of her own. This close to a performance she barely noticed who else might be present.

There was just time...Jude walked over to Josh and touched him on the shoulder. He looked at her questioningly.

'It is all right isn't it?' she said. 'You will come back?'

'Of course!' he said. 'I'll be back in less than ten minutes!'

She had expected something more profound; something that said he understood. Some kind of subtle 'Au revoir' but instead he looked at her as if she were slightly crazy.

Then Marta's voice echoed out across the stadium: 'Please welcome The Miracle Man himself — Josh Goldstone!'

Jude's cell phone rang and she answered it automatically, stepping out of Josh's way as he walked into the tunnel leading to the pitch.

Then she stopped dead, momentarily paralyzed and deaf to whoever might be calling. Confusion held her like a vice. Someone pushed past, to see what was going on outside. She didn't notice. *Her cell phone had rung.*

'Stop!' she yelled at the top of her voice. 'Simon, stop him! That's not Josh!'

Andrew's voice on the phone, speaking anxiously, was cut off as she dropped both phone and bag and raced out of the door. Simon was hesitating but now Jude *knew,* she could see that Josh didn't look quite right; as if his body was half an inch away from his energy.

'Lucifer!' she yelled. 'It's Lucifer! We've all been hypnotized!

Simon dived, grabbing hold of Josh's arm and the new security people jumped on them both. There was a complete fracas just at the entrance of the tunnel. Marta and the people on the other side of the pitch could see that something was going on but not what.

'Go on!' hissed Jude to Barbara Abbas, who was hesitating. 'Go on — on your own. It's quite safe.'

To her great credit, Barbara did just that — and the security men managed to swing Simon and the Josh figure back inside the tunnel and out of the public gaze. They had both men spread against the wall before Barbara had reached the central podium. As his face slammed against concrete, Lucifer lost his connection and it was clear to everyone exactly who he was. 'You bastard,' hissed Simon. 'What have you done to him?'

'Let Simon go!' ordered Jude. 'He is Mr. Goldstone's security officer. You *know* that. This other man is an impostor.'

Barbara had now reached Marta on the stadium. Marta's face was panic-stricken. Where was Lucifer? She had no script for this; she didn't know what to do or to say. Was he in trouble? Was he hurt? Was the real Josh here instead?

But she didn't have to say a word. Barbara Abbas greeted her with a kiss on both cheeks and stepped up to the microphone.

'I'm sorry — Josh has been delayed,' she said. 'Can you make do with me for the moment?'

The woman had true star quality and made the request in a tone that expected a massive 'Yes!'

The crowd, who had only anticipated seeing her anyway rose in a second wave of thunderous applause until Barbara raised her hands for silence and nodded to her team.

At once, the backing track for the national anthem began and, after reaching out to give Marta's hand a reassuring squeeze, Barbara Abbas began to sing.

Chapter Forty Nine

'We've been arrested,' Andrew said when Jude called him back. 'Someone reported the three of us as using drugs; cocaine was planted on us last night when we went out to eat.'

'You went out to eat? You were supposed to stay safe!' Jude was furious.

'Oh for God's sake, we'll deal with that later,' said Andrew with unaccustomed irritation. 'The snitch told the police this morning and there was a raid on the hotel. There was nothing we could do.'

'Aren't you supposed to be allowed a phone call?'

'That *was* my phone call,' said Andrew dryly.

'Okay, was there any of the substance found on Josh?'

'No, some in a drawer in the room — and some in my jacket pocket.'

'Right, I'll get a lawyer. Hopefully we can get Josh bailed and here for half time.'

'Er — and us?' said Andrew.

'*You* can be sorted out later,' said Jude.

'Can I help?' asked a smartly-dressed man at her side. He was Joe Ramathea, a major financier for one of the competing teams, a lawyer and a noted philanthropist.

'Oh yes,' she said, recognizing him at once. 'Yes, please. You must have been sent by heaven.'

Lucifer, meanwhile, was proclaiming all innocence. It was just an illusion to amuse the crowd, he protested. He would have let them see that it was an illusion once Barbara had sung.

'As if even you could fool a whole stadium!' said Jude spitefully. 'And how exactly did you manage to stop Josh getting here on time?'

'Nothing. That was just luck,' said Lucifer.

'Really?' said Jude. 'So how come you were spotted putting cocaine in Andrew's jacket pocket last night?' She was bluffing.

'Don't be stupid,' said Lucifer but his face blanched.

'Oh I'm not stupid,' said Jude. 'We'll get you; don't worry. You'll not get away with this.'

But he would and both she and Lucifer knew it. Thwarted though the boy was, he could read Jude's energy clearly. Her defenses were lowered by fright and what he saw lifted his spirits. What did his plans matter now? Josh would be dead this very day. He felt a great rush of adrenaline. There was only one strand of light in Jude's mind and it was linked to her cell phone. Lucifer's eyes narrowed, realizing she could abort the mission at any time. Suddenly he lunged at her, grabbed her bag and emptied it out. There was just enough time to seize the phone and smash it before security took him to the floor.

In half an hour, the real Josh, together with John, arrived at the Stadium looking slightly crumpled but none the worse for being arrested. With them was Joe Ramathea who had only really offered to help because his daughter collected autographs but who had taken to Josh on sight. The two men were talking animatedly as they climbed out of the car. Jude wondered at Josh's ability to live in the moment.

She couldn't resist hugging him when he turned to greet her.

'Just trying to check it's really me?' he joked.

'Yes I guess so,' she wiped an uncharacteristic tear from her eye.

'Hey!' Josh gave her another swift hug. 'No regrets — huh?'

John gave him a questioning look but there was no time to talk; they had to get into the building and sort it all out for Josh to go on the pitch at half time.

'Though why it's so darned important, I don't know,' John complained.

'Shareholders,' said Jude vaguely. 'Josh — did you hear about Lucifer?'

'Yes, Joe told me,' said Josh. 'Is there time for me to talk to him, briefly?'

'Well, if you're not going to get changed or anything, there's five minutes.'

'Okay, can you find a room and bring him to me?' 'Yes — we've kinda been keeping him captive.'

'Is Maude-Lynn here?' asked Josh *à propos* of nothing.

'No, she's in LA — she's picking Mary-Beth up from the airport. Sorry, I forgot to tell you.' She didn't like telling the lie.

'Oh.' Josh took in a long breath. 'Well take me to Lucifer then.'

'Right.' Jude turned on her heel and walked away. Josh gestured to the stunned John to stay where he was and followed.

'What the hell is going on?' asked John to the air.

'So,' said Josh as he was ushered into the room where Lucifer's hatred was a palpable energetic force that would have knocked most men flying but he was posing as cool and calm, leaning back against the wall.

'I'm not going to talk down to you,' said Josh. 'I'm going to talk to you as an equal.'

Lucifer curled his lip. 'And why wouldn't you?' he said. 'You're no different from me.' He managed to bite his lip to refrain from laughing at Josh. The poor sap didn't know what was going to happen to him and then Lucifer would be triumphant.

'Just a little,' said Josh gently. 'Okay, I'm going to give it to you straight. You are going to come out with me at half time and face the consequences.'

Lucifer made a face. 'Consequences? What consequences? I haven't done anything wrong.' But he was momentarily scared. Had Josh and Jude cooked up something between them? Dammit, he just couldn't read Josh's energy. Then he remembered that he had destroyed Jude's phone. It wasn't Lucifer who was the target and she would never dare make a public call to change any of her plans. The danger was there but maybe he could even spin it for his own good by looking a hero?

Josh rubbed the ball of one foot on the floor and took a moment before speaking. 'You've hurt people,' he said simply. 'You've used power to manipulate and you've betrayed; you've misused great talents. You are cruel.'

Lucifer sneered. 'Quite the super-hero aren't you?'

'Let's cut to the chase, Lucifer,' said Josh, leaning down. 'You would rather rule in hell than serve in heaven. But evil is ultimately chaotic. You cannot out-maneuver love; you don't have the stability or strength. Love will always endure and evil will always destroy itself.

'I don't know what your plan was — did you intend to kill me after you had fooled the others?'

Like quicksilver, Lucifer was on his feet, his face contorted with rage.

'Oh you are going to die!' he said. 'You're the one who's betrayed. I would have discredited you. I would have proved *you* the fake. I had it all worked out. I will still win, you fool, and I will take every ounce of power that is yours.'

'Fine,' said Josh. 'You've made your choice. You get to share everything that is mine. Come on. We'll go out onto the pitch together — a united front. You can have my power — willingly you can have it.'

Lucifer's arrogance was such that he didn't question what was happening; as far as he could see, Josh was just showing the typical wishy-washy weakness of the good. He wanted conciliation and nice stuff to happen. Well, Lucifer could bite his hand off at that and stand there to watch the destruction of his foe.

Together the two men walked down to the executive lounge. Jude, who had been waiting outside the door, walked behind. She said nothing; she had no idea what was happening but didn't dare say so.

Marta was standing in the executive suite, hesitant but trying to put on a brave face. Poor woman, she was having terrible doubts and did not know what to do or where to look.

'Hello Marta,' Josh said easily. 'You look lovely. There's nothing to worry about.' He patted her hand gently and released it as though she were a child.

Marta flashed a look at Lucifer but, confident again, he smiled at her. 'No worries,' he said easily.

Reassured, she stepped backwards, aware of the time factor and that both she and Barbara were going out again to talk live with Josh on the re-built podium and then Barbara (that consummate professional) would sing another song. She and Barbara left the room together with Simon following so he could watch ahead as security for Josh.

Everyone else stood silently, subconsciously knowing that something momentous was happening.

'Lucifer and I are going to go out together,' said Josh to the sound of several sharp intakes of breath.

As they looked, Lucifer seemed to swell in energy and Josh faded slightly.

'Oh dear God,' said John stepping forward. Josh just looked at him and John stopped as though a solid wall had sprung up in front of him.

Time stopped too. Afterwards, every one in that room found it impossible to explain what actually happened. John actually saw the shield go up around the two men containing the energy of each and protecting everyone outside it. There was a glow of fire and light and a rustling sound ('like wings' said Joe Ramathea later). Josh faded and faded and Lucifer grew and grew.

And then for a moment, there was nothing.

'Okay,' said Josh, with a tight smile. 'Perfect timing. Lucifer, are you coming?'

The angelic-looking young man beside him looked perplexed.

'Lucifer?' he said. 'Er...my name's Isaiah. Um...where am I?' He reeled slightly and then fell in a dead faint.

Josh grimaced as though feeling a spasm of pain.

Thirty seconds later, as he stood at the side of the entrance, waiting for the last of the players to jog past him and the announcer to begin, Jude caught up with him.

'Are you okay?' she said.

'Yes,' he said, looking at her directly. There was a deep

tenderness in his dark brown eyes and part of Jude felt a frisson of fear. He looked really fragile, almost sick.

'You will come back, won't you?' she said.

'No Jude,' he said gently. 'I did that bit already.'

'And now...' Marta's voice echoed across the stadium. 'Ladies and gentlemen...I'm delighted to present to you the one and only...The Miracle Man. *Mister* Josh Goldstone!'

He walked out into the sunshine, tall and surprisingly graceful, waving to the crowd who, realizing that the man who raised people from the dead and liberated countries was actually there in front of them, leapt to their feet with a tumultuous cheer.

Jude stood, blind and deaf to the noise. Several stadium assistants nagged at her to get back into the executive club; she was in the way of the caterers and journalists. Automatically, she walked with them and accepted a second glass of red wine from the waiter as she found herself back in the room.

He would be coming back. Surely, he would be coming back. Of course, he would be coming back. That was the whole point of it, wasn't it? Wasn't it? Oh my God *what had she done?*

She grabbed her bag and scrabbled for her phone. She must stop it! It was all wrong. She must text the signal to abort. But the phone wasn't there. She stood, numb and terrified.

Something was happening. She couldn't register what; her mind had gone completely. Someone brushed past her, knocking the glass of red wine in her hand so that it fell, splashing scarlet like blood, all over the white carpet.

She didn't hear the crack as the bullets raced across the heads of the cheering fans. She didn't see Josh's body blasted off its feet, backwards, off the podium onto the grass. She couldn't have seen anything even if she had looked, for her eyes were drowned by tears.

Marta screamed, her voice higher pitched than the shouts around her. Her face, immortalized across millions of television screens, crumpled in horror. Barbara Abbas whirled round and pulled her away as she took breath for the second scream and they both fell from the podium to the grass, as if in slow motion, away from the bullets' trajectory.

But there were no more bullets; they had done their job in front of the shocked crowd and the millions of viewers.

Despite her terror, Marta struggled to get to Josh, calling his name again and again but now the security men and women were moving fast and whisking Lucifer and the women away amid the pandemonium. Only Simon could get near to Josh; Simon, dazed and shaking, staggered down the steps, sick to his soul, and fell at the side of his master's body.

Maude-Lynn stood, transfixed, at Los Angeles International staring up at the 20ft plasma screen above the arrivals gate as Mary-Beth walked through the green customs channel.

She didn't have to say anything; her face said it all. Mary-Beth looked up at the screen, which had gone blank as the Network cut the feed.

'Superbowl. Normal service will be resumed as soon as possible,' it said.

Maude-Lynn put out her hand to her friend; she didn't know what to say.

'Josh?' asked Mary-Beth quietly.

Maude-Lynn nodded and took hold of Mary-Beth's left hand. She felt the unfamiliar bump of a ring and glanced down briefly, noting a slender band of green jade on the third finger. Some part of her noticed too that Mary-Beth seemed to glow with health and that her face had taken on a more rounded look. At that moment, the screen burst back into life with a live studio broadcast. Alan Baylis began relaying the news that Josh Goldstone had been shot at half-time in the Superbowl.

'Unconfirmed reports say that Josh Goldstone has been shot but that no one has confirmed how serious his injuries might be. No one else is believed to have been hurt. Police and ambulance are at the scene now.

'There is no more official news yet — but we now cross to our Sports correspondent, Steve Howells, in Seattle. Steve, what does this mean for the Superbowl? Can they continue with the game or will they have to set another date and start again?'

The two women stood, holding tightly onto each other watching and waiting while people around them exclaimed and shouted if they had understood what had happened and, if they had not, got on with the normal business of greeting loved ones, complaining about lost luggage or fussing about where to find the nearest cash machine. Life goes on; it always goes on.

Maude-Lynn reached for her cell phone and hit speed-dial for Jude but Mary-Beth gently took the phone away from her and closed it.

'Jude won't answer,' she said. 'Nobody will answer. And if they *did* answer, then he would have to be dead, wouldn't he?'

Maude-Lynn nodded at the logic of this statement. She felt totally numb.

'Well, let's hold on to that hope then,' said Mary-Beth although she knew she was just comforting her friend. She could still hear Josh's voice telling her, just one year before, that he had just a short time to live.

'And you *did* love me,' she whispered to herself.

'Okay,' said her friend. 'There's a car waiting. Where do you want to go?'

Chapter Fifty

Had there had been anyone he could have talked to about the last weeks of his life, Josh would have said it felt like being pulled in on a homing-beam. It wasn't unpleasant — it was a liquid silver beam of light that infused his body and soul and comforted and blessed as it pulled. But the planet Earth is a lovely place to spend a lifetime and he was so sorry that he would soon not be able to feel the velvet, pulsing beauty of a living rose petal, appreciate the sensual taste of Belgian chocolate, see the glory of a sunset or experience the joy of holding a lover in his arms.

His body resisted the knowledge of his impending death — as did his ego. There would be no further use for either of those; they truly did die. Surely, they both nagged at him, there was some alternative? Couldn't he just go back into hiding? Couldn't he use his undoubted power to cut that cord off? Couldn't he just refuse to go? But no, his soul was inextricably linked with that homing beam and his soul was almost pining for the greater home. The pull grew steadily stronger and surrender was the only possibility.

How could he tell anyone? They would only fight the idea of his dying (and encourage his ego to fight it too). Perhaps Jude would understand but her lesson, this time, was to deal with the consequences of her actions. How many lifetimes had members of Jude's soul group come back to learn how to handle the task of being the deliverer?

For years, in this life as Josh Gardener, he had pondered the story and legend of Judas Iscariot and the word 'paradidome', the Greek that meant 'to hand over' just as much as it did 'to betray'. He had read all the alternative texts — *The Gospel of Judas, The Last Temptation of Christ* and some long out-of-print novels by authors who secretly knew a thing or two but hid it in a page-turning story.

Jude was not betraying him; she was doing what she could to help him fulfill his destiny and, as he had to go anyway it was best to make it public; that way it could be seen to have been done. There would, of course, be conspiracy theories (and here he wasted a moment of precious life with a thought of irritation about Lucifer and wondered if there was anything he could — or should — do about that problem of evil. But no doubt, if he could, the opportunity would come). He wondered a little who it would be who would have the task of killing him — who would order it and who would carry it out. But that wasn't really important. They would be just part of this particular package and the consequences would be returned to them. What might be more interesting would be who had been tempted and decided not to act but even pondering that was a waste of thought when there was so much precious life to be experienced.

In one final burst of passion for the Earth, he managed to run away for four days just before the Superbowl, leaving a note for Simon (but confiding in John and Andrew that he just needed a break and begging them to cover for him). In an uncharacteristic burst of extravagance, he chartered a Lear jet to take him to Florence, Italy and then hired an unobtrusive Fiat to drive himself through the winter-chilled, undulating landscape of Tuscany with its sentinel cypress trees, black naked vines and ploughed fields of promise. He stopped at the hilltop, walled town of Montepulciano where he found a basic bed and breakfast hostel in the heart of the cool gray stones of history, speaking creditable Italian to the incurious host as he picked up the keys to his sparsely-furnished room on the top floor. There, he sat for a long time on the dark-wooden window seat looking out of the window at the breathtaking views of patchwork fields under the ice-blue sky and savoring the anticipation of fresh pasta, local wine, olive oil, truffles and — for the first time for him in Italy — the local salami and ham.

He spent two days just looking and walking; cherishing the cobblestones beneath his feet and tracing his fingers over the Etruscan stone carvings that formed the stone brick bases of houses and shops. He meandered into all the local bodegas and accepted slivers of the local cheeses and drank the local *nobile* wine. He ate bruschetta with olive oil and garlic in the nineteenth century Caffé Poliziano at the top of the town, appreciating the elegant wood-lined walls with mirrors and pictures, and the palms and lamps and, securing for himself the best table by the window, gazed his fill over the Valdichian countryside. He drank Italian coffee — not because he particularly liked coffee but because it belonged to Italy and Italy's angel and, as such it was a holy icon of the land — and he reveled in Italian ice-cream savoring every glorious touch on his taste buds. He ordered cases of wine as gifts to be delivered in a week's time for everyone he could think of with love (and that was a lot of people — six *bodega* managers had very good holidays that year) and inhaled his fill of the winter glory of Italy.

On the last day, back in Florence, he wrote his will in a hotel room overlooking the River Arno and got two staff to witness it. On his final wander through what he thought was probably his favorite city, he laughed again at the ludicrous hands and feet on the copy of Michelangelo's David in the Piazza Signoria, decided against queuing for the Uffizi and bought Mary-Beth a gold and enamel peacock brooch on the Ponte Vecchio. The brooch caught his eye for no reason at all except that he wanted to get her something and had no idea of her tastes in such things. He found a lawyer's office and managed to lodge a copy of the will with them for safekeeping; the other he couriered to Mattie to arrive on the day after the Superbowl.

That night, he meandered through the streets, mingling with the few winter tourists and the relaxed, elegant and sensual inhabitants of the city, reaching the square of Santa Croce where he had a plate of Italian meats and a glass of Montalcino *nobile* at his favorite *Boccadama* restaurant. Then he walked, soft-footed, silent and in adoration of their beauty, through the streets of Florence, watching the changing colors of the lights, the people and the night until dawn, saying goodbye and thank you. At last, he slept like a baby with his arms wrapped round the extra Egyptian cotton pillow on his antique walnut double bed until the 10am wake-up call told him it was time to go.

All the way back, alone in the passenger cabin of the jet, he watched the lands and the seas of the Earth below, loving it and thanking it. A pod of whales waved their tails at him in the Atlantic and he felt immensely blessed. He never knew it, but that flight of love did more to heal the Earth than years of alleviating carbon footprints — just as he never knew that his eight months in China cleared 85% of that country's pollution.

He arrived in Seattle the night before the Superbowl and laughed to himself that his last supper with John and Andrew was a pizza in a bar. He was sorry that Maude-Lynn wasn't there (though not that Mary-Beth was away — it would have been just too hard to observe her bravery) and sorry too not to say goodbye to his parents. He had considered telling them and stopping off in London but he didn't need the emotional pull of their pain — and London wasn't safe; he was known there and the paparazzi kept a watchful eye on Joe and Maria's home. Instead he wrote them a letter and sent them flowers. It was silly, he knew but there wasn't exactly an etiquette to follow.

By the morning of the Superbowl, despite the drama of the arrest, he was totally serene. The pull of the homing beam had alleviated in Italy — a stay of execution, he thought with a smile — but now it was an unrelenting call, tugging, tugging. He found it hard to focus in a world that seemed to be built of shadows — he had never realized how fragile it was before. He could just put out one finger and touch anything solid and it seemed to ripple. He wondered whether he had any free will left; every sentence the police said to him; all that John and Andrew said, seemed to have been pre-ordained, just waiting for the mouths to open before it could be observed.

He liked Joe, the lawyer, who had a powerful, benign energy field and who asked sensible questions and, on the last car journey to the stadium, he was entranced by the dichotomy of the fragility and the shadows and, in contrast, the colors of everything outside the windows of the car. It seemed as though the Christmas lights, still hanging in the otherwise drab winter Seattle streets, resonated with hidden splendor like stars in a distant galaxy.

It didn't worry him that they missed the National Anthem; he was aware that technically he should have been there earlier, but the homing beam could not be denied. He had no need to worry. It would all still happen as it should. He smiled quietly to himself at the concept of anxiety.

But once they arrived at the stadium and he sensed the malignant energy of Lucifer, Josh's psyche snapped to attention. The laconic, easy morning where Andrew and the others had seemed to move in slow motion and their confusion and irritation were like motes of dust circling in the air, shifted into a metallic clarity of vision that tasted so sharp that his teeth were set on edge. *Lucifer*.

Around him, strength from another world formed itself so that he was armored in light. They weren't instructions exactly that filled his mind but he knew that he was being asked to do one more thing before the final tug, the final docking. He couldn't leave Lucifer's evil in the world without him.

'Of course,' his spirit said to the all-embracing Love.

As Josh and Lucifer stood together in the executive club before walking out onto the pitch, with Lucifer exultant with the desire to win, the protective amour within and around Josh dissolved with a softness of down, and the gentleness of a lover's hand. It began to absorb the horror, the hatred, the ferocity of Lucifer's damaged soul. And Lucifer, sensing weakness, attacked, pouring psychic acid through Josh's very being. Malignant etheric dendrites attacked every neuron of his brain; every understanding he had ever had of love, tenderness and hope was dissolved in demonic glee as Lucifer and chaos rampaged inside of him. This was the meaning of hell, darkness, loathing and despair. A dull numbness waited beneath the pain and that would be the living death that awaited him.

For a moment, he succumbed to the feeling of betrayal. Where now was the great power and love that had lived within him these last two years? *Now* it left? Was his final sacrifice to be so terrible — so eternal? Because, for sure, this hell would never end.

But Josh had become who he was because he had always, at heart, been a good and kind man. Deep, somewhere almost intangibly tiny in his mind, one iota of compassion remained. Tentatively, it opened its eye. How horrible Lucifer's life must be. How could he help being who he was if this was the pain, the wiring of the mind, that he had to live with? It wasn't his fault; he was possessed. He didn't know what he was doing. He couldn't. This was such a wonderful, beautiful world that any mind that could find such a need to hate in it — and such a wish to destroy others — must be mad. And there were so many of them! Through Lucifer's terrible energy he felt and absorbed all the fear, anger and hatred of Earth's humanity.

'Oh God, forgive them, they don't know, they don't *know*,' he thought.

At that moment, Lucifer's devil locked fully into Josh, freeing Lucifer's soul to start again. Josh couldn't see what had happened; he couldn't see anything; couldn't hear or understand anything except the pain; the all-embracing agony. But even so, the compassion shone deeper than the anguish and hate and it felt the calling of the silver pathway home.

Home. Come home.

Jude said something to him and he was vaguely aware of answering. Then, with every nerve vibrating with pain, he walked out into the stadium, managing somehow to place one foot in front of the other as though he were a normal man. Every bone, muscle, tendon of his body was screaming in agony. His skin was on fire; his eyes blinded; his heart blackened and broken; his head encased by barbed wire twisting ever tighter.

'Follow the silver, follow the silver,' whispered the echo of hope in his mind and he climbed the podium. At the top, vaguely aware of the noise around him he positioned himself where the light was brightest. It exacerbated the torture but he knew he had to embrace it, own it and allow it. He threw his arms wide and his head back.

'It is done,' he whispered.

Dying was so easy; so very, very easy and such a blessed relief.

He felt the blows of the bullets as they thumped into his chest and knocked him backwards but the pain of torn flesh was clean and clear, cleansing him from the agony of Lucifer's mind. He saw himself fall and the horrified faces around him as though he were a standing spectator, fascinated by the sight of his own ending.

Such compassion filled him, such peace. This was not his place but he loved it so. Slowly, as people ran around panicking, the image of mortal life began to fade and the cord tugged him into the well-remembered tunnel of light. Oh it was good! Like sliding into a hot bath on a cold winter's night; like diving from a cliff into clear, cool water. Eagerly, he began to flow towards the brightness at the end to the One.

Maria Gardener screamed. Joe came running from the living room to where his wife stood in the kitchen of their London home, tears running down her face.

'Josh...' she said and fell clumsily onto her knees. 'It's Josh...Oh God! I *know*. I always knew I would know. I knew it would be one day but not now! *Not now!* Not *today!* I can't bear it; I can't bear it.'

Her husband knelt by her side, embracing her and resting his gray head on hers. 'You'll bear it,' he said. 'You were the chosen one. You were the only one who could ever have borne it.' And he too began to cry. He didn't need to ask. The police would come soon enough, wearing grave faces, to tell them the details. After all, hadn't she always been right?

On the first day, before the post-mortem could be carried out, Josh's body vanished from the mortuary. No one could explain it; everyone suspected it had been stolen but there was no possibility that anyone could have got in or out without being seen. The world held its breath.

On the second day scuba divers in Lover's Cove, Lake Mead, Nevada found a decomposed male human body in a previously unknown crevice under the ledges of the reef 50 feet down.

On the third day nothing happened.

Nothing happened.

Not one crime was committed; not one person went hungry; not one war was fought. Nobody realized it but the whole world felt strangely at peace. The news networks managed to fill their time with reports of how Josh had not risen from the dead (as if anyone believed he would!) and continued speculation about who had shot him. Without those bits of non-news, they would have been completely stuck.

After a week or two, the nine-day-wonder of a Miracle Man's life and death was replaced by human beings starting up their chaotic lives again. But something had changed. For one day; for one whole day, nothing had happened. And that was the greatest miracle of all.

Josh Gardener died with his wife Gemma Goldstone on Friday 21st March at 12.37pm when their Aston Martin V8 Vantage crashed over the Hoover Dam. It was just three days before the long delayed, state-of-the-art Colorado Bridge bypass was due to open...

References

1 Translation of the Hebrew from *Tanakh, The Holy Scriptures*, (Philadelphia, Jerusalem: Jewish Publication Society) 1985.

BOOKS

MySpiritRadio